The author is a retired police officer who has had a lot of life experience. He was married to his first wife for thirty years and they raised four children. Following a divorce, he married again and divorced just three years later. Apart from writing, and pouring out his heart, he plays the piano, loves gardening and has carried out a lot of DIY building projects in his spare time. He is a 'people person', and has always taken a keen interest in behavioural psychology and relationships.

Bruno Beaches

SCRABBLE BABBLE RABBLE

AUSTIN MACAULEY PUBLISHERS™

LONDON • CAMBRIDGE • NEW YORK • SHARJAH

A CIP catalogue record for this title is available from the British Library.

ISBN9781398436237 (Paperback)
ISBN9781398436244 (ePub e-book)

www.austinmacauley.com

First Published 2022
Austin Macauley Publishers Ltd®
1 Canada Square
Canary Wharf
London
E14 5AA

Chapter 1

Liam was not very good at English. It was his native language and he spoke it reasonably well, albeit with a rather slow, stinted delivery and his vocabulary was acceptable enough, but his reading, writing and comprehension were below SATS key stage two-level. During English classes, his teacher, Mr Blanchflower, assigned Kevin to assist him on a one-to-one basis. Kevin's command of the English language was well above average and he readily assimilated the task of trying to help Liam pick up facets of grammar, new words and to use better sentence construction. Liam was 29. Kevin was 48.

Mr Blanchflower was a kind, caring man who had been an English teacher since leaving university many decades earlier and now he was officially retired. However, he still did some occasional supply teaching for local schools and devoted himself to three regular afternoons per week at his local prison. This was because he loved the English language, he loved teaching and he liked to keep himself busy and to feel that he was still making a difference. He didn't like the idea of just allowing all the skills he had built up over forty years just going to waste when he could still use them to make a valuable contribution to society. As a single man, retirement was definitely not the pot of gold at the end of the rainbow.

He slowly walked up to the scruffy ancient desk at which Liam sat, with Kevin's bulky apple-shaped body perched awkwardly on the far side.

"Liam, how are you getting on?" he asked softly.

"Not bad, sir. It's just a bit difficult actually writing. To be honest, I don't ever write in real life."

"I'm sure, but who knows how better writing skills might help you outside one day, Liam?"

"I don't know who, sir," he responded uncertainly.

"No, that was a rhetorical question, Liam. That means it was asked purely for effect. It didn't require an actual answer."

"What?"

Mr Blanchflower looked at Kevin, who gave him a weak, knowing smile. Kevin, who was wearing an official green tabard to reflect his assistant status, had been assigned by Mr Blanchflower to help Liam. He would read out short sentences from the Sun newspaper for Liam to write down and then Kevin would carefully explain about any errors, of which there were many, even though it was only the Sun newspaper. It was slow work, but productive and Kevin seemed to have a good temperament for this rather frustrating task. Also, anything was better than being banged up all day long in your cell. Mr Blanchflower noticed that some of the class were becoming rather noisy and discerned that it was time to refocus them.

"I'll explain a little later, Liam. Just let me address the class first."

The setup appeared didactic, with twenty-five ancient wooden desks, complete with highly marked, scratched and engraved lids, facing the front of the class, with an inmate sitting alone at each desk, apart from the very few who had mentors alongside them. There were never any empty desks because classes were always oversubscribed. In fact, Mr Blanchflower did very little didactic teaching.

Over the years, he had acquired masses of teaching materials, as they had been routinely discarded from schools, due to another change of curriculum, or a new secretary for education, or sometimes due to a change in political correctness. The materials were still ideal for use in the prison classroom setting, where he needed as wide a choice of materials as possible. He preferred to set each student specific studies to do, whilst he methodically perambulated the room, monitoring progress, or lack of it and providing a steer where needed. He was a very proficient teacher, benefitting as he did from such long experience and a natural aptitude.

The skillset in the room was mostly, unsurprisingly, low but still quite varied. He usually had three inmates like Kevin to help him. White-collar criminals were a massive boon for the system in a lot of classroom settings. Discipline inside a prison classroom was surprisingly far better than in any normal school and for that, he was very grateful. It made his job so much easier. Inmates were given small weekly allowances for attending any courses they could get booked on to and they were loath to risk those, plus, any misbehaviour would most likely affect their 'incentives and earned privileges' (IEP's) detrimentally and IEP's were guarded very carefully. Attending school here was a privilege.

Mr Blanchflower stood at the front of the room and momentarily looked over the top of his reading spectacles. He had a very self-assured presence and despite being a very tall manly man, he had learned over the years to use his personality and reasoning skills to deal with any challenging situations that came his way. His presence and demeanour magically gained respect. A hush quickly descended upon the room and he spoke, with panache.

"Sometimes, students lose sight as to why studying and improving English is so important. Please, allow me to remind you of some of the very important reasons. English is a very rich and complex language. It allows us to think broadly, in all kinds of spheres; poetry, law, love, the sciences, art, everything really. It is also what equips us to accurately express ourselves to others and for us to understand the complexities of other people's speech or writings. The use and understanding of language can be fine-tuned almost indefinitely. The more we master it, the more powerful we are."

"The pen is mightier than the sword!" a voice bellowed out from the back of the room.

Jason was leaning back in his chair looking very pleased with himself, grinning broadly.

"Precisely, Jason. Thank you for that very apposite quote. That is so very true."

Mr Blanchflower took no exception to any positive contributions from the floor at all. In fact, he was grateful. It showed that students were listening, thinking and engaging and he would do nothing to discourage that. He continued, "Incidentally, who knows what 'apposite' means?"

Nobody answered. The assistants knew to keep quiet unless Mr Blanchflower asked them directly.

"Any of my assistants?"

Mark answered boldly, puffing up a little in his green tabard.

"It means very suitable and pertinent."

"Yes, Mark. Thank you."

Addressing the class, he said, "I'm sure you all know the word 'opposite', so why not 'apposite' as well?"

He paused to allow the words to sink in. Then he continued.

"In George Orwell's classic novel, *1984*, he describes how the totalitarian government was constantly wearing down language by removing literature from their culture and what writings had to remain, were drastically simplified. The regime had an ongoing programme to obliterate the memory and use of as much vocabulary as possible. They ensured that in general, fewer and simpler words were being used. They wanted language to devolve into a simplistic, unsophisticated, child-like form of communication. The objective was to simplify language so much that without sufficient words to resort to, people's thinking skills would be reduced and the less they thought the more autonomous and compliant they would become.

I think that is a fantastic insight into the importance and significance of language. Incidentally, I would thoroughly recommend you all to read that particular book, *1984* and his *Animal Farm*. They are easy to read and provide incredible insight into the human condition. Really, I can't recommend them highly enough. They are in the library here. I keep adding copies!"

This provoked some tittering.

"So, back to my point. The broader your language skills, the better able you are to think and express your thoughts. Agreed?"

There was a broadly cohesive response of 'yes sir' from the group.

"Consider this statement: I didn't kill your cat."

He paused, in order to ensure that the class realised that the statement had finished.

"Just five words, but depending on which word I emphasise, it could be interpreted in five different ways."

There was murmuring, perhaps disbelief and surprise from the assembled flock.

"What does it imply if I emphasise the word 'I'?"

He looked at the class. They were quiet.

"Say the phrase, emphasising the 'I' and tell me what you think."

The class erupted in twenty-five men saying the same thing, over and over, to themselves and to each other. After a few moments, he called them to order.

"Anyone?"

A very young-looking lad near the front spoke up.

"That you didn't kill the cat, but maybe someone else did."

"Precisely, Darren. Thank you."

Darren sat back looking pleased and a bit cocky.

"And if I emphasise the 'didn't'? Say it in your head."

After a short pause, "You're just denying it as we all did."

There was an eruption of laughter.

"Exactly, Steven. An emphatic denial of guilt."

He waited for the laughter to die down and then moved on.

"And what if I emphasise the 'kill'?"

There was silence for a while, as each member spoke the phrase in their mind emphasising the particular word kill, then thinking about how it sounded. A different voice answered assertively.

"I might have injured it but I certainly didn't kill it!"

There was more laughter. The answer had been expressed theatrically, comically.

"Quite right, Conrad. Well done. And if I emphasise the word 'your'?"

Again, a short pause before another member belted out.

"I might have killed a cat, but it certainly wasn't your cat!"

More laughter. Perhaps the idea of killing cats was amusing.

"Exactly, Tony. Thank you. And finally, what if I emphasise the word 'cat'?"

After another thoughtful pause, another answer.

"I didn't kill your cat but I did kill something else of yours."

Again, more laughter. The class was enjoying this exposition.

"Yes, Gavin. Well done. So you can see how just by emphasising a different word in the same short phrase can bring a completely different meaning to it, five times in fact with just five words. This is why writing skills are so important. Somehow, we need to be able to transfer these kinds of subtle nuances to what we write too. Admittedly, it may not always be possible, in which case you simply have to be very careful about what you actually write. Don't write about killing cats."

There were chuckles. Then Mr. Blanchflower asked a question.

"Can anyone explain the word 'nuance' for the class please?"

There was a stony silence. Mr Blanchflower looked at Kevin. He suspected that he would be able to explain, but he needed encouragement to come out of his shell, otherwise, Mark would happily answer again for everyone. Kevin was only in his third week at the jail and this was his first English class. It was the Monday afternoon one and they were also held on Wednesday and Friday afternoons. He had not yet settled down. He was visibly shy, coy and self-conscious. The silence and the expectant stare drew him out. He spoke quietly, reddening.

"It refers to very slight changes of meaning, like slight changes of shades on a colour chart."

"Excellent, Kevin. I couldn't have put it better myself."

More light laughter, with Liam and the other nearby student patting Kevin on the back, making him go even redder in the face. Mr Blanchflower continued.

"With face-to-face communication, how much information is conveyed in the words themselves?"

Murmurings erupted around the room.

"All of it?"

"Nope. 'Fraid not. Give me a percentage."

"Ninety percent?"

"Nope."

"Are you talking about NVC's?"

"Now you're talking."

"I've heard that NVC's make up most of the communication."

"Yes. It is said that NVC's, i.e. non-verbal communication, make up over eighty percent of our communication. Who can describe an NVC?"

There was silence again. The room was captivated in thought. Eventually, it was Jason who piped up again.

"Body language."

"Be more precise."

Another pause.

"Tone of voice."

"Thank you, Gavin. Anyone else?"

"Facial expression."

"Absolutely. What else?"

There were murmurings, but no more concrete answers, so Mr Blanchflower prompted.

"What about the way you might be standing? Or how loudly you're speaking?"

Malcolm piped up, which was good because he was generally rather reserved.

"If you're shouting that means you're probably cross."

"Yes, Malcolm. Thank you. Or if you're trying to be affectionate, you might be speaking softly. Anything else?"

"If you've got 'em by the throat, you're probably being threatening."

More laughter and looking around at themselves in merriment.

"Quite, Jason. At that point, it sounds like you wouldn't be needing much in the way of words at all. The body language would be doing all the talking. So, my point is that when we are talking face to face, we communicate very largely with the look on our face, the intonation of our voice, our body position, whether it is open or closed, whether we are loud or quiet, or whether we are holding somebody by the throat."

More laughter.

"So what happens when we write things down?"

Jason again, "You can't be aggressive or menacing?"

More chuckles. "Not necessarily Jason. It's just harder to convey your feelings and emotions with just words on paper. I'm sure on the outside, you all text loads, yeah?"

There was a rumble of affirmation in the room accompanied by lots of nodding.

"Ok. So have any of you sent texts, which later on you found had been misinterpreted?"

Again, lots of talking amongst themselves before John interjected loudly.

"My missus always gets me wrong. I fukin' dread texting her."

"Yes, John. It's a very common problem. I don't mean about people all texting your missus."

Before he could finish, there was a round of good-humoured laughter before he continued.

"I mean in general, with people being misunderstood when they text. My point is this, that to be more effective when writing texts, e-mails, or, God-forbid, real letters, the better your command of the English language, the more successfully you represent yourself, the less likelihood of a misunderstanding. Is that important?"

There was a big joined-up 'yes sir' from the class.

In effect, Mr Blanchflower was giving the class some light relief. He took classes with them from 1.45 p.m. until 3.45 p.m. and that was quite a long time. Inmates weren't the best people at concentrating for a long period of time, so he always tried to introduce some anecdotes to amuse them in the second hour after they'd already taken a comfort and smoke break. He got the impression that most of them thoroughly enjoyed his classes anyway, at least in comparison to just being isolated in their cells watching daytime TV, which would likely be the only alternative. Moreover, he was a professional and he wanted to make the experience as beneficial and enjoyable as possible. He respected his students, prisoners or not.

"Ok, I'm going to tell you a story about the great Winston Churchill, who was a man of great wit. He was sitting in one of the many plush lounges in the Palace of Westminster—that's the houses of Parliament to you and me by the way—when a colleague came over to him and started caressing the top of his bald head. This colleague then said, 'Ooh, that feels just like my wife's bottom.'"

The class sniggered. Mr Blanchflower carried on.

"Mr Churchill then caressed his own bald head and said emphatically, 'Oh yes, so it does!'"

Most of the class roared. Not all of them. Some didn't get the punch-line and other inmates started to explain it to them. Then Mr Blanchflower interjected mischievously.

"Oh no, that was the wrong story. I meant to tell you another one."

The class laughed some more. Mr Blanchflower gave them time to enjoy their merriment. Prisons don't have a lot of merriment generally and he did his best to lighten the atmosphere for his students. He carried on with the more relevant anecdote.

"Ok. So Mr Churchill is handed a big fat dossier from one of his colleagues for reading in due course and he said to this colleague 'I'll waste no time in reading that.'"

The class looked a little bemused.

"What did he mean?"

There were a few low whisperings but it seemed they were being non-committal.

"Anyone?" Mr Blanchflower wasn't giving anything away yet.

Darren spoke up again. "He meant that he would get on and read it soon?"

"Ok, Darren. Could be. Anyone else with a different interpretation?"

Surprisingly, it was Liam who piped up.

"He meant that he wouldn't waste any time fukin' reading it. That's what he fukin' said, innit?"

Yet more laughter.

"Well done Liam. You spotted the double meaning. And you, Darren. You're both right. Churchill deliberately gave the man an ambiguous answer, which was actually rather clever, I think. Who can define the word 'ambiguous'?"

Gavin piped up. "It means that it could be interpreted in different ways, depending."

"Very good, Gavin. Thank you. You see, sometimes we say what we know we mean to say but unless we're really clear, someone else might interpret it differently, maybe because of the mood they're in or maybe because we have been unintentionally ambiguous."

"Yeah, my missus is always in a frickin' mood."

"And I'm sure you're not the only one John. So, what could Mr Churchill have added into his statement to be exact about his intentions, either way?"

Much pondering seemed to be occurring before Darren explained his way of thinking.

"He could have said that he would waste no time in getting on with reading it."

"Yes, Darren. By inserting one or two extra words that intention would have been made crystal clear. On the other hand, he could have said that he would waste no time in actually reading it. Again, that would have been crystal clear the other way. So what is my point?"

"Make sure we think about how we come across?"

"Yes Ron, especially when you're writing something. Look at what you've written and try to see it from someone else's perspective and ask yourself if it makes crystal clear sense to them, not you, because the English language can be very subtle sometimes and can be subject to interpretation."

Mr Blanchflower observed the class. He felt that they had received his lesson well and that he had laboured his points sufficiently. Nobody looked particularly confused, so he carried on.

"Right, going back to our exercise with killing the cat or not, as the case might be, we were exploring the effect of emphasising one particular word verbally. How do we do that in our writing?"

There was another stony silence.

"What do we do to a written word to demonstrate that we are emphasising it over and above the others?"

Still, no answer. It was time for the Kevin-stare again, who similarly to earlier, blushed over before answering.

"Write it in italics?"

"Spot on, Kevin. Thank you. I presume most of you are fairly computer literate. How many of you are doing some kind of computer training here?"

About half the inmates raised their hands.

"Good. Well if any of you don't know how to do the italic thingy, please ask your computer teacher to show you. It's really very simple. Right, well, that's enough from me for one day. Please carry on with your tasks."

He walked over to Liam again and had a discussion about rhetorical questions. After going over a few common examples, Liam got it. He then took Kevin to one side.

"Kevin, I'd like to get Liam playing scrabble during association time. It would be really good for him. Would you be willing to help?"

Kevin looked a bit surprised. He found association times awkward as he hadn't made any friends yet, so he generally went just to sit quietly at the back of the room to watch the big telly and have a change of scenery. He was wary of mixing. These people were most definitely not his type and he was very out of sorts. On the other hand, he was not going to be awkward with one of the instructors whom he'd only just met that afternoon.

"Ok," he replied thoughtfully. "Who else will join us?"

"I'll put a notice on the notice board and we'll see if we get any takers."

Association time usually ran from 6p.m. to 7:45 p.m. after tea, which was taken inside the cells and before lock-up for the night. Like everything inside, it always depended on enough staff being available for the event to go ahead reasonably safely and was subject to change at very short notice. It was permissible most evenings and prisoners could freely congregate in the association room of their wing for games and socialising. They could also visit the library. There was a pool table, a table tennis table, a table football and a cupboard containing a wide variety of board games, including scrabble.

At 3:45 p.m., Mr Blanchflower declared the class over. Officially, there was still an hour of class time left, so some inmates would remain. A few volunteer mentors from the Shannon's Trust were waiting outside in the corridor to come in and do one-to-one reading with some of them for half an hour or so. Mr Blanchflower was also happy to leave Kevin working with Liam and the other white-collar assistants, Christopher and Mark, with their charges, if they were happy to carry on. About twenty of the class filed outside into the corridor where Officer Larry was waiting. Each inmate spoke to him in turn. Some might be allowed to go into the exercise yard for a smoke, some to the library, but most would saunter straight back to their cells for lock up before tea collection after 4:45 p.m.

Chapter 2

Tuesday evening and the association room was buzzing with noise. About a hundred inmates were socialising. Not actually socialising necessarily, as most were just watching the huge flat-screen TV at one end of the room but some were sitting around the small tables just talking or playing games. There were no comfy chairs or settees here. They would be too easy to secrete things in and would potentially pose a security risk. If an inmate desired comfort above all else, he would have to go to his cell to relax on his two-inch thick plastic mattress. All the chairs here were simple, basic, uncomfortable plastic ones with sturdy metal frames and legs. Easy to inspect. Easy to clean, and difficult to pull apart, just like the tables. The table tennis, the pool table, and the table football were always in much demand but there was a pecking order for those and the weaker inmates only got to use them when the more dominant inmates had had enough, or weren't around.

The prisoners looked like a patchwork of colours. They almost all wore the standard grey jogging pants but most of them wore their own tops, which were mostly very colourful. They were not allowed to have dark clothing inside prison because of the risk of emulating officer uniforms. Those in standard kit wore grey or blue tops. Personal tops were a part of the privilege structure. Inmates were given a little bit of individuality back as a reward for good behaviour.

Then there were the contrasting haircuts. The only rule here was that you kept your hair smart and clean. In the past, long hair had been disallowed, because of the risk of smuggling contraband in it, but that rule had become much more lenient in recent times, so long as hair was kept hygienic. A shaved head was very popular, not because it was favoured by the authorities but because it looked hard. The visiting wing barber was always busy. Finally, as a lot of inmates were wearing only T-shirts, a great many varied and colourful tattoos were on show, on arms, necks and in some cases, faces and heads.

There were only six officers present and they spent most of their time standing around, socialising with each other, but always side-glancing cautiously. They might have appeared to be distracted by their own company but they were discreetly vigilant. Similarly, amongst the inmates, ethnic groups all socialised amongst their own kind. You could look around the room and see several pockets of black or brown, amongst the majority of whites. Anyone who broke the unspoken race rule was called a race-traitor. 'Loyalty' was big. Integration was not. On further inspection, you could even delineate the white groups by language. The eastern Europeans, of whom there was a surprisingly significant representation, also stuck together. There was safety in association but any gang formations were strongly thwarted by the staff to avoid future tribal conflict. Sometimes it might be necessary to move certain inmates to different wings to prevent undesirable associations from developing.

Officer Prowse came over to the far end of the association room where the tables were situated. He awaited the scrabble volunteers to arrive. Mr Blanchflower had asked him to get things organised, on his behalf. Ten names had gone very quickly onto the list yesterday evening after it had gone up and officer Prowse had contacted each subject when they had been collecting their tea. There would be two games of four participants with the last two on the list going onto the reserve list. He had asked the eight players to meet him there in the association room at six-fifteen this evening. He divided up the volunteers and provided them with two games. Kevin and Liam would be joined by Denis and Terry. The other four were packed off to play on a table a bit further away.

Mr Blanchflower took it upon himself to augment prison English accessories. He had never attended the association room when it was in use, but he was allowed to inspect accessories on request when he was attending during the afternoons English lessons. The staff appreciated his interest and support and Mr Prowse, in particular, seemed to admire and affiliate with Mr Blanchflower. Some officers were completely cynical about trying to help inmates develop in any way, even though the official dogma was to look after them with humanity and help them lead law-abiding and useful lives in custody and after release.

If he felt that new games could be added to the association room stock, he would look out for them in charity shops. Similarly, he would often turn up with bag loads of fresh books for the wing library, which he had acquired from the serendipitous charity shops. He chose stories about life in general, up-lit, biographies, inspirational life stories, but not murder mysteries and whodunits, of which the library had plenty already. He had started doing this several years earlier when he was incensed that the then education secretary, Chris Grayling, had banned inmates from receiving books as gifts from friends and relatives on the outside because it was contributing to too much luxury! Mr Blanchflower felt that was so counterintuitive and short-sighted, it beggared belief.

Fortunately, the decision was overturned by a court shortly afterwards, when it was ruled that inmates were entitled to receive materials of interest to them and their particular studies and prison libraries couldn't possibly cater for all tastes and requirements on their own. He didn't mind spending a little of his own money on such a good cause. He was a single man with a good pension. He owned his own home and was relatively well-off. He despised parsimony.

Denis was a white male in his mid-sixties, who normally lived alone. He found it very tiresome living cheek-by-jowl with so many other males. He preferred the company of women. He was the proverbial 'ladies' man'. He was rather small and diminutive, but he kept himself surprisingly fit, mainly with cardiovascular exercise. He maintained a smart, dapper appearance, which suited his clean-cut looks. He was always clean-shaven and had short thinning hair of a distinctive salt and pepper hue. His features were still quite distinctive, despite the sagging process having taken effect in recent years. In his youth, he would have appeared quite handsome, no doubt. He was one year into a four-year term for fraud.

Terry was much younger than Denis, being late thirties. He normally lived with his partner, Valerie, but had no kids. His trade was painter and decorator and apart from his occasional stints inside, he had always worked very solidly since his late teens. He'd had a very average education via the comprehensive school system and it became clear early in his education that his forte would be practical work rather than academic or administrative.

He was very distinctive looking due to his curly, ginger, shoulder-length hair and his very large build. He was six foot three and muscular. That was a very helpful asset inside the prison environment. These days, a lot of young men easily exceeded six foot but they hadn't filled out yet like Terry had. Like Denis, he regularly made efforts to keep fit but he was more into weight training and building muscle. Also like Denis, he was a non-smoker. His vice was drinking because its effect on him could be undesirable, as he had a rather fiery temper. Through hard steady work over the years, he had done quite well for himself. He owned his own home and drove a Mercedes car. He was only two months into an eighteen-month sentence for GBH.

Liam was serving a sentence for supplying class-A drugs. He was about seven months into an eighteen months sentence. Kevin was the newest and he was facing the longest stretch. He was a mere two weeks into an eight-year sentence for causing death by dangerous driving. He looked older than he was because, over the years, he had not looked after himself. He worked, ate, slept and worked again without taking the time out for self-development or any kind of fitness activity. Now he was quite chubby and as he was not a tall man, he looked fatter than he really was. He did have a good head of hair, however. It was thick and dark brown, to which his heavy dark-rimmed glasses were well suited. He looked particularly scruffy in prison clothing, as none of it fitted him well.

They each sat at one face of the square table. If Denis was north, Terry was east, Liam south and Kevin west. Denis spoke first and very brightly.

"Well, this should be interesting! I haven't played scrabble for an age. I'm Denis, by the way."

They all shook hands and introduced themselves, apart from Kevin and Liam, who obviously were already acquainted.

"I hope you're all crap at this," Terry interjected, "because I hate fuckin' losing."

The others all went quiet. Terry was a menacing presence. There was always something scary about a broken nose on a man, especially a man of this size. Terry noted the silent look of fear on all the other faces.

"Only kidding guys," he added, smiling.

The others relaxed a little, uncertainly. Many a true word is spoken in jest!

Denis made a move to get the game started.

"I take it we all know the rules?"

Affirmative mutterings and nods apart from Liam, who just sat quietly.

"Great. Can I make a suggestion? The person with the longest first-word starts because that makes the rest of the game easier."

The others looked around at each other. No one had an objection. Denis continued.

"Also, a player gets a double-word score if he uses up all his tiles. That's in the rules. Ok?"

Again. Compliance and they took turns to delve into the green bag for their first seven tiles. As they inspected their lot, looks of concentration and frustration overtook their faces, apart from Liam, that is. He just looked like his usual nonchalant self. He would make an excellent poker player. Kevin reluctantly spoke up. He was just passing on a message from Mr Blanchflower.

"Mr Blanchflower has asked if we each make an attempt to tell a story using the words we place on the board."

The others all looked surprised. He hoped no one would query this because he didn't want to seem argumentative.

"That's not in the rules," Denis offered rather contrarily.

"I know," Kevin replied gently, very nervous not to offend anyone. He was still nervous of everybody in the wing, especially the big men like Terry.

"Mr Blanchflower simply suggested it. He said it's a good way for us to learn to be more expressive and to get thinking."

He looked at Denis and nodded slyly towards Liam. He didn't want them thinking that he thought that they needed development. It was for Liam.

"Who the fuck is this Blanchflower bloke?" Terry enquired loudly.

Liam spoke up in his usual slow monotone voice.

"He's the English teacher. He's a good bloke. You don't fuck with him."

"So you want to do this story thing?"

"Why not, Terry? I mean, it depends on what words you get, doesn't it? I mean, if you spell out pussy, you could probably tell a story about a bit of pussy, couldn't you?"

The others all laughed. It relieved the tension.

"I see," Terry continued. "It's going to be that sort of game, is it? Ok."

Denis interjected.

"Let's just see how we get on. I don't fancy it myself."

"Yeah, but if you do one, you should get extra points, yeah?" Liam added.

"Fair enough, but how many?"

"I don't fukin' know, do I? I've never played fukin scrabble before, have I?"

Liam smiled and added.

"That was a rhetorical question, by the way. No need to answer."

Terry and Denis looked a bit nonplussed. Kevin smiled. Terry broke the short silence.

"Come on then, you tossers. Are we going to play or not?"

Liam asked slowly and seriously.

"Terry, was that a rhetorical question?"

Terry looked very directly at Liam sitting to his left.

"Can we just get on with the game, you dense fucker?"

Denis was looking pleased with himself and asked

"Has anyone got a word yet?"

There was silence as others focussed on their tile racks.

After a while Liam spoke.

"I've got one."

"How many letters?"

"Three."

Denis let out a little bemused snort, without intending to. He quickly covered his mirth by adding.

"Anyone else?"

Kevin offered "Five."

"Terry?"

'Hang on y'fucker. Don't rush me."

Denis hung on silently, for as long as Terry needed.

"Six!"

"Seven." Denis countered immediately.

They all looked at him in disbelief.

Terry chided him. "Why didn't you just say that in the first place?"

"In case anyone else had seven."

He happily placed his tiles down. A 'Y' on the triple letter score in the middle line then the rest of the letters to make 'gainsay' across the board. He proudly proclaimed, "That's a double word score for going first and another double word score for using all my letters."

He added up the score and claimed an impressive seventy-six!

"What the fuck is a gainsay?" Liam queried.

Denis could see that this was going to, possibly, become tedious. Kevin stayed quiet. He wasn't going to risk any conflict with anyone.

"It means that you can't say anything against something. Like, you can't gainsay that I didn't just score seventy-six."

Liam drawled out his thoughts.

"Wait a minute. You said that if anyone goes first, they'd get a double word score and you said that if they used up all their letters, they'd get another double word score and then you went first and used up all your letters on the first go. Doesn't that strike you as pretty fukin' fishy?"

Denis giggled. He knew that this looked like he had fixed it but he hadn't.

"Liam, it was just luck of the tiles and skill. Of course I didn't fix it! I just had a very lucky start."

Liam wasn't convinced.

"It seems very fishy to me, especially as you're a professional conman."

Denis looked embarrassed. Inmates didn't normally make reference to each other's crimes, not unless they wanted to provoke trouble. It was one of the unwritten rules. The exception of course was for sex offenders, but they kept on their own wing, for their own protection. Terry piped up.

"Liam, let's give him the benefit of the doubt for now, yeah? If we find out later that he cheated, we'll break his arms then, ok?"

Liam looked sullenly at Terry before quietly agreeing. Denis's eyes betrayed just a little terror. Terry was slightly excited. He could still get his six-letter word down. It crossed Denis's word on the second 'A' going down the board.

"Domain." he read out proudly as he totted up his eighteen-point score, which also included a double word score. Liam looked at Denis, who was writing down the score.

"I don't want that old fucker keeping the score. I don't trust him. Kevin, you do it."

Kevin looked embarrassed. Terry looked sternly at Denis, who readily handed over the scoresheet to Kevin.

"Whatever." he conceded, holding up his hands in all innocence.

Liam added 'awper' downwards beneath the 'G' of 'gainsay' and felt the need to explain.

"You know. When someone is looking at you and you say 'what are you fukin' gawping at, you gawper?'."

"Yes, we get it, Liam. Very good. How much?"

Liam asked Kevin to score him. He'd gotten a 'W' on a triple letter score, so all in, that came to twenty. Then Kevin took a few moments to add his own word. He put a 'P' on a triple letter score at the extreme left-hand side of the board and placed 'partner' across Liam's gawper, crossing it on the 'E'. He also got a double word score.

"Thirty," he said as he simultaneously wrote it down.

"The end of round one, gentlemen and the scores are?"

21

Terry looked at Kevin expectantly.

Kevin hesitated. He was loath to annoy Terry, even if it was only by reading out the scores.

"In reverse order, Terry eighteen, Liam twenty, me thirty and Denis seventy-six."

Liam laughed. "I'm beating you, Terry!"

"Early days yet bro, early days." Then he added. "Can anyone do a story from their word?"

"Certainly not me," said Denis.

"Not me," from Liam.

"Nor me," added Terry, "But Kevin, you can do something with 'partner' yeah?"

"You think?"

"You look like you're married."

Kevin wondered how he could tell. He'd surrendered his wedding ring on entry, as was required, for safe-keeping. Then he realised that the tell-tale paleness and indentation of where his ring had been for twenty years still disclosed his status.

"Ok. Maybe, but I'll want bonus points."

"How many?"

"Fifty!"

Denis piped up immediately. "Fifteen maybe, but not fifty."

"I'm only doing it for fifty. That will put me in the lead."

"Vote," Terry succinctly announced, raising his hand in approval.

Obviously, Kevin raised his hand too, but so did Liam.

"Carried," announced Terry.

Denis huffed disapprovingly, but they all looked at Kevin expectantly. He looked straight ahead of himself, gaze low, as if he were looking at the board, but his eyes appeared strangely vacant. He spoke in a low sullen tone. They could only just hear him over the general buzz of sound in the huge room.

"I met my wife when I was twenty-six. I married her two years later. Before you knew it, we had two kids and I was supporting all of us on one wage. I worked bloody hard, long hours, but I managed. I was an industrial photocopier salesman, you know, more or less all my life. Some nights I would stay away in a hotel. It was too far to come home the same day. It was on those particular evenings that I used to drink out of boredom. I wasn't normally a drinker. On one of those occasions, I was drinking in town, you know, for a bit more atmosphere, but when I was driving back to the hotel, I caught the kerb coming out of a roundabout and mounted the pavement. I ended up crushing some poor woman pedestrian up against a wall."

He went silent. The others were all silent too. They realised that this was hard for him. Kevin's eyes started to water up.

Liam implored him in a loud whisper, "Don't fuckin' cry, Kevin. If any of the other cunts in here see you crying, they'll be picking on you every five minutes and you're already a soft target."

Terry patted Liam firmly on the chest.

"Shut the fuck up, Liam, you dunce."

Kevin blinked and tears squeezed out of his eyes and rolled down his cheeks. He continued.

"Of course, I stopped and did what I could to help. Someone called an ambulance. It seemed to take an age for that to arrive. At about the same time, the cops arrived. I got breathalysed and nicked. To cut a long story short, I got done for causing death by dangerous driving because I was over the limit. I destroyed two lives that night. That poor woman's and my wife's. Now I'm in here for God knows how long and meanwhile, she's suddenly got no income, no one to pay the mortgage and two teenage daughters to bring up on her own. I love that woman, but I've fucked her life up completely."

He fell silent, just about holding himself together. The others, who had all been inside before, instinctively recognised Kevin as a suicide risk. He was not the sort to cope well in prison, which was such a stark contrast to his normal life and experience.

"Jesus, Kevin. This isn't supposed to be a confessional," hissed Denis, feeling embarrassed for him.

Liam put an arm across Kevin's back. "Don't beat yourself up too much, mate. It could have happened to anyone."

With that, he got out a couple of smokes and handed one to Kevin.

"That deserves a bat, mate."

Kevin readily accepted the fag. Smokes were precious inside. They were the best illicit currency and to buy a week's supply took up most of a person's weekly allowance. Liam was being very generous. He got up and sauntered over to the officers and asked for a light, which he was duly given. Strictly speaking, smoking was not allowed outside of the cells but in practice, that rule was generally relaxed, especially in the association room. The whole fragile penal system, balanced on a give-and-take framework. He re-joined the scrabble team and lit Kevin's fag from his own.

"God," said Terry, "follow that."

There was quiet. The non-smokers busied themselves with their new tiles. Liam just seemed mesmerised by his fag and Kevin was lost in thought, taking occasional deep drags on his. After a while, Denis broke the silence.

"Well, I suppose it's my go again."

He wanted to come up with words that could not possibly form the basis of any story, certainly not a personal one. He placed a 'V' on a triple letter score next to the 'O' of domain and completed the word 'volume', with the 'M' also on a triple letter score.

"That's twenty-five, Kevin?"

Kevin snapped out of his thoughts to an extent and wrote down Denis's score. Terry was quite quickly ready with his vertical word for the top right-hand corner. With a "B" on the triple word score square, he made 'before' by using the 'E' of volume. The 'O' landed on a double letter score.

"Before," he stated boldly. "That's twelve times three. Thirty-six."

He seemed very pleased with getting a triple word score, yet his actual score was not particularly high. A few moments later, Liam steadily placed four tiles on the board.

"That's handy," he said sluggishly, "I was wondering where to put my word 'hand' and you've helped me out, Terry. Thanks for that mate."

He placed 'hand' on the end of 'before'. It formed another triple word score. Maths was not Liam's strong point. He looked at Kevin.

"How much did I score mate?"

Kevin totted it up. The eight of 'hand' added to the eleven of 'before' made nineteen, on a triple word score.

"Fifty-seven! Excellent score, Liam"

Terry interjected. "Liam, you're not nearly as thick as you make out, are you mate?"

Liam took that remark in good humour and looked proud of himself, but really, he had been very lucky. Kevin spent some time playing with ideas. He had a 'J' which was worth eight points and so he was looking at various alternatives to maximise the score using the 'J'. He settled on a rather fortuitous use of all his letters, including a blank. He crossed the first 'R' of 'partner' with a vertical 'majority'. The 'A' got a double letter score and he had to use his blank tile for the 'Y', but the whole word sat on a double word score and as he used up all his tiles in one go, he got another double word score. He totted it up so the others could hear. Seventeen. Double word score. Thirty-four. Another double word score. Sixty-eight. Terry whistled.

"Man, you're quite some operator, you fat fucker and I thought you were nodding off. How do the scores look after that round then, pumpkin?"

"You, fifty-four. Liam seventy-seven. Denis one hundred and one. Me, one hundred and forty eight. Denis looked crestfallen. He thought that he was going to breeze through this to certain victory against this rabble but he was already being trounced. Liam stood up and unexpectedly announced that he had to go.

"We'll carry on tomorrow night yeah?" he said imploringly.

The others were taken aback by his premature departure. There was about half an hour of association time left but nobody wanted to force anything. Denis picked up the conversation.

"Ok, mate. See you tomorrow, same place, same time, funnily enough."

Kevin had already started to scrawl down the words on the board so that they could reconfigure them the next day. Then he dutifully cleared away the board.

"I take it that new tiles for each of us tomorrow is ok? Saves writing down what we've got now."

Both Terry and Denis affirmed. They, obviously, didn't particularly like their current letters.

Terry put a very large hand on his shoulder.

"You ok, mate?" he enquired as sensitively as he could manage.

"Yes, Terry. Thank you."

"What are you going to do now?"

"I think I'll return to my cage early. I'm feeling pretty tired out."

"Ok, mate. You look after yourself, yeah?"

"Of course, Terry. See you tomorrow."

Chapter 3

Like all the others, Kevin had collected his breakfast yesterday at tea time and had kept it overnight to eat in his cell prior to unlock time at 8.15 a.m.; Cereals with relatively warm UHT milk. Generally, the cells each had a small kettle for making tea and coffee as well. He shared that with his cellmate, a lanky stick-thin heroin addict called Mac. Mac was sullen and seemed depressed all of the time and barely spoke. He didn't leave the cell much either, which meant he was locked up for most of each day, just dossing or watching the tiny cell TV. Kevin found his depression catching and was always desperate to escape that cell as soon and as often as he could. Strictly speaking, he shouldn't have been bunked with a druggie, known as a fiend, inside. That was against official prison policy, but due to limited practical options and the proliferation of druggies, that policy regularly fell by the wayside.

The first opportunity for him to escape the cell was at 8:15 a.m. for half an hour exercise in the outside yard, so long as the weather wasn't too inclement. He was not a man given to exercise, but he would go out into the yard purely for a change of scenery, although the word scenery was hardly the apt description and for some actual fresh air. The yard was surrounded by tall grey walls but at least they could see the sky. The other inmates out there were in pairs or small groups and he felt odd being alone, but he felt safe enough because there was always an officer or two in the yard. In his previous life, he had been far too busy working and driving all over the place to fit in anything to do with exercise. Hence his overweight out-of-shape body, which showed all the signs of premature heart attack, stroke, or diabetes. The fact that he was a regular smoker didn't help.

He had completed the obligatory new-arrivals 'rehabilitation of offenders' course over a week ago, so now he was ready to be put to work. This Wednesday morning, following his precious half an hour outside, his personal officer, Mary Jacobs, introduced him to an inmate who was permanently on the cleaning team—a relatively old prisoner in his fifties, called George—who was going to show him the ropes for cleaning duty.

All routine tasks within the prison were carried out by inmates and inmates who worked earned about twelve pounds a week on top of their ordinary allowance of ten or fifteen pounds, depending on how long they had been inside. Courses were better than working. They only paid slightly less and were far more interesting and might even benefit the attendee in due course on the outside. Wages were added to an inmate's cash account called their canteen.

Kevin's basic allowance of ten pounds a week would increase to fifteen pounds after about one month. He would need that money just for fags. Any wages he earned would be in addition to his account. Relatives were allowed to deposit funds into an inmate's cash account but the inmate could only actually access a certain amount each week, ranging from four pounds to twenty-five, depending on their 'Incentives and Earned Privileges' status.

On the canteen sheet, they could put in a weekly order for toiletries and other essentials provided they had sufficient funds of course. There was no credit in prison and no cash. Cigarettes or drugs were the unofficial currency.

Kevin found everything about prison degrading and insulting, apart from helping Liam learn to read and write better. That was the only thing so far that he derived any satisfaction from. Cleaning shower blocks, floors and toilets would be most degrading.

He found the inmates scary, the food disgusting, the routines depressing, the smells unpleasant, the surroundings inhuman, the officers disinterested, the television programmes dull and repetitive and he couldn't even sleep properly. There were too many strange noises. He missed his family dreadfully. He missed curling up in bed next to the warm comforting body of his wife. He missed her support and her female company. He missed his lovely daughters painfully and having choices about what he wore, what he ate, where he would go, what he would do and who he would see. He missed being a real human being, amongst people he could understand and whose language he could speak.

He didn't think he could carry on like this for months, let alone years. He could feel his stress levels sky-high, constantly. He was far too timid for prison life and he lived in constant fear. He knew that even just the anxiety he felt was really bad for his health and if this was life now, he didn't want to live.

After two hours of mopping floors and cleaning toilets, showers and sinks, it was time to go to the serving area at the kitchen to collect a plastic bowl of mush which they called dinner and like everyone else, he had to take it back to his cell to eat it whilst locked up for an hour and a half.

He noticed that Mac didn't even always go out to collect dinner, which helped to account for his stick-like appearance. He was on meds for his drug habit and maybe they suppressed his appetite too. One thing was for sure, Kevin would lose weight inside too. Yesterday afternoon had been mind-numbingly and soul-destroyingly dull and tedious. He had been banged up in his cell with the vacant Mac and a small TV which provided just a little entertainment.

Normally an inmate wouldn't be eligible for any afternoon classes until he had been inside, trouble-free, for a month. The only reason he had access to the afternoon English class so soon was because his personal officer had pulled some strings, knowing that he would be beneficial for Mr Blanchflower as an assistant and unbeknown to him, she was worried about his mental health. She hoped that the class would lift his spirits as Mr Blanchflower was well known for being a great tonic. This afternoon, Kevin would be attending his second English lesson and for that, he was very grateful.

After the class, which he had to admit, was actually quite enjoyable again, he went to the serving area to collect sandwiches for tea and breakfast for the next day. Prison officers stood around in strategic places, ensuring that inmates were going in the right direction at the right time. Any discrepancies in the well-practiced routines would soon be noticed and draw interest. After all, the officers were bored too and if anything could break their monotony, they would pounce on it. They always worked the same wing, with the same inmates, so as to become familiar with them, their routines and their characters. Even inside a prison, each person was still an individual and needed to be understood, if things were to go as smoothly as possible. Tea was consumed back in the cells, under lock and key.

Association time, from 6p.m. to 7:45 p.m., was the final burst of 'freedom' for the day. He arrived in the association room before the others and set up the scrabble board with the words of yesterday. Next to arrive was Terry. He still smelt of shower gel and looked fresh. He had showered just before tea after a hot afternoon working in the laundry room. Prisons were keen on hygiene. Showers here were available whenever inmates were allowed out of their cells. In fact, if an inmate was found to be unhygienic, he could incur a penalty and both the staff and inmates would somehow ensure they changed their ways. Nobody wanted stinking people walking, eating, or sitting around them.

"Hello, pumpkin. How was your day? He enquired brightly of Kevin.

Kevin looked at him sullenly. "The English lesson was the good bit. Everything else was awful, abysmal, dire, depressing, atrocious and diabolical."

"Oh, not too bad then," he answered cheerfully, interrupting his diatribe and sat looking around the room to watch inmates as they filed in. It always paid to know who associated with whom. The coteries that formed inside were called cars. If you fell out with one member of a car, you fell out with all of them. Denis sauntered up with too much energy for a man of his age.

"Yo dudes," he declared, trying to be trendy as he pulled out a seat.

"We're not in a fuckin' cowboy film, you ninja-bandit," Terry answered rather abruptly.

Denis was not going to be an easy man to warm up to. Even in prison there is scorn for some types of prisoners and it was known that Denis was an offender who financially exploited lonely, little old ladies. That wouldn't win him any respect here, although it was unlikely that he would actually incur the physical wrath of other inmates like a sex offender would.

"Ok," he responded, a little bemused. He sat down and asked Kevin for the bag and efficiently grabbed seven new tiles. Kevin followed suit.

"Aren't we going to wait for Liam then?" Terry queried.

"He's late." Denis answered, smiling, "That's his lookout. It means we get more time to work on our tiles."

He kept his head down, focussing, glancing from tiles to board and back again. He wanted to get his lead back. About five minutes later, Liam shuffled over and sat down quietly. They all stared at him silently. His face was a mess. He had a black left eye, complete with a very bloodshot eyeball, fat swollen lips and a puffy reddened left cheek. Only Kevin was fairly clueless as to how this would have happened and it made him even more worried for himself. Terry suddenly looked very angry. He hissed.

"Do the screws know about this?"

"About what?"

"I take that as a no."

This was not a matter for discussion. They were just a scrabble rabble, playing scrabble-babble, not a car, or some other kind of brotherhood. Kevin gingerly handed Liam the tile bag and placed his rack in front of him. Liam looked at the board and announced in his usual pedestrian manner, that he wanted to tell a story; only his pronunciation was not nearly as adequate as usual, because of his puffy lips.

"Is that allowed?" asked Denis innocently.

"Why the fuck not?" replied Terry. Then he looked at Liam.

"With your word 'hand'?"

"I actually made 'beforehand'," Liam corrected him.

"Ok. So you mean your word and my one, yeah?"

"Yep."

They were all gobsmacked that Liam wanted to talk in his condition, so much so that they completely forgot to argue over how many bonus points he might acquire. Then he started, speaking very slowly.

"I grew up in the country, right next to a farm. When I was a kid, we would play in the fields, playing chicken with the cows or bullocks and stuff like that. We would often climb up massive stacks of straw bales in the barns and make dens in them. We could spend hours there, hiding and pretending things."

Denis interrupted him. "You're supposed to be using the word 'beforehand'."

Terry gave him a dirty look, but Liam slowly continued.

"Just wait. I'll get to that point, you cocksucker. As I was saying, before I was rudely interrupted by some cunt, I and a few friends spent loads of time playing in the farmyard. The old farmer would chase us out when he saw us, but most of the time, he was clueless as to where we were. Anyway, in one of the barns was a huge grain silo and it had a narrow little metal ladder going all the way to the top on one side of it. It was scary climbing up it. You can imagine. It was about a hundred feet tall and I was only eight.

Anyway, we used to climb up it for a dare. One day, when I got to the top, I saw that the silo was full to the top with grain and I climbed over the top to stand on the grain. Trouble is, I sank right into it like it was quicksand. Eventually, my friends realised that something was badly wrong and they went and fetched the farmer. He called out the fire brigade. One of them was lowered into the silo with breathing gear on, on a rope. Apparently, he went right under the grain too and after a few minutes though, he managed to fish me out. We were both hoisted out but they thought I was dead. They reckon I had been without much oxygen for about half an hour.

An ambulance took me to the hospital anyway and in the ambulance, I seemed to revive just enough for them to realise that I actually wasn't dead and they nursed me back to health over the next few weeks. So here's the word, 'beforehand', Denis. Beforehand, I was a normal bright little boy, but afterwards, I was a little bit slower and had to go to a special school."

He sat there, cool as a cucumber. No emotion. It was all so matter of fact.

"Well, that was a cheery story, wasn't it" laughed Denis loudly. "Who thought that scrabble-babble could be such a fun game, such a barrel of laughs?"

Terry looked at him and chided him

"You're such a fuckin' sociopath, Denis!"

"Whatever. I'm just not sure that we need more depressing stories. This place is depressing enough already."

Liam piped up.

"It's not a depressing story Denis. It's a miracle that I'm still here. I'm a miracle."

"Yeah, ok, Liam. You're a miracle, just like the baby Jesus."

"Exactly," Then he asked, business-like, "How many points?"

Terry spoke quietly, "Gotta be worth fifty."

Kevin nodded approvingly. Denis huffed disapprovingly but didn't say anything else and Kevin recorded a bonus of fifty. He looked at Liam and was shocked to see that all that talking had made his lips start to bleed. He looked at Denis and, in a subdued voice, said, "Your go."

Denis was well ready with his next word, 'home'. He placed it horizontally across the 'M' of 'majority', the 'E' was on a double letter score and the 'H' was on a triple word score.

"Ten times three," he announced proudly.

Kevin recorded the thirty. Now it was Terry's go. He was trailing badly and needed a good story score to keep himself in the running. He studied the board seriously, blanking out the distracting sounds of the room. Prisoners, in general, learned to blank out sounds and discomfort, otherwise, how would they ever get any sleep? His face lit up as he energetically placed 'oxygen' at the bottom left-hand corner of the board, crossing the blank 'Y' of 'majority and getting the 'O' on a triple word score. He totted it up.

"Fifteen times three. Forty-five! Eat your heart out, Denis."

"You're such a jammy bugger," Denis retorted, staring at the word, wondering if he could have done better on his last go. Terry continued playfully.

"I could do a good story on oxygen or the lack of it, but Liam's already done that one."

He chuckled. Liam answered slowly, "You wouldn't tell it as well as I did, dump truck."

Now it was Liam's go, but he checked with Terry first to see if he wanted to do a story.

"What? With oxygen. I don't think so, mate."

They all looked at the board, all secretly hoping that Liam would find a good opportunity. Liam asked, "Is there such a word as 'oxygenated'?"

The other three all looked gob-smacked.

"I was going to try to put 'date' down somewhere, and then I wondered if oxygenated was a proper word."

Kevin piped up enthusiastically.

"Well done, Liam. That's a great word."

He checked Liam's letters and helped him spell it out correctly. Terry was not so pleased.

"Liam, are you deliberately trying to wind me up, you tart? You keep nicking my fuckin' words! You're living dangerously, mate."

Denis joined in, but affirmatively.

"That's exactly how to play the game, Liam. Good play. I think that's going to give you a great score."

Liam put his four tiles on the bottom line at the end of 'oxygen', the 'T' covering a triple word score and Kevin totted it up.

"Eighteen times three, Fifty-four!"

Denis stood up. "Well, that calls for a cup of mud. Anyone? Mud? Diesel?"

He looked at each of them in turn. Kevin declined, but Liam asked for diesel and Terry mud. Denis weaved his way to the far side of the room, where he collected three polystyrene cups of prison coffee and tea from the two urns and then returned to the table precariously. Kevin was earnestly pouring over his letters and the board. He had two high-scoring letters, a 'Z' and a 'Q' and he hoped to get one of them on a triple word score, but he soon realised that wasn't going to be possible. The best he could do was get the 'Q' on a double letter score, so he settled for that, placing 'quoth' vertically in the upper left quadrant of the board on the extreme left, using the 'H' of home.

"Twenty-seven," he announced. Not too impressive really, considering that he had used a 'Q'.

"Hang on a minute Kevin," Terry queried, "You can't just make words up."

"Yeah," added Liam. "What kind of an animal is a quoth anyway?"

"It's not an animal Liam, it's old English for to say, or quote, like sayeth."

"But we don't use old words like that anymore."

"Doesn't matter Liam, it's still in the dictionary."

"What fukin' dictionary?"

"I know we haven't actually got one, but trust me, it's in there."

"It sounds like it comes from Shakespeare," added Denis, trying to sound knowledgeable.

Terry shook his head and then said. "Oh well, I don't suppose it matters. You got a shit score out of it. How are the scores looking then, at the end of that round, pumpkin?"

"You, Terry, ninety-one. Denis one hundred and thirty-one. Me, one hundred and seventy-five and Liam one hundred and eighty-one."

Liam laughed with a glint in his eyes and teased them, "Watch and learn boys, watch and learn."

He got out a cigarette.

"You got any bats yet, Kev?"

"I've run out, I'm afraid. I've been smoking much more than normal. I'm so fukin' nervous of this place. I've ordered some on my canteen but they've not arrived yet."

"Look bud, I can stump you up a few, but you've gotta pay them back, ok? Or else you'll be my Junebug."

The others laughed. Kevin didn't know what he meant, but it didn't matter because he could tell that he was only joking. So far, Liam was the only person he'd met in the prison whom he actually trusted. He seemed too thick to be devious. He actually seemed to have a good heart.

"That would be great, mate. I'm hanging."

Liam went off to an officer for a light and came back with two lit fags. One for Kevin.

Denis was loath to do a story, but his competitive side forced him to.

"Ok, it looks like that if I don't do a story, I'm going to trail all of you low-lifes and I can't allow that to happen."

"You've got to use 'home'," Terry reminded him.

"Yeah, I know, I know."

He was quiet in thought for a few moments whilst the others watched him expectantly. Then he started.

"I was very young when I got married. Just twenty. It was a bit like that in my day."

Liam interrupted him. "Denis, can you really remember that far back?"

He and Terry sniggered.

"Funnily enough, Liam, yes. It's not that easy to forget that you got married once, even if it was over forty years ago and you keep trying to forget. Then, just like Kevin, I found that before too long, I was the proud father of two kids. I was a successful businessman even back in those days and I was making good money. I bought us a nice cosy little cottage in a popular little village and everything was rosy in the garden, literally."

Liam interrupted him again.

"You haven't used the 'home' word."

"Fuck, Liam, do you have to be so pedantic? So I bought our first home, o.k.? A cottage and then a few years later, when the kids were nine and ten, the missus told me that she didn't love me anymore and wanted me out. In those days, women always, but always, got custody of the kids and kept the house, even though I'd paid for everything. So I had to get out. I didn't see a penny from that house until my youngest turned eighteen. Basically, I bought my darling wife a lovely little cottage and she screwed me out of it. There. That's my happy 'home' story."

"And you've been getting your revenge in ever since, eh, Denis?" Terry interjected, laughing.

"It's not like that Terry," he answered quietly and then asked for his bonus.

"Fifty points, please, Kevin."

Terry jumped in again. "Hang on; it's not automatically fifty points. We vote on it. What do you think, Liam?"

"Well, it obviously wasn't as interesting as my story or Kevin's. Forty?"

Denis remonstrated immediately.

"What do you mean it's not as interesting as your story? I think it is."

"It wouldn't be fair for the rest of us to be swayed by your bias, Denis," Terry announced. "Vote, forty?"

He, Liam and Kevin all held their hands up.

"Carried."

"You're a bunch of conniving losers," Denis fired off sullenly.

Kevin tried to cheer him up. "You've got one hundred and seventy points now, Denis. Right near the top and it's your turn again."

Denis was not impressed but knew there was no point in arguing. He examined his replenished letters. The board was good. Nice and open with long words. It was just a question of making good use of it, but his letters were a bit weedy, too many vowels. He needed to use the 'Q' that Kevin had left available before anyone else did. From that 'Q', he placed down six tiles horizontally to make 'quietly'. He was happy with that. It covered a double word score giving him thirty-eight.

"Nineteen times two Kevin."

"That gives you two hundred and nine."

Denis smiled broadly. Terry's head was down. Concentrating. He was struggling. He only had three consonants. At this point, the four members from the other game came over to inspect their board. They had just wrapped up a game and wanted to see how this other lot was doing. The board was facing Terry, as it was his go, so the interlopers stood mainly behind him, which of course, was totally off-putting.

"Jeez, look at these words. What do you lot have for breakfast? Thesaurus?"

Liam looked confused. "I've never tried that."

Kevin spoke quietly to him.

"It's a type of dictionary, Liam, which gives you all sorts of alternative words, close in meaning to the one you search on."

"Oh," he thought out loud. "We don't need one of them," and he took a large drag on his cigarette in a kind of superior way.

"Fuck me," said another voice. "How did you make such long words?"

Denis explained. "You are allowed to add to words already on the board, so long as it makes another proper word."

One of them counted up the letters in the two longest words.

"Ten letters!" he exclaimed in sincere admiration. "Twice! You guys are a bunch of geeks!"

"And you lot are a bunch of nosey cunts! Now fuck off, back to your kindergarten table. I'm trying to think."

Terry looked quite cross. They were distracting him and he didn't like the way they were standing right behind him. It made him genuinely uncomfortable and he wanted them to go. He turned around and gave them a mean stare. They moved back smartly and returned to their own table. Denis laughed.

"Good choice of words, Terry," he said, amused. "I think our scrabble is working."

Terry got back to thinking.

"I'm going to be creative," he said, as he placed down his tiles.

In the top right hand corner, he placed down 'creat' to join up with the first 'E' of 'beforehand'.

"There you go, Liam. Now all you've got to do is stick 'pro' in front of it and you've got 'procreate'. Taylor made!"

"Oh yeah," Liam replied. Just my sort of word. "I like procreating."

The others tittered. Terry picked up the last of the spare letters, bar one.

Now Liam was focussing. He didn't have a "P" or an "R'. That was a blow. But he had an 's' and wanted to put it on the end of 'domain'. The space at the end of 'domain' was a double word score.

"Kevin, can I put a word beginning with 'S' on the end of domain, so 'domain' becomes 'domains'?"

"That's brilliant Liam. It means you get scores for both words and they're both on a double word score."

"Ok," Liam answered, slightly excitedly and he placed 'slob' across the end of 'domain'.

"How much is that, Kevin?"

"Slob is six times two, that's twelve, plus 'domains' is ten, times two, makes a grand total of thirty-two."

Liam picked up the last spare tile. That only gave him four letters for the next round.

Terry expressed his surprise. "Liam, when did you become the grandmaster of scrabble?"

"It's just a gift, Terry. Get used to it, baby."

Liam was ahead now on the scoreboard, except that Terry had yet to do a story. It was Kevin's go. He checked out the triple word score opportunities, but again, he couldn't get on one. He still had that 'Z'. He had to use it. There were double word scores beneath 'slob'. That's where he had to go. It wasn't hard. He placed 'laze' vertically beneath the 'B' of slob to make 'blaze'. The downside was that his 'E' was right next to a triple word score at the far right bottom corner, which someone else would get the benefit of, but the upside was that he had used his 'Z' on a double word score. Thirty-two points.

"And the points at the end of that round are?" Liam enquired, genuinely interested.

"You're ahead, Liam, with two hundred and thirteen. Then Denis with two hundred and nine, then me with two hundred and seven and I'm afraid you're trailing Terry with one hundred and twenty-seven, but you've yet to do a story."

"Ok," he agreed. "I'll do that tomorrow. I've got some enquiries to make now. But I can't use my word, it's too skanky. I'll use Liam's 'slob' if that's ok?"

"I have no objection," Kevin quickly added, deferentially.

"And if I objected, I'd get voted down, as usual," Denis said dismally.

They all nodded in total agreement on that point and then Liam answered.

"I don't mind you using my word Terry. I'm not proud and I'm happy to help you out, mate, seeing as I'm so far out front."

"Ok, tomoz!" Terry said, as he got up and walked off purposefully.

Chapter 4

The next day, after breakfast and unlock, Terry's day began in the gym, which was always used to maximum capacity during all out-of-cell times, apart from some weekend hours. It was popular with inmates because it was the one thing they could participate in and actually show some benefit from, provided their sentence was long enough and they consistently applied themselves. Muscle building is a very slow process, especially on prison rations. No gains would be particularly noticeable before about six months of hard work in most cases, but even though visible gains were hard to come by, inmates felt better for becoming fitter and stronger and for doing something useful with their time.

Obviously, some inmates seemed to progress much faster than others, but they were the ones managing to get hold of illegal steroids. Prisons are notorious for their illicit drugs. The management, in general, had long since seen the benefit of gyms from their own point of view. They provided aggressive inmates with a legitimate way of expending their excess energy and aggression, as a result of which, they should be more manageable and less trouble.

Here at Wingnut, the particular officer assigned to oversee the proper use of the gym was known as Jelly, because when he spoke, his copious jowls wobbled just like jelly. Applications to be allowed to use the gym went to him via an inmate's personal officer, who would have to sanction it as a viable part of the inmate's overall rehabilitation programme. Obviously, it could be used as a tool to help incentivise the inmate in other areas of his prison life.

Terry usually managed to be allocated two weekday morning sessions and maybe an extra one or two at the weekend, depending on overall demand. On two of the other mornings each week, he helped in the painting and decorating class, assisting the trainer. So, he was only banged up one morning per week, which wasn't too bad at all. He needed to keep himself busy because he was going to be incarcerated for some time. He still had seven months to do prior to be considered for parole on a licence, so long as he kept his nose clean whilst inside.

In the decorating class, his thing was to emphasise preparation. Most participants wanted to hurry their tasks, to see the end results without adequately preparing. He could also vouch that with such skills and dedication, one could earn a reasonable living from it.

After a shower and lunchtime lock up, he repaired to the laundry room where he worked every weekday afternoon. Each weekday morning, immediately after the first unlock, inmates could leave laundry outside their cell for cleaning if it was their day for a change. They only got to have laundry done once per week each. The laundry would be divided into two specific types: 'kit' and 'private clothing'.

The kit would be placed in a communal plastic dumpster for the wing. It comprised prison-issue bedding such as their green poly-cotton bed sheets, pillow-cases, bright orange blankets and towels and prison-issue clothing, such as the grey jogging trousers, blue t-shirts, boxer shorts and grey jumpers or sweatshirts. Some prisoners would have additional prison-issued overalls; 'browns' for those working in catering, 'whites' for the laundry, 'blues' for those working in maintenance, 'greens' for prisoners who are cleaners or wing painters and 'maroons' for those allocated outside.

Then there were differently coloured tabards for those doing other special jobs. These include tabards for 'insiders' (peer mentors), 'listeners', 'toe by toe' mentors (adult literacy), wing reps, violence reduction reps (anti-bullying), diversity and equality reps. These roles weren't necessarily filled, they would only be filled by inmates whom prison staff felt were particularly suited for the role.

On completion of the laundering, inmates wouldn't get the same items of prison kit returned to them. They would be issued a receipt for what they had handed in by an officer or an orderly and could go to the stores to have their items replaced. The downside of this efficiency was that not all kit was in the same condition. Some were old, worn-out, stained, or perpetually smelly and that might be what they were given from stores to replace the more reasonable stuff they had submitted for cleaning.

The communal wash would include items that might be heavily soiled with urine, faeces, blood, semen, vomit, or mucus. Big industrial washing machines and dryers were used and so, different items from different inmates all got mixed up in these big loads. A significant number of adult prisoners were actually incontinent, either as a result of illness, age, or mental health problems. Dealing with bedding that has been wet during the night was a daily chore for most prison laundries. Sometimes soiled sheets or garments were put into sealed dissolvable biohazard bags, for special cleaning, and sometimes not.

Inmates with sufficient funds could usually access 'private washes'. The wing laundry orderly would collect their clothes separately and wash them separately in a clean machine, possibly even using their own preferred washing powder and softener, but for everyone else, the best they could do was put their own private clothing into a net laundry bag with a tag on it to show their wing and cell number. This personal washing would go into a large load of similar nets which would all be washed and dried together, but at least the clothing was kept in its net to identify the owner. The nets should be returned later the same day unopened, with the contents now washed and dried.

However, because the clothing stayed in the nets throughout the process, items would rarely be returned properly dry, which gave the inmates the headache of having to dry their own items inside their cells. With the smell of stale smoke, food and dank wet clothes, the wing had a peculiar smell to it. The only way an inmate could guarantee getting his own laundry back smelling fresh, clean and neatly folded, was to pay under the counter for the private wash service. Payment, of course, was not in cash, which was not used inside prisons, but goods or other favours.

For those unable to pay for such exquisite luxury, they still had another choice. Detergents were available for purchase in their canteen, so if they so chose to, they could wash their own items of clothing in the cell sink, which was not easy, because such sinks were so small and there were no drying facilities. However, it did mean they could avoid changing their boxers for replacement pairs, which had been worn by every other prisoner in the wing before them. The constant changing of clothes for items that had already been worn by all and sundry was part of the process of humiliation for being a prisoner and also demonstrated why inmates would prefer to wear their own clothing if they were allowed to. That would help restore a little of their dignity.

Terry worked the laundry with two other inmates under the supervision of an Operational Support Grade (OSG) officer, whom they referred to as 'Slinky', because he had an uncanny knack of moving around without anyone noticing. OSGs were the equivalent of Police Community Support Officers (PCSOs) in the police service. They were uniformed and had an official capacity, but undertook the more menial tasks of prisoner supervision and therefore didn't warrant being paid the full whack of a prison officer salary.

Later on, the scrabble rabble reconvened shortly after 6 p.m. Same time. Same place. Same people. Another routine to kill time. They had months to kill, years even. Kevin set up the board from his notes as he awaited the arrival of the others. As they turned up, they grabbed seven new tiles each and sat pensively. Terry was the last to arrive. He selected his tiles but then announced that he had his story to tell to start the session off.

"Are you sitting comfortably, boys and girls? Then I shall begin. Once upon a time, there was a terrible slob. He lived in a family, but he didn't do anything to help his family. He just took advantage of them. He didn't give anything back. He didn't help with any of the household chores. He didn't provide anything. He just spent his time amusing himself, mostly playing video games. He had dropped out of education but was completely disinterested in finding work or bettering himself in any way. He was sixteen years old."

Denis interrupted him. "One of your kids, I presume?"

"I don't own up to having any children, Denis," he answered dryly and continued. "This slob annoyed his parents to no end. His parents argued a lot anyway and he often had very loud slanging matches with them. He was driving them to distraction with his indolence and insolence. One day, as he often did, the father lost his temper with this lazy lad and was shouting at him with all his might, gesticulating wildly and going red in the face. The lad just insolently ignored him, slouching in an armchair, refusing to take his eyes off the TV screen, but right there in front of him, the old man blew a gasket and dropped down dead. He was only fifty-eight."

He stopped talking for effect. The others remained silent, their expressions goading him to continue.

"That lad was me and that was my father. Two days later, I was down the job centre and I found an apprenticeship in decorating and the rest is history."

"Hallelujah!" exclaimed Denis. "Another happy uplifting story. How truly thrilling this game really is. We ought to change its name from Scrabble-Babble to Scrabble-Misery, or maybe 'Pass me the Cyanide now'!"

Liam, however, was moved. He put a hand on Terry's shoulder and said quietly, "Mate, don't blame yourself. That's what most sixteen-year-olds are like. I was like that at sixteen and I'm still like it now, at twenty-nine."

"Yeah, thanks for that, Liam. That makes me feel a lot better—not!"

As usual, Kevin remained silent. He didn't want to say anything that might offend anyone. Then he thought of a positive response.

"That's gotta be worth fifty points," he stated. Liam agreed. Denis was noncommittal and Kevin added fifty points to Terry's score.

"Now you're on a hundred and seventy-seven, Terry."

They all started focussing on the board again. It was Denis's turn in a new round. He used the top right-hand segment of the board. He placed a 'W' above the first 'E' of 'create' and 'EK' below. The 'W' was on a double letter score and the 'K' landed on a double word score.

"That's fifteen times two," he proudly announced.

That left him just four tiles.

Terry was eying up the gift of a triple word score at the bottom right hand of the board and sure enough, he had a word. He placed 'FR' horizontally on the left of the 'E' of 'blaze' and an 'E' of his own on the other side. His 'F' covered a double letter score and his 'E' covered the enticing triple word score.

"That's eleven times three!" he said, impressed with his effort. He had just three letters left.

"I suppose all of us could do a story including the word 'free'," he chuckled.

Liam was next. He took his time. Terry chided him.

"Come on, Liam. There must be loads of places you can go."

Liam looked unsure, "Is 'delve' a word?"

Kevin answered, "Yes, Liam. It means to dive into something in the sense of finding out about it."

"I thought I'd heard it somewhere."

He placed his word vertically across 'quietly', placing 'D' followed by a blank representing an 'E' above the 'L' and 'VE' beneath it. The others all looked surprised. That was an unusual word for Liam.

"What's that worth, Kevin?"

"Well, 'D's on a triple letter score. So is the 'E', so that makes fourteen."

"And I get a double word score for using all my letters up," he added proudly.

"No, you don't," challenged Denis. "That's for when you use up all seven."

"No, you said that if we use up all the letters on our rack, we get double word score and that's what I just did."

Denis already looked defeated, "I suppose that if it goes to a vote, I will be ganged-up on as usual."

Kevin tried to be helpful.

"Denis, I think that you do get extra points for being the first one to use up all your letters."

"Double word score then," Terry decided and Kevin added Twenty-eight to Liam's score.

"That's the end of the game," Kevin announced. "What have you guys got left?"

"Wait a minute," Terry interrupted. "Don't we all get to finish off our letters?"

"Only if we'd agreed that at the beginning of the game, Terry. Under normal rules, the game ends when the first person finishes and the rest of us have to deduct the value of our remaining letters from our scores."

"Oh. I'd have played differently if I'd known that, pumpkin," he added unconvincingly.

Denis had tiles adding up to seven, Terry four and Kevin four too. He deducted those numbers from their scores and announced the results in reverse order.

"Me, two hundred and three; Terry, two hundred and six; Denis, two hundred and thirty-two; and Liam two hundred and forty-one. Well done, Liam. An amazing performance."

"Yeah, you can thank me later, Liam, for all the words I gave you," Terry added.

"Yeah, but really I should have won," piped up a rather surly Denis.

"If I'd got fifty points for my story, like the rest of you did, my score would have been two hundred and forty-two and I would have won."

Terry chided him. "Stop being a pussy, Denis. Liam beat you fair and square. Take it like a man, if you can imagine what that's like."

Kevin expressed his surprise, "Well, I have to say, that turned out differently as to what I expected."

Liam responded astutely, "What, you didn't think I could possibly win, Kevin?"

"I didn't mean that exactly, Liam. It's just that your English isn't the best, but you played a blinder of a game. Well done, mate. I'm really pleased for you."

Liam smiled broadly and proudly. He wasn't used to coming out on top of anything or being complimented.

"Well, we've got plenty of time for another game," Denis interjected keenly. "Next time, I'm not going to be so kind to all you fuckers."

Terry stared at him fiercely.

"No offence intended," he quickly added and he and Liam started clearing away all the tiles, replacing them back into the mysterious green bag.

The following day, Friday, Liam and Kevin had the pleasure of attending another English class during the afternoon. Mr Blanchflower had written a few phrases on the whiteboard as follows.

Subordinating conjunctions.

Derivational suffixes.

Adverbial dependent clauses.

Prepositional phrases.

Modal auxiliary verbs.

After the class had all entered the room and settled down, he unfolded his arms and spoke.

"Please read the phrases which I have written on the board."

He watched them, observing how nonplussed they were.

Darren shouted out. "I thought this was the English class, not the double-Dutch class."

The class laughed. Kevin was averting his gaze away from Mr Blanchflower. He didn't want to be asked any questions about them. He had no idea what they were. Mutterings turned into subdued chuckling. Mr Blanchflower continued.

"These are just a few of the many mind-boggling terms used to describe English grammar. Can anyone explain any one of them?"

Absolute silence and Kevin was visibly shrinking in his chair.

"Well, don't worry, because neither can I!"

There was relief of laughter and Kevin stopped trying to squeeze his rather bulky persona into his tight chair.

"My point is this. One can get very easily put off trying to get one's grammar correct if one focuses on this kind of terminology. It confuses the heck out of me and I'm an English teacher!"

More laughter.

"So, please, whatever you do, don't look at this sort of thing. It will put you off. Learning grammar is really just a matter of doggedly learning how things are meant to be, just like when you learn to spell weird words like laughter or psychology. You really don't need to know this kind of terminology to describe it. Honestly, it really does confuse me. But, using good grammar is what is important."

Then he threw out a question.

"How do you give the impression of being hard?"

There was a wave of sniggering before Darren made a point.

"The cold hard stare!"

Mr Blanchflower gently nodded and more answers quickly followed from others.

"You turn to face them and square up looking fearless."

"You walk at them and push them back, taunting them."

"You tell them to fuck off or else!"

"You lock your gaze without blinking and stand your ground."

Mr Blanchflower picked up the reins.

"Ok. So you are no doubt all skilled at turning on the hard look when you feel like you need to. So how do you give the impression of being educated?"

There was silence until someone answered, "But we're not educated."

"You're more educated than you realise. You know how to look hard even though inside you may not be feeling so hard."

Knowing tittering rippled through the class.

"But have you ever worked out how to appear more educated than maybe you are?"

Silence. He carried on.

"This is why I want to emphasise the importance of grammar. If you get your grammar right, it works wonders as to how you are perceived."

Jason piped up.

"Yeah, but does that matter for people like us?"

"Do you apply for anything? A job? a loan? a grant? housing? benefits?"

He paused and let the relevance sink in. Then, "In my humble opinion, you're going to be treated more favourably if you come across better educated. It's called unconscious bias. Good grammar presents you well. I'd like to think that in time you can all find jobs outside for yourselves. Of course, that depends largely on what skills you have, but also it's about how you present yourself. Really. I mean, how would we have such cretins running the country if the top jobs depended on skill?"

There were affirmative chuckles. He looked around the class. They were still all paying attention, so he carried on.

"You've all learned prison slang and can talk in a way that is gibberish to me, right?"

The class sniggered.

"Which means that you all have the ability to expand your vocabulary and polish up your grammar too, yes?"

Nodding of heads and approval, except from Kevin, who had a point to make. He spoke.

"Sir, you talk about people here improving their skills, to be better able to get a job on the outside, but some of us have always worked hard and done all the right things to get and keep a job. In fact, some of us have spent our whole lives faithfully chained to the grindstone, but this system has actually robbed us of all that and has probably made it almost impossible for us ever to get work again."

You could hear a pin drop. Mr Blanchflower looked at him sadly.

"Yes, Kevin. What you say is perfectly true and I am sorry about that, I really am. I just do what I can to help those I can help."

He gave a small shrug of the shoulders. It was a tricky topic. As an afterthought, he added, "If you think of any way I can help you, Kevin, please let me know, but you are atypical here."

He then carried on with his lessons. He started with one of his favourite bugbears; the difference between they're, their and there and your and you're. He explained their respective uses and laboured the point using the whiteboard until the class all seemed able to choose the correct use for a particular phrase. Then he talked about apostrophes and commas and when to use them. How to choose between its and it's. When he thought he had tormented them long enough, he released them for a comfort and smoke break, during which he asked Kevin how the scrabble was going. Kevin reported that it was going well and seemed very beneficial for Liam in particular and as an opportunity for himself to get to know a couple of the other inmates. Mr Blanchflower was pleased that it was working out well. When the class reconvened, he started off with a couple of his amusing anecdotes, as was his style.

"Ok, just a reminder of something we touched on last time, about being misunderstood. Listen to this comment, 'My therapist told me to write letters to all the people I hate and then burn them. I did that, but now I don't know what to do with the letters.'"

Eruption of laughter. Then another one.

"A wife sent her husband to the grocery store to get some milk. She said 'Go to the store and buy a bottle of milk. If they have avocados, buy four.' Half an hour later, he returns with four bottles of milk and says, 'They had avocados'."

Further eruptions of laughter, although as usual, they didn't all get it immediately.

Then he carried on.

"In the title of her famous book on grammar, Lynne Truss manages to make a point about the improper use of the comma in the actual title of the book. She uses the dictionary description of the Panda bear, which says that it eats shoots and leaves. In the title, she inserts a comma after 'eats' which changes the sentence completely. She comically describes the panda entering a restaurant armed with a gun. It eats first, then shoots the gun and then leaves the premises. Eats, shoots and leaves."

More laughter.

"Incidentally, I'd love for you to have a look through that book. I've put several copies in the library. She explains grammar in a simple witty way. You won't do better than having a look at her book, really."

Chapter 5

During the evening the association room was surprisingly not too noisy for conducting a scrabble game. The TV was at the far end of the hall, so its sound was not overbearing. The guards ensured that the inmates didn't turn it up too loudly. Bursts of annoyance or excitement from the pool table and the table football were sporadic enough to be unobtrusive. The table tennis games seemed to be always conducted with a great deal of decorum and calm resignation and the distant, regular, rapid clicks of the ball on bat and table were strangely quite soothing. For obvious reasons, there was no dartboard and the rest of the inmates conducted their conversations and other games in a reasonable fashion.

There was little excitement or elevated sound. Too much of that would only draw the screw's attention. Some inmates moved around occasionally, having bored of the TV and wanting to see what everyone else was doing. During evenings and weekends, this was where the inmates could indulge happily in some degree of normality and any din was tolerable, if not welcome.

The four scrabble players had sorted out their next set of letters for a new game and their faces were furrowed with the machinations of juggling letters in their minds. Denis looked frustrated.

"I can only do four," he announced disappointingly.

"It feels like you've somehow set me up. I can do all seven!" announced Terry, smiling broadly.

"Can anyone else do seven?"

Liam and Kevin shook their heads, unsurprisingly.

"And you're never going to believe my word," Terry stated as he placed 'violent' across the middle of the board, using a blank for an 'E'. He laughed as he took his turn. It seemed weird for him to get that word. He totted up his score. He had the 'V' on a double letter score, so the word came to thirteen.

"Thirteen times two for double word score, times two again, for using all my letters. That makes fifty-two."

Liam whistled.

"There ya go, Liam. Now all you've got to do is put an 'LY' on the end!"

Liam laughed energetically. Terry looked alarmed.

"You're kidding me! You haven't got them, have you?"

Liam laughed all the more. Terry looked angry. He didn't like setting Liam up.

Liam laughed even more as he saw Terry getting vexed.

"You're messing with me, aren't you? Come on. What have you got?"

Liam calmed down and put his letters on the board, vertically, starting at the 'V' and spelled out 'vibrant'.

"You twat," hissed Terry.

"Kevin, does that mean colourful?"

"Not strictly, Liam. It actually means to vibrate, but it's kind of morphed in meaning whereby good vibrations imply good energy, so colours could be said to be vibrant."

"I knew it had something to do with colours. What did I score, mate?"

"You got twelve on a double word score. Well done. Twenty-four."

Liam pulled a fist down, "Yes!" even though it wasn't a particularly good score.

"Terry, are you going to do a talk on 'violent'?" Liam asked expectantly.

"Maybe, mate. Be an easy one for me to do." He chuckled. "Let's see what everyone gets in this round first."

Kevin forced himself to be very brave by his standards. He was about to add to Terry's word. He quietly preceded 'violent' with 'non'. That got him on a triple word score.

"Thirty-six," he stated very quietly.

Terry looked shocked and stared at him directly.

"Kevin! I'm not here to make this game nice and easy for you lot!"

"Sorry, Terry. It was just too good an opportunity to miss."

Denis laughed. He found these antics amusing in an aloof way. Now it was his go. He was feeling mischievous. He could probably earn more points elsewhere, but he couldn't help himself. He placed 'LY' on the end of 'nonviolent'.

Terry almost exploded. "Now you're just taking the piss! Come on! I'm not here just to put words down for all your benefit. Come on! I don't just use your words and I don't like you nicking mine, you dumb fuckers!"

Denis defended himself. "Terry, it's ok. It's the way the game is played."

Liam was sniggering and Kevin was working hard to disguise his smile.

"You're a bunch of cunts, the lot of you."

"Kevin, that got me twenty-one."

Kevin kept his head down as he recorded Denis's score. Then he summed up the scores.

"Denis, twenty-one. Liam, twenty-four. Me, thirty-six and Terry, fifty-two. Who's going to do a story?"

"I'm not having any of you mingers nicking my fuckin' word for a story. I'll do one," Terry announced ungraciously. He gathered his thoughts for a few moments.

"Violent. I'm afraid I could do a lot of stories on that one." He chuckled to himself.

"Ok, I'm going back to the incident that led to my longest incarceration. About eight years ago, I had just started going out with the babe who I'm still with, actually, Valerie. She's a good bird. I wasn't living with her yet, but was staying over occasionally, you know, like you do before they get their hooks into you good and proper."

Liam sniggered.

"Anyway, I had a key for her flat. She was happy for me to drop in any time. One night, I'd been down the pub with some mates for a birthday bash, but I returned to her place after. It wasn't that late, about midnight. I let myself in and things just didn't feel right. The kitchen light was on, the TV in the lounge was on, but she wasn't in there and I could hear sounds coming from her bedroom. So I didn't say anything. I just crept quietly towards her bedroom. The light was on in there too.

I could hear a bloke talking quite loudly to her. He was calling her names, you know the kind of thing; slut, tart, bitch, slapper, bike, minger. The sort of stuff you would call your girlfriends, Denis."

Denis huffed disapprovingly.

"Anyway, the door was ajar. I pushed it slowly open and saw her tied to the bed with her own tights. She had one of those old-fashioned wooden beds with small posts at each corner. She was spread-eagled like a star, on her back, partially clothed, each limb tied to a different corner."

For some reason, the other three players were spellbound. They had never stumbled upon anything like this themselves and were silently rapt. Terry looked around to make sure nobody else was listening. All those nearby were engrossed in their own affairs, so he continued, quietly, as they all leaned in.

"He had also used a pair of tights to gag her too. I could see that she looked terrified. Her face was red and puffy. Man, I can feel the red mist descending right now, just thinking about it."

The veins in his neck started to bulge a little. The others all sat back a bit.

"I stood there watching him for a moment, his tight little buttocks squeezing in and out like a little white balloon being shaken on a stick, as he fucked her furiously. She just stared at me over his shoulder with such big wide bulging eyes. He must have sensed her tensing up 'cos he looked around to see me. He got off her immediately and moved over to the window. He was naked and put his hands up in front of himself defensively. 'You don't understand,' he said in a feeble, pathetic, squeaky little voice. I just said two words. Slowly. Meanly."

Liam interrupted him.

"Why did you say, 'slowly, meanly'? "

"No, you tosser. Let me finish. I spoke slowly and meanly. What I said was, 'untie her'."

Liam was laughing. "That's a great example for our next English lesson as an example of a misunderstanding."

Denis told Liam to shut up and Terry gave Liam a fierce look. "I don't think so, Liam."

Then he continued dramatically.

"He rushed over to her and struggled to unknot the tights. He was fumbling and shaking. He was struggling because he'd tied her up real tight and because he was obviously terrified of me. I shouted at him, 'come on, you cunt. I said, 'untie her!'" I saw that he was pissing himself. After a minute or so, he succeeded and she leapt off the bed, pulling off her gag and stood behind me.

She actually had the presence of mind not to get hysterical. She just hissed, 'my ex!' I kept my eyes on him as he retreated to the window again and I told her to go shower, which she did, without hesitation. I walked over to this complete cunt and grabbed his cheeks. His face cheeks Liam, not his butt cheeks."

The others laughed. It relieved the tension a little. Terry smiled at his little joke, then continued.

"I head-butted him in the face, quite a lot, as I told him what I thought of him. And what I was going to do to him. Then I started punching him in the face.

I think, I'd already broken his nose, but as I punched him in the mouth, I felt teeth breaking. He was pissing on my leg, he was so scared, but I ignored that. That was a small price to pay for the immense satisfaction I was getting from breaking his bones. I didn't smack him on the chin. That would have just knocked him out cold, and I wanted him to be conscious and terrified.

After a while of slowly smashing his face in, I could sense that he was going to pass out anyway, so then I opened the door that led out onto a little balcony. Obviously, there were railings there to make sure nobody fell over the top. We were two floors up and I heaved him over. When he landed on the concrete outside, you could hear a leg break. Have you ever heard a leg break?"

He didn't expect an answer. It was a rhetorical question.

"It makes a really loud crack."

The three other players were rather stunned. Kevin was almost wetting himself in sympathy. Liam broke the silence.

"Did you kill him?"

"Nah. He survived the fall with just a broken leg, a broken pelvis and a fractured skull and of course, his face was already a right mess."

Denis looked rather astonished. "How much bird did you get for that?"

"Initially four years, but my solicitor got that reduced on appeal, given the extenuating circumstances, to three."

Denis didn't think that was nearly long enough, but obviously, he didn't say so.

Kevin managed a weak "Attempted murder?"

"Funny you should say that, Kevin. They charged me with that initially, but they couldn't prove that I actually wanted to kill him. My defence was that I just wanted him out of the flat the quickest way. I wasn't necessarily trying to kill him. In the end, they just went for GBH with intent."

"Well," said Denis, "Remind me never to go near any of your girlfriends."

"He was raping her, Denis."

"Fair comment. Did he get done for that?"

"Too complicated, what with him being her ex and all. The consent issue would have been too contentious, apparently and the fact that I nearly killed him was also a consideration."

"So he got off scot-free?"

"Not exactly. Valerie got a message to him telling him that she wouldn't press charges, because one day when he thought he was safe, I would turn up out of the blue and quietly kill him. He lives in constant fear."

The mood was subdued. Liam broke the impasse.

"Sixty points."

Kevin nodded. Denis also agreed.

"Yeah, that was quite a story. You made the bit up about throwing him out of the balcony though, right?"

Terry looked at him disbelievingly and answered dryly, "Why would I?"

"OK," Denis said slowly, looking down at his letters, wondering how anyone could be quite that violent.

"And it's my go again," Terry said cheerily.

After a few minutes of study, he placed 'puddly' down vertically, using the 'Y' of 'non-violently.'

"Double word score makes twenty-six."

Liam asked, "What's puddly?"

"You know. There are lots of puddles."

He nodded. "What, like puddles of urine and puddles of blood?"

"Yeah, or maybe even puddles of rain."

Liam focussed on his own letters. He had a 'Z' and he wanted to make good use of it. He studied the board intensely for a couple of minutes. The others were patient but relieved when he finally placed 'boozey' down vertically across the first 'O' of 'non-violently'. He felt very pleased with himself. He had cleverly managed to place his 'Z' on a triple letter score. Kevin totted up the score.

"Brilliant, Liam. Forty!"

Liam pulled a fist again. "That calls for a bat. Want one, Kev?"

"Very kind. Thank you."

Liam stood up victoriously and went off to find a light. Kevin's letters were all low value, apart from a 'J', so he busied himself looking for 'J' opportunities. It didn't take him long. "Japan" horizontally across the 'P' of 'puddly'. Only fourteen, but it was on a double word score.

"Twenty-eight," he mumbled as he wrote his own score down.

"Hang on," contested Denis loudly. "You can't use place names."

Kevin defended himself. "Actually Denis. You can. They changed the rules about nine or ten years ago"

"Really? I didn't know that." Denis appeared thoughtful.

Kevin qualified himself. "But I would suggest we don't use people's names, because these days there are so many weird and wonderful new names being given to kids. You would be able to put down more or less anything."

Denis was happy to bow to Kevin's superior knowledge. Liam returned and he and Kevin puffed merrily away, as Denis scoured the board for some kindness for his own weak letters. He was feeling despondent, convinced that he couldn't make a high score with anything on his rack, but eventually, he spotted a great opportunity. Using a blank as an 'R', he placed 'endanger' down across the 'N' of 'vibrant'. The second 'N' and the 'E' were both on double letter scores and the 'E' was over a double word score and he had used up all of his letters.

He excitedly summed it all up.

"Eleven. Double word score. Twenty-two. Double again for using all my letters. Forty-four." He chuckled smugly.

Kevin announced the scores. We're all on sixty-four or sixty-five, except Terry, who's on one hundred and thirty-eight."

Liam and Denis both whistled.

"You can't beat my stories boys," Terry explained proudly. "So who's going to do one for that round?"

There were no takers. They all looked a bit vacant. Terry mused.

"I don't suppose anyone's been to Japan?"

To their surprise, Denis spoke up.

"Actually, yes, I have."

"Denis, can you do a story on Japan?"

"Well I could, but I'm afraid it wouldn't include beatings, attempted murders, rapes, people being starved of oxygen, or people dying from road accidents or heart attacks. It would just be about a holiday. I don't know if that would be acceptable given the present company."

Terry answered on behalf of the other three.

"Don't be a tart, Denis. We don't mind you telling a nice civilised story just before bedtime so we don't get nightmares, but can you make it interesting?"

"That depends on whether you can show a little interest in cultural matters."

Liam interjected, "Wot ya sayin', Denis, that we're not cultured?"

He and Terry laughed, but Kevin looked embarrassed. Then Terry spoke.

"Denis, I'm sure we'd all like to know a little bit more about Japan. Please, give it a try."

Denis looked resigned but not hopeful, but he was willing to try to engage them on a more cultural level.

"Ok, well, I first went there over ten years ago. I enjoyed it so much; I went again about five years ago with a lady friend. Japan is so different. It has an ancient culture that is very contrasting to the West. There is a depth of respect for nature, people and places that you don't see over here and you feel it everywhere. It's difficult to describe. There's a kind of historic dignity which is eminent everywhere. It's like what we pay lip service to, they really mean it."

Liam interjected, "You mean like a cooked breakfast. The chicken makes a contribution, but the pig makes a sacrifice?"

Denis pondered that, not quite seeing any correlation, but he affirmed anyway.

"Yes, Liam. Like that."

Then he continued. "They have hardly any crime over there."

Liam and Terry both laughed at that. They found the concept amusing.

"The women are coy and respectful and dignified. They always dress beautifully, often wearing the traditional Kimono. The streets are spotless and you can leave stuff sitting around and nobody tries to steal it."

"Sounds like someone might put it in a bin though" Liam joked. Denis continued.

"You wouldn't have to lock your bicycle up if you cycle to the shops."

"Weird," Liam mused.

"They take great pride in their food and they actually make a point of eating healthily, unlike over here, where everyone seems to want shit food. They have fantastic parks. They love nature and plants. They kind of venerate them. The architecture is different and beautiful.

You can't help but be fascinated by the place. It's a weird mixture of new and old. Obviously, it is a very progressive high-tech economy. It's the third biggest economy in the world, yet at the same time, it reveres its history and culture immensely. The countryside is fantastic. The vast majority of the country itself is mountains and forest, which means that almost all of the population live in the cities and the countryside is pristine. The country comprises of thousands of islands, although it is mainly three big ones, which are roughly the same size as the UK, yet their population is twice ours."

"Blimey" exclaimed Terry. "I thought our islands were overpopulated."

"Everything about Japan is astonishing. People there tend to live longer than people in other countries. That's probably mainly down to their healthy diet. They are racially more pure, with very little immigration. You and I would struggle to identify foreigners there, because they are mostly Asian, you know, from China, Korea, or the Philippines and they all look similar to us, though not to the Japanese.

They have lots of fabulous temples and shrines, usually in stunning scenery. They are very spiritual people. Most of them practice Shintoism and Buddhism, but they don't go to church like people do in the west. It's a more private thing where they go through personal rituals at temples or shrines, to connect their spirit with that of their ancestors. That sort of thing. Shintoism is virtually unique to Japan."

"Denis, did anything interesting happen when you were there?" Liam asked, not altogether mischievously.

"Like I said at the beginning Liam, no blood and guts, but of course it was interesting. The Japanese bend over backwards to accommodate you. They make you feel very special. The excursions are fab. They have shows of geisha girls, samurai warriors. They were a warrior nation with a lot of integrity you know. They are big on integrity and principles."

"Doesn't sound like the place for you, Denis." Terry joked. Liam sniggered. Kevin managed a coy smile.

"Yeah, well, I had a fantastic time and I would recommend the place to anyone if they want to experience something a bit more classy than Costa del sol."

"Is it expensive, Denis?" Terry asked.

"Yes, it is rather, but then you are paying for a five-star experience, Terry. It's not cheap there in any sense of the word."

"How long does it take to get there, Denis?" asked Liam.

"Well, I've always done a direct flight, which is about twelve hours. That ain't bad considering that it's about six thousand miles away."

Their minds were beginning to float far away into another world of exotic places, food and people, a million miles away from prison. Denis's enthusiasm for the place was, in fact, quite infectious. He would have liked to open up a laptop and to show them some images of the attractions he had been to in Tokyo, Kyoto, Kobe and Osaka, but that was just a fantasy in itself. Denis finished off his brief account.

"After two weeks away in Japan, returning to the UK is like coming back to a land of yobs, filth and ignorance."

"That's not a very nice thing to say about our beloved country, Denis," Terry protested.

"Just saying. That's what it feels like for the first few days back until you get used to it again."

"Is that it?" Liam queried.

"I think that will do for now, Liam."

"Nothing about ninja warriors fighting to the death and Samurai beheadings?"

"No, Liam. I did say at the beginning, it was not going to be about blood and guts."

Kevin asked the other two.

"How many Points? To be fair, that was interesting. I know very little about Japan, well, apart from their photocopiers, of which I know a lot."

"Yeah, Denis. You missed out the bit about Japanese photocopiers," Liam joked, laughingly.

"Please, Denis, save that talk for another life." Terry joked. "Forty?"

"Why not fifty?" Denis protested.

"It wasn't a bad effort Denis, but it lacked zing! What d'ya think, Liam? Forty?"

"Yeah, I agree," answered Liam. "Forty, because he didn't include anything personal. Denis, you didn't say anything about the old lady you went with."

"She wasn't that old" Denis protested.

"How do we know?" Liam replied. "You didn't say anything about her and we know your MO."

He and Terry laughed and Denis looked rather annoyed, but he wasn't going to divulge anything personal about the holiday and so Kevin recorded forty.

"I told you, I returned to a land of yobs" Denis finished, quietly.

The game continued. It was Terry's go and after some deliberation, he placed 'merged' vertically over the 'G' of 'endangered', gaining a triple word score and thirty-three points. Liam surprised them all with 'mimic' horizontally across the 'M' of 'merged'. He had to ask if it should be double 'm', but he was assured that he had spelt it correctly. He had managed to get his 'M' and the 'C' on triple letter scores, which gave him a total of twenty-three.

The others couldn't help thinking that he had the luck of the Gods, but then Kevin played a blinder. He found 'Threaten' vertically in the top left-hand corner using the second 'N' of 'nonviolent'. It was on a double word score and he used up all of his seven letters and the last 'E' was alongside the 'B' of 'boozey', which gave him another five points. In total he scored fifty-three.

Denis felt under pressure as usual, as he entered the last go for this round. After examining many possibilities and incurring a little wrath from Terry for being so indecisive and taking too much time, he went for 'fresh' across the 'E' of 'threaten'. The 'F' sat on a double letter score and the 'S' on a double word score and so he obtained a reasonable score of thirty.

"Score please, Kevin." Terry announced authoritatively.

"Liam, eighty-seven; Myself, one hundred and seventeen; Denis, one hundred and thirty-five; and you, one hundred and seventy-two."

"Yes!" Terry proclaimed as he punched the air. "Eat your hearts out, girlies. So that leaves Liam and Kevin yet to do a story, though. Gentlemen?"

Kevin looked at the latest words. "I don't think I could do one on any of those words. Can I see what turns up in the next round?"

"I don't see why not, Kevin. It's entirely your choice, but you are going to need the points if you're even going to get near my score."

He smiled at him with a happy, smug self-satisfied look on his face.

"Liam?"

"Same for me, I think, mate."

Denis wrapped things up in his inimitable efficient manner.

"I think we should do the next round tomorrow. We've only got about ten minutes left tonight. Let's start fresh tomorrow."

"Good call Denis, but tomorrow is Saturday. Who's got visits?"

Denis shook his head.

"My bird ain't coming in so often now that I've only got two months left,' explained Liam.

Kevin looked sad. He said in a low subdued voice. "Susie's coming in to see me tomorrow. Her first visit."

"Jesus Kevin, You're supposed to be happy about someone coming to see you. You look like you're going to be hung tomorrow. Cheer the fuck up!"

"I'm sorry Terry. I'm just not looking forward to it. Her seeing me in here." He almost added 'with you lot' but was pleased to check himself in time.

"What time is the execution pumpkin?"

"Eleven."

"Ok. Well my Valerie's coming in tomorrow too. I'm seeing her at two, so what's a good time to reconvene?"

"I've got all day mate," Liam offered.

Denis was more precise. "I've got stuff to do in the morning, so shall we say three o'clock, before tea?"

Liam laughed. "What stuff you got to do Denis? You're just killing time like the rest of us. You're such a fuckin' poser."

"No, I've got stuff to do Liam. I'll see you all at three."

"Whatever."

Chapter 6

The next day was Saturday. Visiting day. Kevin was out of his cell as soon as he was allowed, as usual, at 8:15 a.m. He reported to the exercise yard, which, in the absence of work and classes, would be available for most of the day. Of course, there would be the mealtime lockdowns, as always.

It was an early October morning. Overnight it had been quite cold, although the day held the promise of sunshine and warmth. He was barely comfortable in just his prison t-shirt and jumper and had to keep moving to generate some heat. The yard was a little bigger than a basketball court, predictably surrounded by its four huge walls. He couldn't see out anywhere, but he always loved to see the sky, even if it was cloudy. He marvelled at how quickly something so relatively insignificant on the outside, such as simply seeing the sky, had become so precious on the inside.

A few other early starters were outside too, meandering around in twos and threes, catching up with each other's news. Kevin wondered how anyone found anything much to talk about each new day. He wandered around ignoring them, lost in his own thoughts. In less than three hours, his dear wife, Susie would be visiting him for the first time and he was cogitating on how that would feel, both for him and her. He had mixed emotions.

On the one hand, surely it would be lovely to see her, having been denied her friendship, support and comfort for the past three weeks. On the other hand he felt a sense of hopelessness. Her visit wasn't going to change anything. As a newcomer, he would only be allowed to see her once a fortnight for the first three months. Given how long each day felt, let alone weeks and months, her visits would pale into insignificance. He wondered if they would feel like nothing more than a tantalising illusion that would do more to cause despair than gratification, being so unreal and no longer a part of real life.

In a way, he didn't even want to see her, because of an overwhelming sense of shame and guilt for what he had put her through and for whom he had become, an incarcerated prisoner. Did he really want her to actually see him like this? In prison garb? Despite having been married to her for twenty years, he was now feeling bizarrely tentative and hesitant about seeing her.

After a long hour circumnavigating the exercise yard repeatedly, he went to the association room. A lot of the inmates were watching football on the big TV. Football was obviously a staple choice for the majority of them. Kevin felt not the least bit interested in a sport of any kind. He much preferred documentaries. He didn't think he was going to see many of those in the association room. Apart from his scrabble associates, he had made no friends yet and he felt restless and out of sorts. Nobody had made an effort to befriend him and he hadn't found anyone he wanted to make friends with.

He grabbed a mug of mud and then approached one of the guards and asked for permission to visit the library. So long as there was an officer available to staff it, it would be open for most of the weekend. The youthful gruff officer gave him permission, but before Kevin moved on, he quickly checked regarding the visit arrangements later on. He was told to report back to the association room twenty minutes before his visit was due to start. That gave him an hour to kill in the library.

He couldn't settle. His mind wouldn't focus, no matter how hard he concentrated on trying to read. He changed his book five times, but nothing was capable of arresting his thoughts. The waiting time was rather gruelling. He felt no excitement, only apprehension. Finally, it was time to return to the association room where he reported to one of the officers, mentioning his impending visit.

The officer seemed a bit put out. He would have to escort Kevin off the wing into the central part of the prison, where the chapel, the medical room and the visiting room were situated. Kevin considered saying that if it was too much trouble, he didn't mind not going, but a little bit of pride kicked in. He wasn't going to be denied his most important right because someone was being a bit lazy and he looked the officer determinedly in the eye, expectantly.

The officer led him off a bit reluctantly through the concrete wing and several sets of iron-railing doors set in iron railing partitions, which still operated on an old-fashioned lock and key system. It was a slow, noisy, cumbersome process. Kevin presumed that modern prisons would now all have electronic doors, but most UK prisons were over a hundred years old and hadn't had a lot of modernisation done to them. Apparently, the voting public doesn't like the government splashing out lots of money on the welfare of people whom society chose to incarcerate.

When they got to the corridor outside the visiting room, he was handed over to one of the officers supervising visits, who took him into an adjoining waiting room. They both sat at a desk. The officer had a pen and paper.

"Name?"

"Kevin Spartan."

"You new here?"

"Yes."

"Been inside anywhere else?"

"No."

The officer looked up, surprised. That was unusual. He looked at Kevin properly for the first time. Kevin felt like he was being barcode scanned. The officer was looking into his soul.

"First visit then?"

"Yes."

"Who?"

'Wife."

"Name?"

"Susie Spartan."

"Age?"

"Mine or hers?"

"Hers."

"Does that really matter?"

"Yes."

"Forty-three."

"You from C wing?"

C wing was reserved for sex offenders. Kevin was taken aback. He didn't know how to respond appropriately. He put himself in Liam's or Terry's shoes and considered what they would say in answer to that question. Then he replied, quite certainly, "Fuck off!"

"Just wondered."

That seemed to be the right answer. The officer continued, matter-of-fact.

"Are your pockets empty?"

"Yes."

"Stand up."

The officer checked his pockets and quickly frisked him.

"Ok. Sit down again. You need to know the rules. In a minute I'll take you into the visiting room. There are lots of small tables in there with two chairs at each one, opposite each other. The tables are separated by a reasonable distance, so you should be able to ignore all the other people in there. It will be busy with other prisoners in there having their visitors too.

Once you are sitting down, your guest will be led in. She too will have been searched and will be carrying nothing. You may hug her briefly on arrival but then you must both sit down facing each other and not touch again and stay that way for the duration. Definitely, no kissing. You can have up to one hour. Remember, you do not touch again under any circumstances. Do you understand?"

"Jawohl!"

Kevin surprised himself. He didn't know where that came from. It was a Pavlovian response and he looked a little sheepish.

"Sorry. That just slipped out."

The officer gave him a dirty look and continued.

"Visits are a privilege. If you break any of the rules, you will be sanctioned. Don't try to talk to any of the other prisoners or their guests. That is strictly forbidden. Do you understand all of that?"

"Yes."

"Ok. Let's go. By the way, you have to wear one of these."

He handed Kevin a red tabard to put over his jumper.

"Do I have to? It's a bit inhuman isn't it?"

"Yes, I'm afraid so."

Kevin reluctantly donned the tabard and was led into the visiting room. It was large, about the size of a small village hall, with about thirty tables in neat rows and columns. It reminded him of when he took exams at school in the school hall. Quite a lot of other prisoners were already in there waiting and some already had their visitors present. Several officers were standing around the edge of the hall, watching the proceedings quite intensely. Obviously, this was one of the most likely areas in which an inmate might acquire some contraband and plenty of contraband did manage to find its way inside.

He sat nervously, butterflies making his stomach rumble. He was sweating a little without feeling warm. He gazed towards the door which admitted visitors. His insides lurched up and down as various other visitors were led in and then he saw her. He immediately felt emotional. It was like a sudden shock to his system.

Over the past two weeks, he had been doing his utmost to forget about her. She looked lovely. She was wearing a bright colourful dress and had clearly made an effort to look her best without overdoing it. That would be contrary to prison rules. Female visitors were not allowed to dress provocatively.

Kevin was overcome. He placed his arms on the table and lowered his head onto them to hide his sobbing. Susie was escorted over to him by an officer who stood by her until she was seated. She reached out to touch his arms.

"No touching, ma'am, I'm afraid," the officer explained sadly.

"Look at him. He's so distraught."

She now also had tears rolling down her cheeks. She experienced his pain.

"Ma'am, please, just stay seated and refrain from physical touch."

She didn't want to get thrown out, so she withdrew her hands and the officer backed away. She looked intensely at the top of Kevin's head. His shoulders were rising and falling with his sobs.

"Darling, it's ok."

She really didn't know what to say. She'd never seen him like this. He had cried at the birth of each of their daughters, but those were tears of joy, of wonderment, of pure awe. In front of her now was a man in deep, abject despair.

"It's ok, Kevin, my darling. We are going to get through this."

She so wanted to hold him, to connect with her person, her spirit and not just her words, but she had to be restrained. She knew Kevin, well enough, to know that prison was going to be the most vile and intolerable experience for him. She knew that he was a soft, gentle, kind, law-abiding man, notwithstanding his one misdemeanour, but she was shocked and troubled to actually see him like this, a broken man. She wanted to sob too but felt the need to be as strong as possible, for him.

"Darling, it's lovely to see you. I know this is emotional for you. It is for me too. It's ok. If you need to cry, do it. We've got a whole hour."

There were other inmates and visitors in the room and no doubt Kevin was attracting their attention with his weak, pathetic behaviour, but she totally ignored them. She was only there to care for her husband, who was still buckled over the table, hiding his face.

"The girls send their love. They would love to come and see you too, but you're only allowed one visitor at a time, apparently."

Hearing mention of his daughters firmed him up a little. Without looking up he weakly asked how they were.

"They're doing fine. They both send their love. They both want to come and see you."

He looked up at her, his eyes puffy, red and wet.

"I'm so sorry." he said, in a rather squeaky voice.

Instinctively, she took his hands in hers and answered gently.

"Darling, what's happened has happened. It's been very sad and difficult, but we still have a life to look forward to after this is all over."

That's as far as she got before the officer was upon her.

"Ma'am, I can't keep warning you, please, no touching, or you're out!"

"I'm sorry, I was elsewhere. Sorry."

He gave her a kind and imploring look. He really didn't want to cut her visit short.

"It's ok," she reassured the officer. "I'll be more careful."

Kevin was starting to feel annoyed now. He didn't relish someone ordering his wife around.

"Tell me how the girls are."

"Well, obviously, they're back at school now. I think the first week was hard for them, you know, getting teased a bit about you."

She looked at him apologetically. She had to be realistic. She didn't want to try to fool him. Then she carried on more brightly.

"The second week was better. You know what kids are like these days. Attention spans of goldfish, what with their blessed smartphones and social media. Really they're fine and they've both been very mature about it. I'm really proud of them."

She looked at him and smiled.

"You're not looking too bad, hun. You've lost weight!"

"The food in here is really shite."

"Well, I don't mean to be rude, hun, but losing a few pounds won't do you any harm."

She smiled again, mischievously.

"Maybe even a few stones."

Her resilience impressed him.

"How are you coping, hun, financially?"

He was genuinely very worried about the finances, as he had been the sole wage earner.

"I'm screwing the state for every penny of support I can get. They're paying the mortgage and the council tax and I get an allowance for the girls because they're still dependent and I've found a part-time, online job, proofreading."

Kevin almost managed a smile. He was relieved that she was fighting her corner so well. She always had been so sensible and reliable. He had always worried privately that he had disappointed her with their rather dull tedious life, revolving around his dull tedious job, living in their mediocre house on his median wage, but right now, dull and tedious seemed wonderful, to both of them.

"Proofreading what?"

"It can be anything. Mostly commercial reports. The firm I work for handles stuff for all sorts of different companies. Luckily I'm a pretty quick reader and as you know, I'm a stickler for my grammar. I get the impression that a lot of the reports are written by people for whom English is a second language if you get my drift, so there's plenty for me to get my teeth into. The money's alright really and I can fit the work in around the girls. It's working out ok, hun."

Kevin was much relieved to hear this. Susie then enquired very sincerely about him.

"How are you coping in here, dear?"

"Well, I can't say it's easy. I don't fit in at all. They're all criminals in here, you know."

She gave a little laugh.

"Yeah, don't let them turn you into one."

"It's so tedious. The only thing that isn't so bad is the English class."

"Oh, are you finally learning to read and write?"

"Very funny. No, I help by mentoring a lad called Liam. He's a nice lad, really. He's a bit slow. Had an accident when he was young and I help him improve his English. It's the only time I feel like I am doing something useful anymore."

"Oh, that's really good darling. Well done."

"Actually, I quite enjoy the lesson too. The English teacher's got a great sense of humour and I admire the way he plays the class. It's a real skill to watch."

"That doesn't sound so bad."

"Yeah but that's just a few hours a week. The rest of the time is real shite, oh, apart from the scrabble. That's just about tolerable."

"Get you! Scrabble? I can see that I'm going to have to brush up on my English. Who do you play that with?"

"Well the whole point was to do it to help Liam learn, so obviously him, plus a psychotically violent nutter who's really big and scary and an old geezer who defrauds vulnerable old ladies for a living. Nice people."

"Sounds like fun."

"Yeah, a barrel of laughs in here."

They went quiet for a while as they just looked at each other. Then Susie affectionately said.

"I really miss you, hun."

"I miss you too, babe and the girls."

They carried on talking. It was surprising how much they had to catch up on and the hour flew by. A bell rang and visitors around the room began to stand up and walk towards the exit. All the inmates remained seated, obvious in their bright red tabards. Susie didn't want to leave him. Their time together had disappeared far too quickly. She knew how vulnerable he was. If she had her way, she would willingly stay with him to help him through this. That's how much she loved him. As she stood, she spoke.

"Kevin, I'll come and see you as often as I am allowed to. I love you very much."

"I love you too, hun."

As she walked away, he started to sob again. He felt lost without her. It was a wrench for her to walk away from him.

Several hours later, at 3 p.m., it was time to finish that scrabble round. Kevin was there first, getting the board ready as usual, then Liam and Denis appeared, but they had to wait for Terry, who was delayed because of his visit. The others got their new letters and mulled them over whilst they awaited him. Following his visit from Susie, Kevin was feeling very low indeed. She had reminded him of what he was missing. It was unbearable. He felt listless. He had only turned up for the scrabble out of a sense of duty to the others. When Terry finally appeared, he, by contrast, was very jolly.

"You look pleased with yourself." Liam stated.

"Of course. Just seen my babe. She's crazy for me."

"I should think she is if you almost kill people for her." Denis offered jovially.

"Now, now, Denis. Careful what you say, mate. What we talk about here, stays here, Yeah?"

"Of course." Denis immediately assured him.

"Liam?"

"Absolutely!"

"Kevin?"

"I wouldn't dare repeat a thing." he stated, in all honesty.

"Good. Right, if I'm not mistaken, it's my turn."

He fished out another seven letters from the bag and quietly mused on them. After a while, he started laughing.

"What you laughing for?" Liam asked, bemused.

"You're not going to believe this," Terry answered excitedly.

He placed his letters across the top left-hand side of the board, incorporating the first 'T' of 'threaten'.

He made use of a blank to represent an 'M' and wrote the word 'estimate'. What was particularly lucky was that the first letter 'E' and the last letter 'E' were both on triple word scores.

"I'm on two triple word scores. Does that mean I multiply by nine?"

Denis was the first to react.

"Crikey! Admittedly I haven't played a lot of scrabble in my time, I'm more of a chess man myself, but I have to say, that's the first time I've ever seen someone get two triple word scores. And you've used all of your letters!"

"You, jammy bugger!" exclaimed Liam. "You should do the lottery."

Kevin didn't know the answer, but he volunteered his thoughts.

"Well, I suppose, it's only fair to get the triple word score twice, as you've landed on two triple word score squares."

In actual fact, the word itself was very low scoring, all the letters being worth only one, apart from the 'I' which was on a double letter score, making initially a score of only eight.

"Eight times nine," Terry announced proudly. "I think that's seventy-two, plus double word score for using all of my letters makes one hundred and forty-four."

He leaned back on his chair, raising his arms into the air.

"Hallelujah, it's a miracle! Follow that, girlies."

It was Liam's turn.

"I don't think anyone can follow that," he said in his usual droll tone.

He had an "X' and was looking at all the possibilities that he could see to make use of it. He seemed defeated.

"If only I also had a 'C', I could make 'exclude'."

Kevin looked at him and said, "What about 'exude' then?"

"Exude? Is that where you write 'exclude' but you exclude a couple of letters in the middle?"

"No, Liam. It means to leak slowly or to emit."

"Ok, Kevin. If you say so."

He placed his word across the first 'D' of 'puddly', getting the 'U' on a double word score.

"Yes!" he proudly exclaimed, punching the air as usual. "How much, Kevin?"

"Twenty-six."

Kevin was ready to place. He had already seen his opportunity. He placed an 'A' next to the 'Y' at the end of 'boozey and made 'acre' vertically down the bottom left-hand corner, getting the 'E' onto the triple word score. That wasn't a bad effort, considering his mind was elsewhere and because as Terry was already uncatchable, he had little interest in the game right now.

"Is 'ay' allowed Kevin?"

"Yes, it's Scottish for yes."

"I didn't think foreign words were allowed."

"Liam, the Scots speak English, believe it or not. They just speak it in a way we find very hard to understand and they have a few extra words which we don't use, like ay and wee."

"If you say so, Kevin."

Kevin totted up his score. Six plus three sevens.

"Twenty-seven."

He replaced his letters and informed the others that there were now no spare letters left.

Denis knuckled down. He was feeling defeated. He had a 'Q' and no 'U' which was like having a great big present which you're not allowed to open. In fact, unless he got really lucky with someone else's 'U', it was going to count against him. However, he soldiered on. He placed an 'S' on the end of 'exude' and that alone gave him fourteen and the 'S' was the first letter of a vertical word 'swig'. The 'W' was on a triple letter score, so that word gave him another sixteen.

"Thirty please, Kevin."

That wasn't a bad effort, but he was still trailing, bearing in mind Liam and Kevin had yet to do a story.

"Scores please, Kevin," Terry asked.

"Liam, one hundred and thirteen. Me, one hundred and forty-four. Denis One hundred and sixty-five and you, three hundred and sixteen."

Terry laughed again. This was really good for his spirits. He was unassailable. He only had six letters and they were each only worth one each, so his next play was inventive rather than high-scoring. Alongside the vertical 'swig', he vertically placed 'soil'. That gave him 'is', 'go' and 'soil'. The 'O' was on a triple word score, giving him two, nine and twelve.

"Twenty-three please, Kevin."

Liam was back in the hot seat. He didn't take him too long. He placed a 'U' in between the 'T' of 'non-violently' and the 'C' of mimic with a 'K' beneath the 'C' to spell 'tuck'.

"Ten," he said quietly. Nothing to shout about, but he really did have an awkward set of letters. Kevin still had six, but opportunities on the board were thinning. He managed to get 'vroom' down vertically, using the 'O' of violent and the first 'M' of 'mimic. The 'V' was on a triple letter score and that added up in total to eighteen.

It was now Denis's go.

"Guys, I don't think I can do much. I've got a 'q' but no 'u'."

"Tough titty, Denis," Terry sniggered. "Just use what you've got and stop complaining like a spanked girlie. We'll just take off ten at the end."

"Just doesn't seem fair," complained Denis petulantly, as he scanned the empty spaces on the board. At the top right-hand corner, he placed 'FI' vertically over the 'N' of 'Japan' to make 'fin.' It was on a double word score. Twelve.

Terry was quick. He placed an 'O' just under the 'S' of 'estimate'. It was on a double word score. It was also next to the 'H' of 'threaten', so he got two scores of four and ten, which wasn't bad for one 'O'.

Liam still had five letters. He saw a good place for his 'W', placing it directly above the 'H' of 'fresh', with an 'O' beneath, to make 'who'. The 'O' was on a double word score, so he scored a reasonable eighteen, but he still had three letters left.

Kevin placed 'AP' under the 'T' of 'estimate'. The 'P' was on a double letter score, giving him eight points, but the game was not yet over, as he still had one letter left. Denis had just an 'O' apart from his useless 'Q' and he placed it to the left of the 'R' of 'merged'. It was also over the second 'N' of 'endangered', giving him four points. Terry had just one 'I' left and he put it next to the 'F' of fin. Five points and game over.

Liam stood up. "I'm bushed. I need a fag. You coming, Kevin?"

"Sounds like a plan."

"What about your stories, guys?" enquired Terry rather disappointed in the break.

"We'll have a look at it when we get back, Terry," and with that he and Kevin were off to the exercise yard.

Terry stood up. "I'm going to watch a bit of footie until they get back, Denis."

"Good idea. I'm going to powder my nose."

Chapter 7

In the exercise yard, Kevin asked Liam how he found visits from his partner.

"What d'ye mean? Do I like her visiting me?"

"Yes."

"Yeah, I like to see her, but it's not the same as being outside with her. It's a bit pointless, really."

"Do you think she likes to come and see you?"

"Yeah, course, she does, mate. We've been together for four years. I know she misses me. At home, we spend all our time together and she gets lonely without me."

"Did you find it hard when she first started coming?"

"To be honest, mate, I can't remember. I've been inside quite a few times whilst I've been with her. The important thing is that she waits for me. She doesn't take in a Sancho."

"Sancho?"

"Y'know. Jody. Boyfriend."

"Yes, of course."

"Is that what you're worried about, mate? Your good lady going off with some other bloke?"

"No, Liam. Not for a minute. I trust her with my life."

"Oh. Is she a bit of a minger then?"

"Liam, No! She's actually still very attractive but I know that she would never be unfaithful to me, even if I'm in here. I just had very mixed feelings about seeing her today and I wondered if that was normal."

"Nothing's normal in here, mate. We're all different. The only thing you can do is, whatever it takes for you, to get through it."

They finished their fags and returned to the association room and waited for Terry and Denis to re-join them at their table.

Terry spoke. "Guys, none of you can get anywhere near my amazing score but you need to fight it out for second and third. So, who's going to do a story?"

Despite his sour mood, Kevin volunteered. He could do with the distraction.

"I think, I can do one on 'threaten'," he announced.

"Nice one, Kevin. You're gonna surprise us with a bit of aggro?" Liam mused.

"Hardly. As you know, I work as a photocopier salesman. I mean, I used to work as a photocopier salesman. Been doing it for years and years, but also as you all well know, life doesn't always go smoothly."

They all acquiesced sincerely, seriously.

"So, several years ago, the boss of the firm that I was working for at the time decided to go bust."

Liam didn't understand. "What do you mean, he decided?"

"It's a scam, Liam. The guy was loaded, but he was one of those sorts who had no morals whatsoever and if it appeared to him that he could benefit financially from going bankrupt, he would. He didn't give a shit about his creditors or his employees."

"And they call us criminals!" Liam declared. "And I suppose he just started up a new company after that."

"Precisely. New names on the papers. New bank accounts. Same sort of business. Apparently, it's easy if you know how and you have no scruples and you get all your debts wiped off."

Denis was being unusually quiet.

"What bastards they are," Terry stated, "yet we're the ones doing time!"

"Anyway, I only mention that to explain how I lost my job and a month's wage, I might add. So, I was desperate and I found a van driving job with one of those big online retailers who keep an army of white-van-men on the road. It was a bit weird right from the start.

At the interview, the dispatch manager explained that I wouldn't be working for them, but with them. I wasn't self-employed but neither was I employed. I would be a partner. I didn't have a contract but was a kind of franchisee, but I didn't have to actually buy the franchise. I would be paid via some third-party umbrella company. It all confused the bejesus out of me. I think it's what they call the gig economy and I have to admit that I was totally unfamiliar with it."

"Sounds like shit, Kevin," Terry commented.

"It was, Terry. The only bit I understood was that I was on a fixed daily rate of eighty pounds and that's what I needed. It didn't start well. I was required to turn up at the depot at 8 a.m., to load my van, go out and do my deliveries and I expected to return at a reasonable time. All the drivers were herded up outside the warehouse at 8 a.m. It was like a refugee camp. Most of them were eastern European and could barely speak English.

We just stood around outside in the cold for two hours until all the deliveries had been sorted into rounds inside the warehouse. Then, when they finally opened up the doors, there was a mad rush to fetch trolleys of boxes and to load up the vans so we could actually get out on the road. It took me at least twenty minutes to load up the van. They give you this electronic device that tracks your movements. It also has your list of packages on it and it's what customers sign on for delivery and they can send you messages on it. They gave me about two hundred packages, which seemed like a lot, but I cracked on.

It was a nightmare. Some of the numbering on modern housing estates doesn't make any sense and you can waste a lot of time trying to find one particular address. The ones with just house names are the worst. You literally have to crawl through a village checking every single house name and of course, they don't all have their signs up. It made me think that house names should be abolished and all houses have numbers and in the right order. It became even more difficult as night fell and I was struggling by torchlight. At that time of the year, it was getting properly dark at about five o'clock. I felt under enormous pressure all day long. No time to stop for a bite to eat or a drink even. I felt guilty just stopping for a piss behind a tree. Then halfway through the afternoon, I got a message threatening me. Sorry, I've taken ages to get around to the key word."

"That's ok," said Liam. "You got there in the end. What was the threat?"

"That they wouldn't pay me!"

"What?" exclaimed, Terry. "Why?"

"What they said was that you could only return to the depot when you had finished delivering all of your packages or after being out for twelve hours and if you didn't comply with that, you wouldn't be paid a penny. It was a general message that went out to all the drivers."

"Fuck that!" Denis said. "Talk about taking the piss. That's what I call a proper con!"

"Well, that's what I thought, but they had me by the short and curlies. I needed the money. So, I had to carry on till eight pm. You couldn't just stop somewhere. Your device was monitoring your movements and they expected you to be on the move the whole time. If you took an unscheduled stop, they would phone you up and ask why you weren't moving! Then when I got back, I had to reload a trolley with all the packages out of my van that I hadn't delivered and book them back into the warehouse. That took another twenty minutes at least."

"How many?" asked Terry.

Kevin laughed. "The vast majority of them. Of my two hundred, I must have returned about a hundred and fifty!"

The others all laughed too.

"I tried again, the next day, to see if I could be more efficient and again, by mid-afternoon, I got the same threatening message. I suppose I wouldn't have minded so much if I was going to be paid for the extra hours, but I was on a flat daily rate. I had to do over twelve hours work for eight hours pay, without a fucking break and by the time I got home, I was starving and shattered. I barely had enough time or energy left to say hello to the missus. Any plans for the evening had long gone down the plughole."

"So out of order," Terry added.

"I managed the third day, but I was still having to stay out twelve hours because I was still returning with most of my parcels. It was such enormous pressure and with the threat of not being paid. At the end of the day, I was totally shattered again. I'd felt rushed all day long and I was hungry and thirsty and desperate for some R&R."

"What happened in the end?" Denis asked.

"There was no way I was going to be exploited like that every day. At the end that day, I returned the van keys to them and told them to stick them where the sun doesn't shine."

"You little tinker, Kevin!" Terry exclaimed. "And you went back into sales?"

"Yes, as soon as I found something suitable."

"Great story," Liam enthused. "Shows how the other half lives."

"Yeah, I enjoyed that. Gotta be worth forty points." offered Denis.

"Denis, don't be so tight!" Terry chided him. "Fifty points. Hands up."

Terry, Liam and Kevin all raised their hands. Denis grunted.

"Scores please, Kevin."

"Well, after taking off what we've got leftover, which is ten for Denis, one for me and four for Liam, Liam's got One hundred and thirty-seven, Denis, one hundred and seventy-one, me, two hundred and nineteen and Terry, three hundred and fifty-eight."

Terry stood Arms straight up in the air and did a twirl of victory. He wasn't afraid of making a spectacle of himself. He sat down and asked Liam if he wanted to do a story now.

"No, not really, Terry. There are no words there that come up to my standards."

"Oh, ok, Liam. Maybe next time, eh?"

"Hopefully."

Sunday, mid-morning, Kevin was mindlessly sitting in the busy association room facing the TV and not watching the football that was on. He was lost in his own little world, still mulling over Susie's visit and what he was going to do with the rest of his life. Two officers meandered in and singled him out.

"Kevin, you need to come with us."

Kevin immediately looked confused and concerned, but he dutifully arose and followed them. After marching along the wing to the same locked gateway he had passed through yesterday for Susie's visit, he became more concerned.

"Excuse me, but what is going on?"

"There's been an incident and we need to talk to you. Just wait."

He was led silently through the railings and into a corridor on the left and then to one of the rooms on the right. Before entering the room, he was thoroughly searched. Inside, sitting at a big heavy desk was the wing Custodial Manager, Mr Bramley, known colloquially as Mr Pip. Kevin had never met Mr Bramley before, but he understood that he oversaw disciplinary and procedural matters. He was invited to sit down opposite Mr Bramley and one of the escorting officers left the room, whilst the other remained, standing by the door as a guard.

It all felt very serious and Kevin was very nervous indeed. He was a grown man, yet felt like he was back in school in front of the headmaster, about to hear a proclamation of some corporal punishment.

Mr Bramley was probably a bit younger than Kevin, in fact. He turned on a voice recorder and with both elbows resting on the desk, planted his chin on his hands. He spoke in an even, purposeful manner.

"Kevin, you occupy cell number twenty-one, yes?"

The tone alarmed Kevin further.

"Excuse me, do I need a lawyer?"

That put a bored expression on Mr Bramley's face.

"Kevin, you're in prison. We own your ass. If I don't like your behaviour, I can confine you to your cell for twenty-one days, straight. I can put you in solitary confinement. The governor can add an extra forty-two days onto your current sentence if he wants to, no questions asked. We give privileges and we take privileges away. Are you feeling more in context now?"

"Yes, sir." Kevin was crumbling already. He felt incredibly vulnerable.

"If I ask you a question, you answer it. Is that clear?"

"Yes, sir, but I haven't done anything wrong, I can assure you."

"Kevin, I haven't said that you have, have I?"

"No, but it feels like you think I've done something wrong."

"Kevin, please, don't over-think. Just answer my questions, ok?"

"Ok."

"How well do you know your cellmate, Mac Street?"

"I didn't even know he had a surname. He's very quiet."

The irony, thought Mr Bramley.

"I know you've only been here for a few weeks, Kevin and I understand that you keep to yourself, but you share a cell with Mac, so you must have got to know him to some extent."

"Not really, sir. He's always kept to himself too and he's very quiet, sort of always spaced out."

"What do you mean by 'spaced out'?"

"Vacant, dreamy, sleepy, in his own little world, like he's constantly sedated. He doesn't interact with me."

"I see. And what do you know about what he does with his time?"

"I have no idea. After unlock, I always get out of the cell straight away, partly to get away from him. I find him depressing. He seems to just want to stay there and daydream. I haven't seen him during most days. He doesn't do the same jobs or classes as me. In fact, I haven't got a clue what he does."

"I see. What do you two talk about when you're locked up together?"

"Nothing."

"Nothing? I don't think you're being honest with me, Kevin. You must talk about something."

He stared hard at Kevin.

"No, really. He has the TV on or is asleep and I just read. I don't even see him. I'm in the top bunk."

"So do you know anything about what he does at all?"

"Nothing. Really."

Mr Bramley was quiet for a while, then spoke again.

"Kevin, as we speak, your cell is being thoroughly searched. Are we going to find anything we shouldn't?"

"Certainly not on my account."

"But you think Mac might have something?"

"That's not what I meant. I meant that I can only speak for myself."

Mr Bramley thought for a while, then, "How was Mac this morning when you got up?"

"Still asleep, as usual."

"Did he eat his breakfast?"

"Not as far as I know."

"And when you left your cell, how was he then?

"As far as I know, still asleep. It's not my job to wake him up."

Mr Bramley looked very intensely at Kevin, assessing his emotions, his character even. Kevin felt most uncomfortable and asked a question.

"The officers said that there had been an incident. Am I supposed to know what this incident was?"

"That's what I am trying to ascertain Kevin, whether you know about this incident or not."

Kevin sat quietly. Mr Bramley looked at his watch and then turned off the voice recorder. He spoke to the officer.

"Rodney, take him to get dinner, then allocate him another cell. I don't want any inmates going near cell twenty-one. You can transfer Kevin's belongings for him to his new cell after the search is finished. Also, I want that cell locked and not accessed by anybody after the search. Is that quite clear?"

"Yes, sir. No problem."

"You are released, Kevin, if you know what I mean."

Mr Bramley smiled at his little joke and started making notes on some paper. Kevin was led back to the canteen and allowed to eat his meal there whilst a new cell was sorted out for him. After dinner, when the other inmates were unlocked, he was shown his new cell. His few things had been transferred for him, so it appeared to be home from home. The only difference was that he had a new cellmate, whom he was yet to meet, called Roger. He had the top bunk again.

He quickly checked and rearranged his meagre belongings and then retired to the association room, to think. He seemed to have plenty of thinking to do. After a while, Liam sought him out.

"Mate, I'm sorry to hear about your celly."

"What happened to him?"

"Didn't they tell you when they took you off for a grilling?"

"No."

"Maybe they think you're a suspect."

Liam laughed at the implausibility of it. "Kevin, the Wingnut strangler!"

"Liam, what the fuck are you talking about?"

"Mac is brown bread. Got back door parole."

Kevin wasn't too sure about the vernacular but got the brown bread reference and he was shocked.

"He's dead? How did that happen?"

"There are no rumours going around yet, so probably it was either his brake fluid or he got hold of some very strong gear."

"Brake fluid?"

"Yeah, the shit medication he was on."

"What? Legit medication?"

"Yeah, the stuff the doc' dishes out. I'm sure they use people in here for experimentation."

Kevin was silent. He barely knew Mac, but the fact that the man he shared a cell with was now suddenly dead was most troubling. He wondered all the more what kind of a dystopian world he had been thrust into. He pondered the situation and took advantage of Liam for some clarification.

"Do you think he killed himself?"

"Nah. Usually, the screws are hot on the signs of being suicidal and they'll put you in the segregation block, where they can watch you on CCTV twenty-four seven. It looks very bad on them if someone manages to kill themselves. Most do it by hanging."

"What do you mean, 'most'? How often does this sort of thing happen?"

"Quite often, Kevin. Some people lose the will to live in here, but they don't normally succeed on their first attempt. Killing yourself takes practice if that makes sense."

Kevin was gobsmacked. This place was more dire than in his worst nightmare.

"What's going to happen to me?"

"What do you mean?"

"They think I'm a suspect."

"No, they don't. You wouldn't be allowed to mix again if they thought that. You're in the clear, mate. The police have already been. They guarded the body until the undertakers arrived to remove it. You didn't notice?'

"No. I had no idea. What will happen now? I mean about poor Mac."

"Not a lot if he's dead."

"I mean about an investigation."

"They'll wait to see what the autopsy reveals, I suppose."

"Will we find out how he died?"

"Not officially, but someone will find out and it will hit the rumour mill pretty quickly."

Liam's attention span had come to an end.

"Got any bats, mate?"

"As it so happens, yes."

They wandered off together into the exercise yard for a relaxing smoke. Kevin got through two fags, one after the other, which was very extravagant, but he was feeling super-anxious and a little spaced out.

Chapter 8

Monday morning and back to normal. Liam spent the morning in the kitchen and had English in the afternoon. Kevin was straight on the cleaning after his half an hour in the exercise yard, also with English in the afternoon. Terry had expected to be in the gym that morning, but Jelly had failed to turn up for work and as there was no other staff member to replace him, the gym was cancelled and so he was banged up for the morning. Thankfully, he got out after dinner for laundry duty. Denis was helping the computer class in the morning, but as he was due to use the gym that afternoon, he ended up under lock and key for the afternoon.

Kevin had got into the habit of showering at about eleven thirty in the morning, in between his cleaning job and collecting dinner. He liked doing it that time because often he was the only one there. Previously, when he had showered during the evenings because he had no choice, he found that other inmates would invariably mock his pale flabby body. He understood that. His body was embarrassingly out of shape and he was ashamed of it.

He was Billy no-mates and that made him a target for fun and bullying. He also understood that a lot of the inmates had very low self-esteem and in their ignorance, they felt they could raise their own status slightly by belittling or bullying easy targets like him. Often, the inmates showering next to him would urinate on him. Or just spit on him. He hadn't reacted. Apart from being a symbol of ridicule, it was possibly also intended to provoke a reaction so that they would have an excuse to hit him. He dealt with it philosophically. He hoped he was annoying them by just ignoring them. He was, after all, getting hot clean water on him at a much faster rate than their weak streams of stale piss and spit. He wasn't actually being hurt. He was merely being insulted. If he reacted, he would probably get physically hurt and that would be far worse.

Part of prison life for him was accepting as nonchalantly as possible that he was an easy target and that a lot of inmates derived pleasure or significance from mocking people like him.

When walking the corridors, he had learned to keep his distance from others because, for rather a lot of them, it was fun to swiftly swipe the glasses off someone like him as they passed by and smash the glasses to the ground. It was as though glasses were a sign of privilege and they had to show their disrespect for it. It reminded him vaguely of the days of Pol Pot back in the seventies in Cambodia, where people who wore glasses were bludgeoned to death as obvious enemies of the new Marxist, 'ground-zero', agrarian regime.

Currently, his glasses were still in one piece. The frames were big and sturdy and could take a bit of punishment. Unfortunately, both lenses had cracks in them. Fortunately, an optician service visited the prison weekly and each time someone managed to damage his glasses, they could be fully repaired within two weeks. The damage became less likely after the optician replaced his glass lenses with plastic ones, and he became far more circumspect about where and when he wore them.

They all reconvened in the association room at six o'clock to start their third game of scrabble-babble. When they got together, there was the expected expression of grievance and cussing about the gym, but Liam was more interested in how Kevin had got on with his new celly.

"Yeah, I did have a chat with him last night, Liam. I think, I need to make a bit of effort this time. He's even older than me! By quite a lot, actually. His story made me quite sad. He sounds more like a social misfit to me than a criminal."

Liam came from the same town as Roger and he knew a lot about him.

"He wasn't too bad when his mum was still alive. He's always lived with her, she looked after him, as a grown man, I mean, but when she died, he kinda lost the plot. He's a bit slow, you know."

This, from Liam!

"Well, of course, he may not have been very truthful with me, but all he mentioned was petty stuff, like shoplifting, urinating in public, breaching ASBOs, stealing ladies underwear off clotheslines, with a bit of criminal damage thrown in for good measure, when people annoyed him. Hardly stuff you would expect a man to be incarcerated for."

"That's about the sum of it, Kevin, but he doesn't learn. He keeps re-offending. That's why eventually he ends up in here with us real criminals."

He laughed.

"Don't forget, we're all innocent, Liam, especially Denis," Terry interjected.

They all laughed, except Denis, of course, who always felt that he was being singled out as particularly bad, despite him being so superior to them all.

"Shall we get on with the game?" He queried.

"You in a hurry for another thrashing, Denis?" Terry said gleefully.

"I'll have you know, I've been playing with kid gloves on to save upsetting you lot. Remember, discretion is the better part of valour!"

"Discretion is the better part of valour? It's a game of fukin' scrabble, Denis!" Terry added.

"Can you lot stop talking bollocks and start sorting out your letters?" Liam chided.

They all went quiet as they considered the serendipity of the bag. Eventually, Denis interrupted the machinations.

"I can only do four letters."

Liam and Kevin confirmed that they could do no better.

"Me, then." said Terry placing 'jeers' across the middle of the board.

"Twenty-four."

Liam was next. After a while, he asked Kevin if 'bosom' was spelt with 'us'. Kevin corrected him and stated that 'bosom was, in fact, spelt with 'os'. He added, "Funny you should ask about that. It reminds me of how I first learned the correct spelling. It sounds like it should be spelt with 'us', but I was told that when you suck a bosom, your mouth always makes an 'O' shape."

Denis laughed. "You kinky beast, Kevin!"

Kevin looked embarrassed and stared at his letters, intensely.

Liam placed 'bosom' vertically over the 'S' of jeers.

"Ooh, Liam, you gonna do a story about bosoms?" Terry goaded him.

"Maybe, Terry. I like a good bosom story."

Fortuitously, the 'B' and 'M' both landed on triple letter scores, which gave him a reasonable score of twenty-one.

Kevin was quick. He placed an 'S' on the end of 'bosom' and used it to start his word 'sexy'.

"Wow! Looks like we're gonna get some much better stories, fellas," Terry said excitedly.

Kevin stated his score.

"Ten for 'bosoms' and double word score for 'sexy' makes a total of thirty-eight."

"Nice one, Kevin," Liam enthused in genuine admiration.

Denis's letters did not fit together well, so he did well to find a word incorporating the 'X' of 'sexy'. He spelled out 'oxide' vertically on a double word score which gave him twenty-six.

"Your turn for a story, Liam," Denis reminded him.

"Ok. Can we do one more round before I choose?"

Nobody minded that and they continued. It was Terry's go again, but he had mostly vowels, so he knew he wasn't likely to score highly. Instead, he managed a vowel-rich word in order to get rid of them. Using a blank for an 'S' he placed down 'jealous' vertically beneath the 'J' of 'jeers'. That only got him fifteen. He looked a little subdued, after his amazing performance in the last game.

Liam also only had low-scoring letters. He placed down 'untrue' using the 'U' of 'jealous' for his second 'U'. The 'N' lay over a double word score, which gave him only fourteen in total, but his spirits lifted when he fetched a 'Z' out of the bag for his next go.

Kevin was quick as usual and made for the triple word score on the bottom right-hand corner. He placed 'spit' across the bottom of 'oxide', making that word plural. The 'S' was on a double letter score and the 'T' was on the triple word score. As soon as the others saw him get onto the triple word score, they all moaned and groaned. He seemed to have a gift for benefitting from those spaces and it was frustrating for the others. 'Oxides' earned him fifteen points and 'spit' twenty-one more.

He muttered "thirty-six" as he recorded his score.

Terry gave him a playful push. "You're too good for us, Kevin."

"I haven't won a game yet, Terry. Maybe this one will be my turn."

"Not if I can help it," Denis responded as he studied his tiles.

"Got something, really, good, Denis?" Terry enquired.

"Not yet. I'm still looking."

"I thought you meant you had something already, you plonker."

Denis took his time. Eventually, he saw his opportunity and energetically placed 'breaker' vertically from the top line alongside the first two letters of 'bosoms'. The join made 'be' and 'or', together worth six points, but his main word was on a double word score and he had again used up all of his letters.

"Eat your hearts out, girlies," he announced. "Double word score on thirteen makes twenty-six, plus double again for using up all my letters, makes fifty-two, plus another six for 'be' and 'or'."

Terry was not amused. "Denis, you tart, I don't know how you're doing it, but I know you're fukin' cheating."

Denis laughed in an exasperated way. "Why would you say that?"

"No one gets to use all of their letters up hardly ever, but you seem to manage it every game."

Denis laughed some more in frustration. "How would I cheat?"

Terry fixed his stare on Kevin, who was sitting next to Denis.

"Kevin, be honest. Have you been swapping letters with that fucker?"

Kevin shifted uneasily on his hard plastic chair.

"Of course not, Terry. I wouldn't help a cheat." he checked himself. That sounded accusatory and he hadn't meant it to sound like that, although of course, he had been right the first time.

"I meant, I wouldn't help someone to cheat."

Terry wasn't convinced. Now Denis had an impressive lead.

"Scores please, Kevin."

"Liam, thirty-five. Terry, thirty-nine. Me, seventy-four. Denis, Eighty-four."

Terry resented having just half of Denis's score.

"Liam, I think it's time for your story. You've got loads of good words to choose from."

"Too many, Terry. I can't make my mind up."

He perused the board. "To be or not to be," he thought out loud.

"Do you know any Shakespeare?" Denis queried.

"None."

'You'd better not do that one then," he laughed.

"Ok. I've decided."

The others were quite impatient to learn which word he was going to use.

"Bosom!"

They all relaxed and sat back in their chairs, but only a little, as they were stiff upright chairs.

"Well, you remember my story of my accident, yeah?"

"Of course," the others all mumbled.

"Well, for a while, I lost the use of most of my physical and mental skills. I had to have specialist physiotherapy and training for a while, but I made fantastic progress as you can see from the magnificent specimen sat in front of you today."

Terry interrupted him. "Just get on with the fuckin' story, Liam."

"Well, after a few months, they thought I was ready to return to school, but I couldn't go back to a normal school. I had to go to a specialist one and it was residential. I stayed there on school days but went back home at weekends. It was one of those big grand old stately homes that had been changed into a boarding school. I quite liked it there actually. There were loads of sports, although I was crap at sport, I still loved it and the food was fabulous and I got on pretty well with most of the kids in my year."

"Liam, when are we going to get to the bosomy bit?"

"Denis, you're such a perv! Just wait you old fukin perv. We'll get to the bit for you pervs soon. So, as I was saying before I was rudely interrupted, I enjoyed it there. I made some good friends.

We slept in small dormitories. I mean, originally, they were huge bedrooms in a stately home, but for the school, it made sense to stuff at least ten beds into one room. There was loads of space. So there were about ten of us in my bedroom, all aged eight or nine and we had a matron who oversaw daily practicalities, like washing, laundry, making sure we had the right kit for the day, etcetera. She would also make sure we bathed or showered at the end of the day and went to bed on time.

Obviously, she was a substitute mother figure. I don't know how old she was. To an eight-year-old, she was quite a big lady, but she was really kind and thoughtful. She would make sure we were all settled in bed before turning the lights out. It wasn't totally dark. We always had a night-light on. A lot of the boys were scared of the dark. Pussies. One thing I didn't do was wet the bed."

"That started more recently, did it, Liam?" Denis joked.

"Fuck off, Denis. I don't have a weak bladder like you do. Anyway, after turning the lights off, she would stay in the room and sit on one of the lad's beds. I didn't really know what was going on. I was supposed to be going to sleep after all, but then one night it was my turn.

She sat on the edge of my bed facing me. She undid her blouse and in the very weak light I could just about make out the large mounds of her breasts. She put one hand behind my head and lowered one breast into my face. She nuzzled my face into her. It felt really nice, so soft and warm.

Strangely, it was very comforting. I didn't know why, but it just was. I suppose the intimacy of it gave me a warm glow inside. Then she pulled my face into position by her nipple and told me to suck her. She took my hand that was closest to her and placed it on her other breast and asked me to squeeze her nipple, which I did. She kept telling me to squeeze harder. This went on for about fifteen minutes. She would swap which breast I was sucking or squeezing. Eventually, she asked me if that was nice and smiled at me. I said that it was very nice and she got up and left."

"Is that it?" queried Denis.

"What do you mean 'is that it?'?" Of course, that was it, you perv. I was only eight."

"No, what I mean is what happened other nights. It doesn't sound like it was a one-off."

"You're right. It happened on many nights, but she liked to treat everyone fairly equally and I think she had other bedrooms that needed her breasts too, so we all got a turn every now and then."

Terry asked, "What did the other boys make of it?"

"Y'know, Terry, that's the weird thing about it. None of us ever spoke of it. It was like a guilty secret that none of us wanted to talk about like we were all embarrassed about it but I'm sure we all enjoyed it."

"I suppose because you were so young."

"Liam, you got her phone number?"

They all laughed. This matron sounded like she would be good for fantasies.

"Fifty points?" Liam asked.

There was a consensus of agreement, even from Denis. They took a quick comfort break and Terry and Denis risked a mug of the canteen tea. Then it was time for the next round and it was Terry's go. He worked with the 'B' of 'breaker' as it was on the top line and gave access to a triple word score. He managed 'birth'. The 'I' was on a double letter score, so he scored three times eleven. Kevin recorded his thirty-three.

Liam was next. He had a 'Z' and was determined to find a home for it. He was a bit slow but eventually found 'crazy' horizontally over the 'A' of 'breaker'. The 'Z' sat on a double word score.

"I don't know why a 'z' is worth ten. It's always easy to use it. What did I score, Kevin?"

"Thirty-eight, Liam."

"Yes!"

Kevin was quick as always. He placed 'vending' horizontally across the 'D' of 'oxides'. The 'V' was on a double letter score and the 'I' on a double word score. That gave him two times sixteen.

Denis looked perplexed. He had fresh letters to contend with and spent some time rearranging them to try to find a good opportunity. Fortunately, he had picked up a blank which completed his good luck. He hesitated and looked gingerly at Terry. He didn't quite know how to say what he had to say.

Terry read his expression.

"Denis, don't tell me you've got another sevener!"

Denis looked sheepishly at him as if imploring his credulity.

"I don't fuckin' believe it. How could you have just picked up seven new letters and miraculously they just happen to make a word? Nobody does that twice in a row without cheating."

He was looking cross and just a little bit dangerous.

"Terry, I just got lucky. I'm only able to do it because I picked up a blank."

Liam interjected. "Denis, are you sure you've spelt it right?"

"You tell me."

He placed his letters down on the bottom left-hand side of the board. Everyone was curious to see if he really was going to use up all of his letters again. Using the blank as an 'R', he placed 'laughter' vertically across 'untrue' at the 'T'. He totted up his score. The 'L' was on a double letter score. The 'H' was on a double word score.

"That's twelve times two, twenty-four, times two again for all my letters, forty-eight!"

Inside, he was quite jubilant, but on the outside, he looked nervous of Terry. He was genuinely a little bit scared. If Terry really believed that he was cheating, he was quite capable of dishing out some nasty punishment.

Terry looked inquisitively at Kevin.

"Kevin?"

"Of course I didn't help him, Terry. I think we were all watching him very carefully. It looks genuine."

Denis was very grateful for Kevin's support. After pondering the situation for a few moments, Terry enquired, "Scores?"

"You, seventy-two; me, one hundred and six; Liam, one hundred and twenty-three; and Denis, one hundred and thirty-two."

"Fuck that!" Terry said rather loudly, frustrated.

Kevin tried to console him, "But you've still got to do a story."

"Yeah, but so have you and conman Denis."

There was a moment's silence. Nobody wanted to aggravate Terry. Then he carried on more quietly.

"Anyone want to do a story?"

Liam jumped up. "Actually, guys, I've gotta go. We'll carry on tomorrow night. Same place, yeah?"

"Very funny, Liam," Terry said.

Liam walked through the room and left. Terry observed him leave.

Denis bade them farewell and went and sat in front of the TV.

Terry looked at Kevin.

"Are you sure he's not cheating, Kevin?"

"As far as I can tell, Terry, unless he's some kind of magician."

"Well, he does look remarkably like Paul Daniels."

They both laughed.

"I gotta go, Kevin. You look after yourself, yeah?"

"Of course, Terry."

Terry got up and walked out of the room. Liam had turned left towards the toilets, so he also turned left. As he walked down the corridor, two inmates walked briskly towards him. They avoided eye contact. They were both carrying towels and one was still rearranging his clothes.

The corridor led ultimately to the exercise yard, but just before that, on the right-hand side was the entrance to the toilets and showers. He walked purposefully into them. There were six toilet cubicles on each side. There didn't seem to be anyone there. He walked past them into the changing area which was just a big open area with benches and hooks on the wall, just before the shower area, which was a large rectangular room, with five showers down each side, with another four on the far wall. The shower area was completely open. No cubicles or barriers. An inmate was standing at the shower room entrance, fully dressed. He put his right arm straight out towards Terry.

"You don't want to come in here right now, mate," he said dryly.

Terry put his right over the top of the protruding hand and cupped his fingers into the man's palm, with his thumb across his knuckles and swiftly forced the hand into a wrist lock. The challenger leaned forwards to alleviate the intense and sudden pain of the wrist-lock, with his arm locked straight out to his side. Terry reinforced the control with his other hand too, holding the man skilfully in a position whereby he couldn't move. Then with alarming force and precision, he delivered a huge knee strike to the man's upper arm, which popped it out of its socket with the ease which someone else might pod peas. The man fell to the floor moaning loudly. The pain was unbearable.

Terry continued moving purposefully into the room. He could see Liam pinned up against the far right-hand corner by a lad he only knew as Steve, who had a firm hold of Liam by the front of his sweatshirt. Terry's attention, however, was on the third bandit who stood between him and Steve.

The guy immediately squared up to him as he strode forward steadily. Presumably, this lad was not expecting Terry to lash out immediately. Perhaps he thought that there was going to be some sort of polite discussion or stand-off, but no. As soon as Terry was in his fighting arc, he smashed an enormous right-hand punch into the man's sternum, taking him completely by surprise. He felt things give in and crack. Weakly, tenderly, the young man fell to the ground, struggling to breathe clutching his chest awkwardly.

Terry well knew his power and his skill. As a teenager and into his twenties, he had practiced various martial arts and he knew how to maximise the power of a blow and right now, he, absolutely, knew that he had disabled two men, without question. He focussed on the third. Steve. He grabbed him by both face cheeks and smashed him lightly against the right-hand wall. This gave him the peripheral vision of the other two, who were both still laying on the floor, in great discomfort. He didn't need to watch them out of the corner of his eye. There was no question that they were incapacitated. It was just instinct. Steve was far too sensible to try and fight this giant of a man.

For Terry, the clamping of face cheeks in his huge vice-like hands was his preferred technique to have a quiet close-up personal chat with someone. If he wanted to, he could lift a person clean of his feet whilst gripping his face. Not many people can do that. As he stared intensely down into this man's face he barked out gruffly, "Liam. Go."

Liam walked silently and compliantly out of the shower room and back to the association room.

"What's your name, cunt-face?"

The man managed a very muffled 'Steve'.

"I know that, cunt-face. Steve what?"

Again, with his cheeks clasped so tightly, it was difficult to say anything, but he managed a very contorted 'Steve Devenish'

"Well, Steve Devenish. I, really, don't like you or your mates. You've been picking on my mate, Liam and it's not the first time, is it? That makes me so fucking mad."

He banged Steve's head hard against the hard tile wall but not too hard. He didn't want to knock him out. His own senses were very alert. He could feel the adrenalin enabling him. He knew exactly where the other two were. Apart from being still aware of them within his peripheral vision, he could hear the first one moaning and the second one struggling for breath. They were absolutely useless to Steve now.

"You've caught me in a good mood, Stevie baby. I could smash your putrid little brain out all over this wall if I wanted to and to be honest, it's what I feel like doing, but I'm going to be kind this time."

He banged his head against the wall again, only this time harder.

"Do you understand me, cunt-face?"

Steve mumbled affirmatively. He banged his head again.

"So you and I are going to come to a little friendly agreement, ok?"

More mumbling. Another bang against the wall.

"Ok. If anything else happens to my mate, Liam, or any of my other mates for that matter, I'm going to bring your sorry little ass in here and I am going to splatter these dull creamy walls bright red and white with your brains and blood."

He banged Steve's head against the wall again, even harder.

"Do we have an understanding?"

Steve was getting quite dazed now. He mumbled.

Terry gave his head one final bang on the wall then threw him powerfully to the floor. He looked at the three of them intensely. He had to remember their faces well, very well. None of them dared move. When he was quite sure that he had assimilated as much information about their appearances as was necessary, he started to move slowly. He stood over the second one.

"What's your name, fucker?"

"Jo."

He put his foot on his chest and pushed just a little bit. Jo grimaced painfully.

"Jo what, fuck-face?"

"Jo Ashley."

"If I find out that you're lying to me, you cunt, I'll do a lot worse than break a few ribs."

Jo replied very weakly and painfully, "I'm not lying."

Terry moved over to the first one.

"Name? Cunt!"

"Palmer Trinket."

Terry said no more. He took in one last look of them all and left. It was nearly bang-up time, so he went straight back to his cell like a good little boy.

Chapter 9

The next morning, immediately after unlock, Kevin made his way to the exercise yard as usual. Quite a few inmates got there first thing. Perhaps they were the ones who hated being cooped up the most. He wanted to talk to a particular inmate, whom Liam had identified as Lenny.

Lenny regularly attended the yard. He was about forty years old. He had an uncommon alertness about him as if he was constantly on the verge of carrying out or had just carried out some misdemeanour. He always appeared shifty and somehow carried a look of being anti-authority. He constantly had minders around him. He was not tall or thick-set, yet he looked strong in an athletic way. He was lean and wiry, with extensive tattoos. Kevin had noticed that his arms and hands were both covered in ink and he guessed that his body was thick with them elsewhere. They were visible enveloping his upper chest area and his neck. His hair was cropped and revealed even more tattoos on most of his head, although on his face were just a few small blue markings such as stars and tears near his eyes. He had a wispy scruffy beard and went by the nickname of OG which stood for 'original gangster', which was some sort of accolade in prison. All in all, he had a menacing air about him. According to Liam, on the outside, he had been quite high up in a drug supply chain.

It was cold in the fresh air. Kevin would have liked the benefit of a jacket, but in prison, you don't get issued with clothing which you might need if you were 'going out'. He wandered around for about ten minutes before he spotted Lenny enter the yard with two of his lackeys. Inside they were referred to as road dogs.

Kevin was nervous about approaching him. He was afraid that he or his road dogs might just assault him just to evidence their superiority. Inside the prison, it was one big hierarchy and he was in the 'untouchable' class. He gradually got closer to them as they shuffled slowly around the rec. Lenny stopped to light up a cigarette and Kevin decided that this was as good an opportunity as he was going to get to cold-call the guy. As he approached, the two road dogs turned to face him. One stepped up to him and pushed him harshly backwards.

"What's your game, fucktard? Look at you, you fat, flabby piece of shit. What you doin' coming over here? You want to get molly-whopped?"

The man had a mean strained look on his face. Kevin was at least satisfied that he himself could not possibly look like a threat of any kind. Everybody could see that he didn't fit in this place and that he was an uninitiated, isolated, lost newbie.

"I just wanted to ask Lenny something."

"You don't approach OG without being told to you thick bastard. Now fuck off right now before I smash all your teeth in."

With that, he clenched his fists and puffed up his chest. Kevin had noticed that his challenger had a few front teeth missing himself. He was quite petrified and didn't want to risk losing any of his own teeth, so he quickly put as much distance between them and himself as possible.

Lenny hadn't even looked at him. Kevin was deeply frustrated. He needed a big favour and he didn't know who, or how, to ask. Liam would be able to help him but he didn't want Liam to be privy to what he had on his mind. He felt so useless. He needed to speak to people, to establish some useful contacts, but he lacked the street-wise know-how. This world was simply too alien for him. After His half-hour was up, he returned to his cell to get quickly changed into his cleaning overalls and he reported to George.

Mid-morning, Terry was fetched from his laundry duties and taken to Mr Bramley's interview room. The evening before, the two injured inmates had reported their injuries to one of the guards, only because they actually needed to see a doctor. One was genuinely struggling to breathe and the other was in dreadful pain and needed his arm resetting. They had been taken to the treatment room, where they had to wait for an on-call doctor to arrive. Of course, he seemed to take forever to get there. Neither of them had provided a reasonable explanation for their injuries, just the usual nebulous 'I fell over' or 'I bumped into something'.

However, as the injuries were deemed to be quite serious, the CCTV had been examined to throw light on the events. Mr Bramley didn't like not knowing what was going on in his wing. Unfortunately for him, CCTV only covered the corridors. Cameras were not allowed in cells generally, or in private areas such as toilets and showers, by law.

He had already interviewed Liam, who had been seen going in and out of the showers, as had the injured parties. Liam had also been evasive and unhelpful, of course, but Mr Bramley was far more interested in Terry, who had also been identified on CCTV. He asked Terry all the obvious questions. Terry simply explained that he had gone to the toilet block for a crap and predictably denied any knowledge of seeing Liam or the other three inmates in there.

Mr, Bramley was not a stupid man. He had been doing this job for a long time and his instincts were good. He didn't doubt for one moment that it had been Terry who had inflicted the summary justice, but he appreciated that some degree of self-regulating on the block was sometimes a good thing. He was mostly puzzled as to the relationship between Terry and Liam. He had the gut feeling that Terry was protecting Liam but couldn't fathom out why. Liam was a druggie and Terry wasn't, or at least had never revealed any indications that he was. Nothing in prison happened without a reason, but after interviewing both Liam and Terry, he was none the wiser. He calmly expressed his reservations.

"Terry, I'm never happy when I feel that I've been lied to. I'm not stupid. I know you all have your code of so-called honour. However, if we have serious assaults here, I have to inform the police and I don't like it when they get called into my prison to do an investigation in my own backyard. It's rather embarrassing. Can you understand that?"

"Of course, boss."

"Well, on this occasion, it looks like the injuries were mere accidents. Tripping over their shoelaces or something like that and the injuries could have been a lot worse, so the police won't need to get involved. I'm more concerned if I feel that someone has been out of order. It might be that you did us a favour last night. I really don't know, but suffice to say I'll be watching you very closely. I don't want any more trouble and these things have a nasty habit of escalating. If there's more, I might have to transfer you to another wing, or worse. Do you understand?"

"Of course, boss. Crystal clear."

"Very well. You are dismissed."

The day passed without further incident and the scrabble four reconvened after teatime. Neither Terry nor Liam mentioned their visits to Mr Bramley and both Kevin and Denis were too socially isolated to have heard any rumours. Kevin set the board up and reminded Terry that it was his go. They all selected new tiles and settled down to the biggest cerebral challenge of the day. Terry reminded Kevin that it was his turn to tell a story.

"Ok. Let's see, what this round turns up."

Terry placed 'flora' on the bottom left-hand corner, over the blank 'R' of 'laughter'. That was not a big score, but it was on a triple words score, which gave him twenty-one points. Liam spent a while exploring possibilities and he settled on a rather clever play. He placed 'angelic' across the 'G' of laughter and the 'L' of 'jealous'. It was a double word score which earned him twenty points.

"That was well spotted, Liam." Kevin encouraged him. "Very clever, slotting your letters between two other words."

Liam sat back, smiling, feeling very pleased with himself. Now it was Kevin's turn, but the board was getting quite tight. He actually failed to find a good word and settled for 'fail' horizontally on the left-hand side of the board, joining up with the 'L' of laughter. The only redeeming factor of this miserable word was that it sat on a triple word score, giving him twenty-one points. Now it was Denis's turn and he was annoyed.

"I can't believe it. I've got the feckin' 'Q' again and no 'U' of course, so I can't feckin' use it. That's so wrong!"

"It's karma, Denis," added Liam.

"What's that supposed to mean?"

"Denis, don't you know what karma is?"

"Of course, I know what karma is, you retard, I just wondered what you meant by it."

Terry interrupted him, "Now, now, children, can we stop squabbling and just get on with the fuckin' game, please?"

Denis gave Liam a dirty stare, before focussing on the board. He struggled and finally only managed a score of ten. That pulled his lead in a bit. He placed 'peace' down vertically at the top of the board, using the 'C' of 'crazy'. He took the last letter out of the bag.

"No more spare letters, lads."

Terry summed the situation up. "That's the end of another round, guys, so Kevin, you really need to do a story. You've got loads of good words to choose from. How about sexy?"

The others chuckled.

"I don't think so," he replied sedately. "I'll do 'fail'."

"That's a bit morose, isn't it?" challenged Denis, but then he added, "But maybe for you, it's an apt word."

Terry responded quickly, "Shut up, Denis. Let him do whatever he wants to. We didn't stop you doing fuckin' 'Japan', did we?"

No more was said, as they relaxed to hear Kevin out.

"Well, just to give you a bit of background, I had two siblings. I was the middle one. I won't bore you with the details about my parents, but suffice to say that neither of them was ambitious and they simply had no ambition for us kids either. I didn't realise it at the time but I think they were unconsciously preparing us all to fail. They didn't mean that to happen, I don't suppose. It was just a result of their attitudes.

Anyway, I grew up without any confidence. I was not, naturally, good at anything, certainly not sport and they never entertained any notions of encouraging us to learn an instrument or take up meaningful hobbies. So, all three of us just drifted through school. We all failed our eleven plus. I wasn't achieving much at my comprehensive school, but a stroke of luck was taking up psychology. I only did that because I liked the look of the lady teacher who taught it."

"Kevin, you sexy tiger!" exclaimed Liam.

"Hardly, Liam, but she was nice. Anyway, I really enjoyed the subject and one particular lesson she did, really impacted me. It was about mindset. I don't know how much of it I can actually remember now, what, about thirty-five years later, but it was a seminal lesson."

"What, seminal as in semen?" Liam asked laughing.

"Nothing to do with semen, Liam, although now that you mention it, I think the origin of the word is something to do with semen but I was using it in its context of being the cause of a big change or development, but not in the sense of making babies. Basically, she was explaining about how we can be partly in a fixed mindset and partly in a growth mindset. It's like an internal struggle going on inside our heads. Obviously, one side dominates and which one it is, affects our ability to achieve."

He stopped to look around his companions, to see if they were glazing over yet. To his surprise, they all looked interested, so he carried on.

"The way she explained it made me realise that I had been brought up in a fixed mindset way. That meant that I felt that my abilities were limited, that I was born with certain fixed skills or lack of them and that I wouldn't be able to change that or add to them. It was like school for me was just grading my abilities but not really developing them.

So, challenges were to be avoided because they might illustrate my shortcomings. If something didn't come easily to me then I believed that it wasn't right for me. I began to see that I had been choosing to fail. It was my own attitude that was causing me to fail. She taught us that it was possible to move more into a growth mindset way of thinking, where you view challenges as an opportunity to develop and not something to hide from. Where failure is just a step towards finding the path to success and not something to feel ashamed of. She educated me that where I lacked a certain skill for a task, I could put the effort and time in to learn it. She provided lots of examples of very talented people and showed that their talent wasn't something they were born with, it was something they developed through years and years of devotion and hard work.

She was the first person to make me believe that I could grow academically and in other areas of my life, if only I actually believed that it was possible and was determined to learn and develop. She mentioned things I hadn't heard about before, like the plasticity of the brain and life-long learning. I'm not saying that I went on to become a genius, obviously, but I will never forget the massive impact that one lesson had on me in helping me to change my attitude and expectations about success and failure."

He went quiet and thoughtful. He had just delved way back into half-forgotten memories that were now stirring him.

"Nice one, Kevin." Denis offered. 'I thought that was going to be another miserable story, but actually, it was quite uplifting."

"Yeah, that was good, Kevin," Terry added. "I'll try to remember that story for when I have kids one day."

"Thank you, guys. I take it I get fifty points?" Kevin queried.

They all nodded.

"Scores please, Kevin."

"You, ninety-three; Denis, one hundred and forty-two; Liam one hundred and forty-three; and me, one hundred and seventy-seven."

"Last few letters, boys," Terry declared as he resumed his quest for a place on the board. It took him a little while to find something with his awkward letters. He managed 'gawp' at the top of the board using the 'P' of 'peace. The 'W' was on a triple word score, which gave him a respectable score of thirty.

"Look at that, Liam," he announced. 'I've stolen one of your words!"

"You know I don't mind you learning from me, Terry. You've got a long way to go still."

Now, Liam applied himself. It was really difficult for him because his spelling wasn't the best.

"Kevin, is 'suave' spelt with a 'w'?"

"No, Liam, it's a rather strange spelling. S-u-a-v-e."

"Ok," muttered Liam, as he placed 'suave' horizontally across the board to meet the 'E' of 'peace.' The 'S' was on a double word score and he worked out for himself that he had scored sixteen.

"That's a good word for me," Denis interjected brightly.

The others just looked at him blankly. Kevin took up the reins. He kept shuffling his tiles. For once he was not quickly finding inspiration.

"Come on, Kevin. If you don't go soon, I'm going to drop down dead," Terry exclaimed in frustration. "At the end of association time, the screws will be wandering around doing the mop-up and they'll come across a table with three skeletons sitting at it."

"Sorry. I'm doing my best."

A few minutes later he placed 'doting' vertically down the right-hand side, marrying up with the 'G' of 'vending'. As was often the case, he was on a triple word score and his 'N' was on a double letter score. That made three times nine, but unfortunately he had one letter left.

Denis was keen to try to use all his remaining tiles. Head down, he cogitated seriously. He quickly realised that he couldn't use them all because of his 'Q'. Frustratingly, he had the right letters to make a word using the 'U' of 'suave', but there wasn't enough space. The 'Q' was going to count against him again. He placed 'it' beneath the 'G' of 'gawp'. The 'I' was on a triple letter score, giving him a grand total of six. Terry put 'nt' after 'be' scoring just six as well. Two letters remained with him. Liam placed 'moo' next to the 'D' of doting. The 'M' was on a double letter score. That gave him a score of ten, but he still had one tile left.

"God almighty, is this game ever going to end?" exclaimed Terry, frustrated.

It was Kevin's turn. All he had left was a 'W'. There were two 'E's available in 'jeers' and he placed his 'W' above the one which had a double letter score on it.

"That's nine for me, times two for using all my letters up. Eighteen."

He then deducted three points off Terry. Two from Liam and eleven from Denis.

"Let's do the final stories before we tot up the scores Kevin. It's your turn, Denis."

"Oh. Ok," Denis seemed to have forgotten about doing a story. He perused all the words to find the best one for him. After spending a few moments choosing his subject, he started.

"Are you sitting comfortably, boys and girls? Then I shall begin."

Terry and Liam frowned at him.

"What word are you using?" Liam asked.

"Ah, wait and see. All shall be revealed."

Liam and Terry looked at each other, wondering what Denis was on. He continued.

"Quite a long time back, when I was in my early forties when the internet wasn't quite as ubiquitous as it is now, I operated a home distribution business of health products. I advertised mainly through local papers and people would phone me with enquiries and orders. Of course, I employed a few people to help me but sometimes I would visit potential customers in person, at their homes.

One such person was a rather lovely young lady called Jane. She was married with two young kids and was a bit of a health freak. I liked her and so I visited her as regularly as I could. You know, I would deliver her products personally, that sort of thing. Anyway, there came a point where she asked if she could meet me for a drink one afternoon. Of course, I said yes and that became a regular thing. Before long, I was visiting her just to give one."

Liam interjected, "One what? A free sample?"

He laughed.

"You could say that Liam. A portion, a session with my manhood. It was always during the day when her toddlers were at school and her old man was out at work."

Another query from Liam, "Denis, were you with anyone else at the time?"

"Of course, I was. I had a girlfriend. Jane was just an occasional daytime thing."

"Ok."

"Anyway, after a while Jane started telling me that she loved me and that she was dissatisfied with her husband and started talking about us getting together properly. I played along with this because I was loving banging her. I didn't think

100

she was serious about her and me but in time she told her old man about us. You could say that the shit hit the fan and it wasn't long before they separated."

Terry asked a question. "Denis, this is all vaguely interesting but what has it got to do any of the words on the board?"

"Patience, Terry. I'm nearly there. So after she and her husband split up, she wanted to get together with me. I had to tell her that that was totally out of the question. There was no way I was going to take on somebody else's kids and we stopped seeing each other. So my word is 'breaker'. I broke up someone's marriage."

As he said this he beamed with pride. The others clearly didn't share his sense of enjoyment and surprisingly, it was Kevin who verbalised their mood.

"Excuse me for not feeling as thrilled as you look Denis but what was so good about that?"

"Well, not everyone could have pulled that off."

Kevin looked surprised.

"Surely you weren't intentionally trying to break up their marriage, were you?"

"No, of course not. What I meant is that you have to be someone special to pull a babe away from her hubby."

He was still smiling, proudly.

"And you don't feel any sense of guilt about that?"

"Of course not. Why should I? She was doing precisely what she wanted to do. If it hadn't been me, it would have been someone else. I didn't make her do anything she didn't want to."

He looked at the three of them quizzically, not understanding their misgivings even slightly. He continued, "What? You wouldn't have done the same thing in those circumstances?"

They all remained silent. Kevin, as a married man, felt particularly horrified at Denis's apparent callousness but he remained quietly composed. He saw no point in beating any kind of drum. What was done was done.

"Fifty points?" asked Denis.

They were quiet.

"You mean my story was worth sixty points?"

"Thinking forty, Denis," Terry offered dryly.

"Why?"

"Well, to be honest, it lacked any real punch and it was a rather unedifying story."

"What and throwing someone out of a second-floor window is?"

"I think so, Denis, given the circumstances." He paused and then added, "You need to work on your content and delivery, to bring it up to our group standard."

"That's bollocks!" Denis barked out crossly.

"Forty, guys?"

Three hands went up and Kevin recorded forty.

Chapter 10

Liam and Kevin strolled off to the recreation yard, they said, for some fresh air, but when they got there, they filled their lungs with toxic carcinogenic fumes. Terry remained with Denis. He was rather curious about the man.

"Fancy some mud?" Terry enquired of him.

Denis was surprised at the offer and brightly accepted. Terry went off to get their drinks and returned to the table.

"You're an unusual guy, Denis. You are obviously an educated, able man. You say you've run businesses and all that, but here you are, stuck inside with all these incapable, useless, lowlifes. How did that happen?"

Denis felt uncomfortable at his direct approach.

"Well, it's a long story, Terry. It's mainly because of confusion about my intentions after I get involved with girlfriends."

"Misunderstandings over money?"

"Exactly. Misunderstandings."

"It's happened before though?"

"True, but I'll have you know, I've only been convicted twice. There were two other cases where I got found not guilty."

Terry wasn't interested in pursuing some kind of amateur investigation. He just wondered how he coped.

"Do you find it lonely in here, I mean, generally, the inmates are young enough to be your sons and grandsons and there aren't other businessmen here, not legit businessmen I mean."

"Yes, Terry, it is and probably for Kevin too. I can't really relate to people here. I just keep my head down and get on with it."

"Do any of your girlfriends visit you in here?"

Denis gave a knowing laugh.

"No, mate, I seem to have got on the wrong side of them."

"But you do have a regular visitor, don't you?"

"Yeah, that's my dear ol' mum. She's eighty-four you know. It's a two-hour journey by train for her to get here. I'm always telling her not to bother but you know what mums are like. She comes religiously every fortnight."

"That's nice, Denis. She sounds like a dear old lady. Not being rude about your age, mate, but are you afraid you might die in here?"

"Fuck off! I'm not that old and I've only got one more year to do. I keep myself in great shape."

"Just wondered. You seem motivated enough. I reckon you must have something to look forward to on the outside."

Terry smiled at him playfully, but Denis was starting to feel suspicious about what Terry was trying to find out about. Indeed, he had a pot of gold to look forward to but he wasn't going to mention that.

"Just life and freedom, Terry. Life and freedom."

Meanwhile outside Kevin was picking Liam's brain. The telling of and listening to stories had stimulated them all mentally.

"Liam, you've been inside before, haven't you?"

"Lots of times, mate."

"How do you deal with being locked up like this?"

"In what way?"

"You know, with the boredom, the inactivity, the orders, the control, the shit people in here, no offence."

"None taken, mate. You couldn't possibly have been referring to me. Well, for me, life on the outside isn't so wonderful, so being inside, not so bad either."

"Really? You really think that?"

"Obviously, I prefer to be outside but my normal life is pretty boring. I don't do anything apart from feeding my habit and watching TV really."

"But you've got a girlfriend."

"Yeah. What about her?"

"Well, doesn't she make your life feel more fulfilled when you are with her?"

"I suppose, but really, our relationship is more practical than anything. Together, it's easier to get council accommodation and social security and to organise drugs. Also if one of us accidentally overdoses, the other one will call an ambulance. That comes in handy sometimes."

Kevin was astonished at the matter-of-fact way he spoke of overdosing.

"Has that ever actually happened to you?"

Liam laughed. "Yes, mate. A few times. Illegal drugs are not like things you buy in the chemists. There's no label telling you exactly what's inside it or how strong it is. Sometimes, you get ripped off and end up buying mostly talcum powder, but sometimes the gear is really hot and you end up taking too much in one go."

This was a world Kevin had no idea about.

"And if you accidentally overdose, what can an ambulance do?"

"Nothing, Kevin. Not the ambulance, but the people inside can help."

"You know what I mean, twat."

"A big shot of adrenaline brings you back if they catch you in time."

Kevin was astounded that anyone would dice with death, for kicks.

"Is the high worth the risk?"

"I don't chase highs, Kevin. If I did, I would be on ice, crystals, snow, powder, rocks. Know what I mean?"

"Not really. So what are you on?"

"I just use smack, scag, brown, call it what you will."

"And that doesn't give you a high?"

"Kevin, haven't you ever tried anything?"

"Only nicotine, if that counts and that is an expensive pain in the arse."

"For an educated man, Kevin, you're pretty fuckin' ignorant. No offence."

"None taken, Liam. This is not my field of expertise. So why do you take drugs?"

"Smack is what the counsellors call a depressant, Kevin. It allows you to escape any pain, physical or mental. Simple as that. It wraps you up in soft, spongy, cotton wool and takes you to a safe dreamy place far away from anything bad. Problem is that when you're a user, you feel like shit between fixes."

"Emotionally?"

"No, physically. The longer you wait for a fix, the sicker you feel."

"Such as?"

" Nausea, vomiting, the shits, cramps, muscle aches, can't sleep."

"Doesn't sound like much fun."

"It ain't. It's evil."

Kevin had never felt the need to experiment with drugs. He didn't even drink very much normally.

"So why don't you give it up?"

Liam laughed. "For exactly the same reason you don't give up fags mate. And going cold turkey can last for a week. That's a long time to feel like you're dying. Too long."

Kevin had to think about that for a while. He remembered that there had been times when he had tried to give up smoking but the draw was too strong. He was beginning to understand Liam a little bit better. He spoke quietly.

"I'm sorry, mate. I'm not being judgemental, just trying to understand you and learn from you."

"It's ok, Kevin. I'm not ashamed of who I am or what I do. These things all depend on how you were brought up, who you made friends with and the kind of things they did. You got two daughters, right?"

"Yes," Kevin admitted, rather alarmed at where this was heading.

"You ain't gonna stop them trying stuff. Drugs are everywhere. It all depends on what they get offered, where they are, what their mates are doing."

Kevin made a mental record of discussing this subject with Susie the next time he saw her. He felt panicky that he wasn't going to be around when his daughters might be needing him the most. Liam continued, "You don't like prison, do you?"

"Liam, I hate it so much. Everything about it; the bastard screws; The bastard inmates, no offence, the bastard rules, the bastard smells, the bastard regime, the bastard boredom, the bastard food…"

"Yeah, I get it, Kevin. I'm here too, don't forget."

"Sorry. I shouldn't be sharing my misery with you. I'd just like to know how you all tolerate it."

"You just have to get used to it, Kevin. Simple as."

Liam finished his fag.

"We need to go in, mate. Bastard lock-up time."

The following morning, whilst mopping corridor floors splattered with slops of dinner from the previous day, his attention was taken up by an inmate standing in his cell doorway, enjoying a smoke. The smoke smelled strangely sweet. Kevin presumed that it was some form of cannabis. He had only recently learned that there were new synthetic forms of the stuff which were much stronger than the original plants. The user was in his early thirties and had that characteristically gaunt, malnourished appearance of a habitual drug user. Kevin sidled up to him.

"Mate, could you help me get some gear?"

The man's stance changed immediately from relaxed and lounging to erect and agitated.

"What the fuck? Are you a grass or something?"

"No please, I just want to know where to get some stuff."

"You gotta be kidding me. I know a puritanical prig when I see one."

"Well, do you know anyone else who would help me?"

"Fuck off, you fat cunt!"

With that he withdrew inside his cell, turning his back on Kevin, who was left quite bewildered. He carried on mopping the floor, feeling totally useless and rather fat.

The rest of the day passed by with its routine of drudgery and predictability. As prisons go, Wingnut had an admirable record of getting its inmates involved in work and classes. The governor, Dr Villan, was a highly educated man with two degrees and a master's and a doctorate and he believed passionately in education, even for prison inmates.

He had been in charge of wingnut for eighteen months. It would soon be time for a career-enhancing new post for him, but whilst he had been there, he had actively routed out officers who had been obstructive about prisoner engagement and there had been quite a number of them, the old school who considered prisons to be simply placed to segregate the dangerous from society and to punish the undeserving. Hence the only inmates, who spent most of their time locked up during the day, were the ones who effectively chose to be.

Today was the only morning during the week when Terry was locked up for lack of other commitments. Liam was always occupied apart from Tuesday afternoons, Kevin was only locked up on Tuesday and Thursday afternoons and Denis was locked up on Tuesday, Thursday and Friday mornings. Dr Villan insisted that all inmates had at least one half-day locked up, just to remind them of what they were mostly being spared.

The evening arrived and the four reconvened at their scrabble table. They had completed their third game, apart from Terry telling a story, so that was set to be the first event of their short evening together. The board was out but clear of any letters. Denis had started to get out his new tiles.

"Hang on sweetie," Terry interrupted him. "I can't have you lot working out your new words whilst I'm occupied storytelling. You're going to have to wait."

Denis had thought it was worth a try, but he wasn't going to argue with Terry and he demurely replaced his tiles back into the bag. 'Fuck,' he thought. 'I had an 'X'.' The thought had momentarily crossed his mind of secreting the 'X', but he decided that the risk wasn't worth it. It was only a fleeting game after all and he needed his fingers in the longer term.

They all settled down expectantly. Terry was discovering that he rather liked telling stories.

"I wasn't academic at school but I did love history and I still do. What do we learn from history boys?"

Denis, "It repeats itself."

"Yes, but more poignantly, we learn from history that we don't learn from history."

Kevin chuckled. Denis huffed and Liam was nonplussed.

"What word are you using, Terry?" Liam enquired.

"All will become apparent, Liam. Be patient. I'm going to tell you the story of one of the most amazing journeys ever undertaken."

"Must be one of the Apollo missions," Denis interjected.

"No, Denis, a journey on this planet. Now stop interrupting, you dozy fucker and let me get on with it."

Denis tried to manage a smile and went quiet.

"It's the story of Ernest Shackleton."

Kevin and Denis were both familiar with the name and his fame but only in a rather vague way. Liam had never heard of him, but he didn't say so.

"He was a seafaring explorer. His family motto was 'by endurance we shall conquer' and so he called his ship 'Endurance.' It was an old-fashioned wooden ship with cloth sails. It seems to me incredible that back in the old days, men were willing to risk their lives setting out into dangerous, often uncharted seas in such simple vessels. But there we are, their spirit of adventure must have been enormous.

Nowadays, we think that we're brave if we walk to the shops in the rain. Anyway, Shackleton wanted to sail off to the south Pole. If my memory serves me right, a Norwegian exploration crew had got there for the first time a few years earlier, just before our own Scott of Antarctica, but Shackleton still wanted to get there too. He would have been only the third person to get there.

He took a crew of twenty-six and set off in 1914, on the first day of world war one. They took with them sixty-nine sledge dogs, for when they would

108

sledge over the ice to the pole itself. By November 1914, they reached the whaling isle of South Georgia. Remember, whaling was really big in those days. Picture Moby Dick. The whalers warned him that the sea to Antarctica was packed with more ice than they'd ever seen before. It wasn't a good time to go any further south but Shackleton was determined. They set off again and spent another six weeks forcing their ship through the ice floes, but by mid-January, the Endurance was trapped in the ice. The tragedy was that they were only one day shy of their landing point on the continent.

For the next nine months, the ship drifted along with the ice floe, unable to escape its entrapment. As the months passed, the ice slowly crushed the ship. By October, they had to abandon it. The ice was literally crushing it and breaking it up. Then they slept on the ice in thin linen tents. At this point, they only had enough food to last them four weeks and as their food began to run out, they hunted penguins and seals. By the end of March, more than a year after becoming trapped on the ice, they were forced to eat all of their dogs.

In April 1916, when the dog burgers had run out, Shackleton decided to use the three lifeboats they had saved from the mother ship to sail to a tiny, barren island called Elephant Island. After seven days at sea, the crew finally reached land for the first time in 16 months. Even that journey was a miracle of navigation in tiny lifeboats. All the crew was still alive, twenty-six of them plus one lad who had stowed away. But now they would all be doomed if they stayed on that little island and doomed if they ventured out to sea, so Shackleton felt like he had to gamble his own life trying to get back to South Georgia. The problem was that it was 800 miles away, across treacherous seas and now they only had a single usable lifeboat."

Terry stopped to check the others were still with him.

"You lot still with me?"

They all made affirmative sounds. Liam asked if the word was death.

"Liam, do you see the word 'death' on the board?"

"No."

"Well, it can't be that then, can it, you retard? So, to carry on with this epic journey, Shackleton took two of his men and set off. That they reached their intended destination eight hundred miles away was quite simply a miracle of navigation. To this day, given their crude instruments, their voyage has been called the greatest boat journey ever accomplished. It took them seventeen days."

Liam was curious. "How did they actually know where to go?"

"Well, apart from their crude instruments, Liam, I suppose they must have navigated by the stars at night. Basically, it was a miracle."

"That's amazing," Liam mused.

"Their troubles were not over yet, Liam. They had landed on the wrong side of the island, so now they had to hike from one side of the island to the other, overcoming five thousand foot peaks and they had no equipment apart from a few ropes and hardly any rations left. It would be a twenty miles journey over icy mountains and glaciers. Shackleton was afraid that if they stopped to sleep, they would freeze to death. The temperature was probably something unimaginable, like minus thirty. Somehow, they summoned up the energy and determination to march on and climb for thirty-six hours straight and guess what?"

"They all fell down a ravine?"

"No, they actually made it to the whaling station, ragged, haggard and exhausted, but alive."

"Then what happened?"

Liam was engrossed.

"I suppose, they built up their health and reserves at the whaling station, plenty of whale meat to beef up on, if that's the right word and then the priority was to rescue the rest of the crew abandoned on Elephant island. Shackleton borrowed a ship at the whaling station and set sail. The conditions were so harsh that he had to abandon his first three attempts, but eventually, on his fourth attempt, in August 1916, he succeeded in getting to his men. How many of the original crew were still alive, do you think?"

Kevin piped up. "If my memory serves me well, I think they all were."

"Yes, Kevin. They had all survived, camping under the upturned unseaworthy lifeboats and surviving on fish and penguins."

"That's amazing," Liam added. "Was that real penguins or penguins the biscuit?"

He chortled at his own weak joke.

"Shut up, Liam!" Terry said, getting back on track.

"Yeah and you think that life is hard in here! Then they all sailed back to England, arriving in October 1918, two whole years after they had left. They all survived, well, apart from the dogs, of course."

"So, what was your word?" Liam asked.

"I haven't got to that part yet, Liam."

110

"What? I thought that was the end. A happy ending, especially for Denis."
Denis sneered at him.

"Ok, so this is the footnote. After Shackleton and his two colleagues had climbed over South Georgia Island on foot and arrived at the whaling station, they reflected together on their epic journey. Shackleton himself was convinced that a fourth person was mysteriously with them but he never mentioned it to the other two. But then one of the other two expressed exactly the same thoughts to him, as did the third. They had all been aware of a fourth person with them, who helped guide them across that terrible terrain.

Shackleton expressed a deep belief that 'providence' had guided them, not only across the snowfields but across the stormy sea between Elephant Island and South Georgia. So, what's my word, Liam?"

Liam looked at the board carefully. After a while, he tentatively offered 'angelic'?

"Yes, Liam. They had been joined by an angel."

Chapter 11

Terry was awarded a well-deserved fifty points for his story, but Kevin was still way out in front on the scoreboard and was the clear winner, with two hundred and twenty-two points, Denis coming second with one hundred and seventy-seven, Terry right behind him with one hundred and seventy-six and Liam only just trailing with one hundred and sixty-seven.

"Denis, you're the only one yet to win a game," Terry proclaimed rather disdainfully.

"The show ain't over yet, buddy."

"Denis, be a darling and get us some mud. All that talking has made my throat dry."

Denis got up and strolled over to the urns. Liam started rolling a spliff, whilst Terry turned to observe the room. He pondered human nature, reflecting on the fact that most inmates did the same thing each evening with the same colleagues. People were such creatures of habit.

He thought about the affiliations that were apparent from where people sat and who they associated with. The strongest bonding occurred because of ethnic identity and then there were shared interests, similar backgrounds and geographical connections. Some of the inmates were overtly effeminate and they stuck together and although they were often a source of shielded amusement, they weren't overtly victimised like they would have been twenty years earlier. Sexual variations had become far more acceptable throughout society, including inside prisons.

The saddest individuals were the ones who failed to bond. Sometimes little coteries formed of two or three of the leftovers. Nobody picked them for their team and they gelled just because they were the leftovers. The others referred to them mockingly as the dregs and of course, they got bullied a lot. People like Denis and Kevin were so different that they would often serve their term without making any bonds at all.

The same went for the inmates who were suffering from serious mental health issues. Often, the only people they bonded with were their personal officers. Being forced into a community of trapped diverse people could be a very lonely place indeed.

Terry noticed that Steve, Joe and Palmer always stuck together and would usually sit near the front of the room watching football. He'd also noticed that they had a connection with Lenny and his henchmen, but Lenny didn't scare him in the least. Strangely, the people he was getting closest to were here on the scrabble table and that was a pure chance occurrence.

When he was in the gym, he always made an effort to be friendly with the blacks. Although they varied in stature quite considerably, they were all well-defined and muscular and as a team, could be very menacing. The biggest of them was a former boxer called Mace and he was about the same size as Terry. He was doing time for manslaughter. There was an unspoken mutual respect and acknowledgement between the two of them, just because of size and sensed skills. Without a word being spoken on the subject, tacitly, they kind of weirdly knew that they could depend on each other if the wheel came off.

Just as Denis returned with the coffees, there was an eruption at the other scrabble table. The board was on the floor and two of the players were standing vigorously exchanging punches. As the rest of the room noticed the fracas, the noise level went through the roof. Cheering, shouting, jeering and banging on tables. They all stood up to be able to see the fight better. Fights were always great entertainment and were to be wholeheartedly encouraged. No one cared who was winning. It was just great to see some action.

All the officers in the room diverted to the fracas post haste and it wasn't long before the two protagonists were pinned to the floor by four officers. The other two began to wander through the room telling people to calm down and sit down or else association time would be cancelled for them all. The din slowly subsided as they resettled, watching the two offenders being marched off to their cells. No more association time for them for a week or two.

"At least we haven't got to that stage yet," mused Denis with a broad grin on his face.

"Better hope we never do, Denis. I reckon that even Kevin could whip your little ass."

Terry and Liam laughed. Kevin just looked embarrassed, as he often did and Denis looked offended, as he often did.

"Girlies, are we ready for another wordy onslaught?" queried Terry.

They all got down to it, grabbing seven letters from the bag. Denis was a bit miffed. He didn't get that 'X' again, but after a couple of minutes, he announced that he had a six-letter word. The others all capitulated. None of them had found any inspiration at all and Denis placed 'attack' across the middle of the board with the 'K' on the double letter score.

"That's seventeen times two please, Kevin. A word for you, Terry."

"Not all seven letters, Denis? You're slipping, mate," Terry taunted him playfully.

"There's plenty of time, bud."

Terry went next. He placed 'graph' vertically across the second 'A' of 'attack'. That put both his 'G' and 'H' on triple letter scores, making twenty-three. Liam was next and as usual, he took his time. Terry and Denis maintained their patience by focussing on slowly sipping their coffees and anticipating their own next moves on the board. Finally, Liam placed 'jaded' vertically over the 'A' of 'attack.'

"That's clever, Liam," Kevin encouraged him. 'You got the 'J' on a double letter score and the 'D'. That gives you a healthy twenty-four. Well done." Liam punched the air joyfully.

"I'm beating you, Terry," he said smiling.

Terry looked at him in disbelief.

"One word and one point, Liam."

Kevin was beavering away and soon came up with his word. He placed 'berated' horizontally joining the 'D' of 'jaded,'

"Only twenty," he muttered.

"What does that mean?" Liam queried.

"It's posh for 'tell off,' Liam,"

"Ok. I'll remember that for when I next need to tell Denis off." He chuckled.

"What are you going on about, Liam, you retard?" Denis responded immediately.

"Language!" Terry scolded him. "We're playing a civilised game of scrabble here, Denis. No insults. Just a little berating is allowed."

Terry and Liam sniggered and Denis looked put out. Kevin sensibly cut across the vein of antagonism.

"Your go, Denis."

Denis got his head down. It didn't take him long to find a way of exploiting the triple words score below the 'B' of 'berated'. He placed vertically 'broth'. The 'R' was on a double letter score.

"Three times eleven please, Kevin," he requested rather smugly. He was moving into a good lead and now it was up to Terry to rein in that lead if possible.

"Sorry guys, but I'm fucked. I'm not kidding. I've got all vowels. I think I'll change all my letters."

Kevin pulled him up. Terry, you haven't tried yet. Come on, you might find something."

"You think?"

"It's worth a go. If you use your turn to change all your letters, you'll score nothing."

Terry reluctantly explored the board. After a short while, he spoke.

"Well, I'd better get all constants next time."

"Consonants," Kevin helped him.

"Yeah. Them."

He placed two 'E's between the 'J' of 'jeers and the 'R' of 'graph'. They both sat over the 'T's of attack and one was on a double letter score.

"Actually," he announced rather proudly, "That ain't too bad. I get twelve for 'jeer' and five for the two 'et's. Seventeen."

"Hang on," Denis interrupted. "You can't have 'et'. That's French."

"I didn't mean it in French, Denis. I meant it in English, as in 'I et something for breakfast'."

"But that's spelt 'ate'."

"Not if you pronounce it 'et', not 'ate'. I et it. Then, it's spelt 'et'. Obviously."

Terry seemed determined but Denis wasn't ready to back down.

"What do you think, Kevin?"

Kevin didn't want to get himself dragged into arguments but now he had been called on to opine. As always, he tried to be discreet and diplomatic.

"Well, Denis. If we had access to a dictionary, we could determine the correct answer, but I think that in the absence of a dictionary, we should give Terry the benefit of the doubt. He has done rather well to use just two 'E' so creatively after all."

"I don't get why you two are always kissing his arse."

Terry looked at him sternly.

Kevin smiled and said quietly "Haven't you noticed how big he is?"

He then wrote on the scoresheet.

"Seventeen it is then,"

Liam was next. As always he took his time, but all of a sudden, he began to laugh.

Terry looked at him sternly. "What's up with you, you faggot?"

Liam laughed some more, then said, "You're not going to believe this."

Using the 'H' at the end of 'broth' he spelled out horizontally 'honestly' using a blank for the 'L', which he gratefully kissed as he placed it down.

He stood up with his arms in the air. "The winner," he exclaimed confidently.

"Sit down, you jerk! We've only just started. The rest of us might get beginner's luck too," Terry chided him.

"How much, Kevin?"

Liam was genuinely excited.

"Well, the 'E' is on a double letter score, so you get fourteen for the word, forty-two for a triple word score; double that for using up all your letters. Eighty-four!"

"Fuck that!" Terry exclaimed, turning away on his chair, as if in disgust. Denis looked rather gutted. He needed to win this game. He was beginning to consider ways of scuppering the play. Liam stood again as if to reinforce his superiority. Terry physically grabbed him and pulled him back onto his chair.

"Sit!"

Liam chuckled happily.

Kevin placed his tiles down immediately. He was usually very quick, but this time, more so, and his 'G' got on a triple word score. He placed 'ing' on the end of 'attack'.

"That's sixteen times three. Forty-eight."

"Is it my imagination Kevin, or do you seem to almost always get a triple word score?"

"Definitely, your imagination, Terry. I think you'll find that you're the one who most often gets that."

Terry eyed him suspiciously. It felt like Kevin was always getting them.

"Ok, so what are the scores?"

"You, forty; Denis, sixty-seven; me, sixty-eight; and Liam, one hundred and eight."

"Fuck," terry hissed in a subdued fashion. "I think it's maybe time for a story. Whose turn is it?"

"It's Liam's turn," Kevin noted.

"Oh fuck," Liam exclaimed. "Is it really?"

Denis interjected. "Yes, Liam. You haven't done one since you were sucking matron's big bosom, remember?"

He sniggered. Liam sniggered too.

"Ok, let me just look at the board."

He carefully pondered the board, like he was about to select a specialist subject for the mastermind.

"Well, to be honest, guys, I'm struggling a bit. I might be able to do something with 'berated' though."

"Go for it!" encouraged Denis.

"Ok, it's about my partner Kaz, before I met her. I've been with her for about four or five years. Before I met her, she had been a single mother of three young children. Don't ask me about the fathers. I've never tried to find out. That's not my business. I didn't meet her until after the incident I am about to tell you, Ok?"

"Yeah, just get on with it, Liam," Terry asserted

"Ok. Well, she had these three young kids as I said and she was a junkie, like me. She managed being a single mum and a junkie quite well apparently. She would get a hit when the two older kids were at school, which meant that she only had to make sure the toddler was occupied whilst she was out of it.

This seemed to work ok for a long time, but of course, one day, something went wrong. She was completely out of it. Usually, the kid would keep itself occupied indoors, but on this one occasion, this little toddler managed to get out of the house. He wandered off outside. They lived near a stream and the kid fell into it and drowned.

When Karen came round and realised that her kid was gone, she was hysterical. She called the police, who soon found the body. She was arrested for child neglect. Her other two kids were taken into care immediately and she hardly saw them again. Eventually, they were adopted, so for the past few years, she hasn't seen them at all. So I suppose you could say that she was berated for her neglect."

"God, Liam, how did she cope with that?"

"Drugs. She likes to be out of it."

"Did you ever meet her kids?"

"No. This happened before me."

"How does she feel about herself?"

"Terrible, I suppose. She didn't want to lose any of her kids. You know what mums are like."

The listeners went quiet as they speculated on how dreadful this poor woman must have felt.

"Did she get punished?"

"You can't punish a mother more than depriving her of her children, but yes, in addition, she was put on probation for two years, not that that is like punishment, really."

"How is she now?"

"I think she just wants to die."

They all went quiet. Then Kevin spoke.

"I think that deserves fifty points. It was very impacting."

There were murmurs of approval. Liam brightened up.

"Kev, did I get the word right?"

"Well, you were restricted by the board, Liam. Your story might have been better suited to 'punishment' or 'consequence' because of the severity of the situation. 'Berate' is rather more light, you know, where nothing more serious than a good telling off is required like you forgot to put the rubbish out, or Terry berates Denis for being pompous, or something like that, but it's ok. It's in the right vein."

"Great." He looked distracted. "You fancy coming outside for a bat, you old fag?"

"Sorted, you young fiend."

They both stood up to leave. Terry offered to get Denis a hot drink which he accepted. When Liam and Kevin got to the exercise yard, Liam spoke.

"Kevin, I'm hearing that you have been asking people for gear."

Kevin looked highly embarrassed.

"I'm sorry, Liam. I didn't want you to find out about this, I really didn't."

"Mate, the walls have ears. There are no secrets in here. Even the screws know most of what is going on. Everyone thinks you're a weirdo. No one knows you or trusts you, so no one's gonna help you."

"That's nice, I'm sure, but I thought that prisons are awash with drugs?"

"They are, mate. But they are also populated by inmates who generally don't want a month or two added to their sentences for supplying a punk like you."

"So why am I treated differently?"

Liam laughed. "Mate, you are from another world. All the rest of us in here either know each other or know someone who knows people in here. That creates a certain amount of trust and a pecking order and a system. You're completely outside of that system, you wuss. No one knows you, therefore no one trusts you. How do they even know you're not a grass or a plant?"

"Oh, come on." He was rather exasperated.

"Anyway, Kevin, what do you want gear for?"

"I really don't want to talk about that, Liam."

"You could have asked me."

"I absolutely don't want to involve you, Liam."

Liam thought for a moment. He was a slow thinker, but he seemed to have a reasonable degree of intuition.

"I'm pretty sure you're not trying to get a habit, so that leaves self-harm. Kevin, don't tell me that it's so bad in here that you want to do a Dutch?"

"Liam, I really don't want to talk about it."

"Ok, Kev. It's your funeral. Oops, I really didn't mean to say that Kevin. I mean, it's your life, but take some advice from me, mate. Don't go near OG again. He's always looking for opportunities to enhance his reputation. He's a complete cunt and to him, you're just fodder. He'll hurt you just to big himself up. You got that?"

"Yes, I rather got that impression myself."

"And if you keep cold calling people, it won't be long before someone shanks you."

"Oh dear. I don't like the sound of that."

He physically recoiled.

"And, if you survive the wound, you'd definitely get a nasty infection which you might not survive. Nothing in here is clean, especially sharps and blades."

"I suppose, not."

"Don't forget, Kevin, a lot of stuff is kept safe by being stored up someone's arse."

Kevin pulled a face of disgust. "Delightful."

"You can make some pocket money, Kevin, if you want to, by hiring out your own pouch."

Kevin looked at him horrified. Words failed him.

"Just sayin', in case you need to earn some favours."

"I don't think I'll get that desperate, Liam."

"Well, you never know. Just giving you the heads up pumpkin, but listen, man, real talk, don't think about topping yourself. Life is a gift no matter how shit it is for the time being. Things change. We all have a future. You'll get used to prison life. We all do, well, most of us."

He realised the hollowness of his words as he spoke them. He had only a few days earlier explained to Kevin how common an occurrence, suicide was, inside prison, but there was nothing more he could think of saying right now. They returned to the game.

They got another round done before it was bang-up time. Denis was next with 'lampoon' which he placed vertically down the right-hand side to the 'N' of 'attacking'. That was on a double word and it scored him a total of twenty-six. Terry followed with 'amaze' vertically over the 'A' of 'berated'. That also was on a double word score, earning him thirty-two points. Liam placed 'screen' horizontally by attaching the 'S' on the bottom of 'graph'. That scored him twelve points for 'graphs' and sixteen points for 'screen' which was on a double word score.

The final effort in the round from Kevin was a vertical 'sniffs' over the 'N' of 'screen'. He had to use a blank to make the second 'S'. This got him onto the triple word score at the bottom right-hand corner of the board, which scored three times eleven. Liam was still streaking ahead on the scoreboard. They disbanded for the evening.

As Kevin returned to his cell, he was in a thoughtful mood. Roger was already in there snoring away as he always did. That was just one more tiny straw on Kevin's back. Roger's snoring disturbed his sleep every single night.

He, really, couldn't see himself surviving in prison. He was at that time of life when, with the best years behind him, it was easy to feel that he was a failure. His achievements didn't count for much and the world would be a better place without him. He felt so guilty about abandoning his wife and daughters by being imprisoned. He was convinced that they would have a better life with him out the way, making room for someone better and more reliable than him.

He had to be brave and noble and selfless and do the right thing for them. He couldn't be violent to himself. He totally lacked the guts for that. He had never been violent to anything or anyone and he certainly wouldn't have the guts to inflict pain upon himself but he could very happily put himself quietly and permanently to sleep. He wanted to visit that place that Liam had described as being soft and spongy, a safe dreamy place far away from bad things, like failure and despondency and then stay there. With that comforting thought, he drifted off to sleep, despite Roger's snoring.

Chapter 12

The next day after tea and unlock, Kevin went to the association room to get the scrabble board ready. The games cupboard hadn't been unlocked. He approached one of the officers to ask for it to be unlocked.

"No scrabble for you guys tonight, I'm afraid."

Kevin was surprised.

"Why not?"

"I'm sure that you noticed there was a little eruption over one of the scrabble games yesterday."

"Yeah, but not ours."

"Sorry, mate. The boss has closed down the games. We don't want a repercussion of last night."

"Do you think it's fair to tar us all with the same brush?"

The officer grimaced.

"Look, ol' fella. It's not your place to question the rules. There was disorder and now there are sanctions. No more scrabble for a while. Simple. Is that such a big deal?"

"Well, yes, it is actually. We all rather enjoy it."

"I don't think you're here to enjoy yourselves, do you?"

Kevin looked him in the eye. Officer Jenkins had cold eyes and was not known for empathy. He was old-school. Kevin discerned that trying to reason with him was pointless. He walked back to the table to await and inform the others. Denis was the first to arrive.

"Oh," he reflected when told. "So, some other delinquents lose their rag and we get sanctioned for them. Great"

After that Terry and Liam arrived, and they were more matter-of-fact about it. This was the kind of inconsistency they were used to experiencing and seeing in prison.

"Well," Terry said thoughtfully, "What shall we do to overcome this little setback, gentlemen? Kevin, what does the growth mindset do?"

"That's a very good question, Terry. It would see this as a learning opportunity. We have to learn to adapt and not just cave in to defeat."

"Ok. Sounds good. How?"

"Yeah, let's not let them beat us," Liam offered.

"Well, we could all just carry on by doing a story. I've got the words all written down."

"Good plan, Kevin. Show us the words."

He got his note out and read the words, slowly, thoughtfully, as it was his turn. The only word on the board which stirred anything in him was 'amaze'.

"I mentioned in an earlier story that I got married when I was twenty-six but I said nothing of how I met my beautiful wife. It was an amazing story."

Denis interrupted him.

"I'm not sure, I want to hear this. I think it's going to be too smarmy. It might make me wanna puke."

Terry answered for Kevin. "Shut up, Denis, you dumb fuck! You're the one who moans about miserable stories and now you're going to hear one that is amazing. Don't judge till you've heard him out. Carry on, Kevin."

Denis shrugged. Kevin continued.

"Well, to be honest, I was never a ladies' man like Denis was."

"What do you mean 'was'?"

"Ok, Is, then. I'd been to university and I had quite a few friends who were girls, but no big romances or particularly meaningful relationships, so I was still quite shy and uncertain around women. Then I started working in sales and most of the people I pitched to in the business field were men. I had started to buy my own little flat and the job was going well, but I knew that I was underdeveloped in the relationship department and so I decided to do something about it. I took up a few new hobbies, like rambling and chess."

Liam laughed and interrupted him with some degree of genuine surprise.

"Kevin, rambling is for old people. Surely you knew that? And you were in your twenties or did you want to meet more mature women, you kinky beast?"

"You're quite right, Liam. I was only meeting much older people, so it didn't really work for what I wanted and as for the chess, I was friggin' useless at it anyway and the players were almost all blokes too."

"Why didn't you just go down the pub?" Terry asked.

"I really didn't have the confidence for that, Terry. Not on my own. I was far too self-conscious. Then, I got chatting to a guy at work about my conundrum and he told me about a mate of his who was also a bit geeky but he was an avid amateur photographer. He had advertised his services for glamour photography and apparently, he had loads of responses. After that, he was always meeting lovely young ladies desperate to get some decent glamour pics of themselves. This struck a chord with me. I felt that I could do that too but I would have to build up my photography skills, so I enrolled in an evening photography course."

"Kevin! I always knew you had a pervy side to you!" Terry laughed out. Then he asked seriously.

"Was it a glamour photography class with lots of nude women to photograph?"

"No, it was just a basic course about how to take good pictures generally. It covered all the technical aspects of cameras, you know, what effect different aperture sizes have, depth of field, exposure values, compensation, shutter speeds, ISO values, lens focal lengths, wide-angle, telephoto, light metering, you know, stuff like that."

"Shut up, Kevin. You're sending me to sleep," Terry protested.

Liam looked rather vacant but Denis was right there with him.

"Fascinating stuff, Kevin. I much prefer to shoot in manual mode myself. Aperture-priority naturally."

Terry interjected. "Can we please get on with the story before you two start playing with each other as you whisper sweet F-stops into each other's ears?"

Kevin picked up his thread. "Ok. Well, suffice to say I really got into it. It kind of complimented my work with photocopiers in a way. That was quite technical too and I liked the technical stuff. I found the technical creativity of a proper camera really interesting. It was an exciting time to be getting into photography, actually. They were just beginning to bring out automatic-focus lenses and cameras were starting to go digital. I don't suppose you remember the old film cameras, do you, Liam?"

"What?" Liam replied with a very confused look on his face. "I just use my mobile, mate. It's got twelve megapixels in it."

Terry asked a question.

"As a matter of interest, Kevin, what did you study at uni'?"

"Business studies. I thought that would help me get a decent job."

"And did it?"

"Depends on what you call a decent job, Terry. Anyway, getting back to my story. There were mostly guys on my course and just a few ladies. The blokes all seemed to have the very latest, flashy, film SLR cameras which were very expensive. The new compact digital cameras weren't really any good for photography classes, bizarrely enough, because they were so simple to use. They were fully automatic. No knobs to play with."

"Ooh, Kevin, I didn't know you hung that way," Liam teased.

"And they were frighteningly expensive when they first came out as well. I had only treated myself to a reasonable second-hand SLR. What I'm trying to get across is that all the other blokes had much flashier equipment than me and seemed to know more about cameras and pictures than I did and so of course, they were altogether more impressive and confident than I was, but that was ok, because I was only there just to learn about photography.

One of the girls on the course, Susie, was outstandingly attractive and all the guys were always trying to impress her, you know, with the size of their lenses and their ultra-fast shutter speeds. It was a bit pathetic really. They were a bit like animals at the start of the mating season. It reminded me of those David Attenborough films where the birds of paradise put on the most spectacular shows and flit around the females so that the one with the most impressive jig and plumes got to copulate."

"And were you too?" Terry asked.

"What? Like an animal?"

"Yeah, you know, dancing around, showing off your equipment and all that. Trying to win her sexual favours."

"Not at all, Terry. She was far too nice for me and I knew it. I was polite to her, of course, but I wasn't showing any particular interest in her. I really wasn't. There were a few other girls on the course but it was Susie who the guys hung around, tongues hanging out, salivating, staring, rubbing their groins. The course went on for quite a few months. We would experiment with taking pictures between classes and bring our best photos into class for analysis by the others each week."

"How did your stuff rate, Kev?" Denis queried.

"Not very well, I'm afraid, Denis. The others seemed to get much more artistic shots than me, but then, I think they had more experience already. For me, it wasn't a competition. I was there just to learn. Period."

Liam piped up. "Were they glamour pics, Kevin?"

"What, naked women you mean?"

"Yeah."

"No. It was all very tame. We were just shooting scenic stuff, or interesting angles on everyday stuff, or playing with different exposures, or getting silhouettes, or blurred backgrounds. Stuff like that. You may not understand this Liam, but this was in the days before guys were routinely sending girls dick-pics."

"But you said, you wanted to get into glamour photography."

"Eventually, Liam, eventually, but I wasn't ready yet. I would have to learn many more skills first. Anyway, these guys were coming onto Susie whenever they got the chance, but as far as I knew, they weren't getting anywhere.

Then one day out of the blue, she got chatting to me at the end of the class and ended up asking me if I wanted to go for a drink afterwards. I was literally shell-shocked, I was so surprised. I must have looked like a right dick. I couldn't think of what to say. My mouth must have dropped open because she put her fingers on my chin and moved them up to close my mouth. 'Am I that surprising?' she asked."

He laughed at the memory. "I was amazed that she asked me out, of all the guys there."

"And the rest is history?" Denis asked.

"And the rest is history," Kevin confirmed proudly, smiling thoughtfully.

"Well Kevin, you da man!" exclaimed Terry and he leaned over the table to give Kevin a big high five.

"I wonder what she saw in you, Kevin?" Denis asked. That sounded rather insulting but he didn't mean to be.

"Sorry, that came out wrong. I meant, I wonder which of your many qualities she was particularly attracted to?"

Terry turned to Denis. "I'm sure he ain't going to want to give you any hints, Denis, you dozy fucker."

Liam spoke to Kevin. "You've been a very lucky fellah, Kevin."

The contented, pleased look fell away from Kevin's face.

"I don't feel very lucky, Liam. Look at me now."

"Fuck off, Kevin. This is just temporary. You've got everything to look forward to. You need to count your blessings, mate. A beautiful wife. Your own home. Kids. A proper job."

Kevin looked at him in rather sad disbelief. He only felt like he had completely fucked up his life and had lost everything. He said nothing. Denis asked him a question.

"Did you ever get into glamour photography then?"

"No, Denis. I don't think that would have gone down too well with Susie. I never even told her that I had once harboured that idea at all. That might have scared her off. I didn't want her thinking I was a perv like…" He stopped just short of naming anyone. Terry and Liam Laughed, but Denis wondered seriously who he was insinuating.

They spent the rest of their association time drinking tea or coffee, smoking and exchanging amusing little anecdotes of their lives. Kevin seemed to have opened a Pandora box. Now they all wanted to tell stories about their first girlfriend, or their funniest encounter, or their most disastrous shag.

For the time being, they forgot all about the scrabble game. Even Denis revealed some ancient truths about himself. It was one of those rare occasions where the mood was just right. Imperceptibly and inexplicably, normal reservations and caution just melted away. They felt strangely comfortable revealing themselves and delighted in the mirth and merriment their little anecdotes brought to themselves and the others.

By bang-up time, none of them could remember an evening when they had felt so relaxed, so engaged and just plainly entertained by merely talking and sharing. They had shared a beautiful evening of camaraderie together. Human beings levelling with each other openly and honestly.

The following Friday morning went routinely as always; Kevin cleaning, Liam cooking, Terry gymming and Denis reading in his cell. At noon they all collected dinner and returned to their cells to be locked up for an hour and a half, whilst they ate. They would be unlocked if they had an afternoon occupation to attend. Kevin and Liam had English to go to, Terry the laundry and Denis the library.

When Kevin's cell door was unlocked after dinner, he found Lenny and two of his torpedoes, Bennett and Devenish, loitering nearby. They quickly ushered him back into his cell.

"Fuck off, Roger!" Lenny snapped.

Roger got off his bunk in a rather cumbersome fashion but he was moving as quickly as his racked old body would allow. He said nothing as he scrambled out of the cell towards the rec. Kevin backed up to the bunks, almost trembling.

He sensed big trouble and he was confused. Lenny stood at arm's length in front of him and delivered an almighty slap to his face, knocking his glasses clean off his face. Kevin recoiled to one side and put his hand to his face.

"Stand up straight, you fat fucker!" Lenny hissed.

He then delivered an equally hard back-hander to Kevin's other cheek but that didn't make his glasses reappear. Similarly, Kevin recoiled again.

"What have I done?" he asked, expressing his confusion.

"Nothing, you disgusting fucktard. I just want to make sure you're paying attention."

Kevin made no reply and just looked at him, very scared. Lenny's face was quite revolting this close-up. His wispy beard looked dirty, his skin looked unhealthy, greasy and blotchy, his teeth looked mostly bad and his tattoos looked a mess. Kevin really didn't like standing this close to him.

"Someone is going to give you something to hide. You will make an incision in your mattress and hide it in there. You will be given a tape to cover up the cut in the mattress and you will guard said item with your life until one of my boys comes to fetch it."

He slapped him across the face again. The torpedoes stood around nonchalantly, keeping an eye on Kevin and the corridor.

"Do you understand?"

"Yes," Kevin said quietly.

Lenny delivered another backhander, as if practicing his tennis.

"Speak up, you vile punk!"

"Yes," Kevin said more firmly.

"And not a word to anyone. If that item goes missing or if anyone learns about it, you will be brown bread by the next day. Is that clear, fucktard?"

"Yes, but how will I know if it's one of your boys collecting?"

Lenny looked angry and struck him yet again.

"Don't be such a cunt. No one else will know about it, will they?"

"Of course."

Lenny stared at him hatefully, hissing between his clenched brown teeth, before turning and leaving, his henchmen closely in tow.

Kevin sat on the lower bunk and cried. He felt scared, hurt and so alone. It took him fully fifteen minutes before he felt composed enough to go to the afternoon English class. He didn't feel like going there at all but he felt even less inclined to stay alone in his cell. He felt too vulnerable.

128

By the time he arrived late, after making feeble excuses to the officers in the corridors, about his lateness, Mr Blanchflower was in full swing.

"Come in, Kevin. We were just discussing how we learn."

Kevin sat and Mr Blanchflower carried on.

"So who can give me an example of how we learn?"

Darren piped up "Going to school."

"Yeah, but I want to break it down. Actually, how do we learn?"

"Copy people?"

"Yes, Conrad. Think small children."

"Experiment with things?"

"Yes, Darcus, but how does a child get most of its information?"

"By chewing things?"

'Ok, think a bit older."

"From its parents?"

"Yes. Does the process change as we get older?"

"Hope so, my parents are both dead!"

The class laughed.

Another student interjected. "You had a head start mate. I never had any parents."

More laughter. Prison Humour could be quite dark.

Another quip. "You're both so privileged. I was never born."

Hysterics now.

"You think you had it bad? When I was a mere sperm, my dad was having oral sex."

More fodder for the raucous laughter.

Mr Blanchflower chose to take the reins back at that point as that thread could go on endlessly, although it was very good for developing their creativity.

"Yes, all very good. So, initially, we learn everything from our parents or whoever is supposed to be looking after us, but as we develop and we need broader input, we draw on other sources, such as other people, friends, teachers, television programmes, books, our own experimentation, etcetera. So, what limits our learning, with so many resources at our disposal?"

"Money?"

"Do you really think so? Maybe, in terms of some formal education or really top-notch education, but libraries are full of books and borrowing them is free.

Then there's the internet. I suppose that most of the sum of mankind's total knowledge is freely available on that."

"Ability to read and write."

"Absolutely, Gavin. It's probably true to say that most of what we learn is by reading, which is why I want to make sure we all improve our literacy whilst, we are here. What else?"

"Willingness to learn?"

" Yes and what determines that?"

"Whether you're interested?"

"O.k. And what impacts on that?"

"Need? Vision?"

"Opportunity."

"How distracted you are by other stuff."

"What you actually want to do with your life?"

"Yes, all very good answers. There are different impact factors for all of us depending on our circumstances but there is one core model I'd like to make you aware of. Who's heard of Maslow's hierarchy of need?"

The class went silent. Inmates looked around to see if anyone had a hand up. Nobody did.

"Come on, I only want to know who's heard of it. I'm not going to ask anyone to explain it."

This time, Kevin's hand went up.

"Great!" exclaimed Mr Blanchflower. "Tell us all about it, Kevin!"

The class erupted in mirth. As they quietened down, Mr Blanchflower continued.

"Only kidding, Kevin. Just my little joke. Well, Maslow's hierarchy or pyramid of needs provides us with a succinct, diagrammatic representation of how we need to climb up a pyramid to reach the pinnacle in order to reach maximum personal development."

He drew a big pyramid on the whiteboard behind him and divided it into five segments.

"The big base segment represents our basic needs to simply stay alive from one day to the next, such as food, water, sleep, fresh air."

He wrote 'basic physical needs' in that section on the diagram. The class watched, almost in awe.

"The next level up represents safety and security, such as a shelter that can protect you from storms, wild dangerous animals and maybe even wild dangerous people."

The class tittered and he wrote 'safety and security' inside the second tier.

"The next tier is to do with social needs. The need for love and affection, a sense of belonging."

He wrote 'love, affection, family' inside tier three.

"Who can have a stab at what the next level is?"

"Kevin, can!" some wag called out.

"Apart from Kevin."

"What you get good at as an individual?"

"That's a very good suggestion, Conrad. Yes, it's about self-esteem, status, being confident in yourself and building an image that you are pleased with."

He wrote 'self-esteem/status' in tier four.

"Anyone has a guess at what the top tier is?"

"Sex?"

The class laughed accompanied by a chorus of whistling.

"Actually, Conrad, that would be in tier three, with love and belonging, so quite low down really."

He turned to the board and added 'sex' alongside 'love, affection, family' in tier three.

"According to Maslow, sex is a fairly basic social need although not all people need sex to feel loved and appreciated, of course."

"Yeah. Priests don't need sex to feel loved and appreciated, well, apart from with choirboys and any other kids they can get their hands on."

The class erupted in laughter again.

"Ok, let's not get hung up on the sex! Anyone else? The top tier?"

"Becoming the pope?"

More laughter.

"Well, for the pope, yes, but not for the rest of us mere mortals. The top tier is called self-actualisation, or self-fulfilment."

He wrote that alongside the top tier which was too small to write inside.

"That top tier means being the best you can be, achieving your full potential. So why is all of this important?"

There was stony silence.

"Ok. Well, I'm no psychologist, as Maslow was. He wrote this theory way back in the early forties and it's still a good tool to shed light on how we develop and learn as human beings. His proposal was that you couldn't move up a tier until the needs of the lower tier were met first. That certainly is easy to see lower down. If you don't eat, you starve and obviously, you can't progress much from that.

Then, before you start looking for friendship and love, you would want to find somewhere safe to live first, so you can survive from day to day. That's tier two. Does this make sense so far guys?"

There were lots of affirmations and nodding of heads.

"I think the next two tiers are the most important. He suggests that you won't begin developing your own persona and self-confidence until you've got a supportive community around you. How many of you feel that you grew up with a supportive community around you?"

He looked inquisitively around the room, only to see most faces looking sad and rather lost.

"My priest was very supportive," Jason offered.

"Yes, Jason. I can see a theme developing here, but I don't want to go into details about your backgrounds. I'm not here to stir up sad memories but I do want you to think about this whole subject so that when you get a chance to become more reliably established in one of these levels, which might have been precarious for you in the past, you try to do so.

Life is a constant journey of learning. The idea is to help you see the importance of the lower levels that you need to feel comfortable with your achievements in levels one, two and three, before you have any realistic chance of moving up into tier four or maybe even five one day. Do you see that?"

The class murmured some degree of acceptance.

"I don't know how many people actually get to the top and fully raise their potential. Probably very few, actually. Obviously, there are all sorts of other potentially limiting factors but I have no doubt that all of you in here today can reach tier four if you put your minds to it. Any questions or comments?"

"Yeah, what's this got to do with English?" Tony playfully enquired.

Some of the class tittered and some of them told him very firmly to shut up. They wouldn't tolerate Mr Blanchflower being mocked.

"Well, Tony, I like going off-piste sometimes into a little bit of sociology or psychology. It's all good fun! But more importantly, it's got everything to do with whatever subject you want to learn. I want you to be able and willing to learn more, whether it's English or anything else that's useful to you.

I know that a lot of you haven't had ideal beginnings in life but that doesn't mean that you shouldn't aspire to climb the pyramid of self-development in the future. I hope that by understanding how it works will help you to find ways of filling in the gaps in one tier so that you can move on up to the next tier. Before I became a teacher I was allowing myself to just drift. Maybe I struggled to build my tier three before I was finally able to move up to tier four."

The class was quiet, thoughtful and absorbent. Someone aired their thoughts, admiringly.

"Mr Blanchflower, surely you have reached the top tier?"

"Who knows, Malcolm. Who knows? That's probably not for me to comment on."

Liam piped up, very proud of his knowledge.

"Sir was that a rhetorical question?"

"Yes Liam. Very good."

Chapter 13

Scrabble was off on Friday evening and throughout the weekend, which therefore passed very tediously. On Saturday, Liam had a visit from Kaz and Denis had one from his lovely old mother, Edith. That broke their days up a little but the rest of the weekend was spent just trying to occupy themselves with all the usual other options. Kaz was quite excited as Liam would be due for release on licence soon, as long as he carried on staying out of trouble. Their actual meetings together were always rather dull, as neither of them were big talkers and they were both tranquil types.

Liam was unusual insofar as his work as a catering assistant extended into the weekends. The inmates still needed their dinners and therefore, he would work either a Saturday or a Sunday morning. This week it would be the Sunday. It earned him extra privileges which he took as art classes. It also meant that he was only required to work on three weekday mornings.

Terry managed to secure some gym time and even some time on the pool table during the evenings. Kevin struggled the most to kill time. As much as he resented cleaning toilets and floors during the week at least that kept him busy. He didn't associate well, for a variety of reasons; his age; his middle-class background; his lack of a criminal track record and criminal associates; his personality, which wasn't well adjusted for dealing with new people, or change. He kept a very low profile, yet the main incident of the weekend involved him.

On Saturday afternoon, whilst he sat in the association room reading, he was approached by the two Lenny's aids he had briefly encountered the previous afternoon, Bennett and Devenish. He was ordered to go take a shower. He knew he had no option but to comply.

He returned to his cell, trembling slightly and collected his towel and shower gel and then proceeded to the showers as instructed. He was full of trepidation. Two inmates whose names he didn't know were already in there showering and one of them told him to strip and get in the shower. This he did, feeling most uncomfortable getting naked in front of other people. When naked in broad daylight in front of strange people, he was extremely self-conscious about his copious and blubbery, pale flesh. He was insipid-looking and he didn't even have much body hair to help him look a bit more manly. He got under a shower and started to wash.

The other two got out quickly and dried themselves and dressed. A third inmate then entered the changing room. He quickly moved an item from within his towel and gave it to one of the others. It was going to be a slick operation. This mule then began to strip as Kevin was sternly ordered to get out and get dry and dressed as quickly as he could. As he dressed, the item was placed inside his towel. One of the inmates reminded him of his orders.

"Fucker, you know what to do with it. The tape is on the blade. Just make sure no one else knows about it, ok, or you know what will happen to you?"

"Yes," he answered meekly.

They left smartly and as soon as Kevin had dressed, he scurried back to his cell. He definitely didn't want to get caught in possession. He lay on his bed, trying to look as inconspicuous as possible. The fact that he was in his cell when he didn't have to be might look suspicious in and of itself.

Facing the wall, he unwrapped the item enough to reveal the blade. It was about six inches long, an inch and a half wide and very sharp. It was evil-looking and surprisingly heavy. He had been led to believe that 'shanks' inside the prison were concoctions of filed down bits of metal from sundry sources such as bits of metal chair legs or even just sharp bits of solid plastic attached to makeshift wooden or plastic handles, but this was a pucker, serious, real knife.

He used it to cut a small slice in the plastic cover of his mattress on the wall side. He then cut into the dense foam to create a sheath for it. He peeled off the short section of blue tape that had been stored on the blade and rewrapped the knife before forcing it into his mattress. When he had finally managed to conceal the whole length of the knife rather clumsily inside the foam, he covered the cut with the tape.

The knife would be easy to find if anyone had a mind to search his cell. It made quite a lump inside the thin mattress. He made sure the mattress was discreetly covered with the blanket before getting up and returning to the association room. He was very nervous. He may have made his mind up about a way of escaping prison but at the same time, he didn't want to get into any trouble that might make prison life even more intolerable whilst he still had to endure it.

Come the evening, he was rather grateful that there was no scrabble-babble. He was afraid that Terry or Liam might notice that his demeanour was different, more fretful, more tense and uneasy than usual and he didn't want to be grilled. He was never comfortable lying to anyone.

Monday morning, he was able to leave his cleaning duties a little early. At eleven o'clock, he had a scheduled meeting with his personal prison officer, Mary Jacobs. This would be his third one-to-one meeting with her.

All inmates were allocated dedicated personal officers with whom they could discuss matters with some degree of confidentiality and they were supposed to meet weekly. The initiative had been conceived in recent years to help build rapport between inmates and staff in general and it was hoped that problems could be identified early on and dealt with before there were any serious consequences. Officers received appropriate training and support to help equip them for this new mentoring role.

Mary was about thirty-five years old and had been a prison officer for almost ten years. She seemed to enjoy her job and showed genuine concern for her charges, "Well Kevin, how have things been this week?"

"Wonderful."

Mary looked at him a little sternly. "Kevin, these meetings with me are only going to be productive for you if you can be honest with me."

"I don't know what I am supposed to say. I absolutely hate it in here with every single fibre of my body, soul and spirit."

"Well, have you had any issues which I might be able to help with?"

"Can you get me out of here?"

She looked at him blankly. "Sorry for looking so drab, but they all say that and it gets really boring."

"Yes, I expect they do. Sorry. I don't mean to be obstructive, boring, or so predictable. I am grateful that you are here for me to talk to, but really, the situation is just so dire, a little bit of fine-tuning is not really going to help."

Mary was concerned about his sullen, gloomy attitude. It was her job to help steer him into a more positive frame of mind.

"Kevin, you've got to focus on the fact that it's not forever."

"Eight years in here is forever."

"Now, Kevin, you're exaggerating and you know it. You know that you will be paroled halfway through."

Kevin's face and attitude brightened up not a jot.

"And halfway through your prison time, you will be moved to an open prison. That will be far better for you."

"That's still two years away and it's still a prison."

"Come on, Kevin, think about what you were doing five years ago. Hasn't that time flown by? And we're only looking at two years. How old are your daughters?"

"Thirteen and fourteen."

"I bet it seems like yesterday when they were still just babies."

"That's different. You don't want the time with your kids to fly by. But you do in prison."

"Ok, Kevin. I'm not going to force you to talk about anything, so long as you are fully aware that I am here for you to discuss anything of concern to you, ok?"

"Ok."

"Right, well there is something I have to talk to you about."

She looked at him rather seriously. He froze. Had they already found the knife? Inside he was panicking, but he tried to remain serenely composed, waiting with bated breath.

"As of today, there is a new governor, Mr Dibden and he wants to make his presence known. He's going to be the proverbial new broom that sweeps cleaner. They're all like that when they first come here, but he can't change things too much, because the overall ethos of the whole prison service is delivered top-down from the home office. However, he will want to stamp his own personal interpretation of the guidance on the rest of us. We don't expect too many changes though."

Kevin was listening politely. He preferred her doing all the talking rather than him but he was not really at all interested in prison politics.

"Will anything affect me?" he asked, only slightly curiously.

"Well, I am coming to that bit, Kevin. There will be a short-term change that will affect all of the inmates. Mr Dibden has done his homework and he is aware that a lot of officers here are somewhat behind with their online training modules and he's making it a priority that we all get up to speed asap. He wants his new machine to be sparkly clean and efficient. To make time available for officers to get on and study their outstanding modules, prisoner association time is going to be cancelled until we've all caught up."

"Oh," Kevin said rather drily. After considering this news for a few moments, he spoke.

"I don't think that's very fair."

"Maybe not, but it's only temporary."

"That's the best part of the day for us."

"Yes, I know, Kevin. I'm sorry. There's nothing I can do about it. Each inmate will get the chance to discuss this with his personal officer this week."

"What good will that do?"

"None, I'm afraid. Don't shoot the messenger. I'm just letting you know."

"Have you lot got so much training to do?"

"Personally, I've got very little to catch up on but it's true that some officers are way behind. Not everyone loves doing computer training modules as I'm sure you can imagine."

Kevin tried to seem interested.

"I thought you were all fully trained and qualified already."

"Yes, of course, we are Kevin but there's always a little more burnishing that can be done."

Kevin's mind played with the phrase 'polishing a turd' but he didn't voice his thoughts. He just asked, "Why?"

"Politics mainly, I suppose. Changing priorities. New goals. Some genuinely beneficial new initiatives sometimes."

"Is it largely about the organisation covering its own ass, you know, so if something goes wrong, the management can turn around and say that the staff was delivered with the latest appropriate training, so it's not the management's fault?"

"Hark at you, the old wizened cynic!"

She leaned back, smiling, looking at him knowingly. He replied.

"It's being in here that does it. You know what they say. 'To err is human, to blame it on someone else shows management potential'."

"Ooh, that's good. You're wasted in here, Kevin."

Her remark was supposed to be jocular and humorous, but as soon as the words left her mouth, she realised that they were more tragic than comic, because they were so true. Kevin felt it too. There was a moment's awkward silence before she carried on.

"Well, I'm sure it's not just about management covering its ass, Kevin. We have to do a lot of ongoing awareness training. I am sure you can imagine - how to deal sensitively with different ethnic groups, gender issues, religious indoctrination. Stuff like that. Society is changing so rapidly and we have to change with it."

"Got anything for people in prisons who are not criminals?"

"Yes, Kevin. Patience. Open prison. We are more about rehabilitation these days than mere incarceration."

Kevin looked at her blankly.

"Before we finish, Kevin, are you sure there's nothing you want to talk about?"

She looked at him searchingly.

"What happened to Mac?"

"Mac? Who's Mac?"

"He was my celly up until a week ago."

"Oh, the one who died?"

"Yes, that one. How did he die?"

"Well, Kevin, I'm not really supposed to discuss other inmates with you."

Kevin interrupted her. "I'm sure he won't mind."

"Yes, you could say that. Well, as you were his celly, it's only fair that you know, I suppose. It was just a case of overdosing. The autopsy found enough heroin in him to put a horse to sleep."

"That's what we thought."

"I'm sorry, Kevin. That wasn't very nice."

This news of the loss of association time soon leaked out to the inmates who were understandably not happy, especially because no officer could be specific as to when normal service would be resumed. Thus, for several days, although normal daytime classes and work were continued, lock-up time began at 5:15 p.m. and didn't end until 8:15 a.m. the next day. The week passed routinely enough, but inmates were visibly more disgruntled and tensions were building up. Both officers and inmates could feel the atmosphere change.

First thing on Friday morning, in the exercise yard, Kevin was one of the first inmates to be made aware that something was going to kick off later. Bennett and Devenish approached him in the yard. Bennett barked at him.

"Fucktard, you disgusting fat piece of shit. You need to bring our item to the canteen at dinner time today. Don't let anyone know you've got it and don't be late, you revolting blubbery cunt. If you don't show up when you're supposed to, we'll be round later to cut you up into enough tiny pieces to flush you down the shitter where you belong. You got that, fucktard?"

Kevin was almost wetting himself in fear. He nodded.

"Speak to me, you pathetic moron!"

"Yes, I've got it," he replied weakly.

"You act normal and just wait till Lenny comes over to get it off you. Keep it well hidden until he finds you, oh and keep well away from the guards. You got that, shit-face?"

He nodded meekly.

They both gave him their best menacing looks, which they'd been perfecting for all their adult lives, before walking back into the main building.

Kevin was not at all relaxed whilst cleaning. He was watching the clock so carefully. Time was dragging by, but he had to be careful to be on time. If he entered the canteen early that would look suspicious and he couldn't afford to attract the attention of any of the guards. If he was late, he would end up as mince-meat. He got there at his usual time and stood as innocently as he could in the queue. The kitchen orderlies hadn't started serving yet and the queue was building up.

Indeed, this was about to become the flashpoint. About eighty inmates were queuing up in the canteen for their lunchtime meals as usual. There were not many tables and chairs in that area because it was very rarely actually used for dining. The five officers near the serving area stood around chatting, expecting this day to be like any other, only it wasn't.

The three inmates on kitchen duty suddenly and unexpectedly exited the kitchen, armed with wet tea towels. The kitchen OSG Joe Gunner followed them to the doorway, calling for them to come back. He was ignored. There were four CCTV cameras in the canteen, one in each corner. They threw the wet towels up over the cameras. It took a few efforts, but it got done in seconds.

"Hey, what do you think you're doing?" shouted one of the officers, as he moved briskly towards one of the kitchen aids, instinctively drawing his baton. The realisation that something was going seriously wrong dawned immediately on the other officers too. They also drew their batons but this only served to ignite the situation.

All of a sudden there was a roar as inmates began picking up chairs and throwing them at the officers. Tables were overturned. Plates and mugs were added to the ammunition and the officers were herded towards the door. The officers had gas canisters and batons but each of them was in no doubt that they and their equipment were no match for eighty angry, erupting inmates.

They were genuinely frightened for their own safety. They weren't expected to be heroes in situations like this, but to act with discretion and minimise the risk of harm. Their interpretation of that meant heading for the door as quickly as possible. They instinctively moved as one unit, without turning their backs on the venting mob.

OSG Gunner quickly took stock and retreated back into the kitchen, securing the door first and then the serving hatch. He was demonstrating great presence of mind and bravery. He could have made a dash for the main door himself like the officers were, but he chose to remain in the kitchen and to secure it in order to prevent the rioting inmates access to a range of significant makeshift and actual weapons. He was being a true hero, acting in a selfless way which would greatly minimise the amount of injuries that might be inflicted during an insurrection, whilst leaving himself isolated and in potential danger.

The officers had already raised the alarm and were frantically radioing for reinforcements. They did, however, manage to all exit the canteen before securing the door, effectively locking eighty irate, angry, frustrated inmates inside, unsupervised and wishing to vent their wrath in any way that seemed to fit in the circumstances. The noise level was excessive with most of the inmates shouting. They turned on each other. Fights quickly broke out. The red mist descended and fists and boots were flying. Only a few weren't overcome by the excitement and mob fury.

Denis and the other dregs retreated into the corner furthest from the door and huddled next to the wall. Kevin was on the wrong side of the throng. He cowered by the wall next to the corridor, very alone and terrified. He had never in his life witnessed such violence and was stunned by the dramatic escalation. All the other inmates congregated in the centre of the room exchanging wild flurries of kicks and punches. In the heat of the moment, it would have been hard to fathom out how they were choosing whom to fight with or against, but in fact, the action was very tribal.

Terry found himself viciously attacked near the middle of the crush. Steve, Joe, Palmer, Bennett and a few others were targeting him. He found himself under such a flurry of blows that the only sensible thing for him to do was to cower with his forearms in front of his lowered head and to move his body from side to side, unpredictably, in order to minimise the impact and accuracy of the blows and hope for an opportunity to fight back.

He was suffering such an intense and crazed attack that he couldn't possibly risk opening up to form any kind of counter-attack yet. He felt heavy kicks to his legs and realised that they were trying to get him on the ground. He resisted allowing his legs to buckle. That was painful, but to allow himself to go down would be a certain calamity for him. If he went down he would have several inmates taking it in turns to stamp on his head. Even as he was still standing, he occasionally felt a very hard blow to his head. Someone had a sock with snooker balls inside it and was using it as a cosh on him. They really were trying to get him down so they could beat him mercilessly.

Fortunately, the cosh blows were not powerful enough to knock him unconscious but they were shocking and were cutting his head. His adrenaline surged through him giving him a huge wave of strength to resist all the blows and minimise his pain.

Lenny left the frenzied mob on seeing Kevin to one side. He rushed up to him, "Where's the knife, you cunt?"

Kevin bent down and pulled up the relevant trouser leg. He got his right fist around the handle, still wrapped in the cloth and he pulled it gently out of his sock. Lenny was partly leaning over him to see where the knife was.

"Come on, fucktard. Hurry up!"

Kevin then thrust the knife upwards at great speed and with as much force as he could muster, which under the circumstances, was quite considerable, straight into the chest cavity of the hapless Lenny. He released his grip on the knife and moved slightly to one side, astonished at what he had just done. He was just as shocked as was Lenny. He stared at Lenny, mesmerised.

Lenny fell forwards, almost onto him, slowly crumpling to the floor. Kevin sunk onto his haunches right alongside him. Lenny looked intensely into Kevin's face who, stunned, met his gaze. Lenny was trying to speak, but no words were coming out. He tried to reach out with one arm, but his coordination had gone and his arm just flapped like river weed caught in a current. His legs were moving ever so slowly as if he was trying to get up, but again, the coordination was rapidly going and the movements got slower and slower.

Kevin watched as a dark wet pool of blood started to soak Lenny's T-shirt, with drops rapidly oozing onto the floor. Simultaneously he saw the colour drain from Lenny's face. It went pale, then quickly into a grey-white pallor. Lenny's eyes were initially enquiring but soon looked full of fear and alarm. Fear's eyes are very large and intense. Kevin looked silently into them for the few seconds it took for Lenny's head to sink to the floor, with his mouth sagging open and his eyes still wide open, but now suddenly lifeless.

Kevin just wanted to get away. He was horrified. In a fraction of a second all his hatred and resentment from the endless daily humiliations and the penetrating frustration of all the losses that constantly tormented his mind, had channelled their immense bottled up energy into one momentary, unplanned, immense reaction. He stood up and scurried quickly around the edge of the room to join Denis and the dregs in the far corner cowering for safety. They had been successful in staying separate from the massive melee. There were three bodies on the floor in the middle of the fracas and they were being kicked mercilessly.

Terry was still on his feet, but luckily for him, the tide had turned. Mace and his black team had steamed into the frenzy and had targeted Lenny's henchmen, who were for the main part, the ones giving Terry a good beating. The blacks were excellent fighters, seemingly all with considerable boxing skills. Mace had taught them well. Their targets soon fell away and like a giant bear emerging from a stupor, Terry started lashing out too. He was so angry and fierce; no one in his path was shown any leniency.

Soon there were quite a few more unconscious bodies on the ground. The opposition was rapidly destroyed and Terry stood still, taking stock. Arms and legs were flailing all around him.

"Stop!" he shouted as loudly as he could. There was a noticeable lull in the blows nearby him but it wasn't enough.

"Stop!" he shouted again. "We're not hurting them. We're only hurting ourselves."

As he shouted he started pushing the nearby inmates who were kicking unconscious bodies on the floor. He pushed them hard, shouting constantly. Mace joined in, pushing and shouting, his buddies right behind him. Not many of the lads who got pushed stayed on their feet. One idiot lashed out at Terry and was viciously knocked out for his insolence and stupidity. The mood in the room changed, dramatically. The more Terry and Mace shouted, the quieter the other inmates got. They began to withdraw from the melee and group quietly in front of the far wall.

"That's enough!" Terry informed them all.

The fighting stopped almost as quickly as it had started. Sweaty, dishevelled and bloody inmates started to take stock too. They went quiet. They looked drained and tired. Fighting takes a great deal of energy but now the energy was spent. The excitement was gone and most of them looked rather sadly at the seven or eight unconscious prisoners lying awkwardly on the floor. Terry was quite a sight; his sweaty, bloodied T-shirt clung to his muscular chest, revealing his hugeness. His long curly ginger hair was wet and dripping with blood.

"You dozy twats. Look what you've done!"

He didn't know much about first aid, but as a sign of his humanity, he turned to the unconscious casualties and those who were not already on their fronts, he turned them roughly onto their fronts. He at least knew that unconscious people could easily choke if left on their backs. Nobody seemed to be paying any attention to Lenny at the side. He was already laying on his front and it was not obvious that he had a dirty great big knife stuck in his chest and was laying in a pool of blood. His henchmen were either unconscious or hiding at the back of the motley group, nursing their own injuries and trying to keep a low profile now, for fear of further retribution. They had after all been the ones guilty of starting this insurrection.

Terry walked over to the locked door and stood in front of it looking through the Perspex window. There was a sea of uniforms on the other side with Mr Bramley to the fore, megaphone at his side.

"It's over now," he claimed. "I and Mace put a stop to it."

Mr Bramley couldn't see the whole of the room through the small window, but he could see most of it and clearly, the fighting had stopped. The inmates seemed to be forming an orderly bedraggled mass at the far end of the room.

"Ok, well, that's good," he replied confidently, very relieved.

"We'll be coming in shortly with the NTRG. Please try to ensure that there is no further violence."

He didn't want to let on that the National Tactical Response Group hadn't arrived yet. It would take some time to get forty or so specially trained officers together, even for an emergency. The other wings had been locked down to enable quite a number of their officers to be released to B-wing as backup for the NTRG when it arrived. Off-duty officers had also been called in for backup.

"There are men in here who need medical attention."

Terry indicated the bodies lying listlessly on the floor, not realising that he himself, with a large amount of blood dripping down his face also looked like he needed medical treatment too.

"Yes I can see that, Terry."

Mr Bramley remembered Terry well from their interview. He was surprised that Terry had played a part in quelling the disturbance. He continued.

"We have medics at the ready but we can't risk them going in until the prisoners have been secured. The sooner the NTRG gets here and the more you all cooperate, the sooner we can help the casualties."

Terry appreciated that Mr Bramley had a bit of a dilemma on his hands. The inmates could easily kick off again, especially if not enough force was available to secure their compliance. The casualties would have to wait. Mr Bramley himself was more concerned about rescuing the OSG isolated in the kitchen.

Some of the inmates had retrieved the chairs which had been flung around earlier and were sitting down examining their bruises and cuts. Others were sitting on the floor. The rest just leaned against the walls. There was definitely a subdued air in the room now. They knew that their fun was well and truly over. Now they would have to pay.

Fifteen minutes later, the NTRG arrived. They entered the room in formation, with small shields on one arm and a baton in the other. They were bedecked with protective clothing from head to toe, with helmets and visors. They looked extremely menacing and competent. The regular officers entered the room behind them, also brandishing their batons. The inmates would be utterly foolish to take this lot on and they knew it. The officer in charge of the unit had a megaphone and he barked out his orders.

"Everyone stand over at the far wall facing it!"

The inmates casually obeyed.

"Put your hands behind your heads and interlock your fingers."

They slowly complied.

"Now, kneel down and face the floor."

This they did too. A few of them with damage to a leg only knelt on one knee, but most knelt on two and the tactical officers walked slowly and carefully forwards, picking their way over or around the unconscious casualties. They stopped about six feet away from the first of the inmates.

"You will be removed one by one. If any of you make a sudden move or resist, you will receive baton blows and will be disabled. Is that clear?"

There were muffled mumblings, with a few loud 'Cunts!', 'Bastards!' from some of the inmates, but none of them were putting up any resistance.

Two particularly large powerfully-built NTRG moved in front of the line of their colleagues and grabbed the first inmate like he was a rag doll. They withdrew back through their ranks and handed him over to regular officers behind them, who marched him off to his cell. This process continued very efficiently, one by one, as the unit commander maintained control throughout the process, with regular instructions to the remaining inmates to stay quiet, keep calm, maintain their kneeling position and only face the floor. There were no further incidents. Fifteen minutes later every single inmate was secured back in his cell and the NTRG job was well done. They stood down.

Prior to incarceration, each inmate was searched for weapons and inspected for injuries. All of the walking wounded were locked up. They would be examined and treated soon by prison doctors and nurses. The priority now was for the ambulance crews to attend to the unconscious first and they weren't allowed into the canteen until the very last prisoner had been removed, for their own safety.

Then the four crews rushed in. Further crews had been summoned but were still to arrive. Between them, the present paramedics examined all the unconscious casualties as comprehensively as they could, before selecting which four should be removed first. Those were then placed carefully on trolleys and moved to the hospital, each escorted by a prison officer.

As the paramedics attended the injured, Mr Bramley himself approached the kitchen door and informed the OSG Gunner inside that it was now safe to come out. The officer came out, looking very relieved that the ordeal was over. Mr Bramley applauded his quick thinking and bravery copiously. He was very proud of him.

Before leaving with the fourth casualty on a trolley, one of the paramedics took Mr Bramley aside.

"Mister, that one over there by the wall, he's a goner."

"What?" Mr Bramley replied, rather shocked. He had presumed they were all unconscious.

"You mean dead?"

"Fraid so, boss. I've checked all his vital signs. None! And he's got a dirty great big knife stuck deep inside his chest and he's lying in a pool of blood. I didn't move him at all."

He then got back to his trolley and left. Prison officers who were competent in first aid sat or kneeled next to remaining unconscious casualties, ensuring that they were breathing ok and to stem any bleeding, as they awaited further ambulance crews. Fortunately, they arrived within minutes of the others leaving and it wasn't long before the remaining four were gone too.

All officers, bar two, were removed from the canteen. They were assigned the job of guarding the crime scene and were instructed to not go near the body, which had already been identified as that of one Lenny Marshall, known colloquially as OG.

Mr Bramley got out his mobile phone and sadly dialled nine nine nine.

Chapter 14

Detective Chief Superintendent Gary Bertrand was a fastidious man. You could tell that just from the way he dressed. He was never seen without his signature three-piece suit. His collar and tie were always immaculately arranged and properly buttoned up, of course. His hair changed little because he had it cut fortnightly. Needless to say, his shoes were always spotlessly clean no matter what the weather. His approach to his work was also meticulous which helped to make him the superb detective that he was. He had a somewhat gaunt look about him as if he worried too much. He was well respected, having successfully prosecuted many complex cases during his thirty-year career as a detective.

It was 3 p.m. and he was holding a conference in the CID major incident room at area police headquarters. It was a large, light, sterile, uncluttered room, not being owned and personalised by any particular group. It was reserved only for major incidents including some murders, and was well equipped with computers, big modern office desks and massive whiteboards. He had already selected the team that he wanted to work with him and they had all been summoned post-haste.

Now they were all sitting in front of him, mostly rather excited at the prospect of playing a part in a major investigation. They had drawn office chairs away from the computer screens to make a group directly in front of him. They already knew that he brooked no eating or drinking during meetings of any kind. He regarded that kind of behaviour as uncouth and sloppy, an unfortunate result of people watching too many American police dramas where in his opinion, the officers were barely any better than the criminals. Standards had to be maintained. He stood as he addressed them. He was always supremely polite.

"Ladies and gentlemen, by now you will all know that there was a murder at Wingnut prison this afternoon."

He spoke with measured solemnity.

"I will be the senior investigating officer and detective Chief Inspector Josephine Colchester will be my deputy."

He indicated her briefly, sitting at his side.

"You are all hand-picked to be part of my team. The fact that this crime happened inside a prison provides us with unique and difficult challenges, some of which I will remind you of shortly. Which of you have investigated a crime inside a prison before?"

A few hands went up.

"Can you identify yourselves please and briefly state your experience for the benefit of the team."

DI Brand started. "DI Gareth Brand. I've been involved in two cases. One was male rape, the other GBH with intent."

He then went quiet and the next colleague spoke up.

"DI Carol Rutherford. I've had two cases as well. One was for the attempted murder of a prison officer, the other was extortion."

"DC Freddy Lane. One case of manslaughter by arson and another of GBH with intent."

DC Lane was the old sweat on the team. He had actually reached retirement age but preferred to carry on working, even though he was effectively only working for a third of his pay.

Mr Bertrand continued.

"For the rest of you, please note these faces. If you have any questions about the peculiarities of conducting an investigation inside a prison, please speak with them, or me, of course. Can I please remind you all that we are a team. There will be nobody making a name for themselves here. Our sole collective objective is to crack the case together as a team. No stars. No competing. No scoring points. Is that perfectly clear?"

"Yes, sir." in unison.

He didn't mention his own relevant experience. He presumed that most of them would know his excellent track record by now.

"I know that these days a lot of officers try to use everything to make themselves look good. For them, everything has to be a rung on their career ladder. If I get the impression that anyone tries to use this investigation for that purpose, they will be off it before you can say 'Lenny Marshall'. Have I made myself perfectly clear?"

"Yes, sir," again, in unison.

"We must all help each other. The key to an investigation like this is coordination and cooperation. Obviously, we will be using the HOLMES computer system for the investigation which I know you are all familiar with. I just want to emphasise that everything must go on there and I mean everything. Hints, suspicions, rumours, gut-feelings, reservations, as well as all cold hard facts. Please don't think that a tiny observation or whatever might be too trivial for inclusion. I can assure you that it won't be. A jigsaw picture is made up of lots and lots of little bits and we're going to need every little piece. Ok, everyone?"

"Yes, sir,"

"Please make sure you are familiar with some of the upgrades on the system. There are the usual links, but for this case, there will also be a link to 'Prison Cloud-Wingnut' which is their own Intel database. Obviously, that should be very helpful to us. Please don't overlook it.

As we speak, the forensic team is at the scene gleaning their evidence. None of you will get to see the body in situ. You will have to rely on the photographs. They will also be shown to a forensic psychologist to see if they can come up with any of their magic predictions."

The team tittered.

"How many of you think that the murder might have been committed by a prison officer?"

No hands went up.

He looked around the room, noting no hands and repeated the question, emphasising the 'might' and simply waited. One by one, slowly, the hands went up. He had made his point but he went on to press his point home.

"I want no bias. I want no preconceived ideas. They only ever serve to hamstring an investigation. At some point, there were prison officers in the same room where the victim was killed, as well as eighty inmates. That means that until eliminated, they too are suspects. No Bias. No preconceived notions. Is that clear?"

"Yes, sir."

He reminded them of the famous flaws of a notorious case.

"I appreciate that some of you may not even have been born at the time of the Yorkshire Ripper but I want to remind you of a very important lesson learned there. Peter Sutcliffe, who was eventually convicted of thirteen murders and seven attempted murders, had been arrested several times during the course of the investigation. There was clear evidence to link him to the murders and some investigating officers were convinced that he was their man, yet he was arrested and released several times to kill again and again. Why?"

Most of them knew the answer, but it was DS Rebecca Swayne who responded.

"Because the senior investigating officer had made his mind up that the tapes they were being sent by a nutter who claimed to be the ripper, were genuine and as a result, he dismissed any suspects that were put before him if they didn't have the same distinct accent as the man on the tapes."

"Precisely, Rebecca. Thank you. And what is the point?"

She continued. "The SIO had allowed himself to have a fixed preconceived idea that blinded him to other possibilities."

"Exactly. Thank you. Please, all of you, remember that case. I don't want you being blinded to any possibilities. You are the eyes and ears and nose of this animal that is going to track down our killer. Holmes is the brain. They got wrong-footed by a nutter and inside our prison, sifting through the lies and deceptions is going to be hard work. Which inmates are telling the truth? Which are just trying to wrong-foot us? Which are truly hiding something? It's going to be complicated. This won't be a walk in the park.

There are no passing members of the public who might be able to provide credible witness testimony. I understand that the CCTV cameras were disabled, but obviously, we will trawl through the footage to see for ourselves. Incidentally, it was because of the huge errors made during the Sutcliffe case that the home office devised the Home Office Large Major Enquiry System for processing all the information in future cases and we're still benefiting from it today.

Another important point for you all to be aware of. There's a particular issue with evidence-integrity inside a prison because of the nature of the inmates for obvious reasons. Any testimony we do get can be easily discredited in court because of our witness's antecedents. They are all proven criminals and liars, so we have to go that bit further to prove the reliability of evidence. Each interview must be totally above board. Solicitors present if requested. Rights delivered without fail.

Once we get a lead we will need to work hard on supporting it with lots of reliable corroboration. We can't afford to put a single foot wrong and there are at least eighty-five people to be interviewed. I want high standards to persist through every single one. Is that perfectly clear?"

Again, another, 'yes, sir,' in unison.

"On the plus side, putting prison officers and any other suspects to one side for the moment, we already have our eighty suspects all locked up, just waiting for us to interview them, which is handy, to say the least. The correctional officer in charge of B-wing is Mr William Bramley. I have spoken to him on the phone and asked that all the suspects are kept locked up until after we have interviewed them. I've told him that I don't want them getting together to make up stories or to intimidate potential witnesses. He has agreed to this but with one rider. He doesn't think he can limit their movements for too long. Maximum of five days probably.

All the inmates are entitled to some exercise each day and I have asked him to supervise that in such a way so that they still don't get the opportunity to talk to each other. That is very demanding in terms of his staffing. Any such restrictions beyond five days are likely to bring an avalanche of solicitors, civil liberties campaigners and all the do-gooders screaming the place down on his head.

So, I have paired you up in five teams of two. You should be able to carry out four or five interviews per day. I don't want you overdoing it. You still need to be getting your downtime to stay fresh and healthy. I don't want any of you getting tired and missing clues. At four to five interviews per day each, we should be done in four days. That gives us one whole spare day in case we need to do some catch-up. Beyond that, we can still keep particular individuals in isolation for longer provided that we can justify it."

He then read out the names of the pairs. They all nodded.

"Ok. Clear so far?"

"Yes, sir."

"The office manager here will be DS Gregory Spires."

He indicated him to the others.

"He will be here in the office as long as any of you are out there doing your stuff. I don't mind him getting tired out."

There were chuckles.

"The regular police prison liaison officer is PC David Burt. He will be entirely at our disposal throughout the investigation. All these details are already on Holmes. Any questions so far?"

"Yes, sir. Has a weapon been recovered?"

"Yes. It was left in situ in the victim's chest cavity."

"Sir, how are we going to divvy up the interviews?"

"That is a very good question, Harry. I don't want it to be random. I want it to be as focussed as possible as follows. There are lots of little gangs inside. I want the same team interviewing all the members of each gang. If any associations or connections become apparent either during the interview or from research, again, I want the same interview team dealing with the connected. That way we will be better able to spot any discrepancies or any joint purposes. As you all well know, discrepancies are our signpost towards something worth digging into. What we do know already is that the disturbance which occurred today was orchestrated. It wasn't spontaneous.

There were three inmates working in the kitchen, preparing dinner for the other one hundred or so inmates on the wing and whilst the majority of the other inmates were in the canteen allegedly waiting for their food, these three exited the kitchen with wet tea towels which they threw up over the CCTV cameras, in a very pre-planned, coordinated fashion. Then the fracas kicked off. I want Gareth and Peter to deal with them and the OSG who was in the kitchen supervising them at the time. Any connections they give us will be interviewed by Gareth and Peter too. That makes sense?"

"Yes, sir."

"Any other questions?"

"Yes, sir, are we looking for other offences?"

"Good question, Tony. Not particularly. We have our work cut out with the murder itself, but of course, other offences may well be disclosed. If they are not particularly serious, please pass them onto the prison authorities via our liaison officer David Burt. If they seem quite serious, record them as a crime as you would normally do and they will be passed on through the system to be investigated through the normal channels, but not us. I don't want anything distracting our investigation. Just make sure that everything goes onto Holmes though for reference."

"Yes, sir."

"I want this investigation to remain fluid. I'll leave you to choose who you want to interview first, based on what you glean from the Intel. You will be able to see who has collared which inmate on the system. Remember, I want to see a connection between the subjects you are interviewing. If there's a clash of interests as it were, I hope you can work it out between yourselves. If not, bring it to me. I'm always happy to play Solomon."

"Yes, sir."

"Any more questions?"

"Sir, will we be interviewing the prison officers too?"

"Good question, Sophie. No, you won't, but I will be, with DCI Colchester. I like to get my hands dirty too, you know. Well, not too dirty."

The mood lightened.

"Remember, this might have been a random killing. There was something of a mini-riot after all and there was a lot of violence. Eight inmates have been hospitalised. Or it might have been premeditated. If it was, there may have been several inmates involved in a conspiracy to murder. I know I don't need to teach you to suck eggs but I want to find out what grievances there were between various inmates, especially any involving the deceased and any of his associates. If it wasn't a random killing, we will need to work out the motivation. And we need to know where that weapon came from. That will help us a lot. Are there any more questions?"

"Yes, sir. I take it we will be interviewing at the prison itself. What are the facilities like there for that purpose?"

"Good question, Robert. They lack the kind of recording equipment we need to use for evidential purposes, so our technical support department is organising the equipping of six offices inside the prison so that they are fit for interviewing. They should be all ready by the end of today. This room will be the major incident room, so when you're not interviewing, I expect to see you here. I want you all to spend the rest of today researching all the inmates you are likely to be interviewing tomorrow. Don't stay too late. I want you fresh tomorrow. I suggest an 8 a.m. start at the prison itself. At the end of the day, I want you all back here by 5 p.m. for a team debrief and a bit of good old-fashioned brainstorming. Any more questions?"

DS Michael Pendleton had one.

"Sir, will the casualties be interviewed at the hospital?"

"Good question, Michael. Given what has happened to them, they might well be our most willing witnesses. I'll know more about their condition tomorrow. I'm hoping that they will be returned to the prison hospital wing before the end of the week. I think it's sensible to leave them until later on when hopefully they'll be back inside."

"Any more questions?"

The floor was silent for a few moments and then DS Tony Bigley suddenly spoke up and the rest of the room groaned, comically.

"What? I just thought of something."

They quietened down and he asked his question.

"Sir, you mentioned the knife. Do we know much yet about any other weapons that were used in the fracas?"

"Good question, Tony. As far as I am aware at this time, the only other weapons recovered at the scene were a wooden cosh made from an old chair leg and a contrived cosh using a sock with two billiard balls inside it. All the inmates were searched on return to their cells and I am led to believe that no further weapons were recovered during those searches. Any more questions?"

Finally, there was silence. Mr Bertrand had one for them.

"How many of you care about the fact that 'Lenny Marshall' was killed?"

There was a bit of mumbling as people thought out loud. Hands went up, slowly at first, but before too long, all bar one. Mr Bertrand looked at DC Stevens and said.

"DC Stevens, your hand didn't go up. Why not?"

"To be honest, sir, I'm not that bothered that a man like him got killed, I mean, we all know what he was like, but I do want to see that the investigation is successful and that the killer is found if that makes sense."

Mr Bertrand looked thoughtful. "I see," he said quietly, gently rubbing his chin.

"Ok, everyone. It's time to get to work."

He peeled away and took DS Tokenforth to one side.

"Harry, I think I made a mistake choosing DC Stevens. I want you to return him to his previous post and select another partner for yourself. One who's suitably qualified, of course and that you work well with."

"Yes, sir. No problem. I'll make a call shortly."

All members of the team found a computer screen and made it their own for now. This office would be their new home for the foreseeable future. They started mining data on their potential subjects, eagerly awaiting the next day when they could start the challenge for real.

Chapter 15

'B' wing had just become very strange. It was Saturday morning, but after breakfast, no inmates were going off to the gym, or the library, or the association room and not even the exercise yard. Kevin didn't miss being out in the communal areas cleaning. No one was going to be out there walking around spilling their food, or visiting the communal toilets and spaying the remnants of yesterday's curry all around the pan sides. But what he was looking forward to was a visit from Susie.

Inmates were discovering that they would only be allowed out of their cells for a little exercise, a daily shower and to be interviewed by the police. All meals would be brought to them in their cells. Kevin reminded a passing officer that he was expecting a matrimonial visit that afternoon.

"Not anymore, pal. All visits have been cancelled. Didn't you know there is a murder to be investigated? You murdering bastards are all grounded for at least five days."

Kevin sank back into his cell. He had actually been looking forward to seeing Susie this time. It might have been the last time he saw her. He was gutted. Prison officers were not happy either. They had to do more menial tasks like serving the food and escorting inmates to and from exercise and showers. A few extra OSGs were brought in to cover any essential work that had previously been done by inmates such as cooking and essential cleaning.

As a result, inmates were becoming a lot more fractious with their cellmates, as well as with officers. It wasn't normal for them to be cramped up so closely with their cellys for twenty-three hours a day. That was likely to cause tension and disputes and the last thing the prison needed right now was more violence. Mr Bramley asked Mr Bertrand if the prisoners could go back to some normality after they had been interviewed but Mr Bertrand was opposed to the idea on the grounds that they would be in a better position to try to influence other prisoners yet to be interviewed.

A lockdown might sound easy for the officers, but in fact, it was harder because apart from having more menial tasks to perform, they had to be more attentive than normal, checking cells regularly for signs of violence or self-harm and responding to more minor scuffles. The tension affected both the inmates and the officers. Relations were strained. The situation had retrograded into a 'them and us' scenario, which is what officers usually worked very hard to dispel. Rehabilitation and mutual cooperation had gone out of the window.

Mr Bertrand was right about the frequency of interviews. Each team managed four or five interviews on day one and the whole team was back in the MIR before 5 p.m. Some had started updating Holmes; others were just doing more research before Mr Bertrand called them into a group discussion. He sat rather excitedly amongst them.

"Progress report, please. Mr Brand, you first, please."

Gareth Brand was a detective inspector with over twenty years of experience. Before joining the police service, he had been a tree surgeon, but he was no longer agile and fit. Far from it. His partner was detective sergeant Peter Starchley who was relatively young, being late twenties. He was more typical of the modern breed of officer, having joined straight from university with a degree in political history.

Gareth couldn't imagine for a moment why anyone would want to study anything to do with politics. Such a dull topic in his book. However, he was pleased that he had been allocated the kitchen staff because he felt that he had been given some of the best meat to chew on.

"Well, the three kitchen aids on the day were Callum Medley, Jason Parsley and Thomas Bennett. Prison Intel clearly shows them all associated with the deceased, Lenny. At various times, they would all associate with him, whether it be in the exercise yard or the association room of an evening watching football. Intel also indicates that Lenny was the top dog and the others were more like his lackeys. They have all been convicted of supplying class A drugs in the past. Two are currently serving sentences in relation to supply, but Bennett is currently in for GBH. They are all believed to be using inside, probably synthetic cannabis, maybe more.

I'll start with Bennett because he's the only one of the three who is an associate of Lenny on the outside and there's plenty of police Intel linking the two for quite a number of years. He was happy to be interviewed without a solicitor. He maintained that he had no idea that a disturbance had been planned or that any violence was intended against anyone.

In relation to the question about his involvement in disabling the CCTV cameras, he didn't deny that it was premeditated but stated that he had no idea why he had been made to do it. He maintained that he had been threatened with violence if he didn't do what he did, but he refused to give any further details of what or by whom. Looking at his Intel, it seems most unlikely that anyone would succeed in threatening him into doing anything against his wishes. He went 'no comment' on any questions requiring details or further clarity. He claimed total ignorance about the knife.

When we asked him about Lenny, he admitted that he knew Lenny on the outside, as a drug user, but denied ever working with him in the supply chain and obviously, in here they are good mates. When we asked him if he had any idea as to why Lenny would have been assaulted like this, I have to say, that he looked genuinely surprised and confused about it. Verbally, he just said no and tried to keep his cool but I'm pretty sure it hadn't been an outcome he had expected. That's just my take on his body language. Other than that, he gave nothing away."

Mr Bertrand asked a question.

"Thank you, Gareth. Peter, what was your take on the interview and please feel free to disagree with Mr Brand if you felt differently."

There was a little laughter as Mr Brand feigned alarm.

"No, I agree with Mr Brand entirely."

Mr Brand mockingly mopped his brow.

"I would reiterate the bit about Lenny. When asked about who might want to hurt him, I agree that he looked genuinely confused and, I thought, actually sad."

"Ok. Very good. Gareth, did Bennett get involved in the violence?"

"Yes, he made no bones about it. He denied targeting anyone in particular, he was just defending himself. He stated that everyone was just hitting everyone. They were all letting off steam because they'd been denied their association time all week. He was nursing a beautiful shiner and his face, in general, looked quite bruised."

"Ok. What about the other two?"

"We spoke to Medley next. He did want a solicitor, but the interview went very similarly to Bennett's. He accepted that he had played a small part in the event, again, under threat. No details about from whom or with what. Again he denied any knowledge of what was going to happen or that violence was going to occur.

Similarly, he admitted getting involved in the fracas. He said that everyone got involved but was unspecific about who he was hitting, or who was hitting him. He also looked pretty roughed up but made no official complaints about anything or anyone. He also claimed to have no idea about anyone wanting to injure Lenny. When I asked him if he was surprised that Lenny had been stabbed, he stated that he really was. It was the only thing he said throughout the whole interview that had any conviction to it."

"Peter?"

"Yes, sir. I got the impression that he was lying all along, until he answered the question about Lenny's death and then we saw some sincerity."

"That's very interesting. Thank you. Anything from Parsley?"

Mr Brand picked up the thread again.

"Nothing else to add really. Just like the other two. He fully accepted doing his bit to disable the cameras but claiming to know nothing about what was intended. He got stuck into the melee as soon as it started to 'protect his mates' and again, genuine surprise about Lenny."

"Great, that's very interesting. Anything else to report?"

"We did interview Bennett's cellmate, a chap called Christmas would you believe, but he was evasive and gave us nothing. I got the impression that he is very scared of Bennett, so it was more or less all 'no comment'."

"Understandable. Who do you plan to see tomorrow?"

"There are four other inmates who also work in the kitchens on various days and because of the kitchen link, we're going to interview them, if no one else gets their hooks into them first. Then, if we have enough time, we'll begin interviewing the relevant cellmates."

"Excellent. That sounds good."

The rest of the debrief went in a similar fashion, each team summing up their interviews to give the rest of the Taskforce a feel for what their subjects had been like under caution. Twenty-two interviews were completed on day one. The general picture established by the end of this debrief was that the word had circulated on Monday morning that there was going to be a 'demonstration', a venting of their tensions, in the canteen at lunchtime but nobody was specifically named in regard to who was stirring the mood.

There was a reference to long-standing tension between various clans. The blacks were no fans of Lenny and his gang and the feeling was mutual. Effectively, this was simply because they were business rivals and vied for custom inside. The Asians loathed the right-wingers who were rabid racists. The racists hated everybody who wasn't on their team.

Then there were various scores to be settled between inmates who had fallen out over anything from being 'dissed' to being the subject of a theft, or a failed deal. Even grudges about who got what privileges, classes, or work were a big deal and could be avenged. The inmates spoke about these things freely. They were a normal part of daily life but they were cautious not to point the finger at anyone directly. Nobody wanted to be labelled a 'snitch'.

Mr Bertrand rounded off the debrief with an update from himself.

"Just to let you know how my day's been. Chief inspector Colchester and I interviewed the OSG Joe Gunner. He was the one in the kitchen just before all this kicked off. It seems that he got on well with all the inmates seconded to kitchen duty. He's actually a very switched-on cookie. He's very cautious about equipment and obsessively checks off everything at the end of each session to make sure nothing goes missing and if he's unsure of anyone, he prevents them from working in the kitchen.

He'd had Medley, Parsley and Bennett working alongside him for some months and he was quite trusting of them. He'd never had any trouble with them before and he had no idea that anything was wrong until they walked out. He hadn't noticed any of them putting tea towels in the sink. The first he knew about anything out of the ordinary was when they were picking them up as they walked out. He was very credible and we had no reason to doubt his word. Mr Bramley seems to think the world of him.

You'll like this. I asked Gunner what criteria he used to determine whether or not inmates might be suitable for kitchen duty and he said, 'The number one criteria is that they are not intent on putting their bogies, nail cuttings and semen in the food.'"

Mr Bertrand chuckled. The team mostly groaned.

"He said this with a completely straight face. He was being deadly serious. How the other half live, eh?"

He then got serious again and continued.

"We interviewed two of the five officers who had been supervising the canteen yesterday. Langridge and Jenkins. They both gave us similar accounts.

160

As far as they were concerned, they were all caught by surprise. Things turned ugly very quickly. They all drew their batons in self-defence and retreated altogether as quickly and safely as they could to the door. They decided almost immediately that the situation was unsalvageable and their objective was simply to escape in one piece. They had a few things thrown at them, but neither of them was injured and they secured the door on exiting, calling in reinforcements immediately.

In fact, you can see exactly what was happening immediately prior to this. There is a link on Holmes to the CCTV recording up until when the tea towels were thrown over the cameras. Unfortunately, none of the footage was any good after that. If it was any good, it would already be case closed."

At the end of day one, nothing has been revealed about potential suspects for the assault on Lenny, nor the source of the knife.

At about the same time as the police were having their debrief, the B-wing inmates were finishing their tea and were settling down to a lonely evening in their cell with just their one cellmate. They would most likely be about to while away the evening hours watching their small TVs, just as they had been doing all day long already.

Mr Bramley was very nervous about the impact of the lockdown on the emotional and mental welfare of his charges. He was doing his utmost to keep them occupied, given his limited options. He had his officers distribute all the board games that were in stock in the association room to the cells. He even bought in especially, fifty new packs of cards so that each cell at least had a pack of cards to play with. He also organised a daily book run from the library so that inmates were offered a new book or two daily.

Liam and his cellmate Colin had just finished watching a fascinating documentary in the Blue Planet series. Of course, their tiny TV barely did it any justice but it was a lot better than nothing. Colin was very bright. He was about five years older than Liam and like him, he was a heroin addict and also like him, he was on a script of methadone whilst inside which kept him fairly mellow. He was not a typical addict. He had benefited from a blessed upbringing in a loving family. He had thrived as a child and as a young adult and had gone on to a good university, obtaining a first-class degree in computer sciences. He had secured a very promising career in the tech industry. Next, he fell madly in love with a gorgeous woman and got engaged to be married.

Nothing in the garden could be rosier. Then tragedy struck. His fiancé was raped and strangled one fateful night, whilst walking home after a late night out with the girls. Colin never forgave himself for not being there for her, even though he was not supposed to be chaperoning her that evening. He was consumed with guilt and despair and started drinking excessively to literally drown his sorrows and his life started to slowly fall apart. Before too long, he lost his job and he spiralled into debt. His family kept bailing him out for a long time but eventually he turned to heroin to kill his emotions and that worked brilliantly and then things went into free fall.

Nobody could trust him anymore and 'tough love' kicked in. He was on his own. He started dealing just to feed his own habit but with his organisational abilities, he soon started dealing as a middle man in much larger quantities, but what he wasn't, was streetwise. It wasn't long before he was caught in possession of a large quantity of a class-A drug and even though it was just his first conviction, he was sentenced to two years in prison because of the large quantities involved. Thankfully, he got on well with Liam, but in prison society, with his privileged background, he was one of the dregs.

"God, that was amazing. Evolution is such an amazing thing."

"Yeah, Colin. That was amazing. I'll give you that but I'm not sure if evolution has anything to do with it."

Colin was sitting on the lower bunk, Liam on the top one. Colin's face contorted somewhat.

"What do you mean?"

"I know I am a bit slow, Colin and I didn't get that good an education and all that, but I just don't understand evolution."

"What is there not to understand? It's a very simple theory."

"Everyone says that, but to me, it's illogical."

"What? Why?"

Colin sounded quite horrified.

"Well, if evolution was true, shouldn't we be surrounded by billions and trillions of blobs of matter that are still in the process of developing into something? Everything I see in the outside world is perfect, well, apart from some of the people I know, of course. I'm thinking all the animals, the birds, the insects, the fish, the plants, etcetera. They all breathe, eat, move, see, hear, smell, reproduce, sleep and heal. They all have instincts that programme them for their particular life. They're all perfect."

"Nothing is perfect Liam. Nothing achieves perfection because it is always evolving into something better."

"But surely not everything can have achieved almost perfection at exactly the same time and all the prototypes disappeared?

"That's because everything has an adaption gene, Liam. That apple tree in the courtyard, it's still evolving. In a thousand years' time, its apples will taste different."

"Yeah, but what about all the in-between things? That apple tree might still be evolving, but it is also perfect right now. It feeds, breathes, produces fruit and offspring, etcetera. What I want to know is, where are the blobs of matter changing into something over the next million years which haven't got very far along the evolutionary journey yet. Where are they?"

"Liam, in the Galapagos islands, there is a lizard which has adapted to living in saltwater. It's the only type of lizard in the whole world that can live in saltwater. Go back thousands of years and it was a lizard on dry land, but for some reason, it ended up on an island in the sea and had to adapt. That's evolution."

"But Colin, it is and was a lizard. That still doesn't explain where all the blobs are."

"That's simply because we're at a stage in evolution where everything appears to be perfect for what it needs to be right now, but it is still all evolving, I can assure you."

Liam still didn't understand. He was rather disappointed. He knew Colin was a very clever person and he had hoped that he would help him understand.

"Ok. Another question."

"Go on. I've got the time," he said with a smile on his face.

"Ok. So, if we go back just a little way down the evolutionary past before we were what we are now, but close. Where we were still evolving, the last few bits of us. How did we survive without all the bits we now rely on to keep us alive? Like our digestive system, our muscles, immune system, breathing, blood circulation, brain, nervous system, all of our organs and senses, such as hearing, seeing, feeling, tasting."

"Yeah, ok, Liam. I get your point. Listen; let me tell you about an 'early earth' experiment some scientists carried out. They isolated a few gases and some water in a sterile glass globe and introduced electricity. The gases and water represented what might have existed after the big bang and the electricity might have come from lightning and guess what some building blocks of amino acids were formed. In time these would have mutated and stuck together to form bigger and bigger organisms and over billions of years, that's how all our bits and pieces were formed. We don't know what caused the big bang but we do know that it kicked off evolution."

"Yeah, but, Colin, I don't want to go back to the big bang. I get that. I want to go back to not long ago when we were nearly what we are now, but some things were still not quite right, say our digestive system, or our immune system. How did we survive without food or without diseases killing us?"

"We would have survived on a cellular basis, Liam. Each cell would have got nutrients from its surroundings from the atmosphere and sunlight. A bit like photosynthesis in plants. As for the disease bit, that's the beauty of evolution, it explains the survival of the fittest. Diseases would have killed off all the weak vulnerable ones, leaving only the strongest versions of us to survive."

"So if we're the strong ones who survived diseases for the past few hundred million years, why do we have a very complex immune system now? Why does every single creature have one? I've heard that sharks are immune to everything!"

"Nature is very clever, Liam. It has made us evolve immune systems so that we can survive newly evolved diseases."

"So it can see into the future?"

"Yes, Liam. That's how evolution works. It seems to know what we will need in the future. That's why we will never stop evolving."

Liam was still disappointed and confused. Why did everybody else get it, but not him?

"Colin, I still can't bet my head around it. Let me ask you another question."

"Go on, mate."

"Ok, so we managed to evolve and survive for millions of years without vital organs and immunity, etcetera, but again, if we go back just a little way, when we were recognisable as humanoids but our sexual organs hadn't evolved yet, how did we breed?"

Colin was quiet and thoughtful. He was thinking up an answer. Liam continued.

"How did every single species evolve to have perfectly matching male and female reproductive organs and how did we breed before they were perfected as male and female?"

"Liam, it's all to do with the X and Y chromosomes in our DNA. Way back, there was just one permutation, either it was XX or XY. Either way, the other combination evolved as well and that led to the difference between the two sexes.

"Yeah, but what I'm asking, Colin, is how did we breed whilst our organs were evolving over millions of years and how at the end of all that time did the male and female match perfectly in every single species of living thing."

"Some worms breed asexually."

"That's a perfectly evolved red herring, Colin. It doesn't answer the question."

"Well, because the XX and XY all started in the same creature, as they evolved, they carried information about the other gender and were thus able to evolve to match them perfectly."

"Like the XX in one creature knew about the XY in another creature and somehow they evolved in a compatible way? Like they knew how the other one was evolving at the same time over millions of years?"

"Yes, exactly. Maybe there was some kind of telepathic information exchange. Maybe millions, no, billions of species disappeared because they didn't get the reproductive thing right. Survival of the fittest, again."

"And how did we breed during that period?"

"I don't know the details, Liam. It must have been a much simpler process before we evolved to be so complex."

Liam was none the wiser. He was feeling quite stupid and confused.

"Ok. I think I get it but I've got another question."

"Fire away, mate." Colin was pleased to be so helpful.

"When Darwin came up with his theory, he believed that the single-cell was a very simple basic thing that by bumping into other simple cells and merging with them, eventually, grew to make more and more complex organisms, right?"

"Yep."

"Well, nowadays, we know that a single cell is not simple or empty like Darwin thought. Science has discovered that every single cell, which itself is microscopic, contains DNA which is billions of bits of complex proteins that somehow carry the code to create life. Every single minute cell contains an incredible blueprint for the creation of every other cell and organ in our entire body. This blueprint, which is in every single animal, plant, insect, etcetera, is more complex than any computer program we have ever created. Surely that doesn't fit with the theory of evolution? Where did all that magic DNA come from?"

"Liam, you have to go back to the beginning again. Each of those original cells that were created in the big bang had a tiny fragment of what would eventually make a part of the DNA. As the cells evolved into more complex organisms, the DNA evolved too."

"That's it?"

"No doubt about it. Surely you've heard David Attenborough explain these things on the telly. He's one of the cleverest men ever to have existed. He understands what was going on the earth six billion years ago. That's pretty damn clever don't you think?'

"Yeah, I suppose so. I just wish he was able to explain things more simply for people like me."

"I think he tries his best, Liam. He's been making programmes about the earth and evolution all his life."

"He's a scientist, right?"

"Yes, one of the best."

"Well, these days as I understand it, scientists, who obviously don't believe in a God or a creator, because they're scientists, have started accepting the concept of 'intelligent design'. I think they've been blown away by the complexity of DNA and the genome, which of course, Darwin knew nothing about. How does that fit in with evolution?"

"Mate, nature is amazingly intelligent. Look at the symmetry of the petals in a rose flower. It's stunning and nature designed that. That's intelligent design. Don't forget that evolution keeps on making things better and better over millions and millions of years."

For Liam, a lot of things simply didn't add up and Colin really wasn't helping, much as he was trying.

"Ok, Colin, I've got one last question which confuses me. You ready?"

'Go on, mate."

"Ok. So, we've been discussing the matter. Physical things, like our bodies, our cells, which we can examine under a microscope. What about our personalities, our emotions, our consciousness if you like. Where does all that come from? 'cos if you dissect a human body, you won't find any of that stuff physically, so they couldn't have evolved like all our cells did. Basically, where did our spirituality come from?"

166

"Of course they did, Liam. They evolved out of our need to survive. We needed to be able to think and communicate for the survival of the fittest to have happened. Necessity is what makes evolution work."

"But what did it evolve out of? It's not cellular. I'm talking about our creativity, our love of music, our humanity, our humour, our ability to love and hate. You can't isolate it or examine any of that under a microscope."

"Exactly, Liam. You can't, but you know it's there. You can't see it or touch it or pass it on to someone else, but you know it's there, so it must have evolved in a similar way, a way you can't actually identify, but you know it happened, just like you know it's there now. Gorillas show love to their young ones, but they don't write orchestral symphonies, simply because they are behind us on the evolutionary tree. One day they will be making fantastic music and using complex language and be painting incredible art and devising sophisticated machines just like we do."

"Really?"

Colin was getting quite excited now and he progressed way beyond Liam's questions.

"In thousands of years' time we will have evolved into spacemen. We will leave this earth with its limitations. We're already starting to go down the road of trans-humanism."

"Colin, I don't want to be a tranny."

Colin ignored him and carried on pontificating.

"Some people already have mechanical hearts and in the future, we will incorporate more and more tech into ourselves, so that we will be part human, part computer. Then we will be looking at immortality because we will be able to constantly renew our parts with better parts. It's already happening, mate, with nanotechnology.

Our universe is thirteen and a half billion years old. We've already had two previous suns which burned out. The current sun has only got one billion years left. That is why we will evolve into hi-tech trans-human spacemen. We will have to if we want to survive as a species because this planet won't survive but evolution will make sure that we do.

Our greatest thinkers and visionaries are already making it happen. Elon Musk is devising computer chips to be inserted into our brains to link us to our devices via Bluetooth. And he's making rockets to take us deep into space to colonise other planets. Bill Gates is developing technology for implanting RFID chips inside us so we can gain entry into places and pay for things without stopping to show anything. He's also devising vaccines that will alter our DNA to improve it.

The military is working on nanotechnology which will course around our veins, monitoring all kinds of stuff and communicating with computers on the outside. It will also be capable of delivering mood-changing hormones and stuff like that. Nanotech will be the cure for depression and any other mental illnesses. What's all that, if it's not evolution?"

Liam was quite nonplussed. Personally, he liked to keep his electronic devices outside of his body and wasn't too keen on the idea of this type of evolution, which was quite ironic really, because he was more than happy to insert alien chemicals into his bloodstream which only had any effect by playing with the chemicals already inside his brain's neurons just to get a temporary fix and that was a lot less noble than saving the human race.

Chapter 16

"Liam, do you know anything about Lenny Marshal's death?"

It was Sunday, late morning and DI Brand and DS Starchley had already interviewed Jamal Hotspur and Labron Wilkinson, two of the other kitchen aids who weren't working on the fateful day. Now it was Liam's turn. He was not concerned. He had done nothing wrong. He could answer their questions without fear.

"I know when and where it happened, but so do you."

"Ok. Please, tell us what happened in the canteen on Friday lunchtime."

"We were just queuing for dinner when the lads helping in the kitchen came out and threw tea towels over the cameras. The officers went for them and the rest of the lads kicked off."

DI Brand waited to see if Liam was going to add anything. He didn't.

"What do you mean by 'kicked off'?"

"They started throwing stuff at the officers. Probably because the officers had their batons out."

"Did you throw stuff?"

"Nah, I'm not that excitable."

"What happened next?"

"The officers scarpered out the door altogether. Then some of the inmates started fighting with each other."

"Do you know what they were fighting about?"

"Nah. It could have been anything. I think they were all just wound up and letting off steam."

"Wound up by what or who?"

"The screws took away our association time last week and everybody was pissed."

"I see. What's so good about association time?"

"For an hour and a half, we get to be human beings again."

"I'm not sure what you mean, Liam. Can you explain?"

"It's obvious innit? We spend all day either locked up, or working, or doing classes. The evening association time is the only time we're allowed to mix and do stuff, normal stuff, with a bit of freedom."

"I see and why did that make the inmates so angry?"

"It's obvious innit? We were being punished for something we hadn't done?"

"So taking your association time away was a punishment?"

"Course. In here, you have to earn privileges but they get withdrawn if you do something wrong."

"So, who was being punished?"

"We all were, but for no reason. We were told that it was because the new boss wanted more time for the screws to do training. That wasn't fair."

"I see. When you do have association time Liam, what do you like to do?"

"Depends. Just sit around watching football with the boys. Play snooker or table tennis. Some of the guys love table football but I'm no good at that. Sometimes we play cards or board games."

"I see. Do you know Lenny Marshal?"

"We called him OG. Yeah, I knew him. You get to know most people inside if you're here long enough."

"And how long have you been here, Liam?"

"Eight months and counting."

"I believe you're due for parole soon."

This brought a big smile to Liam's face. "Yep!"

"So you wouldn't want to mess up at this late stage would you?"

"Nope."

"What was your relationship with Lenny like?"

"I didn't have a relationship with him. That sounds so gay. I just knew him. Basically, I kept out of his way."

"Why?"

"He's one of the big fish in here. He's got a lot of mates and he's a nasty fucker."

"In what way, Liam."

"Come on, mister. You must know what it's like inside. People get threatened and hurt all the time. That's prison life."

"What's that got to do with Lenny?"

"He's one of the top dogs, so you just don't want to get on the wrong side of him. You know all this already. Why are you asking me?"

"Did you get on the wrong side of him, Liam?"

"No. Why would I?"

"I don't know, Liam. All I know is that last Friday lunchtime he got stabbed to death and it is my job to find out how that happened."

DI Brand sat back looking intensely at Liam and DS Starchley took over.

"Hi, Liam. Just to remind you, I'm DS Starchley and I'm assisting with this investigation. Liam, we've been having a look through the prison records and we see that about two weeks ago you were involved in an incident in the showers one evening. What happened?"

"I don't think I can remember."

"It was about 7:15 p.m. on Monday, the ninth of October."

"Sorry, mate. I don't recall anything. Most of the time I don't even know what day of the week it is, let alone the date. I go to the showers most evenings."

"The following morning you were interviewed by Mr Bramley."

"Oh, that. I couldn't help him. Apparently, that evening a couple of the guys got hurt in there, so he told me, but I didn't know anything about it."

"Two or three?"

"He only mentioned two. I only know what he told me."

"Were they associates of Lenny Marshal?"

"I wouldn't know."

"A second potential witness was seen by Mr Bramley, Terry Mako. Do you know him?"

"Only from playing scrabble."

"You play scrabble?"

'Yeah, most evenings. We started about three weeks ago. It was Mr Blanchflower's idea."

"And Mr Blanchflower is?"

"He's our English tutor. He wanted to organise some scrabble because it would be good for my reading and writing, which is not very good."

"Ok, so, how did Terry Mako get involved?"

"Mr Blanchflower put a notice up asking for participants. There was enough interest to fix up two games."

"That was a good response. Who are the other players in your game?"

"An old fellah called Denis and a wuss called Kevin. He's actually quite old as well."

"And did you know any of these players before you all met to play scrabble?"

"No. I might have seen them around but I'd never spoken to any of them except Kevin, of course. I know him from the English class."

"Is his English poor too?"

Liam laughed. "No mate. He helps me. He's well educated and professional, like you two."

"So he does the English class to help people?"

"Yeah. All the pricks in here help the less able in classes if they want to. It gets them out of their cells, dunnit?"

DS Starchley went quiet and Mr Brand took over again.

"Liam, during the fighting that was going on, did you get involved?"

Liam laughed. "Of course. We all did, but I wasn't stupid enough to get in the thick of it. I just stood at the back and did a bit of pushing and shoving and a little slapping."

"Did you see where Lenny was?"

"Honestly, I didn't. It was just a mass of bodies."

"Did you know any of the casualties who ended up unconscious on the floor?"

"At the time, I had no idea who was down. It was only when we all stood back that I could see who some of them were."

"Did you recognise any of them?"

Liam decided that he had helped enough. He did notice who they all were. They included Steve, Jo and Palmer, but he felt that it was wise to seem ignorant.

"I wasn't really looking. I didn't notice."

"Liam. What brought this mini-riot to an end?"

"To be honest, it was Terry and Mace. They started shouting at everyone to stop and they were pushing people back until they did stop. Nobody was going to argue with them two."

"Why not?"

"Have you seen them? They're both fucking huge!"

"I see, so why do you think they tried to stop the fighting?"

"I've got no idea, boss. You'll have to ask them."

"You said Terry and Mace. Are they mates?"

"Not as far as I know. I've never seen them together before."

Mr Brand thought for a few moments, consulting his notes.

"Liam, you've been working regularly in the kitchen for quite some time, yes?

"Yeah."

"Tuesday, Wednesdays, Thursdays and one day at the weekend. Is that correct?"

"Yeah."

"Has anyone ever approached you to ask for a favour?"

"I get asked for sexual favours occasionally, but I'm not a wolf or a Junebug."

He was giving an honest straight answer and was very straight-faced.

"No, Liam, I meant in relation to the kitchen, like getting a knife, or tea towels, or anything."

"Nah."

"Are you sure? You answered very quickly."

"That's because it ain't happened."

"Do you know if it's happened to anyone else in there?"

"Nah."

Brand and Starchley looked at each other with knowing looks. They had no more questions.

"Ok, Liam. I don't think we've got any more questions for you. Thank you for your help. Just one last thing. If you could help us with finding the killer, would you?"

Liam thought carefully about this. It felt like a trick question and he considered his options. If he said no, they'd think he was hiding something and if he said yes, that would make him sound like a snitch and if they thought he was a snitch, they might try to use him. He was taking so long to think about his answer Mr Brand prompted him.

"Hello? Calling planet, Liam!"

Liam looked up. He wasn't sure.

"I don't know. All I can say is that I actually don't know anything."

Denis was getting very bored of being locked up twenty-four seven and it was only the second day of it. He was frustrated. At his age, he was afraid that not keeping fit was particularly detrimental. He had missed his gym session.

Thankfully, he enjoyed reading, but all day long? That was too much and the kind of fayre on daytime TV was mostly crap in his opinion.

His cellmate was a Russian in his early forties called Dimitriy, although, because they were friends, Denis was allowed to call him Dimi. In Russia, only friends are allowed to use your abbreviated name. Dimitriy spoke with a strong Russian accent, although his English was pretty good. He was rather serious, with a dry sense of humour. Denis, by contrast, was often bubbly and conversational and in his boredom, he was resorting to engaging Dimitriy in conversation. As they both lay on their bunks, Denis spoke through the mattress above him.

"Dimitriy, can I ask you a personal question?"

"Yes, of course, you can, my friend."

"Do you ever feel guilty about what you do?"

"What you mean? Fart in bed?"

Denis gave a little laugh. "You know what I mean."

"No. I am innocent."

"Come on, you twat. Be honest for once."

"You mean what you call trafficking girls?"

"Yes."

"Why? You think that sounds bad?"

"To be perfectly honest, Yes. Of course."

"Why you think that bad?"

"What do you mean 'why do I think that's bad. It's fairly feckin' horrible, isn't it?"

"Why?"

"Hey, I thought I was supposed to be the one asking the questions!"

"Tell me why, or I'll come down there and cut your throat."

He could be very menacing, but obviously, he was joking, wasn't he?

"Well, presumably, you take girls away from their home and sell them into sexual exploitation."

"My friend, you presume a lot."

"Well, isn't that true?"

"The girls come from very bad places. They want to get away."

"You arrange their travel, right?"

"Yes and sale."

"Don't you think that sounds horrible? Selling people?"

"Not if they want to be sold."

"I can't believe they want to be sold."

"You are ignorant my friend. I am not trying to be rude but you live in rich country where even poor people have big TV screens and plenty of food and beer. You don't understand life in Russia."

"Ok. So are you saying that these girls are not victims? They're willing participants?"

"A lot of these girls are used for sex at home. Here they do the same thing but have better life. I improve their life."

"Ok. So how do they live here?"

"They live in nice house with other girls. They have lot of friends. They have good food from Lidl. Men like you visit them and fuck them for good money. That is all."

"If you're doing such a kind job, then why are you banged up in here?"

"Because British ignorant. Stupid. In Russia, we have saying 'if you live with wolves, howl like a wolf'. That is what I do. What about you? You thief? In Russia, we kill the thief."

"My case is very complicated, Dimi. I don't think you'd understand it."

"You just fob me off because you are worse than me, yes?"

Denis was starting to feel uncomfortable and went quiet.

DI Carol Rutherford and DS Michael Pendleton had elected to interview the black coteries, of which there were two. A gang of five of African origins and a gang of four from Jamaica. Intel indicated that they kept themselves separate from each other, although there was nothing to indicate that there was animosity between them. In fact, the Jamaicans hadn't made it into the canteen before the trouble kicked off, so it had quickly become apparent that they wouldn't need to be interviewed after all. Rutherford and Pendleton had interviewed four of the African group the previous day and nothing of relevant interest had been revealed. Today, they started off with the last one, Marquis Lebois, known colloquially as Mace.

Mace was a striking example of a man, despite now being early forties. Well over six feet tall, muscular in a body-building way of exaggerated curves and swellings, with massive strength, he was a menacing presence. His professional boxing days were over but he made a good living from debt collecting and dishing out punishments for unsavoury associates.

Because of the environment he worked in and the nature of his clients and targets, very little of his handiwork ever got officially reported to the police, although they had sufficient Intel on him to be well aware of his activities. The fact that he had been convicted of a crime and ended up inside was a stroke of bad luck for him and a stroke of good luck for a lot of other people.

One of his victims proved to have a very weak chin. He was knocked out and fell awkwardly on concrete, suffering an unintended fractured skull. He was hospitalised but suffered a fatal aneurysm a few days later. The evidence against Mace was overwhelming despite little witness testimony and his denials. He was sentenced to ten years for manslaughter just two years earlier.

He declined a solicitor and sat passively opposite the two officers. DI Rutherford was relatively young. She was ambitious, intelligent, officious and capable. DS Pendleton was quite a bit older than her and more experienced, but not career-savvy like she was. Rutherford started the interview off.

"Mr Lebois, is it ok if I call you Marquis?"

"What do I call you?"

"You can call me Carol if you want or detective inspector Rutherford if you prefer."

Mace then fixed his gaze on DS Pendleton. He didn't need to say anything.

"I'm detective sergeant Pendleton but you can call me Michael if you want."

Mace gave them a little smile.

"You might as well call me Mace. Everyone else does."

DI Rutherford spoke first.

"That's an interesting nickname. How did you get it?"

Mace smiled more fully, "You don't want to know."

He had great teeth. Bright white, in such contrast to his very dark skin.

"Ok," she replied slowly. "So let's get straight to business then, Mace. I'm sure you're aware that we are investigating the murder of one Lenny Marshal last Friday. It happened in the canteen at lunchtime. You were one of the people in the canteen at the time. Can you tell me anything about how that happened?"

"Are you interviewing everyone who was there?"

"Yes, of course."

"Not just the boogies or guys with form?"

"Boogies?"

"Blacks."

"Of course not. Everyone. We're looking for witnesses but until we discover the truth, we are treating everyone as a potential suspect as well."

Mace sat quietly, mulling the situation over.

"So, Can you tell me anything about how that happened?"

"Nope."

"Nothing at all?"

"Nope."

"Is that because you don't want to?"

"Nope."

"Why then?"

"Because I ain't seen nothin'."

"Do you know anything about why he might have been assaulted?"

"Nope."

"Did you know Lenny?"

"Nope."

"Surely, you must have had some dealings with him. You've both been living in this wing for over a year."

"Depends on what you call living."

"Call it what you want, Mace. You've been occupying the same spaces for over a year. What interactions have you had with him?"

"Just seen him around, is all."

"Have you ever spoken to him?"

"Nope. Had no reason."

"Do you know anything about him?"

"Not much. He always has dogs with him."

"Dogs?"

"Homies. Crew."

"Do you know anyone who might have a grievance with him?"

"Nope."

"Do you mix much?"

"Nope."

"Tell me about the disturbance on Friday."

"It kicked off after the screws walked out. They were so chicken."

"Do you think they should have stayed?"

"Of course."

"Why?"

"To stop someone getting killed."

"Did you know someone was going to be killed?"

"Nope."

DI Rutherford didn't want to make any judgements on the prison officers or to get drawn into a moral discussion about their actions, or lack of them. She moved on.

"Were you with anyone at the time?"

"My homies."

"Who were?"

"Jamal. Niles. Rashad. Dremonte. You can tell who they are by the colour of their skin."

He smiled again. His teeth really flashed.

"You all stuck together?"

"Of course. We're homies."

"Did you get involved in the violence?"

"Not to start with. We stood to one side at first."

"Then what happened?"

"The big ginger was getting hammered. I like him, so I waded in to help him."

"Are you referring to Terry Mako?"

"I don't know his surname. Terry. The big ginger guy."

"Why do you like him?"

"Dunno. It's just a gut feeling."

"Do you have any connection with him?"

"No. He's often down the gym when we're there. Is all."

"Did you owe him any favours?"

"Fuck off."

"Why did you help him?"

"Because I could."

"You said he was getting hammered. By who?"

"Don't know exactly but I could tell he was being targeted. That ain't fair."

"And you could tell that even though there were over seventy inmates throwing punches at the same time?"

"Yep."

She looked at him rather incredulously.

"What happened next?"

"I waded in and knocked a few honkies off him."

"How?"

"You don't need to know any more than that."

"What about your crew?"

"Dunno. They were behind me."

"Then what happened?"

"There was a bit more Molly-whopping, then Ginger started yelling at people to stop."

"Molly-whopping?"

"Fighting."

"And did they stop?"

"Slowly at first. We had to knock a few more first. Then they stopped."

He smiled mischievously.

"We did you lot a big favour."

"How?"

"We stopped the fighting. We probably saved lives."

DI Rutherford went quiet for a moment, looking at her notes. Her companion spoke, identifying himself again.

"DS Pendleton. Mace, do you know anything about the weapon that was used?"

"Nope."

"Apparently, it was quite a sizeable knife. How could that have been hidden inside a prison."

He smiled knowingly. "No idea."

"Eight men ended up in hospital. Do you know anything about how any of them got injured?"

"Nope."

"But you said that you got involved in the fighting. Who did you hit?"

"I don't know. It was just a mass of bodies. You don't remember a lot of detail when a riot is going on around you."

"I'm sure, yet you seemed to notice what was happening to Mako."

"He's a big guy like me. He stands out."

The officers seemed to have run out of questions. Mace asked them one.

"Will there be one fives?"

Michael answered. "What are they?"

"Prison charges for the infraction."

179

"I can't speak on behalf of the prison service, Mace. I don't know. We are only looking into the murder."

They politely thanked Mace for his cooperation and brought the interview to a close.

Chapter 17

Sunday, early evening, the officers all sat in an informal circle at the MIR. They were engaging in badinage and hastily finishing off their coffees before Mr Bertrand called them to order. As usual, he sat amongst them with DCI Colchester sitting next to him. He crossed his legs and tried to look relaxed.

"Ok. Who's going to start us off? Has anyone cracked the case yet?"

Some rather nervous laughter rippled through the room. Most of the officers had been engaged on major enquiries previously and they felt that this one was being unusually fruitless so far and nobody spoke up. Often, they would soon find potential suspects and the challenge of the case was to find the evidence to identify the real one and provide the proof needed for a court case.

"Ok, so has anyone found any good leads yet?"

Mr Bertrand was being too optimistic and the room remained silent.

"Oh dear," he quietly exclaimed. "Day two and no leads yet. Well, what have we got?"

The silence was awkward and a young DC Sophie Wellsome broke it, trying to be positive.

"Well, sir, DS Bigley and I have conducted nine interviews so far and each subject has provided a very similar account about the riot, which, bearing in mind that they're not mixing, means that there appears to be a lot of consistency. We certainly don't seem to have been offered a load of red herrings and swerve balls."

"Thank you, Sophie. You are counting our blessings. Does anyone have anything positive? Rumours? leads off-record?"

There was another uncomfortable silence until DC Robert Goodfellow spoke up.

"Sir, I honestly think that our best witnesses are going to be the lads who suffered the most. The ones in the hospital. There must be a reason they were targeted and maybe that will link to the attack on Marshall."

"Yes, thank you Robert. You might be right or they might just be the ones with weak chins."

He asked for a tot up of interviews. There had been twenty-four that day.

"Ok, so that makes forty-six interviews in total. That's more than half of our suspects and we still have nothing?"

He was being very challenging. He wanted to keep them on their toes throughout the investigation, not that he thought that they were slacking, but it was his job to keep the pressure on. At the end of the day, it was his investigation and he'd never yet failed to prosecute a murder investigation.

"What about the knife?"

More silence. DC Freddy Lane broke it this time.

"Sir, it seems quite clear that major players get underlings to hide things for them so that they themselves can't be caught red-handed if there's a successful search."

"What kind of things, Freddy?"

"Any contraband really. Particularly, mobile phones, but also weapons and drugs. My point is that this practice is possibly the weak link. One of these stashers might crack and admit to hiding the knife for someone because they themselves don't want to be implicated in a murder."

"Indeed, Freddy, I do hope so. I presume you're all covering this aspect during your interviews?"

Lots of positive mutterings. DS Tokenforth returned to the subject of the seriously injured.

"Sir, what news on the hospital cases?"

"I'm pleased to say that four of them will be released to the care of the prison hospital wing tomorrow morning which means that we should be able to interview them tomorrow afternoon. They'll probably have to be informal interviews. I don't think we can justify removing them from their hospital beds. As for the others, they want to keep them in for one more day's observation, in case of any brain injury."

DS Rebecca Swayne spoke up.

"Sir, Freddy and I have already interviewed four other Indians, so we'd like to take the three injured Indians when they come out if that's ok?"

"Does anyone have any objection to that?"

Nobody spoke up.

"Looks like you can, Rebecca. Bearing in mind that three of the eight knocked unconscious were Indian, I think we need to keep our minds open about the racist element. That might well work in our favour. They might be willing to give something away in retribution. I want to know if it seems that some Indians were targeted and some weren't and if that proves to be the case, I want to know why, ok?"

"Of course, sir."

"Anything else?"

DI Brand spoke up. "Sir, I spoke about the kitchen aids in yesterday's briefing and today, we interviewed the other four aids who weren't working on the day in question. Nothing of interest came up, to be honest. However, we did ask one of them, Liam Ferguson, about an incident that occurred in the showers two weeks ago. CCTV shows that he went in there at about 7:15 p.m. and three of Marshall's closest allies were already in there. The footage from the corridor shows who went in and out and when, but nothing of what happened on the inside. The three inside were Steven Devenish, Jo Ashley and Palmer Trinkett."

Mr Bertrand interrupted him. "The same three that are in the hospital."

"Yes, sir."

"A short while later, Terry Mako entered and then about a minute later, Liam walked out on his own. Five minutes later, Mako exited, again, alone. A few minutes after that, the first three exited. You can see on the CCTV that Ashley and Trinkett were clearly in pain or injured. They weren't walking properly and Devenish was helping Trinkett along. They reported their injuries to an officer. It turns out that Ashley had suffered broken ribs and Trinkett had had his arm dislocated. I wonder if that incident could be relevant in any way."

"Thank you for that, Gareth. That may well be relevant. I have, in fact, spoken to Mr Bramley about all incidents over the past few months. There is a list on Holmes under the prison Intel link. Most of them seem rather trivial, but please do all have a look at them. We can't afford to miss any clues."

Mr Brand asked a question.

"Sir, what did Mr Bramley say about that incident with Ferguson, etcetera?"

"He was under no illusion that Mako had caused the injuries. He's got lots of form for serious violence but the injured parties maintained that they had slipped on the wet floor, so nothing could be done about it. Mako himself denied any knowledge of any incident, maintaining that he simply went to the toilet, but you're quite right, some scores were undoubtedly being settled. We need to bear this incident and any other like it very much in mind."

"Did Mr Bramley indicate what might have been at the bottom of this incident, sir?"

"He was quite sure that it was to do with drug distribution. Ferguson is known to be a runner and a stasher. Bit like what Freddy said earlier about the little fish doing the dirty work for the big fish but he was clueless about Mako's part in it all."

"Surely that's a link to Marshall?"

"Possibly, Gareth, except that there are other big fish in here."

"But Devenish, Ashley and Trinket are Marshall's boys."

"Exclusively?"

"According to Intel."

"Maybe our Intel is incomplete. Let's not jump to any conclusions yet. If we do, we might miss something else."

Mr Bertrand paused to make sure everyone was paying attention.

"Anything else?"

DI Carol Rutherford spoke up. "Interesting that this Terry Mako character has been mentioned because he came up in our interview today."

"Go on."

Mr Bertrand leaned forwards, hungry for some useful information.

"Well, Michael and I interviewed the black contingent yesterday, apart from the big man, Marquis Lebois, whom we interviewed today. Everyone calls him Mace by the way. Well, he indicated that he and his homies were going to stand aside from the violence when it erupted, but he got involved when he saw that Mako, who he calls the big ginger, was getting set upon, 'hammered' in his words, by four or five others and he waded in to help him."

"Why?" Mr Bertrand asked curiously."

"He just said because he liked him. He denied any actual friendship or other connection with him, other than they both use the gym sometimes at the same time. That was it."

"Curious. It's hard to accept that he was acting out of the goodness of his heart or maybe he was. Or maybe he just needed a little excuse to wade in like all the others."

Mr Bertrand thought out aloud.

"Yet it was Mako and Mace who apparently called a halt to the violence. Why would they do that? Where was Marshall at this point? We need to know much more about what was going on with Marshall. Have any of the inmates put him anywhere or with anyone during any of this?"

A sea of blank faces stared back at him. He looked disappointed.

"Ok, so who's down to interview this Mako guy?"

Nobody responded. Mr Bertrand continued.

"In that case, Carol, as there seems to be a potential link between Mako and the Marquis, I suggest that you and Michael do him, ok?"

"Of course, sir."

"I also want to know the link between him and Ferguson. I want to know why he was being targeted during the riot and I want to know why Marquis came to his aid."

"Noted."

"Gareth, as you've done Marshall's associates so far, I want you to carry on with the others, Devenish, Ashley and Trinkett when they come back and you Rebecca will have the injured Indians.

Right, the autopsy report is in. Marshall died from a single knife wound to the heart. The blow would have been more or less instantly fatal so it's likely that he was struck more or less where he was found dead. The forensic team found no evidence of his body having been moved or dragged.

The pathologist suggested that whoever dealt the blow knew what they were doing for several reasons. One, the blow was struck with the blade horizontal, so that it would have met the least possible resistance from the ribs. This is particularly relevant because it was quite a wide blade and could have jammed between ribs if it wasn't presented at the correct angle. Two, the entry wound was actually just below the rib cage, which indicates again that the killer was experienced as he struck a blow that minimised obstruction by ribs. Three, the blow was angled perfectly upwards so that it fully penetrated the victim's heart.

He said that it was clearly intended to be a fatal blow. It was also delivered with a great deal of power to penetrate the cavity so absolutely. The blade went into the body right up to the cross guard of the handle. He also surmised that the perpetrator must have been right-handed from the angle of the entry."

He looked at his team with a slight look of awe. This killer was good.

"The only other thing is that Marshall had cocaine in his bloodstream, but in all honesty, I can't see that being relevant to the killing. I have also heard from the forensic psychologist. She has examined all the information available, especially the photographs and she says that because of the circumstances in which the crime occurred, she can't really surmise anything. She's got nothing to go on in terms of possible motivation, or whether it was premeditated, or the choice of the crime scene, etcetera. So, we have what we have. The rest of you continue through the list as you see best. Let's hope that we turn something up tomorrow."

DS Pendleton surmised something.

"Sir, is it beginning to look like the riot was inspired just to provide cover and opportunity for Marshal to be executed?"

"It looks that way, Michael, given what we know so far, in which case a lot of those scrotes in there know stuff we need to know. The challenge is getting someone to actually speak to us. Any potential witnesses need to be assured that they will be protected. They're probably all shitting themselves at the moment. Offer them the world and its oyster for good witness testimony. And, go over all your subject's Intel again from the knife point of view. I want to know about anyone who's used a knife before, even if it was only to self-harm, or because they had a Saturday job in a butcher's shop or anything!"

It seemed that the briefing was over, but DS Pendleton piped up with one last question.

"Sir, are we hoping for anything positive from forensics on the knife?"

Mr Bertrand answered dispassionately.

"I'm afraid not, Michael. I'm sure there would be lots of DNA on the rag in particular, but there was a riot going on right next to it. Saliva, blood, hair and teeth were flying all over the place. Besides that, the rag could have been stolen from any of the other inmates given the enclosed environment and then there's the laundry arrangements, whereby all their laundry gets bunched together. Therefore, we couldn't possibly establish any integrity regarding any DNA evidence found on the rag or knife and if we had the audacity to try to use it in court, any defence attorney worth his salt would undermine its integrity in seconds and make us look like we're clutching at straws and we don't want that. For us, it would be no more than a red herring. So, no. No DNA from the knife. Anything else?"

The room was silent. It was time to go home.

Monday morning found Terry pacing around his cell very frustrated. Normally, he would be in the gym by now.

"Fuck all this waiting, mate. It's doing my head in."

Grigore chastened him as he lay on his bunk watching Sesame Street on their little TV.

"What you say here? You do the crime. You do the time."

Terry was in no mood to be philosophical

"Grigore, you Romanian tit, whatever we've done, it's not right that we all get banged up just because that OG animal overstepped the mark with someone."

"My friend, this will pass. Remember, adversity is a good teacher"

"I'm not in the mood for any of your Romanian folklore, Grigore. I need to be busy or I'm going to go fucking mad."

Grigore felt sorry for him. Some people were much better at dealing with confinement and restrictions than others.

"You have too much mustard, my friend."

"What does that mean?"

"In my country, we say a man has too much mustard if he gets angry. Hothead."

"That may well be true but I can't change the way I am, can I? You're not helping."

Grigore was one of the many eastern Europeans who entered the UK after their country entered the EEC and after 'new labour' encouraged them to come to England in the late noughties for a better life and their vote. However, for him, the streets were not paved with gold and he soon fell in with a Romanian pick-pocketing team. They were good, too good, and in time a police team was set up purely to target them. The team didn't jump on individual pickpockets. They bided their time, building up the evidence of organised crime and conspiracy to defraud and only when they had enough evidence to press serious charges, did they strike. Grigore was one of the unfortunate members of the Romanians who took a lot of the rap and he was sentenced to twelve months inside.

Terry was no fan of thieves, but in prison, the most important thing is to survive and petty grudges only served to make life harder in the long run, so he was amiable towards Grigore. He himself wasn't perfect and they were in the same boat, just for different reasons.

An officer unlocked the cell door.

"Mr Mako, they want you for interview."

"Hallelujah! Any opportunity to get out of this fucking cage for a while."

The officer led him along the corridor towards the B-wing barrier which he slowly unlocked. From there he led him down the corridor to the makeshift interview rooms. Terry briefly noticed as he passed that some of the rooms were already in use. The officer stopped at a room whose door was still open. Two police officers were sitting with their backs to him, but on his arrival they stood to greet him. The prison officer remained in the doorway.

Terry was surprised that one of the officers was a woman. It didn't seem right, a woman investigating a murder. He observed that she was about his age and was quite attractive. The male detective was quite a lot older.

"Terry Mako?" she enquired formally.

"Yes," he replied. "Why, did you think that they might get the wrong person?"

He smiled confidently.

"Of course not. I'm sure they are very efficient, but we have to check."

She indicated for him to sit down in front of them. After he had done so, she released the escort and the door was closed, but not locked.

"I'm detective inspector Carol Rutherford and this is detective sergeant Michael Pendleton. We're here to interview you about the death of Lenny Marshall last Friday, ok?"

"No problem."

She went on to explain about the recording tapes and that he could have a solicitor present if he so wished. He declined and she turned the tapes on before cautioning him and all identifying themselves again for the benefit of the tapes.

"Is it ok if I call you Terry?"

"Of course. That is my name," he answered with a little gleam in his eye.

"Terry, you've got quite a bit of form for serious violence."

"I already knew that," he answered cheekily.

"That makes you particularly interesting to us in this case."

"Oh. I thought it was because of my good looks and charm."

He smiled. He was flirting with her. She ignored his wise-cracking.

"Can you tell me why you get violent?"

"Wow, that's a big question. Am I supposed to know the answer?"

"It's your life, your behaviour. Surely you know why you do the things that you do."

He thought for a moment. "I just stand up for myself. That's all."

"Is it because of drink?"

"Are you being judgemental?"

"Not at all. I simply want to understand you and what influences you."

She looked at him dispassionately. He was an attractive man, but she desperately didn't want to give him the impression that she had noticed, yet her eyes were a little brighter than usual, her pupils bigger and her pulse quicker. She consciously avoided twirling her hair with her fingers.

"Can you be more specific?"

"Ok, so what motivated you when you threw a man out of a second-storey window?"

He chuckled at the thought.

"I'm sure that you've read my file, in which case you already know the answer to that question."

She decided to provoke him. "Jealousy?"

"Fuck off! I wasn't jealous of him. Why would I be? He was her ex! No. I threw him out of the window because I caught him raping her and I've done my time for that one."

"So, righteous anger?"

"Yeah. That. Exactly that."

"And it was ok to take the law into your own hands?"

"Yeah, justice is far, far quicker that way."

She looked at him slightly disapprovingly.

"Tell me about what you're inside for this time?"

"Why? You already know."

"Yes, but I want to hear it from you. You can help me understand you."

"Is understanding me going to help you find Lenny's killer?"

"Maybe. What have we got to lose?"

DS Pendleton was watching Terry quite intensely the whole time. He was learning his mannerisms, his facial tics, the changes of tone in his voice, the look in his eyes, what he did with his arms and hands. He had learned over many years how people give themselves away with tiny gestures when they were lying or evading something. The more DI Rutherford engaged him in conversation, the more he would understand his body language.

"I was in a pub with Val, my girlfriend, having a few beers. It was a nice pub, not the sort of place you would expect any trouble. Some bloke who'd had far too much came over to us and started pestering Val. I told him politely to fuck off."

DI Rutherford interrupted him.

"When you say you told him politely to fuck off, does that me you used different words like 'please go away' or something like that?"

Terry laughed. "No, I told him to fuck off, but I said it politely."

"I see. Then what happened?"

"He just got more lary. We were sitting down, so I got up, grabbed him by the scruff of his neck, pinned him up against a nearby wall and I told him a few home truths about his parents and then told him where to go."

"But you didn't hit him?"

"No, I didn't."

"So how did things escalate?"

"Like I said, it wasn't the sort of pub known for trouble, but there were a couple of bouncers on the door just because it was a very busy pub. I'd already had an altercation with one of them on the way in."

"Really? That was unfortunate. How did that happen?"

"He was really up himself. You know what some people get like once they get a little power. It goes to their head. He refused me entry unless I showed him my driving licence. He was just throwing his pathetic bit of weight around. Probably trying to impress Val. It didn't work. She thought he was a complete tosser.

Anyway, I argued with him that I didn't have to produce ID just to enter some fucking pub. He insisted that I did and he explained that the reason the pub is called a 'licensed premises' is because patrons have to show their driving licences on entry. He explained that like I was stupid or ignorant."

DI Rutherford gave a little laugh. That was rather funny, she admitted to herself.

"So how did this confrontation transpire?'

"Val agreed to show them her licence and they were satisfied with that."

"So, you've pinned some drunk up against a wall for being inappropriate with your girlfriend and the bouncers come up to you?"

"Exactly. The smaller obnoxious one started grabbing my arm to pull me away. I warned him not to touch me but he carried on. He seemed to have something to prove, or maybe he was deaf, but he picked on the wrong guy. I nutted the drunk, then turned on this obnoxious little fuck. I smacked him so hard, I broke his jaw in three places. He went out cold."

"At that point, did you not think it might be a good idea to leave?"

"I never run away."

She resisted rolling her eyes.

"Ok, so what happened next?"

"The other bouncer tried to get me to the floor. I wasn't going to let him damage my arm or anything else for that matter. So I laid into him too and broke both his cheekbones and his nose."

"And his arm."

"Oh yeah. That too."

She looked at him pensively. It was time to get specific about the events at Wingnut. She got him to explain what he was doing on the day in question before going to the canteen, where he was in the canteen just before the kitchen aids entered and whether he was in company with anyone. Then she asked.

"Do you know Lenny Marshal?"

"You mean, did I know him?"

"You know what I mean."

"Only to look at. I had no dealings with him if that's what you mean."

"Why didn't you have any dealings with him?"

"Because I'm not a druggie."

"I see. Did you see where he was when the trouble kicked off in the canteen?"

"Nope. He's not a very big fellow. He doesn't stand out."

"Ok. So where were you?"

"We all seemed to bunch up when the trouble started. Instinct, I suppose."

"And where were you positioned in the bunch?"

"Quite centrally, I suppose."

"Then what happened?"

"I started to get hit from all sides."

"Do you think you were targeted?"

"I have no idea."

"Terry, why would you have been targeted?"

"I have no idea."

"Surely you would be the last person anyone would just attack for the sake of it, being such a big guy and with a reputation for violence."

"You'd think."

"Haven't you wondered?"

"Strange things happen in prison."

"Who was hitting you?"

"I honestly don't know. I got my head down and my arms up to protect myself. Someone was using a cosh on me."

"How do you know that? You said you had your head down."

"I felt it on my head! It was hard and kinda painful!"

"Ok. What happened next?"

"I noticed the blows becoming less regular. That's when I noticed Mace right next to me lashing out at people who were hitting me and that's when I exploded into action."

"What does that mean?"

"I started hitting out at my attackers."

"And what happened to them?"

"They went down like deckchairs in a gale."

"Who were they?"

"I don't know."

"You don't know because you didn't recognise them or you didn't notice who they were?"

"It was so hectic. So many bodies around. So much action. I didn't notice who they were"

"I find that hard to believe, Terry."

Terry just looked at her with a wry smile and shrugged his huge shoulders.

"Then what happened?"

"I noticed several bodies on the floor. Some of them were still getting a good kicking. That made me really mad. You don't carry on kicking unconscious people. I started shouting at those fuckers to stop and carried on punching people who were still kicking."

"Were some of these bodies on the floor the ones you knocked down?"

"I really don't know. They might have got up. There were already quite a lot of bodies down. I did notice that some of them were Indian."

"Ok, Terry, so you mention seeing bodies on the floor that you didn't recognise apart from some of them being Indian. Did you notice Marshal's body on the floor?"

"Not initially. Not until everyone had moved back. Then I saw him at one side by the wall. He wasn't near us."

"Did you see anything at all happening to him?"

"Nope."

'Did you see anyone at all near him at any time?"

"Nope."

DI Rutherford went quiet for a moment, then turned to her colleague.

"Michael, do you have any questions for Terry?"

"Yes."

He paused as he looked at his notes briefly.

"Terry, would you help us nail the killer if you could."

"Probably."

"Why only probably?"

"Because it's a hypothetical question. I couldn't say for sure unless I knew who the killer was?"

"So you'd be prepared to protect a killer?"

"I'm not saying that. I just can't be certain about the answer to a hypothetical question."

DS Pendleton pondered for a moment again.

"If you knew where the knife had come from, would you tell us?"

"Same answer. It's hypothetical."

"So you'd be prepared to protect some people in here but not others?"

"I'm not saying that."

"Who would you protect, Terry?"

"I can't answer that, can I? It would seem like I'm pointing the finger at someone, wouldn't it? Honestly, guys, I don't know who knifed Lenny."

"Terry, why did Mace come to your aid?"

"I don't know. I've not even had a chance to thank him."

"So you agree that he waded in to help you?"

"It seems that way."

"And you really don't know why?"

"No. I suppose it's just one of those things you can't explain. I think I would have done the same for him. Maybe he sensed that."

"How do you know Mace?"

"Only from the gym. He and his crew are often there when I'm there too. I suppose that sort of thing must build a little camaraderie."

"During the fracas, did you get injured?"

"I had four cuts on my head and lots of big bumps. They all needed a couple of stitches in. The stitches were more painful than when I got cut in the first place."

"Adrenalin or lack of it, I suppose."

"Yeah, I suppose."

"Just one more thing, Terry, what is your connection with Liam Ferguson?"

"We play scrabble together."

"Really?" DS Pendleton couldn't suppress his surprise.

"Yes, it's something we've been doing over the past few weeks when we're allowed to."

"I see. Tell me about the incident in the shower block a few weeks ago with Liam."

"It's like I said to Mr Bramley at the time. I don't know anything about it. I only went in there for a crap. I didn't know that anyone was injured in there that evening."

DS Pendleton and DI Rutherford had run out of questions and blind perseverance.

Chapter 18

Monday afternoon found Kevin lying on his bed trying to play solitaire with a pack of cards. It wasn't easy because the cards kept slipping out of place on the sloping mattress. The whole thing sagged in the middle. He was also finding it very difficult to concentrate on anything. He was feeling terribly nervous and hadn't been sleeping well at night at all. The upside of that was that he found it easy to slumber during the day when the tiredness overtook him.

Roger lay in the bunk beneath him, twisted to one side to watch the TV standing on its little metal desk. He seemed to watch whatever came on next. Kevin found it very hard to talk to him. Roger was seriously educationally challenged but he also seemed to lack personality which might have made up for the educational deficiency to some extent. Quite simply, they had nothing in common to discuss and Kevin found himself exceptionally emotionally and socially isolated. He fretted constantly. There was a surround-sound cinema in his head, replaying the incident with Lenny on a loop. He couldn't stop it or erase it. Someone must have seen him.

He knew from the guards that the police were interviewing every single B-wing inmate in turn. He had no idea how long that would take, but what he did know was that he would be the last. Somebody would drop him in it. Why wouldn't they? Someone must have seen what he did. So the police would interview everybody else to get as much evidence and confirmation as possible before confronting him with fait-accompli. Then what would he do? He could hardly deny it and he would be charged with murder. How terrible for Susie. Married to a double killer. This was unbearable. How could he have done that to her?

He squirmed as his mind tormented him. He didn't even know why he'd done it. It was some kind of atavistic primeval response to a situation that was just too alarming for him to cope with. He tried to think of something else. Susie, the girls, work even. He had never thought that one day he would actually miss

195

photocopiers. That didn't distract him for long. He could occasionally hear inmates being taken out of their cells for interviews, then being returned about an hour later.

He tried reading, watching TV, but nothing released him from his all-consuming thoughts. He considered calling a guard and confessing but that seemed so weak. Why should he just give them his head on a plate? He had, after all, saved someone else's life that day. That knife was meant for somebody and whoever it was meant to be, was now still happily and obliviously walking around. Someone owed him a huge favour. He wondered who it might have been, but he was not privy to prison society and politics and he had absolutely no clue as to whom the intended victim might have been.

He was not a religious man, but now in these weird circumstances, he found himself wondering. Why had he been chosen to hide the knife? Why had he reacted the way he did? It was as if his body had been taken possession of for just a few seconds and as a result, the very course of history had been changed, like he was in a Ray Bradbury science-fiction film. It hadn't really been him. How could a man stab another man without conscious thought? Without intention? His mind whirled throughout the afternoon as usual and into the night when he finally fell asleep, exhausted.

Monday evening at the MIR was time for debrief number three. There was not an air of excitement and Mr Bertrand sensed it. He sat rather soberly in the circle. He looked around at his officers' faces, searching. None of them looked eager to speak. He knew the eager look when someone had something exciting to report.

"Ok," he said stoically, "Who's going to start us off?"

He tried not to sound sullen. DI Brand considered that he had conducted the most significant interviews of the day, so he decided that he should be the one to kick off.

"Sir, Peter and I interviewed the three injured associates of Marshall's this afternoon after they returned to the prison hospital. That was Steve Devenish, Joe Ashley and Palmer Trinkett. We made sure that none of them came in contact with any other inmates and that they were kept apart from each other after the interview. There was a very interesting aspect to the interviews which I will come on to shortly. They had all prepared their story in hospital, no doubt and they all wanted a solicitor present but they did answer our questions.

We didn't start off mentioning the stabbing because, unlike all the conscious casualties, they weren't aware of the outcome of the riot because they were out cold way before it ended. So we approached it from the point of view that we were investigating the riot itself. They all gave very similar accounts, all saying in essence that as soon as the prison officers vacated the canteen, the fighting kicked off amongst themselves. They stated that Terry Mako attacked them all, catching them unaware. They all alleged that it was him alone who put them all in hospital. They didn't explain why they were all mysteriously standing next to him at the time and they all denied throwing any punches themselves. None of their accounts was particularly convincing.

We both felt that they were lying but here's the good bit. When we eventually asked them in turn about what had happened to Marshall, they all appeared blank and confused. They asked something like 'what do you mean?' This surprise was genuine. When we eventually revealed that Marshall had been stabbed and killed, to a man, they all looked shocked and in disbelief. Devenish went quite white. Ashley thought we were joking and to start with, he laughed, but when he realised that we weren't joking, his mouth fell open and was lost for words and he looked stunned."

Mr Bertrand sought confirmation. "So are you saying that they clearly had no idea that Marshall had been attacked and that their surprise indicated something else?"

"Well, it's difficult to say for sure if they expected someone else to have been targeted, but that was the feeling we both got. They were definitely shocked about Marshall's death. They were looking at us as if to say 'how could that possibly have happened?'."

"Ok, thank you. That is very interesting. I take it they denied any knowledge of the knife"

"Yes, sir."

Mr, Bertrand mused out loud. "Is it possible that someone else was the intended target? That still begs the question as to how Marshall came to be the one with the knife in his chest? And who the knifeman was. He had no defensive wounds that would indicate that he knew he was under attack. There had clearly been no fight for his life. No cuts on his hands or fingers, which is most unusual in a case like this."

He was quite confused, but he didn't want his officers to perceive his confusion. He carried on.

"Carol, how did you get on with the big ginger?"

"Well, sir, we spoke to him for quite a while about previous violent incidents, just to get the measure of him and I have to say that he came across the whole time as pretty genuine. He freely answered our questions and his account of the riot and fighting tallies up perfectly with Marquis's. You could tell that he had nothing to hide. He stated that as soon as the fracas kicked off he was targeted by a large number of attackers. We have verified with medical records that he did indeed sustain several nasty cuts to his head which required stitches. We believe they were the result of the billiard ball sock-cosh."

"Do we know yet who was wielding the sock-cosh?"

"Not to my knowledge at this point, sir. "

Nobody else spoke up.

"I take it he didn't identify his attackers?"

"Correct sir, but we knew when he was lying about that sort of thing. He'd have a little smile on his face when he was being economical with the truth. He maintained that he only knew Mace vaguely from the gym and didn't really know why he had come to his aid. He denied any knowledge about where Marshall was and what happened to him and he denied any knowledge of the incident in the shower block a few weeks ago with Ferguson, Devenish, Ashley and Trinkett."

"I take it that he said that with that little smile on his face?"

"Precisely, sir."

"And that was all he said about the Marquis coming to his aid?"

"Yes, sir. He seemed genuinely surprised by it. He just said it must have been just a kind of loose friendship sort of thing."

"Oh, dear. He hasn't really given us anything very helpful, has he?"

Mr Bertrand looked positively disappointed.

"Anything to add, Michael?"

"No, sir, 'fraid not."

The rest of the team gave brief summaries of their interviews too but nothing of interest turned up. Two of the other hospital casualties had been released today as well and they had been interviewed by DS Tokenforth and DC Goodfellow, but their findings were negative. It seemed that inmates Topps and Crystal had been simply in the wrong place at the wrong time and had taken a severe beating each from the others simply because the others were venting their frustrations on them. The mood in the MIR went quite dull but was salvaged by the youngest team member, one DC Robert Goodfellow.

"Sir, bearing in mind what you said right at the beginning of this investigation, about not making presumptions, etcetera, could it have been suicide?"

There was a loud burst of laughter and his fellow offices rocked on their chairs in merriment. Robert looked a little embarrassed but defended himself.

"I'm being serious, sir. Is it possible? Romans used to fall on their swords to kill themselves."

Mr Bertrand smiled broadly.

"Robert. I take my hat off to you. I hadn't thought of that myself, but you are quite right to bring any possible consideration into the mix, however remote it might be. However, in all honesty, given the circumstances and the apparent strength of the blow and how it was struck, I think it's very unlikely, but I will run that concept past the pathologist and see what he says, just to be sure."

It took a little while for the others to settle down. Mr Bertrand asked for an interview count. There had been twenty-three today, bringing the total up to sixty-nine. That left only eleven for the next day, which apart from the three Indians still in hospital, just left the dregs.

Tuesday morning was mop-up time. DS Swayne and DC Lane went off to the hospital to interview the three Indians who were still being kept in for observation, which left just two interviews each for the other teams at the prison. DI Brand and DS Starchley took Colin Smith because he was Liam's cellmate. The others were shared out quite randomly. DS Bigley and DC Wellsome took Kevin and Roger simply because they were cellmates.

As Swayne and Lane drove towards the hospital, Rebecca spoke.

"I can already tell you why the Indians got well and truly hammered."

"I know what you're going to say."

"Chowdry and Dalek are in for a so-called honour killing. Chowdry's actual sister! Dalek's cousin! They beat her up and set her on fire in the garden whilst the rest of the family looked on from the bedroom windows. She was only sixteen for Christ's sake. Because she had the audacity to get herself a white boyfriend. Jesus Christ! How can these people be so sick? Police were called only because neighbours complained about them having a bonfire in their garden."

"I know. It's disgusting. Shame it wasn't them who got the knife."

"At least there's a code of honour inside."

"But poor old Balakrishnan. Probably just the wrong place, wrong time for him."

Rebecca frowned. She agreed that what happened to Balakrishnan was most unfortunate, but she felt nothing but the utmost disgust for the other two and was glad they'd got beaten up. She certainly wasn't going to be bending over backwards in trying to discover who their perpetrators were.

The interview with Roger Brown was nothing more than a formality. Bigley and Wellsome went through the correct procedures and asked him the correct questions, but his answers were dull in the extreme. He had no associations; he noticed nothing out of the ordinary. He was privy to nothing remotely confidential. The poor man clearly had a very low IQ. The only useful information that he could provide was who was in the huddle in the corner hiding from the violence during the time of the riot, which is where he was and even then, he didn't know most of their names. He could only name Kevin and Denis. He was soon packed off back to his cell and Kevin was fetched. He really was one of the very last to be interviewed.

He sat nervously in front of the two detectives. He was still so confused in his own mind that he wasn't sure whether to confess or not. He didn't really care. He just wanted to kill himself. The only people he wanted to protect were Susie and their daughters. He sat quietly whilst the officers turned on the tapes and introduced themselves. They asked him to identify himself, which he did. They offered him the chance to have a solicitor present, which he declined. He was fully willing to take responsibility for himself. Tony spoke first.

"Mr Spartan, is it ok if we call you Kevin?"

"Yes, of course."

"You seem very nervous. Are you ok?"

"Yes. I'm just not used to any of this."

"Yes, we've read your file. You're not exactly a typical criminal, are you? And you've only been inside six weeks, is that right?"

"It seems more like six months, but I suppose you're right."

"How are you settling down in here?"

Kevin thought that was a very stupid question. Only a casual visitor totally lacking in any humanity or empathy could ask such an inane question. He bristled.

"Not at all and I hope I never do."

200

Tony was only trying to build rapport and to fish for information and he continued in the same vein. Kevin was looking at them intensely whilst trying to disguise his terror. When were they going to say 'Kevin. We know you did it. We've got witnesses.'?

"I'm sure it must be a bit of a shock to the system getting sent to prison for the first time at age forty-eight."

They were familiar with his file.

"It's disgusting. I hate it."

"How are you getting on with the other inmates?"

Kevin wondered if this man truly believed that he could just get along with these vile people. He felt like asking him why he kept asking such stupid questions and why weren't they just asking him why he killed Marshal, but he measured his response. He went along with their coy approach. Soon enough, they would nail him.

"I keep myself to myself. I have nothing in common with any of them. I am not a druggie or an alcoholic. I am not a violent man or a terrorist. I am not a thief or a con man. I don't traffic people and I don't kill members of my family because of some crazy twisted fanatical religious or cultural deception. I just had an accident in my car one day, that was all."

Well, he'd said it now. In his diatribe, he had just stated that he was not a violent man because at his core, he absolutely wasn't. The mere fact that he had killed a man didn't alter that. He would stick with that now until they confronted him with the irrefutable evidence that he was, in fact, a cold-blooded killer and then he would crack like a weak, feeble, eggshell underfoot. Sophie felt the tension rising and tried to interject a little more sensitivity.

"Kevin, we do realise that life inside must be bloody awful for you, but as you were in the canteen when a man died, we want to know if you can help us determine what happened."

This was confusing. They were playing a game with him. He would play the game back.

"There was a riot."

"Yes, we know that. Do you know a Lenny Marshal?"

"Only to look at. Liam warned me to stay away from him because he was violent."

"Why would he be violent to you?"

"Because I'm a fish, a pumpkin, a dump truck, a lame duck, a newbie. Easy prey for bullies like him, apparently."

"And why would Liam warn you about him?"

"Liam is about the only person in here that I've got to know. That's because I help tutor him in the English class."

"You get to wear one of those bibs?"

"Yes. A very nice green one."

"Ok, well, as you've mentioned Liam, let me ask you a question. Are you aware of any connection between Liam and Lenny Marshall?"

"I know nothing about anyone's business in here. Like I said, I really do keep my head down. I quietly clean every weekday morning. I help in the English class three afternoons a week and the rest of the time I'm locked up with a man who has the mental age of a ten-year-old but is a lot less fun than a real child."

She smiled. "Yes, we've had the pleasure ourselves."

"What do you do during association time?"

"Play scrabble."

"On your own?"

They all thought that was a stupid question.

"No, I play with Liam, Terry and Denis."

"Terry Mako?"

"I don't know his surname. The big ginger guy."

She seemed more alert.

"What do you make of him?"

"Actually, he's a nice guy, just really scary."

"Why?"

"I don't mean that he intends to be scary. He doesn't, but when he tells some of his stories, I am horrified at how violent he can be."

"I thought you said you didn't get on with anyone, but here you are swapping anecdotes with the big scary man."

"It's not a friendship thing. It's part of our rules for scrabble. Each round, one of us has to tell a story. We call it scrabble-babble."

"I see. That's very creative. "

"Mr Blanchflower's idea."

She looked at him blankly.

"He's the English teacher."

"I see."

"From the stories Terry has shared with you, do you think he is capable of killing a man?"

"I don't think that's a very fair question. We have all agreed that our stories go no further than the players. Anyway, for all I know, the stories might be made up. It's purely for fun."

"I see. That's very loyal of you. Can you qualify that at all, even just a little bit?"

"All I would say, in his defence, is that I get the impression that he's only violent if someone is stupid enough to offend him or attack him first."

"I see. And what do you tell stories about?"

"Nothing criminal. Family. Work. Growing up."

Tony picked up the thread again.

"Kevin, where were you when the riot began?"

Now they were going in for the kill, he thought.

"To start with, I was just in the queue waiting for dinner, but when it kicked off and the others were throwing things at the wardens, I quickly moved to the far corner to avoid being hit by something."

"Which side?"

"The corridor side."

"Why did you go to that side?"

"Because nobody was over there. I just wanted to get as far away from everyone else as possible. It was very scary. They're more or less all dangerous people in here and when there's a riot, they're clearly out of control."

"Yes, that must have been very scary. What did you do in the corner?"

"I just cowered down."

"Was anyone with you?"

"No."

"Did you see where Lenny Marshal was?"

"No."

"What happened then?"

"I just stayed still whilst the riot was in progress. After a while, I saw that there was a group of inmates on the other side hiding in that corner. I saw Roger and Denis there and I scurried over to them because I thought I would be safer in their group. On my own, I felt very exposed."

"I see. Can you remember who was hitting who"?

"You've got to be joking. It was just a morass of bodies shouting, hitting, kicking, screaming and I was only looking for the safest place to go. I'm sorry if I can't help you, but I have to admit, violence really scares me. I'm just not used to it. I know it sounds pathetic but I just wanted to hide. I'll make no bones about it. I am a complete coward."

"No one's judging you for your self-preservation instincts, Kevin. Who knows what any of us would do in those circumstances? Who else was in that corner?"

"Denis and Roger, like I said and a few others whose names I don't know. Oh and Colin. He's Liam's celly."

"I see, Kevin. On a slightly different tack, what sort of jobs have you had in the past?"

"I've always been a salesman. Photocopier."

"I see. Nothing ever physical?"

"No. I don't carry them. I just try to get orders for them. Nothing physical. As you can see, I'm in pretty poor shape."

DS Bigley and DC Wellsome looked at each other. They had no more questions.

Chapter 19

At 4:45 p.m., all the inmates were released from their cells. They were of course rather exuberant. It was Tuesday and the lockdown was finally over after four whole days and they were free to collect their teas and breakfasts as normal. There was much banter and jocular behaviour. There was a strong feeling of demob happiness as they caught up with their mates in the corridor. Four days of total communal isolation had finally come to an end. Some of them were almost dancing. They would still have to return to their cells to eat but they would be freed again at 6 p.m. for restored association time. The word was out that the next day, everything else would be back to normal too.

When association time arrived, the four scrabble players tentatively gathered at their table area. Terry was the first to speak.

"You guys up for some scrabble still? Or are you desperate to do something different now after all this shite?"

"I'm ok for scrabble," Liam offered.

"Me too," added Kevin.

"Suits me," Denis said jovially.

"Ok, so shall we get down to it?"

There was a consensus. They all sat, apart from Kevin who went to fetch the board.

"What a fuckin' few days." Terry mused.

"I thought I was going to go fuckin mad. My celly's ok. It was just not having anything different to do every day."

"It was pretty evil," Denis added. "I think I've done enough reading to last me a lifetime."

Liam commented "You cunts don't know how lucky you are. In some prisons, they're locked up twenty-three hours a day every fukin' day, all the time."

"I'm not sure it's quite that bad these days, Liam," Denis countered, "But I take your point. Generally, it's pretty good here."

As Kevin got the board out, Terry asked him if he still had the details of their last game.

"You're kidding, right? That was a lifetime ago. We'll have to start again."

"That's not fair," Denis protested. "I was way out in front."

"You're such a fukin' liar, Denis. You can't help yourself, can you? I was way ahead of you, you cunt," Liam countered.

"Boys, please. If Kevin's lost the details, then we have no choice but to start again, do we? Wind your tits in."

They all eagerly grabbed seven letters from the bag.

Meanwhile, at the MIR, the mood was very different. Mr Bertrand had gathered in the day's accounts from all his officers. All eighty inmates had finally been interviewed and bizarrely, they still did not have a single suspect. He was subdued and the team felt defeated. They had done what they were trained to do but it hadn't been enough. The murder was still every bit as much a mystery now as it had been on the afternoon of the incident. Mr Bertrand was immensely frustrated but he still had to encourage his team. That was professionalism.

"Ok. I admit that this is a bit of a mystery and it's immensely frustrating at this point. We've had eighty suspects on a plate. We've interviewed each of them and DCI Colchester and I have also spoken with every single prison officer who regularly works B-wing and none of us have turned up a single clue. Not one. This is most unusual. I'll be honest with you. I am rather baffled, just as I am sure that you all are. I think that the best thing I can do right now is to tell you all a little night-time story and then send you all home to bed for some well-earned rest, and to cogitate."

The group tittered.

"How many of you have watched the film *The Enigma files*?"

Most hands went up.

"Good. It's a fantastic film about an amazing man called Alan Turing. For those of you unfamiliar with the film, allow me to summarise it and then I'll make my point. It was set early in the Second World War when the Germans still had the upper hand and were busy conquering the whole of Europe. They benefited from a very sophisticated and unbreakable code for all their communications which was called the enigma code.

British intelligence recruited the brightest minds it could find and got them working in top-secret at Bletchley Manor in an effort to crack the code. They mainly employed linguists and puzzle-solvers with very high IQs for the purpose, but a mathematician, Alan Turing, managed to persuade them to take him on their team as well. God only knows why he thought he could use mathematics to break a language code, but he was convinced that he could do it and he built a machine for the purpose. Again, how his mind contrived such a machine is a complete mystery. It was effectively the world's first computer."

There were gasps of surprise. He continued.

"Yes. Way back in the forties. Basically, Turing was way ahead of his time. However, his machine failed to come up with the goods and the war office was becoming increasingly exasperated with his ideas which clearly weren't working. The problem was that the code was so sophisticated, his elementary computer, which was the size of a big room, was too slow to crack it in one day and each day, the Germans changed the code. He and his team were literally pulling their hair out. Every single day for months on end, they just hit a brick wall. Yet, Turing never lost his faith, either in his own abilities or his computer's, despite the complete lack of progress.

Then one evening, when they were down the pub getting some well-deserved R&R, feeling rather depressed and forlorn, someone not on their team made a passing remark about how they at least knew what the last two words of each missive was - 'Heil Hitler!' This stunned them because none of them had ever thought about that. Someone not on their team had made a casual observation which was the missing link. They raced back to their computer, typed in the fact that the last two words meant 'Heil Hitler!' and bingo! From then on, they cracked the code every single day. All because they focussed on a little bit of information which they had hitherto overlooked."

There were happy admiring noises in the room.

"It's the same for us. We've overlooked some small details, or we haven't looked at something objectively enough, or broadly enough, or from the right angle, or from someone else's point of view. I want to thank you all for all the hard work you've all put in this week. There's no question that you've all worked diligently and professionally but there's still much work to be done. I want you all to go home now and rest. I'll see you all here tomorrow, refreshed and with different glasses on so to speak. We'll look at everything afresh. We need to find that little missing link which thus far we've somehow missed. I'll resist saying 'Heil Hitler' for fear of being misinterpreted. Goodnight and sleep well."

They laughed and noisily dispersed, grabbing their various bits and pieces. The Alan Turing story had been very encouraging. Robert hadn't seen the film and didn't know the story. He asked his partner Harry if he knew what Turing went on to do after the war.

"Robert. I'm afraid that the story didn't have a happy ending. Turing's machine had to be dismantled after the war under the official secrets act and because his work was top secret, he got no public recognition for what he achieved and in those days, it was a crime to be gay."

"What?"

"Yeah, you're too young to remember that. You could be done for homosexual offences right up to the end of the seventies, you know."

"Wow!"

"Anyway, poor old Turing, actually he wasn't that old, well, he was gay and his local police constantly harassed him for being gay and he got arrested. He undertook chemical castration."

"What? The bastards!"

"Yeah, in lieu of prison."

"You're fucking kidding me. After all he did?"

"Yeah. Wicked, ain't it? They reckon his work shortened the war by two years. Anyway, after the war, he carried on developing the computer. He was said to be the father of algorithms and artificial intelligence. Basically, he was a computer genius."

"So, what happened to him after that?"

"Well, no one knows for sure what motivated him, but it's believed to be the oppression he got for being gay. It drove him to suicide."

"No! That's terrible. How old was he?"

"Early forties, I believe. If he had lived on, he probably would have become our own Bill Gates or Steve Jobs, only thirty years earlier."

"That's so fucking sad. Much more sad than us not finding Marshall's killer."

"Yes, Robert, but that is one of the main differences between us and our American cousins. They give their geniuses tons of encouragement and billions of dollars. Here, we just try to destroy them in case they do better than us. Good night, Robert."

The new Warden, Mr Dibden, had learnt an important lesson. If you charge into a new situation and recklessly upset the apple cart, there can be serious consequences. Initially, after his arrival, all the wings had been put on evening lockdowns, but after the riot in B-wing, he was advised to restore the usual privileges in the other wings immediately on pain of further potential disturbances.

Fortunately, he wasn't too proud or stubborn to take advice from his long-standing custodial officers and he relented over association time privileges on the other wings. After all, he now had the worry of a home office internal enquiry being conducted because of the riot and the murder, not to mention the actual police investigation that was currently being conducted. His new posting had not started well and he was worried about the effects it might have on his career. He would do his best to show that the disruption had been caused by tensions, which had been developing in the weeks or months prior to his arrival.

The start of the new scrabble game was somewhat uninspired. After two weeks off, the players had got out of the scrabble way of thinking. The only offering of five letters to start the game off was 'gutty' from Terry which earned him a meagre eighteen points. Liam followed with 'poxy' for twenty-four points because he got an 'X' on a double letter score. Then Kevin managed a reasonable word 'trollop' but only for a mere sixteen points, followed by Denis's 'rivet' for twenty. It wasn't until the second round that things began to fizz.

Terry got 'realize' along the top line, covering a triple word score, for an impressive fifty-one, but to his chagrin, Liam cheekily added 'un' at the start of 'realize' and added a 'D' at the end, earning an even more impressive sixty for 'unrealized', because his 'u' reached the top left corner of a triple word score.

"Liam, how many times do I have to warn you not to steal my words, you thieving bastard?"

Terry expanded his chest and huffed and puffed. He didn't like someone else taking advantage of his word, but of course, Liam's play had been completely legitimate and Terry's tantrum only served to amuse him.

"What, Terry? This is completely within the rules, isn't it, Kevin?"

"Yes, it is, Liam. You can even just add an 's' on some words to get the word score all over again, plus the 's'."

He looked at Terry appealingly.

209

"Doesn't feel right to me. I do all the hard work by coming up with a brilliant word and he adds a couple of letters to it and gets more points than I did. I think we need a new rule whereby if he uses my word, I get half the points."

"I don't think that would work." Kevin offered meekly.

The game was beginning to distract him from the terror he felt constantly of being caught out over Lenny. Terry went quiet, brooding internally.

It was now Kevin's go and he came up with a rather clever 'garnered' using the 'G' of 'gutty'. However, it was a low-scoring word, so even though he had covered a double word score and he doubled again for using up all his letters, he only scored forty. They were all looking to Denis now, to see if he too could raise his game in round two. The 'd' of 'garnered' reached the bottom line, with triple word scores on either side of it, so he obviously focussed there. He soon saw his opportunity and placed 'grandma' on the bottom line, using the 'd', but he had used no high scoring letters, so he only managed thirty-three.

"Ah, that's so sweet, Denis. You thinking of one of your girlfriends?"

"I'll have you know that much younger ladies find me very attractive, Terry. You could say that I'm very versatile."

They all chuckled.

"Scores, please." Terry enquired.

"In reverse order. Denis, fifty-three. Me, fifty-six; you, sixty-nine; and Liam, eighty-four."

Liam stood and did a little twirly jig.

Terry spoke. "Well, we've done two rounds. Time for someone to do a story, I think. Anyone?"

They all scrutinised the words on the board, running them through their minds to see if anything resonated.

"Kevin, what does 'garnered' mean?"

"It means to gather something together, Liam."

Terry asked Denis a question. "You want to tell us a story about you and one of your grandma's Denis?"

He chuckled. Denis huffed. "Dream on."

Nobody felt inspired.

Terry conceded. "Oh, dear, boys. Mr Blanchflower wouldn't be very impressed. We'll just have to do another round then."

It was his turn. After a few minutes, he put 'wronging' down the left-hand side, starting on a triple word score and ending on the 'G' of grandma. He had to use a blank for the 'O', but he had used up all his letters.

"Eat your heart out, girlies. You are witnessing the master at work. Triple word score. That's three times fourteen, forty-two, times two for using up all my letters, makes eighty-four. In one go!"

He looked smug. Kevin remained neutral but Denis looked quite miffed. Liam, however, looked like he had a trick up his sleeve. He had already worked out his next go and Terry's move hadn't affected it. He placed 'shawls' vertically down the board so that the 'S' joined up with 'grandma'. The 'S' sat on a triple word score which meant that he got a triple word score twice. He was rather excited.

"Kevin. How much is that? It's a blinder."

Kevin totted it up. "'Shawls' is thirteen times three and 'Grandmas' is twelve times three. That's a total of seventy-five, Liam, nudging your total score just above Terry's."

"What? I don't believe it. I was streets ahead. You jammy fucker!"

Denis was looking glum. "I shouldn't have left 'grandma' like that. It was a gift for someone. That's my fault."

"Don't fret, boys. Whatever you do, I'm just too good for you."

Liam looked very pleased with himself. Kevin and Denis were beginning to trail badly. It was now Kevin's go and he very quickly put down 'hash' using the 'H' of shawls. His second 'H' was on a double word score. He got twenty. Terry was a little disappointed in him.

"Kevin, you haven't given up, have you? I don't wish to seem rude, but that didn't seem like much of an effort."

"I just had very dull letters, Terry. Sorry."

Terry frowned at him and then addressed Denis.

"Come on, Denis. You've got to be able to do better than that."

Denis knuckled down intensely, but he really didn't come up with much.

He placed 'gluten' down between 'wronging' and 'garnered', using 'G' from 'wronging' and the 'E' of 'garnered'. It was a double word score, yet it scored him only fourteen points.

Liam summed the situation up. "Terry, I think we've got so far ahead, they've got their heads in their boots."

"I think you're right, fellah. Oh, well. Let's not knock them for their lack of resilience. They're not hardened criminals like you and me, Liam. We have to remember that and make allowances for them. Now can anyone do a story?"

The new words didn't seem to add a great deal more potential, but it seemed that Denis wanted to redeem himself a little and he felt able.

"Yeah, I could do one on 'wronging' but only if I get the full fifty points this time."

The others looked around at each other. Denis needed some encouragement, so they all nodded.

"Ok. Listen up. This is basically going to be some excellent advice to you, younger men, whether you're married yet or not."

"Denis, it has to be a story," Liam said.

"It's going to be a story, Liam, but it's a story with a moral purpose. Like a parable in the bible. You remember how I told you the story of my wife getting my house off me?"

There were nods, despite the fact he'd told that story three weeks ago.

"Well, after that, I had to find somewhere else to live. I was very angry with my ex, but it was really important for me to keep seeing my kids. Like I said, they were only about nine and ten. She would have been happy to see me just drift away and lose contact like most separated fathers do, the bitch, but I was determined to be as much of a father to them as I could be, under the circumstances. I couldn't suddenly provide them with a home which social services approved of, so I was limited to just taking them out once a week for the day.

She tried to make it awkward for me, so I had to go to court to get my rights enforced. My weekly visits went on for years. I always stayed in touch with my girls, as often as I was allowed and I carried on providing for them, way after they reached eighteen. They eventually got boyfriends and settled down and then I saw less of them, but my point is this. Some wrongs never get put right. Much as I resented my ex for what she did to me, it nevertheless always felt wrong that she wasn't with me, alongside me, when I was with my girls.

Obviously, I enjoyed seeing them myself, but there was always a sense of emptiness too, because I should have been doing it with their mother enjoying them with me. I think it's to do with the magnitude of creating life. Once you've done that with someone, you'll never find the same depth of meaning with anyone else and then, when you're celebrating that new life in some way, it feels wrong that there's only half of you there. Does that make sense?"

Kevin nodded silently.

Terry commented. "Yeah, I suppose so, Denis. I haven't got kids yet but I suppose I will feel the same way about the mother when I do."

Liam wasn't so sure. "I don't really get it, Denis. You obviously hate your ex, so why would you want her around?"

"I know. It's hard to explain, but when you're around your kids, you just hanker after what it should have been like, for their sake as well as yours and you don't feel the hatred as much as the sense of loss when you're right in that moment. Does that make sense?"

"Yeah, I suppose. Why did she leave you, Denis?"

"That's too complicated to explain, Liam. I think that part of the problem at that time was that Princess Dianna and Princess Sarah Ferguson were both divorcing their royal husbands and I honestly think that encouraged a lot of other women around that time to step out on their own too."

Terry stated matter-of-factly, "I'm not sure that was a proper story though, under the rules of Scrabble-Babble."

"What?" Denis queried, nonplussed. "Why not?"

"Well, you were just saying about how you felt about something. That's not a story, is it?"

"Yeah, he's right, Denis. It wasn't a proper story," Liam added. "Maybe forty points, Terry?"

"Yeah, that's what I was thinking, Liam. What do you think, Kevin?"

"Well, to be honest, I think you're right about it not being a proper story but we did agree beforehand that he would get fifty points for trying."

The other two looked at each other for a moment, then relented.

"Yeah. Ok. We are all men of honour, Denis. Maybe there is a lesson there for you to learn. Fifty points then."

Chapter 20

Wednesday morning found Kevin mopping floors, Liam cooking dinner, Terry in the gym and Denis assisting the computer class. They all never thought they'd be so content doing their work or enjoying their privileges. Even the guards had a bit of a spring in their step. They had more interesting and varied work to do again. Everyone preferred some kind of routine and normality.

Wednesday afternoon found Kevin and Liam in the English class, Terry in the laundry and Denis in the gym. The detectives visits had come to an end.

Mr Blanchflower welcomed his charges back.

"Boys, I missed you last Friday and this Monday. I hope you've all got a note from your mums!"

There was some brief giggling.

"Today, we're going to do a class exercise about vocabulary. Tell me that sounds exciting!"

A few of them shouted out. "That sounds exciting!"

"A lot better than being locked up all day, right?"

There was a loud cheer.

"Ok. I'm going to dish out some cards. One between two. They're all pictures of shoes. Nobody here had a shoe fetish, do they?"

Tony answered.

"Yeah, Malcolm does. I hear he wanks into his celly's shoes most nights."

There was raucous laughter.

Malcolm responded, "At least I don't steal knickers off washing lines at night."

"You said that like there's something wrong with it!"

More laughter.

Mr Blanchflower was giving them a little opportunity to let off steam. He realised that they had all been through an ordeal over the past few days.

"Ok, so what I want you to do, in pairs, is to build up a picture of the person who might be the owner of these shoes. Physical description. Age. What they might do for a job, for hobbies. Where they might live. What kind of food they might eat. How active they are. What kind of fashions they might like, what kind of music. Anything. Remember, this is an exercise to develop your vocabulary, so extend yourselves and be a bit more flowery than usual. I don't want to hear that this bloke had big feet, therefore, he must have been a right big twat."

They giggled. Someone had their own gag.

"Are you sure this isn't to do with the murder investigation? I hear they need our help."

Another outburst of laughter. Mr Blanchflower wondered how they might collectively feel about the lack of progress in the murder case, whether they felt victorious or proud as a group because the police had so far failed to crack the case, or whether it even bothered them that they had an unidentified murderer on the loose amongst themselves. He wasn't going to ask. It was too sensitive a subject for an English lesson. He dished out the cards. There were pictures of training shoes, leather boots, wellington boots, brogues, sailing shoes, plimsolls, Doc Martens, dancing shoes, stilettos, working boots, worn-out leather work boots, boxing boots, running shoes, slippers and skating boots. The class got into pairs and started chatting away noisily. They each had pen and paper to record their descriptions.

"Ten minutes should be enough," Mr Blanchflower added over the din.

When the ten minutes expired he asked for a volunteer to start them off. Andrew stood up and held his piece of paper in front of him.

"Me and Rashid got the stilettos."

There were immediate wolf whistles.

"The shoes are very clean and posh, so we surmise that the owner is either a nice city lady or Malcolm."

More laughter.

"We're not going to describe Malcolm. You all know that perv already. We're going to describe the lady. She likes to dress well. She is sophisticated, so not too young, maybe mid-thirties. She has a clean, sedentary, yes, I said sedentary (the class whistled in admiration), job where she sits around all day long, so she can get away with wearing stilettos at work. She's wearing a tight knee-length skirt. I think they call them pencil skirts, but I don't know why. She has a smart white blouse on and a Jacket to match her skirt. I won't mention her underwear because I don't want to get Tony overly excited."

Lots of sniggering and jeering.

"Her nails are highly manicured because that's one way ladies try to look posh, but her nails can't be too long, or else how would she use a keyboard? We think she eats very carefully because she's very appearance-conscious and she wouldn't want to be overweight. Posh healthy food, probably from Marks and Spencer. For hobbies, we've got her down as a dancer, so she can still wear nice stilettos when she's out. Maybe Tango or ballroom. We think she lives alone, waiting for her dream man to come along, but unfortunately, I'm going to be unavailable for some time, but she's going to wait for me."

Laughter and wolf whistles.

"We think she's got one of those awful little lap dogs for a pet, but when she's out walking that, she wears more sensible shoes and big dark glasses and a long coat, like a different persona. When she's not dancing, we think she goes out for a little drinky-winky with the girls in some trendy bar and for holidays, it's definitely a posh hotel by a sun-drenched beach where she can pose all day in a tiny bikini, showing off her gorgeous body and tottering around in her high-heel stilettos when she's fetching dry martinis."

He sat down. There was a round of applause. He stood up and theatrically bowed to the class.

"Very good, Andrew and Rashid. Sedentary was a very good descriptive word. Who can explain what that means for the class?"

Jason shouted out. "It means you sit around on your lardy arse all day."

"Yes, Jason. Quite. Ok. Who got the worn-out working boots?"

This was Liam and Kevin. Liam stood, staring at his piece of paper. His delivery was slow as always. He both spoke and read slowly, but he was confident.

"They may be working boots but we don't think they belong to a worker."

There was some loud exaggerated oohing.

"No, we think they're dirty and worn out because they belong to a tramp. Now, let me just educate you a bit, boys. They're not called tramps anymore. That might hurt their feelings. They're called street-dwellers or homeless. Ok? Our tramp is old. Maybe fifty. They don't last much longer than that on the cold, wet streets, you know. He's wearing filthy old clothes that are shabby and torn and that match his boots perfectly, so in a way, he's quite fashionable. His hair is long and straggly. Tramps don't go to the barbers like we do remember. He's got a beard because how can you shave without a mirror? His face is ruddy and tough, unlike any of you lot."

There was some hooting.

"His face is leathery from constant exposure to the elements and by elements, I mean sun, rain and wind. He's a loner who moves around the city, shuffling in his broken boots, looking for good places to beg and to shelter out of the rain. His diet is not very good. People give him stuff but it's always fast food. No vegetables and very little fruit and as you know, that's not very good for his health. Some of the money he gets given does go on booze. Come on, guys. Don't judge him. We all drink, don't we? He's actually not that concerned about fashion.

Sometimes people give him quite nice clothing. Sometimes, he might get something almost new from a charity shop and so his stuff doesn't match until it's all worn out and filthy and then it matches perfectly, but he only cares about how warm it is. He doesn't change his pants every day, only when they get really sticky."

The class gave an unanimous exclamation of disgust.

"What? What did I say?"

He continued. "We don't think he even cleans his teeth every day. It's the first thing you really notice about a tramp close-up. His teeth. They're always terrible. Either missing or dark brown and chipped. We don't think he's got any hobbies and a holiday for him would be going to a different city to beg. He might have a dog with him. That helps him get donations and a pet dog is the only creature that is ever going to love him, so he's important for that reason too. He doesn't listen to music but he's very familiar with the sound of traffic. He could tell you what time of day it is by the sound of the traffic, he's that in tune with it."

He had finished reading the notes. He looked around the class for approval, holding an arm up as if acknowledging their admiration.

"Thank you, fans."

"Sit down, you dozy fucker!"

Mr Blanchflower took the reins.

"Thank you, Liam. That was excellent. I particularly liked the bit where he was moving around the city, shuffling in his broken boots. The choice of the word 'shuffling' was very effective. It spoke about not just movement but how he moved. It gave away something of his condition, his age maybe, or his physical limitations. Very good."

"That was, Kevin, sir."

"Yes, well, whoever came up with it. It was very good."

"No, sir, I meant that's the way I see Kevin moving around."

The class erupted in laughter again. Liam prodded Kevin playfully. The class continued along in the same vein for the next thirteen pairs of shoes. There was a lot of laughter and a few nice new words were well and truly learned.

The latest game of scrabble reconvened at association time.

Terry kicked off with 'exceed' using the 'X' of 'poxy' and also making 'et' with the second 'T' of 'gutty'. That earned him twenty points. Liam followed with 'timid' down to the 'D' of 'exceed', earning him a mere sixteen and Kevin followed even more quickly with 'idiot' across the 'I' of 'timid'. His heart really was not in it. He made only fourteen. He replenished his tile holder with the last of the spare letters. Denis made a good effort to score more highly. He managed to use the triple word score at the top right-hand corner of the board, where he placed 'fistic' using the 'T' of 'idiot'.

"Is that something on the autistic spectrum, Denis?" Liam enquired curiously.

"Not necessarily, Liam. Anyone?"

The others were no wiser than Liam, not even Kevin.

"You should know this one, Terry. It means you're handy with your fists."

"Are you trying to say that I'm fistic, Denis?"

"Yes. No offence."

"Well, that depends. Does the word have either a good or bad slant to it?"

"You mean does it have a pejorative edge to it? Or is it merely informative?"

"Yeah, that's what I meant."

"I think it's purely descriptive, Terry, in a neutral way."

"That's ok, then."

Denis only had three letters left, all vowels, so he should be able to use them easily enough, given sufficient goes.

Terry managed 'woofy' from the 'W' of 'shawls'. He wasn't very happy with that, as it only scored fifteen points and he and Liam were neck and neck on the scoreboard. Liam struggled, eventually placing 'bye' over the 'Y' of 'woofy'. This got him sixteen points, as his word hit a double word score, but it left him five letters, three of which were rather high in value. Kevin rather cleverly got a 'Q' in a double word score. He placed 'aqua' over the 'U' of 'gluten', thus scoring twenty-six, but he was still trailing hugely and he had a "J" left over which could count against him. Now it was Denis's go again.

"How many letters have you got left, Denis?" Terry asked.

"Three."

"Come on. You've got to use them all up this go."

He wanted the game to end so that Liam would have letters left over to count against him.

"I can't, Terry. They're all vowels."

He placed a single 'O' next to the second 'N' of 'wronging'. It was also over the 'R' of 'Grandmas' and it was on a double word score. So his 'no' and 'or' made him another eight points. Now, it was Terry's go and he hoped he would manage to use up both of his remaining letters. He did, by placing his 'I' and 'B' between the first 'R' of 'garnered' and the 'S' of 'shawls' making 'ribs' worth eight points because the 'I' was on a triple letter score.

"End of game!" he announced triumphantly. "What are your penalty points please, fellahs?"

'Fuck! I've got fourteen!' exclaimed Liam, very disappointed. He had been so close to Terry, but now he was scuppered.

"Just two for me, Kevin."

"And I've got eleven," Kevin stated quietly. "So the final scores are, me, one hundred and five; Denis, one hundred and fifty-six; Liam, one hundred and seventy-seven; and Terry, one hundred and ninety-six."

Terry stood up and raised his big arms into the air. "Thank you, girlies and only Denis did a story! And he still didn't win! What a total loser!"

There wasn't much Denis could say about that. Inexcusable really, so he stayed silent. Terry was in a buoyant mood. He had won his second game and felt very pleased with himself.

"Anyone want to do a story before we wrap this game up?"

Denis had already done one, Kevin was in too subdued a mood and Liam found no inspiration on the board.

"Well, in that case, then my scrabble babble buddies, I think I'll do one to celebrate my latest victory."

"Hang on," Denis said briskly. "Let me get a cuppa first. Anyone else wants one?"

Kevin declined. He found the canteen drinks unpalatable, but Liam opted for mud. When Denis returned with two cups of mud, Terry began.

What word do you think I'm going to use?"

"Fistic," Denis answered quickly.

"No, Denis."

"Ribs and how to break them?"

"No, Kevin, but both good guesses. Liam?"

"Idiot?"

Terry looked at him quizzically.

"No, Liam. The word is 'bye'."

The others looked a little puzzled, wondering how he would make a story out of that. He commenced.

"Many years ago, obviously before Val, I had a girlfriend called Mary. She had a catholic background but wasn't really practising anymore. Anyway, she was really fit and I got her to engage in sinful activities with me as often as possible and before long, she found that she was pregnant. She wanted to keep the baby and I didn't mind either way. I didn't know what the future held and I wasn't going to be all dictatorial about something as important as this for my own selfish reasons and so I simply accepted what she wanted and my responsibility, of course. I mean, it had been my choice to do her in the first place, hadn't it?"

They all nodded sagely.

"Anyway, in time, we discovered that the baby was not developing well and as time went on, the doctors became convinced that the baby wouldn't survive outside the womb. They blandly presumed that Mary would automatically opt for a termination, but I suppose because of her religious beliefs, or background, she said that was totally out of the question. She went ahead with the pregnancy, knowing for sure that the baby would die soon after birth.

I thought that was very strange. I didn't understand her reasoning at all, you know, going through with a long pregnancy for nothing in the end, but I didn't challenge her wishes. She felt so strongly that no matter what everyone else thought about the situation, God had given her that baby and it deserved a chance at life. I supported her. I had admiration for her love and devotion to be honest, even though I didn't understand it.

She went the full nine months and gave birth to a little boy. I was lucky enough to be there. It was an amazing experience. I had never seen a baby born before. As soon as he came out you could see straight away that he wasn't right. The midwife wrapped him up and laid him in Mary's arms. I sat next to her, with an arm around her.

The medical staff left the room and we both just sat there looking at him. It was the closest thing I have ever experienced to a spiritual experience. I don't have the words to describe what I mean by that. It was just the sense and miracle of seeing this new life, but also knowing that we only had him for a few precious minutes or hours. We both had a sense of purpose in just being with him whilst we could.

Mary spoke quietly to him the whole time, just administering love to him. I could tell that she really loved him. I suppose she had bonded with him whilst he was in her womb for nine months. He was quiet. He didn't cry. Sometimes his eyes opened in short startled bursts, but most of the time they stayed shut. As the minutes slowly ticked by, I could sense that he was fading. Mary knew it too. It was as if she was chaperoning him from one life into another.

At some point, he died quietly in her arms. I wasn't sure when that happened exactly. It was so peaceful and Mary carried on saying lovely things to him, but as his little body went totally limp and we both knew that he'd gone. That's when Mary started to cry, but you know, it wasn't a sad moment. It was like we'd both had the privilege of helping this little baby come out of her tummy and go straight into another world, like he didn't need to stay here for years and years like the rest of us and put up with all the shit we have to put up with. No, I really felt that he had moved on to somewhere good and not just died into nothingness and that we had been given just a short while to meet him and then to say goodbye to him, as he carried on his life elsewhere. It was like Mary instinctively knew it was going to feel like this, but the spirituality of it took me by surprise. I'd never sensed anything like that before, nor since."

He stopped. To the surprise of the others, he was showing tiny signs of choking back tears. He composed himself.

"Now, I need that cup of mud."

He stood up and walked off to the urn, leaving the others feeling a little emotional themselves. That was a story that reached right into their souls and stirred them. Even Denis didn't try to make a crass joke about it.

Day five at the MIR passed without any excitement. Mr Bertrand had charged his task force to go through their own researches and interviews with a fine-tooth comb, to reflect most carefully on every little detail. Then, over the coming days, when they had exhausted that task, he wanted them each to trawl through all the other suspects, starting with the recorded interviews. All eighty interviews had been transcribed by busy support staff onto the Holmes computer system, so anyone on the team could readily examine all of the other accounts. They could even listen to the taped recordings themselves if they so wished, if they thought that listening for clues in the way answers were given might add something.

DI Rutherford and DS Pendleton would fall behind the others with this task, as Mr Bertrand has asked them to return to the prison the following day, to re-interview all the relevant prison staff, in order to see if there was anything that he himself had missed and also to check for any new information whatsoever their end. Then, at the end of the day, he invited them all to watch a video clip.

"Now, some of you, no, most of you have seen this clip, but please don't say a word if you have. I don't want anyone giving the game away! I am going to show you all a very short video. It's only about a minute long and all it shows is a bunch of basketball players passing a ball amongst themselves. I want you each to count how many times the ball was passed during the clip, Ok?"

There were a lot of knowing looks in the group, but also some looks of bemusement. It sounded like a very easy task. They hadn't all seen the clip before and the unenlightened all concentrated very hard. The clip was played. Those who had seen it before were smiling. The clip soon ended.

"Right. How many of you hadn't seen that clip before?"

Just four of them put their hands up.

"Ok. So you four, tell me how many times the ball was passed."

In turn, they each answered 'fifteen.'

"And which of you noticed the gorilla?"

Only one of them put their hand up. The rest of the team laughed.

The other three all gave responses of surprise about any gorilla. There had been no gorilla! If there had been they would have spotted it. They were shown the clip once more and this time they all clearly observed a man in a gorilla suit walking slowly amongst the basketball players for most of the time, but he never once touched the ball. They couldn't believe that they hadn't noticed him the first time. Mr Bertrand spoke with a smile on his face.

"My point is obvious. That clip is always a lot of fun to show when people haven't seen it before. The fact is that about half of the people who watch it the first time don't see the gorilla. The human mind is quite capable of playing tricks on us. Magicians know how to exploit our expectations and use them to easily deceive us. That clip shows that when we focus on one thing, we can so easily not see something else, even though it is obvious. We ourselves know how careful we have to be when taking statements. We have to avoid asking leading questions because people pick up on our implications and begin to think they remember something they actually didn't see. So for you all. Please remember the gorilla. We might miss him if we focus too strongly on our preconceived ideas."

DC Goodfellow spoke up.

"Sir, in that vein, have we adequately considered Bennett, Medley and Parsley? We know that they were Marshall's associates and have perhaps assumed that they were fighting for him during the riot. What if one of them wanted to take over his little empire in there and needed to get rid of him?"

"That's a very good question, Robert. I'll leave that thought with the rest of the team to consider very carefully. We need ideas first, then evidence."

Chapter 21

Thursday morning after breakfast, Liam was escorted to one of the interview rooms by his personal officer, John Herman, for his weekly one-to-one support session. He didn't really connect well with John, who was only a few years older than him. He found him naive and a little condescending and he had no realistic perception or understanding of the druggie world. Mentoring probably wasn't his strong point but it was now a part of his role, so Liam found the sessions to be little more than John just politely checking up on him and more or less just going through a routine.

"I bet you're glad that investigation is over, eh Liam?"

"Yeah, I suppose, although the investigation itself didn't bother me, it was being banged up the whole time whilst it was going on. That was a bit of a drag. Did they get anywhere with it in the end?"

"Liam, I am not at liberty to discuss the investigation with you, but I do have some really good news for you today."

"What, you're changing prisons?"

"Very funny, Liam. No, but you are."

"What?"

"You're due for release before the end of the month, but they're bringing it forward. Your probation officer will be visiting you here on Monday or Tuesday and you'll be out on licence before the end of next week."

John looked at him, smiling, happy for him. Liam was a bit surprised. He hadn't been expecting early release, even though it was only by a few weeks.

"Oh, ok. That's good. I'll have to let Kaz know so she can collect me."

"The probation officer is a lady called Carol Smithers. Do you know her?"

Liam smiled broadly. "Yeah, I know her. She's ok, actually. Bit boring, but quite fair."

"They're not there to entertain you, Liam. So you should get on quite well with her and we shouldn't see you back here on recall?"

"Who knows what the future holds?" Liam replied playfully.

"Well, Liam, with that imminently in the pipeline, I don't think there's anything else we need to talk about, do you?"

"No, I suppose not."

"Unless you want to tell me who stabbed Lenny?"

"Pass."

With that, they both got up and John escorted Liam to the kitchen where he was just a little late for duty.

That evening after tea when the scrabble players met for another game and as Kevin was getting the board and letters out, Liam shared his good news with them.

"Hey guys, I've got some good news."

"Who for?"

"Me, I suppose."

"Finally, they're going to let you have that sex change op?"

"Fuck off! No. I'm being released next week."

They were all surprised. With everything that had been going on, they hadn't paid much attention to the fact that he was in his final month there.

"That's early, isn't it, Liam?" Terry asked.

"Yeah, about two weeks."

"What did you do to deserve that, you jammy bugger? Been grassing someone up?"

"Yeah, you guessed. I told them that it was you wot killed OG."

Liam, Denis and Terry all laughed. Kevin stayed stony silent. He couldn't help himself.

"What's up, Kevin?" Terry prompted. "You that upset about losing your little bum-chum?"

"To be perfectly honest, Terry, I will miss him. He may be a wasted, useless, dense junkie, but he's a nice fellow at heart."

Liam smiled warmly. It was a nice feeling to be liked by someone, but he didn't know what to say because it was so unusual. Terry spoke for him.

"Ah, that's sweet, Kevin. You can always arrange to see him again when you get out in four years' time, if ya still fancy him then."

He then turned his attention back to Liam. "Well, Liam, you'd better make the best of the next few days to try to win another scrabble game, eh? You probably won't find quality people like us on the outside to play scrabble-babble with."

"True," Liam replied, with some degree of sincerity.

They got on with it. As was often the case, Denis came up with the longest word for the first go. Unfortunately for him, it wasn't high-scoring. 'Desire' earned him only fourteen points. Terry quickly spotted 'embark' coming down from the second 'E' of 'desire'. This scored better because his letters were more valuable and he was also on a double word score, making twenty-eight. Liam was next and he had been lucky as he had picked up a 'Q' and a 'U' to go with it. With little delay, he found a place for 'quart' across the 'R' of 'embark'. It was a blinder. The 'Q' happened to be on a double letter score and the 'T' was on a double word score. All in all that came to a respectable forty-eight.

"Liam, the news of your release has cleared your mind!" Terry exclaimed, impressed.

Denis wasn't so generous. "I don't know why I usually go first. It just sets all you knobs up for the big scores. I think I'll let someone else go first next time."

"Now, you're learning." Terry teased.

It was Kevin's go. Was he going to get into the game today? Actually, he was very lucky on his first go. Not only did he have all the letters required to spell 'dioxides' by also using the 'D' of 'desire', but his 'X' fell on a triple letter score and to top it all, he got a double word score for using all of his letters. That made seventy points. Surely a start like that would keep anyone's mind on the game?

"You jammy fucker, Kevin! All your letters on your first go and an 'X' on a triple letter score. Mate, you need to start doing the lottery!"

"Are we allowed to do the lottery in here, Terry?"

"Yes mate, so long as your canteen can stretch to it."

"Hmmm. Maybe I should then."

Now it was Denis's turn again and it was proving to be a lucky game. Using a blank for a 'G' and going across the first 'D' of 'dioxides', Denis placed down all his letters to make 'bleeding'. The 'I' was on a double letter score, but the 'L' was on a double word score, so with his bonus, he scored forty-four.

"What a shame, I didn't have any decent letters like you lucky fuckers. My highest was a two!"

"Stop moaning, Denis, you retard," Terry admonished him. "Count yourself lucky. You used up all your letters. Now you might get some good ones!"

He rather sullenly dragged seven new letters out of the bag. They all watched him carefully to ensure he didn't cheat.

"What? Why are you all looking at me?"

"Just making sure you can count up to seven, ok, Denis."

He deliberately looked up as he picked his new letters, then, "Fuck. I don't believe it. All ones, bar one!"

"Karma, Denis," Liam spoke softly and meaningfully.

"What d'yer mean 'Karma'? This is just plain bad luck."

Denis was not happy. Now, he was really going to struggle to get another good score.

It was Terry's go again and he was eying up the 'Q' of 'quart' on the board as it was hovering over a triple word score three spaces down. It wasn't much of a word, but it did the job. He placed 'uit' beneath the 'Q' to make 'quit' and score an easy thirty-nine. Liam went next and he took his time choosing what to do. Finally, he spotted a rather fine opportunity to place 'peeping' down across the first 'E' of 'bleeding. The first 'P' was on a double letter score and the second lay over a double word score. That earned him thirty points. Kevin was next and he wanted to maintain his lead, especially as he had some really tasty letters. To get a decent score, all he had to do was place 'whi' in the top left-hand corner to line up with the 'P' of 'peeping' to make 'whip' for a triple word score of thirty-six. That was the end of round two.

"Scores, please, Kevin," Terry asked.

"Denis, fifty-eight; you, sixty-seven; Liam, seventy-eight; and me, one hundred and six."

"Ooh, Kevin, you're racing away this time. Anyone want to do a story?"

They all perused the board.

"I thought you might want to do one on 'peeping', Denis," Terry teased.

Liam sniggered.

"Very funny," Denis countered unenthusiastically.

"I don't think there's one there for me."

Nobody seemed keen, so they carried on with the game.

Denis struck lucky again. He got 'lonely' on a triple word score over the 'N' of 'bleeding'. That was thirty points. Then Terry rather cleverly put 'various' down across the 'I' of 'quit', with the 'S' attached to the bottom of 'embark'.

That earned him fourteen for 'various' and another fifteen for 'embarks'. Liam didn't take too long to find 'valve' over the 'V' of 'various'. That was on a double word score and made him twenty-two points.

Kevin was still ahead on the scoreboard, even though it was now his turn to finish the round off. He scored highly again. He made 'jiz' using the 'I' of 'desire'. Both of his letters fell on double letter scores, providing a score of thirty-seven for just two additional letters.

"Mate, that's wicked!" Liam exclaimed. "That was brilliant. You know what jiz is, don't you, Kevin?"

"I think so, Liam. I think it's slang for semen."

Liam laughed. "What? Sailors?"

"You know what kind of semen I mean."

Terry added some additional knowledge.

"I think it refers more to the actual act of cumming on a part of a body, like 'he jizzed on her tits'."

"Yes, thank you for that, Terry. I don't think we need to know about your jizzing fetishes," Denis added.

"Just saying, Denis. Don't want Liam not getting the definition quite right. I mean, this is about improving our English, right? You gonna do a story with that one then?"

Denis laughed. "I don't think so, Terry."

The scores were in the same order as the previous round, except that Kevin had extended his lead.

"Come on. Someone's got to do a story, otherwise, we're just playing scrabble and not scrabble-babble and I did the last one."

The others scoured the board once again. Kevin spoke.

"I can do one. I don't think it's going to be very interesting though. It's kind of banal."

Terry asked him. "Yeah, ok, but will it be more interesting than one of Denis's stories?"

"Oh, yes," Kevin added quickly.

"Well, do it then."

"Ok. I'm going to do two words actually in the same story."

"Ooh, get you!" Liam teased.

"Yeah, but you don't get double points for that though," Denis quickly added.

"Not a problem, Denis. I really don't need the points."

He gave a little smile and continued.

"Well, it goes back about six years when the girls were about seven or eight. Susie had been a full-on mum since they were born, but by now, she was climbing up the walls a bit and she wanted to do something occasionally with just me."

"Kevin, is it going to be a juicy 'jiz' story?" Liam asked cheekily.

"No, Liam, definitely not. Anyway, Susie organised a babysitter, then all we had to do was find something we could enjoy together during an occasional evening. She scoured all the adverts in local papers and found this dance class nearby. Neither of us were dancers but she fancied giving it a try. I wasn't too keen, you know, the typical male attitude of two left feet and all that, but I wanted to keep her happy, so I agreed to it. Gotta say I was really nervous the first time we went."

"What kind of dancing was it?" Denis enquired.

"Modern jive, Denis. I'd never even heard of it."

"Oh yes, I've heard of that, Kevin. I've tried a bit of ballroom and tango myself in the past. I have to say, it was quite fun and I seemed to be a bit of a natural."

"Denis, you're interrupting him," Terry chided.

"Sorry, I'm sure."

Kevin continued. "Anyway, I won't bore you with all the details. What I will say is that it was incredibly sociable. All the other dancers were amazingly friendly and helpful. It was harder for me because the blokes have to learn the moves and the women have to learn to follow the male lead. They pick up their bit far quicker than the men do. It was a strange thing to do though, as a married couple, because you spend most of the evening in the arms of other partners, not your own."

"Wow, Kevin, sounds like great fun."

"Sssshhh, Terry, you're interrupting."

Terry gave Denis a dirty look.

"We carried on doing the lessons once a week and what they called the freestyle weekend dance, once a month, for about two years. We were both getting quite good at it, well, particularly Susie. She was a great mover."

Liam asked a question. "Kevin, if it's not about jizzing, what word are you using?"

"Sorry, I have been remiss. What I should have said by now is that we embarked on a new hobby. Dancing."

"Dancing's not on the board."

"No, Liam. Embark. We embarked on a new hobby."

"Ah. Yes. Now I see."

"And what is the other word?"

"Quit, Liam. Quit, because after about two years of doing it with great relish, we quit."

"Why on earth would you do that? It sounds like you really enjoyed it."

"We did, but Susie suddenly went down with a bad case of vertigo. For a while, she could barely stand up. Dancing was out of the question until she got better but she never fully recovered. We tried getting back into it, but it's the worst thing for vertigo because the ladies get spun around a heck of a lot and that made her feel ill, so we had to stop."

"Kevin, you could have carried on though?"

"Not without Susie. That wouldn't have been fair. We both stopped and we both missed it enormously. That's it. I told you it was going to be a rather dull story. Compared to you guys, I'm afraid I've led a rather dull life."

None of them argued with that. Terry tried to think of something encouraging to say but with Kevin banged up for a lot longer than the rest of them, he couldn't think of anything positive.

"Fifty more points then, Kevin. Your score must be huge by now."

In fact, he had about twice what anyone else had. They decided to leave the rest of the game for the next day. Kevin and Liam went out for a fag and Denis and Terry went off to fetch hot drinks and to watch the rest of the throng doing whatever they were doing.

The following morning, a Friday, was one of the mornings when Liam and Denis were not otherwise occupied and so they were both under lock and key for the morning. Terry was at the gym and Kevin was cleaning. He was looking forward to seeing Susie the very next day. All the visits of the previous weekend had been cancelled because of the lockdown but had been reinstated for this weekend instead. This would be only her second visit to him in about six weeks. After his cleaning was completed and before going to fetch dinner, he got his shower kit from his cell and entered the showers. It was his favourite time to shower because he would probably be alone with no one to mock him.

Unfortunately on this occasion, his peace and quiet was very much disturbed. Thomas Bennett, together with Devenish and Ashley, entered the showers. They were fully clothed. Now that Lenny was gone, Thomas was the new top dog in that clan.

"Turn the fucking shower off, you spastic!" he growled.

Kevin did as he was ordered. He instinctively held his hands over his genitals and faced Thomas who slapped him across the face for no apparent reason. This was a habit he had copied from Lenny. It was useful to humiliate someone without causing obvious injury. It was also rather shocking for the recipient but at least he didn't have his glasses on.

"What the fuck happened to that knife, you disgusting moron?"

Kevin was pleased that he had urinated before entering the shower. He was sure that he would be wetting himself now if he had a full bladder and that would have annoyed Thomas standing so close to him.

"I delivered it to Lenny as instructed."

"You are a lying cunt."

He slapped Kevin again.

"Who the fuck did you give it to?"

"I told you, Lenny, of course."

Thomas stood up real close to Kevin, face to face. He wasn't nearly as repulsive as Lenny had been this close-up, probably because he was a lot younger and had a lot of rapid deterioration ahead of him, but his breath was quite unpleasant, warm, sour and rather pungent.

"Then you tell me how the fuck that knife ended up in Lenny's chest and not in his hand!"

Thomas was grimacing fiercely, his mouth taut, his eyes bulging. Kevin was genuinely terrified of him.

"I've got no idea. I gave him the knife just before the riot started."

At this point, Thomas pinned Kevin against the wall with his left hand pressing onto his right shoulder and he pressed a cold sharp object into Kevin's fat stomach with his right hand. Kevin looked down to see that Thomas was pressing a screwdriver into his rolls of belly fat. He sensed his anal sphincter beginning to twitch erratically. He really hoped that he wouldn't actually shit himself.

"Look, you repulsive fat cunt, if you don't tell me right now who you gave that knife to, you are going to bleed to death right here, right now."

He pressed the screwdriver harder. The terror Kevin felt in the moment didn't entirely anaesthetise the pain of the sharp metal beginning to pierce his skin. He was in no doubt that Thomas was perfectly ready to drive it all the way home. He had a reputation for being very violent and inside, it was important that inmates lived up to their reputations. Nobody wanted to go soft just because they were behind bars. Kevin sensed that his only hope was to somehow bluff his way out of this lethal circumstance. In desperation, he pushed himself way beyond his usual emotional limitations. He had to outsmart this moron.

"You can stick that screwdriver in me, you thick cunt, but you need to know it will be the last thing you ever do."

Thomas laughed, partly out of nervous shock at Kevin standing up for himself and partly out of surprise at what he actually just said.

"Fucktard, are you going to take us all on? You couldn't even handle one of us."

He laughed some more and the others laughed too. He pressed the screwdriver harder. Kevin's mind was racing. He wasn't that bothered about living anymore, but he didn't want to die at the hands of this contemptible thug, nor with the end of a screwdriver stuck into his vital organs. He was thinking at warp speed.

"Why do you think that the big Ginger wiped the floor with your cunty friends over there a few weeks ago?"

Thomas looked shocked. He wondered what on earth Kevin was implying and what he was on.

"Are you fucking delirious? What the fuck are you talking about?"

"You heard me, you moron. Do you think Ginger attacked them because of some weird affection for the hapless Liam?"

"What?" Thomas was having trouble keeping up.

"No, you idiot. He did it because I asked him to. On the outside, he and I have a very significant connection which you don't need to know about. What you do need to know is that he owes me. A lot. I wanted to protect Liam, simply because I like him and I used Ginger to do it. If I come to any harm at all, he will avenge me. If you're stupid enough to hurt me today, I don't think that you and your pathetic grovelling mates will survive the weekend. Now go ahead and stick your fucking screwdriver in me. I will die happy, knowing that you will all be beaten to death soon. Your ugly faces will be smashed to smithereens. You deserve no less, you vile motherfuckers."

He looked intensely into Thomas's eyes. The fact that he actually wasn't scared of death gave him a strength which Thomas couldn't help but pick up on. He misinterpreted that boldness as Kevin being honest. He pulled the screwdriver away from his stomach, somewhat confused. He looked at Kevin for a few moments whilst gathering his thoughts. Things had taken a strange turn and he had to rethink. To be fair, he regrouped his mind quite quickly and on a completely different tack, he said, "I've been told that you want gear. Are you going to put your fat revolting body to sleep, cunt face?"

Kevin just looked at him defiantly, silently.

"Well, fucktard, I'll get the gear to you and let's see if you've got the bollocks to do it. If not, I'll stick this screwdriver inside your guts anyway and that ginger cunt's. I'll sort you both out! And I don't make idle threats."

With that, he gave Kevin one very hard final slap, turned and left. The others quickly joined him without saying anything.

Kevin started to sob. He couldn't help himself. He felt upset, hurt, alone, vulnerable and suicidal. All sorts of horrible emotions rolled into a mass of self-loathing and disgust for prison life in general, and himself. He sank on his naked buttocks and sobbed some more. A few minutes later, some other inmates entered the showers, naked, to actually shower.

"Look at that blubbery retard. What a fucking feeble excuse of a man." one of them cajoled, for no particular reason, but at least they didn't piss on him. Kevin got to his feet and went out to dry and dress. He'd suffered enough humiliation and fear for the time being.

That afternoon he attended an English lesson. As always, it was a great antidote to the mundane and dramatic unpleasantness of prison life. He really admired Mr Blanchflower. Partly because he had such a way with these awful inmates and partly because he possessed compassion that he had rarely witnessed in another human being before. He found him inspiring. He wasn't learning any English from him, of course, but he was learning about integrity, benevolence and kindness. He was particularly quiet and subdued during this lesson but it served as an oasis in a desert of nastiness.

Later, following tea, they continued their game. Once they settled down, Denis placed 'half' across the 'L' of 'valve', on a double word score and his 'F' was also above the 'A' of 'various'. That gave him a score of twenty-five.

Terry was going for the triple word score at the bottom left corner of the board. He placed 'wince' there, joining up with the 'E' of 'valve'. The 'C' was on a triple letter score, so all in all, he scored a rather good thirty-nine. If he was to do a story now, his tally would be just behind Kevin's. On his go, Liam used up quite a lot of letters, but not to much avail. He placed 'butted' down from the 'B' of 'bleeding'. His first 'T' was on a triple letter score, but that was his only enhancement and he scored a mere eleven. As he replenished his letters, he warned the others, "Hardly any spare letters left now, boys."

Kevin didn't need to do much. He simply placed 'et' at the end of 'quart' to make 'quartet' for sixteen points. Then Denis placed but one letter down, an 'R' at the end of 'wince'. It also formed 'far' with the 'fa' above it. That scored him seventeen points and he picked up the last spare letter. Terry used some of the large free space on the right-hand side of the board. He placed 'lanyard' across from the second 'L' of 'lonely' on a double word score to make twenty-two more points. Now, if he did a story, he would be a mere two points behind Kevin.

Liam was trailing everyone, even Denis, but he was about to play a blinder that would change things dramatically. He put 'informs' down the right-hand side of the board, with the 'F' on a triple word score and using up all his letters and in such a way that his 'S' went on the end of 'quartet' earning him 'quartets' too. He got thirty-six for 'informs', seventeen for 'quartets' and doubling those for using up all his letters, gave him a grand total of one hundred and six.

This was even enough to distract Kevin from his pressing worries, and he congratulated him. "Liam, you are the master. One hundred and six! Astonishing. I never thought anyone was going to catch me!"

Liam couldn't help himself. He stood and did a little jig with his hands in the air with a very big smile on his face. It was a double whammy for Denis and Kevin as they both still had seven tiles left and now the game was over with Liam being the clear winner.

Denis had to deduct nine from his score, leaving him one hundred and twenty-one. Terry only had to take off two, leaving him one hundred and fifty-five. Kevin had to deduct seven, leaving him two hundred and two, but Liam's score was a magnificent two hundred and seventeen. They all stood and awarded him a high-five. Denis looked exasperated. He couldn't understand how he had constantly done so badly against these lowlifes. He was the only one not to have won a game thus far, in six games and this time, for the first time, he came last. He wanted to go away and sulk.

Liam proudly announced that he deserved a smoke and invited Kevin out into the yard with him.

"Liam, you carry on. I'll join you in just a mo."

Denis went off to get some diesel or mud and a very vexed Kevin invited Terry to one side, away from prying ears.

"Terry, I have a confession to make. You need to be aware of it."

"Kevin, did you use some naughty words to someone?"

Kevin swallowed hard. "Sort of. Actually, I took your name in vain."

Terry looked puzzled. "Can you explain?"

"I got threatened by someone and I saved myself by pretending that you would avenge me. That we had a connection. I'm sorry."

Terry looked at him thoughtfully, then said

"And?"

"I thought you might be cross?"

Terry thought some more, trying to read between the lines.

"That's ok, mate. You obviously thought on your feet. Well done. You're learning. Everybody in here is full of bullshit. Why not you too, eh? It'll help you get along."

Kevin was relieved that Terry wasn't bothered. Then, after consideration, and as the penny dropped, Terry looked sternly at Kevin and asked rather fiercely,

"Kevin, who's been threatening you ?"

He was perplexed and looked genuinely concerned. Kevin had worked out what had happened when he got cross about Liam being picked on.

"I'd rather not go into that Terry if you don't mind."

"Your prerogative, buddy. Fancy a cup of mud?"

Chapter 22

The following morning, Saturday, found Kevin feeling extremely nervous, because he was going to get a visit from his wife. He wondered how he could feel so equivocal about seeing the love of his life from whom he had become separated for so long. Just like last time, he had trouble filling in the time before she was due to arrive at 2 p.m. He flitted between the library and the association room, always mindful of keeping well away from anyone connected to Bennett's crowd. Just before dinner and even though he had become very nervous of using the showers, he went for a shower to spruce himself up and to shave. He wanted to look his best for her, although he felt like a wreck.

At ten to two, he was escorted to the visiting room and was placed at a central table, where he sat and watched the visitor's door. The room soon became full of inmates. The prison was catching up on last weekend's visits, which had been postponed and was trying to fit in some that had originally been scheduled for this weekend, rather than reschedule all of them. She walked in and he watched her, tears in his eyes. This time he was determined to control his emotions better. In his mind, he knew that this would probably be the very last time he saw her and he wanted to make the most of it.

When she arrived at his table, he stood and they hugged until an officer came over and ordered them to sit and stay apart. She looked lovely. She had a lovely colourful dress on and had clearly had her hair done for the visit. She was wearing his favourite perfume 'fantasy' by Britney Spears. He loved that perfume. He realised how lucky he was to have a woman like this. He had let her down so absolutely, yet here she was trying to look her best for him and she was all ready to do her best to pick up his spirits.

"Babe, how are you? You're beginning to look younger!" she said brightly.

He was of course still overweight, but he had been losing weight quite rapidly and his face in particular was less chubby, making his features stand out better.

"Yeah, sure," he replied, thinking it mere flattery. "But really, you look fantastic, darling."

She did look fantastic. She rewarded him with a lovely smile.

"Well, hun, how are you getting on now? Have you settled down a little yet?"

She looked into his eyes with deep sincerity. She wanted to know that he was finding it easier. Her deep sincere concern rocked him emotionally.

"I'll never settle down in here, honey. The place is evil."

She looked disappointed. He didn't want to disappoint her but he also couldn't lie to her. She would know if he lied to her. He changed the subject.

"How are the girls?"

"They're fine. They are looking forward to being allowed to come in for a family visit. I'm told that we can do that after you've been here three months."

Kevin pondered that. Three months. That would still be six or seven weeks away. An eternity. He never wanted his daughters to see him in there, dressed as a prisoner. Simples. He wouldn't still be there in seven weeks, probably not even in one week, but he couldn't tell her that. He wouldn't be seeing his daughters again. He wanted them to have only good memories of him. They carried on talking easily for the whole hour. She told him how much she missed him and that she was so lonely without him. That didn't help. He didn't want her to be lonely. He would be doing something to put that right. He spoke earnestly.

"Susie, I have a confession to make."

That sounded ominous. She looked at him lovingly, encouragingly.

"This place changes people. I am no longer the man you married."

Her face contorted into deep concern.

"Darling, of course, you are. You're still the same man that I married and I still love you."

"You don't understand. This place has changed me. I am a different person. I do different things."

"She looked at him quizzically, perplexed by what he could possibly mean. She felt sorry for him. Of course, he was struggling with this regime, these people and the fact of being imprisoned. She understood that. She didn't want him to elaborate. She wanted him to fight the notion that this place was changing him.

"Darling. Please, be strong. You can do it. Don't let it change you. I am being strong for you. I will always support you, my darling."

With that, she grabbed his hands and held them. Visiting time was nearly over, so fuck the guards. Within seconds, the bell went and people started moving. She held onto his hands as all the moving bodies screened them. As the room emptied, they stayed sitting, holding hands. A guard eventually came over and invited her to leave, dishing out a dirty look for the holding of hands. They stood, gazing into each other's eyes. Kevin wanted to remember that look forever. Then, she turned and left and he really did feel a little bit stronger. He knew what he had to do.

Sunday morning was Liam's last weekend stint in the kitchen. The rest of the day and Monday passed in usual fashion.

On Tuesday afternoon, Kevin had a session with his personal officer Jacobs.

"Kevin, how are you? Sorry, I missed you last week, but obviously, circumstances weren't normal and the police didn't want any personal meetings to be conducted."

"Yes, I know."

"How was your interview."

"Boring. I had nothing to say. Embarrassing. I had to confess to them that I just hid in the corner and trembled pathetically."

"That's nothing to be ashamed of, Kevin. To my mind, that's just showing a bit of common sense. You didn't get hurt at all, did you?"

"No. I stayed as far from the action as possible."

"Have there been any other problems?"

"You mean apart from my cellmate overdosing and dying underneath me and me getting caught up in a riot in which another inmate died? um, no, I don't think so."

There was no way he was going to let her know about his issues with Bennett. That would mean revealing his part in hiding the knife.

"Oh, that's good. I can assure you, Kevin, that our death rate here is not normally as high as one a fortnight."

"That's very reassuring, considering I'm in for four years."

She looked at him wearily. His sarcasm and cynicism were not easy for her to overcome. She changed her look to a stern one momentarily before asking another question.

"How was your visit with Susie?"

He wasn't prepared for that question and immediately he felt emotional. Being a woman, Mary picked up on his reaction immediately.

"Kevin, what's wrong?"

He remained silent. He didn't want to talk about Susie. He wouldn't be seeing her again and any thoughts of her now upset him.

"Kevin, I can see that something about Susie is really upsetting you. I am a good person for you to talk to about it. Really, I am. I've done Home-Office-approved courses on relationships you know."

Kevin pulled himself together a bit.

"I'm sorry, Mary. I appreciate your support. I really do, but please, I really don't want to talk about Susie, ok?"

"Ok, Kevin. Absolutely. Just so long as you know. Ok, is there anything you do want to talk about?"

"No, not really, but thank you, anyway."

She leaned back on her chair looking at him. In his own way, he was a tough nut to crack. Like many men, she thought, he hid his feelings and inside prison, that was not usually a good thing. She decided to call the meeting to a close and escorted him back to his cell.

Tuesday was very different for Liam. He had a visit from his probation officer. She had to be satisfied that she knew where he would be living on release and that she approved his residence and that he was willing to submit himself to weekly probation appointments. She was very impressed to learn that whilst inside for the past eight months, he had been on a methadone programme with reducing the dosage and he'd recently actually become clean. She was really pleased for him and she would do her best to encourage him into some gainful employment after release. He was due to be released on Thursday at 9 a.m. Immediately after her visit, he phoned Kaz to confirm what day and at what time she could collect him. He was excited and yet strangely, he would miss the camaraderie of being inside.

Wednesday evening, Denis won his first scrabble game. The others had been playing half-heartedly because they wanted Liam to win and go out on a high, but Denis couldn't help but take advantage. However, at least Liam came a healthy second. He had really enjoyed the scrabble games and despite his poor grammar and spelling, he had performed so well and it had boosted his confidence enormously. He had also enjoyed the friendship of the team players. He was very grateful to Kevin for the support he had given him in all the English lessons since he had arrived.

Thursday morning during exercise time in the yard, a lot of the inmates came over to Liam to genuinely wish him all the best. It was cold and grey, but fortunately, not raining. He felt really good. Judging by the number of inmates popping out to bid him farewell, he seemed to be quite popular. Terry and Kevin were the last ones to say goodbye. They both escorted him to the corridor gate with Officer Herman, where they said their final goodbyes. They all felt awkward, not knowing how much emotion to show, yet they all appreciated the sincerity of the situation. Liam was led through the gate and Kevin and Terry watched him disappear through another door.

"I'll miss him," Kevin said quietly.

"Yeah, I know you will, bud, but now you've got to try to make new friends in here. I know it's not easy for a prick like you, but you've got to try."

Kevin gave him a quick glance and casually agreed, even though he knew that he wasn't going to try at all.

That evening association time, Kevin, Denis and Terry met at their usual table out of habit. They sat down and just started chatting wistfully about Liam when officer Prowse came over to them with a young black man in tow, who was grinning broadly.

"Guys, Mr Blanchflower asked if you would be good enough to include young Emmanuel here in your scrabble game in lieu of Liam. Would that be ok?"

The three of them were eminently polite and affable and naturally accepted his company. None of them had ever spoken to him before. He was a fish. He'd only been in there about two weeks, but he had missed out on the excitement of the riot because he hadn't made it into the canteen in time. Emmanuel sat in Liam's chair and officer Prowse left them to it.

Terry explained to the newcomer how they played scrabble-babble. Emmanuel seemed excited at the thought of storytelling. He had spent most of his life in Nigeria, near the capital city of Lagos and in Africa, telling stories was a way of life, quite unlike in the west, where entertainment was more about just watching things. In time, they would find that he was always enthusiastic about telling a story. If nobody else could do a story during each round, he would happily tell one for them.

He was never stumped for one, so they had to limit his storytelling points to one award per game, or else he would have constantly run away with the highest score every single game. He was very demonstrative and his stories were generally centred on nature, mostly wild animals, but sometimes the weather, or plants and only occasionally about people. Telling stories made him feel much more at home. He smiled a great deal and was a pleasure to have on board. He was only twenty-two. No doubt in time, his own story would be pieced together for them via his numerous babbles.

Friday passed as normal. Saturday held a bonus for Terry and Denis who both had their usual visits lined up. Denis always acted as if his mother's visit was nothing more than an embarrassment but if you watched him very closely beforehand, there were little ticks that gave away positive anticipation. Emmanuel would receive no visitors. He had no relatives nearby at all. He apparently had some distant relatives in London but no one close enough to him in any sense of the word to be interested in visiting him in prison.

Kevin was beginning to wonder how long it would take before Bennett would get his merchandise to him. He wondered if he could call it merchandise if he wasn't actually paying for it. His product. He appreciated that it might take a while because since the riot and the discovery of such a large weapon, cell searches had increased both in frequency and vigour. Mr Dibden was paranoid about more embarrassing developments and he was doing his utmost to ensure that the possibility of further embarrassing passage or use of contraband was minimised.

For Kevin, the very thought of actually receiving what he had asked for was disconcerting in itself. He had never injected himself with anything and as he was such a wimp, even sticking a tiny needle into his flesh perturbed him. He only knew the ropes vaguely from having seen this sort of thing done in films, so it was going to be weird trying to get it right the first time without any help. He couldn't ask anyone for tips because he couldn't afford to alert anyone. He had to conquer this task by himself and just hope that he got it right the first time.

Sunday Morning found him flitting between the library and the association room as was his wont. He returned to his cell just after midday with his dinner for lockup time. Roger was already there, scoffing messily and noisily on the lower bunk. Kevin climbed up onto the top bunk where he discovered a strange tobacco pouch. It was nothing to do with Roger who didn't smoke. He sat on his bunk to eat his dinner and acted normally, but when he had finished eating, he lay down, facing the wall, to secretly and eagerly examine the pouch. Within it, there was quite a bit of loose tobacco but shielded inside that was a syringe, a small lump of brown resin wrapped in a dirty piece of paper, a metal teaspoon and a tiny plastic sachet containing a liquid.

From what he had gleaned from TV films, he understood that he had to open the sachet, pour the liquid onto the spoon with the heroin on it too and heat it from beneath to dissolve the brown substance into the liquid. He wondered if you were supposed to let it cool down before you injected it. Films aren't always accurate. They have to move at a certain pace after all. He would need a lighter but he didn't have one.

He was in no mood to carry out the act hastily. Now that he had the apparatus to control his destiny within his hands, his mind focussed on other last-minute arrangements, like, should he leave Susie a note? He was going to do this so that she could be a free woman again and rid herself of her criminal burden. Would leaving her a note add to or diminish her initial anguish? He wanted to minimise her trauma because he did love her very much and he decided that she would probably want answers. So the kindest thing he could do, in addition to actually freeing her was to provide some answers.

He had no pen and paper. For reasons unclear to him, they were strictly rationed inside prison. Even asking for such items could raise suspicions about his intentions. He asked Roger if he had any. Roger said no, but he knew where he could get some.

"Really? Would you mind getting me a couple of pages and something to write with?"

"I think I could do that," Roger responded proudly.

"But Roger, it's very important that you don't say what, or rather who, you want it for, ok?"

"Ok, mate. Mum's the word."

Kevin wondered where that strange but common expression had originated. After dinner time lock-up, they both left the cell. Again, when Kevin next returned, with tea at about 5 p.m., Roger was already there and he proudly handed him two sheets of paper and a half pencil. Kevin scoffed his tea as quickly as possible and got down to composing. The hour until unlock time again passed extremely quickly. He really wanted to stay in his cell and carry on composing but that would look most odd for him, so he left the cell and joined his scrabble buddies as usual. He'd be back before 8 p.m. and he would be able to carry on then.

The games were taking much longer now because Emmanuel talked so much. Of course, Terry and Denis were rude and disparaging towards him as they would have been towards any other player but Emmanuel was getting used to the brutish, British sense of humour and he took their cajoling in the good spirits in which they were intended. Funnily enough, three or four other inmates

242

would now regularly sit alongside their scrabble table just to be entertained by Emmanuel's stories and the cajoling that accompanied them, of course.

Terry and Denis didn't relish the extra attention and were more careful with their own stories because of it, but then the dynamics of the game was always going to be different with Liam gone, especially as he had been replaced with a very different, loud new player and they had to accept that. Kevin's mind was very far from the game and Terry kept telling him to wake up, to absolutely no avail.

Later that evening, after the scrabble session finished for the day, Kevin eagerly returned to his cell to continue getting his thoughts down on paper. By late evening, one sheet was covered back and front with copious notes and the pencil was blunt, but he was nowhere near satisfied as to what exactly to say.

"Roger, how am I supposed to re-sharpen this pencil?" he enquired lamely.

Roger gave a little chuckle.

"I can't do it in here, mate, but I can do it for you tomorrow."

Kevin handed him down the stumpy pencil.

"Thanks, mate. I really appreciate it."

He hid his notes inside the cut in the mattress with the tobacco pouch. This was deeply secret stuff, and the note was sacred.

Monday was particularly exciting for Emmanuel because it was the start of a week when he was being allowed to participate in both the woodworking classes and the English classes. He was very upbeat about anything positive and his happy demeanour cheered up the more miserable and sedate around him. Kevin simply couldn't believe how anyone could be so upbeat whilst inside a shitty prison. It must be something to do with the African mentality, he thought.

After the evening scrabble session and back in his cell, Roger handed him a nicely sharpened pencil and he started using up the second sheet. By the end of that evening, that sheet was also simply covered in notes and drafts. Explaining to a loved one why you were ending your life for them was a much more difficult task than he could ever have imagined.

The next day, as soon as both he and Roger were awake, he asked Roger if he would be able to get him one more sheet of paper and a cigarette lighter. To his surprise, Roger seemed confident that he could.

That afternoon he was due to have another personal meeting with Mary. He wasn't looking forward to it. He didn't want her trying to pry inside his mind. He couldn't reveal to anyone what was really going on inside his mind. It had to

243

remain a secret, or else he would be thwarted. After he had done what he needed to do, then everyone could know how he felt. Nevertheless, he attended the meeting with her, simply determined to be his normal, closed, awkward self. After the usual pleasantries and him not giving away any leads and no proper conversations being developed, as usual, she came up with a surprise.

"Kevin, someone has asked to have a visit with you."

"Susie?"

"No, Karen Smith."

Kevin looked quite bewildered.

"I don't know a Karen Smith. Who is she?"

Mary didn't want to explain. She knew more than she was prepared to let on.

"I can't say any more than what I have already said, Kevin."

"Excuse me, but you haven't said anything yet. Who is she?"

"Kevin, please. I can't explain. All I can do is ask you if you want to accept the visit or not."

"How am I supposed to know that if I don't know what it's about? Why the mystery?"

He started to worry. All of a sudden his thoughts turned to the investigation. He wondered if it was about the knife, or his interview, or something another inmate might have said about him, or maybe the package in his mattress even. Had Roger said something to someone?

"Is she a solicitor?"

"No."

"Police?"

"No, Kevin and please, I don't want to play twenty questions."

"I'm supposed to be seeing Susie on Saturday. Isn't that my allocation of visits all used up?"

"You can have this one as an extra. It could be on Thursday evening."

Kevin wasn't happy about not being given further information

"Why can't you tell me who she is?"

"Because it's personal."

Now he was completely perplexed.

"As my personal officer, do you think I should take this personal visit?"

"Yes, Kevin, I do."

She looked very sincere and now he was more curious than worried.

"What time?"

"Six o'clock? Are you going to accept it?"

He considered quietly for a few moments.

"Ok, I'll take it, but if there are any negative consequences, I won't have any more meetings with you, ok?"

She looked at him slightly victoriously.

"No problem."

"And I'll put a complaint in."

"Thanks, Kevin. I love you too."

She returned him to his cell.

Chapter 23

The following day, Kevin was busy all day with cleaning and the English class, which was rather frustrating because he so wanted to complete his letter to Susie. He was now paired up with Emmanuel in English, whose natural ebullience still exasperated him somewhat.

Roger had managed to get both the items he had requested and he wanted no payment for them. During his spare time at mealtimes in his cell and after the evening association time, Kevin completed his suicide note in his best hand, slowly and with deep consideration. He was finally happy with it and he flushed the two pages of drafts down the toilet. The final missive read as follows.

"My darling, if you are reading this love letter to you then I have already passed on into the next life and you will already know this. I want you to know that I haven't ended my life because of the pure misery that prison serves up, garnished with eternal anguish, pain and regret. No, my darling. My love for you could tolerate and endure anything, even prison and I can be brave. I have ended my life because it was our life, one we began together, as one flesh, over twenty years ago, but because of my folly that life and support has been denied to you. You are now suffering as much as am I and for absolutely no guilt on your part whatsoever. That is my worst crime, my heaviest guilt.

I am convinced that freed from your bond to me, you will soon rebuild your life in a far better way. You are a beautiful, vivacious and capable woman with such a wonderful capacity for love. You may feel upset and even more let down for a short season by my leaving you behind but I am convinced that as that season ebbs away, as it will surely do, you will be grateful to me for releasing you into a new and better life.

Please don't think of me as a coward who couldn't face four long years behind bars. The way things are going for me here, I can't see myself qualifying for parole ever. It is more likely that my sentence will be extended time and again. I fear I might become the new Charles Bronson! really and that is not a prospect I am willing to face myself, nor to subject you to the ignominy and hardship that accompanies it. Tell my daughters that I love them both very, very much and will be watching their progress throughout life from above. I will be their guardian angel and yours too. Thank you for all your love and devotion. It will sustain me in eternity and for eternity.

Until we meet again,

All my love forever, Kevin xx"

The MIR had wrapped up over a week ago, exactly one week after the final interviews had been completed. The team had gone over and over every detail with a toothpick. It had been like they had disassembled a haystack blade by blade to find the needle, only to find there had never been a needle in there in the first place. Then they had double-checked all the blades again, to try to find that elusive needle, but to no avail.

Mr Bertrand couldn't possibly justify keeping the team assembled any longer. They had done a great deal of work and had been very thorough, but with no fresh leads, there was simply nothing left for them to do. They had interviewed on tape eighty suspects and over twenty prison officers had also been interviewed informally, but he had to concede that in spite of all that hard work, they had drawn a blank. Valuable resources had to be deployed elsewhere. Mr Bertrand himself was now OIC in another knife murder but that one would be a relative walk in the park compared to Wingnut. He had CCTV, known suspects, testosterone and gang related motivation, witnesses and conveniently small numbers of people to deal with.

Of course, the Marshall investigation would remain open until solved, if ever and each officer involved in the case could still access the Holmes computer records at any time, should they wish to do so. The OIC was now DI Brand because he and DS Starchley had conducted some of the most relevant interviews during the course of the investigation, but even they had both gone on to other cases.

If there was any major development in the case, Mr Bertrand would get involved again, but that looked eminently unlikely at this point in time. Any new information would be directed in the direction of DI Brand in the first instance. Of course, the whole team felt disheartened. Mr Bertrand had never failed to prosecute a murder investigation and so he was especially disappointed and perplexed. Sadly though, they were all focussing on new cases now.

The following day was Thursday when Kevin was due to meet this mysterious Karen Smith at 6 p.m. Having completed his letter and having the means to end his life quietly and painlessly in his sleep, he was feeling unusually contented. He breezed through the day, having determined that tomorrow, Friday, would definitely be his last day on this ungrateful planet. The best time to administer his medicine would be shortly after lights out, after Roger was asleep, snoring his head off as usual. Then when Susie attended her visit the following day, they could explain to her in person what had happened during the night and give his letter to her instead. That would be lovely. Perfect timing. Almost romantic.

Whilst collecting dinner, he bumped into Terry. His curiosity about Roger piqued.

"Hey Terry, do you know my celly Roger?"

"Not really. From what little I do know about him, I feel sorry for him."

"Yeah, he seems rather unfortunate in many ways, yet he seems to be able to get things done which might be beyond someone like me."

"And you're wondering how he manages that, right?"

"Yes."

Terry looked around to make sure no one else was listening, and then he said quietly, "I don't know this from personal experience, you understand Kevin, but I've heard he does a fuckin' good blowjob because he hasn't't got many teeth."

Terry was matter-of-fact. Kevin was horrified. The thought turned his stomach. He really wished he hadn't asked.

Later on, after tea and having been locked up all afternoon, he was keen to get out and meet this visitor. He was escorted to the meeting room where he sat at one of the side tables. It was very different from a bustling weekend. There was only one other couple present on the far side of the room. They appeared to be a mother and son and were talking very quietly. He had to wait for about five minutes before the visitor door opened and he watched a slightly chubby, scruffy woman in her early thirties approach him with a guard. She was quite unremarkable. She was wearing old jeans and a jumper underneath a brown anorak. Her skin was very pale and her hair was light brown, shoulder-length and looked like it could do with a good wash and comb.

He politely stood to welcome her and invited her to sit. The guard left the room. There was already one other guard in the room and that was quite enough for just two couples. He noticed that she didn't smell very nice at all.

"Thank you for seeing me," she said stoically.

She noted his quizzical look.

"You don't know who I am, do you?"

"I've been told your name, but that's all."

"Oh, they're buggers, aren't they? I thought they would have told you."

"Clearly not."

"I am Liam's partner."

"Oh." Now Kevin was alarmed. Why was she visiting him and not Liam?

"I wanted you to know that when Liam got out he spoke very highly of you and I wanted to thank you personally for befriending him. It meant a lot to him."

"You don't need to thank me, love, he was good company. Did he tell you about our scrabble games?"

Kevin smiled at the memory.

"I couldn't stop him. He called it scrabble-babble because you told stories, right?"

That brought a little smile to her face. Her voice was rather monotone, much like Liam's funnily enough.

"Yes. Liam was a surprisingly good storyteller. It was Mr Blanchflower's idea. He thought it would help Liam master the English language a little better, but in fact, we all enjoyed it."

"Oh yes, he mentioned him too. He admired him as well."

"And how is our Liam settling back in the big wide world?" Kevin asked brightly and jealously.

The smile disappeared from Karen's face. Kevin sensed her sadness and he knew instantly that something bad had happened.

"What's happened?" He asked pertly.

"I suppose that's why they didn't tell you why I was coming to see you, Kevin. They wanted me to tell you personally."

"Tell me what?"

"Liam's dead."

Her cold steady words punched him in the chest. He felt shocked and alarmed.

"What? How?"

"He went to a mate's house the day after his release. The stupid bugger took too much gear. They all got stoned. I'm afraid he's too easily influenced, Kevin.

It was too much for him and it killed him. It's called tolerance, Kevin, or lack of it."

Kevin was too upset to discuss the matter further. He looked down and saw his tears pooling on the tabletop. He rested his arms on the table, laid his head down and sobbed quietly.

Karen carried on in her rather detached way.

"I'm sorry, Kevin. I really didn't mean to upset you."

She sat quietly observing him, unemotionally. She had suffered so much trauma in her own life that was more or less impervious to emotional pain now but she did feel genuinely sorry for Kevin. He carried on sobbing for quite a while. He had liked Liam but his sobbing was partly to do with his own life coming apart at the seams too. The sudden sad news about Liam triggered a release in him. The emotions were all getting rolled into one mass of sadness and extreme disappointment and he felt completely overwhelmed. She didn't touch him like Susie would have. She just sat quietly. She was a patient woman. Eventually, when she saw that his sobbing was ebbing away, she spoke again.

"Kevin, I'd like you to come to his funeral. He would have loved that. Could you?"

Kevin pulled himself together gradually.

"I've got no idea. I'd have to ask my personal officer about that. I don't know."

There was little more to say and Kevin wanted to leave. He stood up and composed himself as best he could.

"Karen, thank you for taking the trouble to come and see me, but I really need to go now. I'm not in the mood for chatting. I'm so sorry about Liam. I can't believe it. I'm so sorry for you too."

He was still fighting back the tears. He just wanted to go and lay on his bunk quietly.

"That's ok, Kevin. I understand. I'll make sure the prison has details of the funeral, ok?"

"Ok. Thank you," and with that, he turned and left the room.

Kevin was far too upset to attend the association room after that for the remainder of his free time. He did indeed just return to his cell where he laid on his bunk, staring up to the ceiling, churning over a mass of thoughts for hour after hour. Liam. Susie. Suicide. Bennett. Marshall. Rebecca. Allison. Life.

Death. Purpose. Detectives. Drugs. Knives. Round and round in circles. By the time he drifted off to sleep, it was way past lights-out time.

He awoke later than usual. He had been in a deep thorough sleep for the first time since entering prison and he felt strangely refreshed. Today was suicide day. He wondered what his last dinner would be. Chilli con carne probably. It was Friday after all. Condemned prisoners in America were always given the most extravagant meal of their choice on the day of their execution. One last final treat. He would like duck foie gras entree followed by vanilla yoghurt cheesecake pots with flapjack crumble and raspberries, all washed down with a nice bottle of Châteauneuf-du-Pape Grande Prebois. Chilli con carne and lukewarm water would have to suffice. Actually, it was better. It fondly reminded him of Liam who used to help cook it..

He quickly ate breakfast, got out into the exercise yard for a fag and then organised himself for his usual cleaning duties. Whilst going through the familiar routine of swiping his mop gradually from side to side for hours on end in an almost trance-like state, he found himself re-evaluating things. The timing of Karen's visit had been extraordinary. The fact that Liam had died accidentally by a method he himself was choosing to die by this very day, now felt like a travesty.

Liam had often told him that he needed to make the best of life and to be grateful for his many blessings. He mused on how lucky he was compared to Liam, whose circumstances and way of life, unintentionally robbed him of his life in his prime. He was beginning to feel guilty about planning to commit suicide, not because of Susie, but because of Liam. As the hours rolled by, he felt more and more strongly that to take his own life was unjust, selfish and a capitulation for all the wrong reasons. Maybe he should try to get through all of this shit. Maybe Susie would be ok with making the sacrifices she had to make on his behalf. Maybe his daughters would forgive him one day. What would Liam want? Should he stay strong for Liam? Would Liam be disappointed if he didn't make it to his funeral?

He walked away from his bucket and mop and returned to his cell where he retrieved the tobacco pouch. He secreted it in his overalls and walked purposely up the corridor to the second floor where Bennett's cell was. There was nobody inside and it was locked. He threw the pouch through the bars onto the floor. He then went back downstairs and found a guard. He walked boldly up to him and announced, "I have a confession to make."

Within the hour DI Brand and DS Starchley were back on the premises. They had immediately dropped whatever else they were doing, had hastily gathered together some recording equipment and rushed to the prison to seize the moment. This was big. On their arrival they were escorted inside to the interview room where Kevin was already sitting, still in his cleaning overalls, guarded by one officer, just waiting for them. They set up their recording device, sat opposite him and started the interview off by introducing themselves and cautioning him. He was offered the attendance of a solicitor which he declined. DI Brand opened up the questioning.

"Kevin, can you give me your full name please?"

"Kevin John Spartan"

He also rattled off his date of birth for them.

"Just to recap on previous events for the sake of the tape, you have been interviewed previously, over two weeks ago in fact, on the twenty-third of October, here in this very room, by officers DS Bigley and DC Wellsome, regarding the death of one Lenny Marshall. Do you remember that?"

Kevin gave a little mocking smile. As if he could forget.

"Of course," he answered politely.

"Can you summarise what you said to the officers then?"

"They were asking me if I knew anything about Lenny's death. He had been stabbed a few days earlier in the canteen and I was present there, at the time, with about eighty other inmates."

"Yes, that's quite correct. And what was the gist of your account to the officers?"

"I told them that I knew nothing about what had happened. They believed me, but I lied."

"Kevin, in what way did you lie?"

"I did know about the knife. I hid it for them."

He looked down, guiltily.

"Ok, Kevin, let's just rewind this and start at the beginning. What was the very first thing that happened which either you knew about, or involved you, that was in any way connected with Marshal's death?"

The events were all still very clear in Kevin's mind.

"It started when Lenny attended my cell just after dinner time lockup on the Friday, a week before the riot."

"Was he alone?"

"No, Thomas and Steve were with him."

"Do you know their surnames?"

"No I don't, but I've seen them a lot. They always used to hang out with Lenny."

"Ok, please, carry on."

"They pushed me back into my cell and Lenny held me against the wall and slapped me around quite a bit."

"Do you know why?"

"No reason. He seemed to just enjoy that sort of thing. I think it was just to scare me and that worked extremely well."

"Why do you think he wanted to scare you?"

"Because he wanted me to hide something for him."

"What was it?"

"At that point, I had no idea. He didn't have it with him. He was just informing me that they would be getting something to me and that I would have to hide it in my mattress for them until someone collected it."

"And he gave you no idea what it was?"

"No."

"Or for how long?"

"No."

"What were Thomas and Steve doing?"

"They were just standing behind him, making sure no guards were coming along, I suppose."

"Did you agree to the proposal?"

"Of course."

"Why?"

"Because I would be brown bread if I didn't comply."

"Is that what Lenny said?"

"Yep and I was crapping myself."

"Why did they pick you to do this for them?"

"Can't be sure, but I suppose it's because I am a loner, weak, vulnerable, unable to fight back, nobody here to support me, easy to terrify, very likely to be totally compliant, and they were quite right about all of that."

"You could have reported them to the wardens."

"Yeah. right. Do you know what happens to snitches in here?"

DI Brand considered that point silently, then he continued.

"So, what happened next?"

"The very next day, during afternoon association time, Thomas and Steve approached me in the association room and ordered me to go take a shower, right then. I did, of course. When I got into the showers, there were two other guys in there. I don't know their names."

"What time was this please?"

"I can't be too exact. It was mid-afternoon."

"Go on."

"They ordered me to strip and get into the shower. They got out at the same time and got dressed. Then another guy arrived and gave them something. They then ordered me out and to get dressed asap. As soon as I had dried, they wrapped something up in my towel as I was getting dressed. They reminded me about keeping it safe or else, kind of thing and they left."

"What happened to the third inmate?"

"He got undressed and got into the shower."

"Do you know him?"

"No."

"So, how did you hide it?"

"I did exactly what they asked me to do. I cut a slice in the side of my mattress and stuffed it inside. They'd even provided me with a little piece of blue plastic tape to cover the cut with."

"Describe the item to me, please."

"Well, it was wrapped up in a grey cloth, so I didn't ever see it properly. I knew it was a big knife because I partially unwrapped it to cut my mattress with it. It was very sharp."

"What was the handle like?"

"I didn't see it. I kept it wrapped up as much as possible but it was big."

"How long was the blade?"

"About six inches, I suppose, maybe seven."

"And how thick?"

"Inch and a half?"

"Then what happened?"

"It stayed there until that Friday, the day of the riot. First thing in the morning I was in the exercise yard when Thomas and Steve approached me. Thomas spoke. He ordered me to bring the knife to him in the canteen at dinner time."

"Did he threaten you again?"

"Of course. He told me that if I fucked up they'd be round later to cut me up into little bits and flush me down the shitter where I belonged."

"And did you believe him?"

"One hundred percent! I could almost taste the toilet water."

The officers remained nonchalant, but they silently empathised with his terror.

"What happened next?"

"At dinner time, I attended the canteen at my usual time and I had the knife stuffed down one sock, still wrapped in its cloth."

"What was happening in the canteen at that time?"

"A queue was forming. Service seemed to have been delayed, so the queue was getting bigger and bigger. That's when Thomas and the other two kitchen orderlies came out of the kitchen and threw tea towels over the cameras."

"What did you do then?'

"The place seemed to erupt so suddenly. I just stood there disoriented in the heaving throng for a few moments. People were shouting and throwing things. Next thing I knew, Thomas was in my face screaming at me for the knife. I quickly bent down and grabbed it and handed it to him."

"So you're quite sure that you handed the knife to Thomas Bennett?"

"One hundred per cent."

"What did he do then?"

"I've got no idea."

"What did you do?"

"I scarpered over to the quiet side of the room to escape all the violence."

"Did you notice where Lenny was at this time?"

"Absolutely, no idea."

"Why are you telling us about the knife now, when you didn't before?"

"Because before, I was genuinely afraid that if I said anything, they'd kill me."

"What's changed?"

"A week after the murder, they accosted me in the showers."

"Who did?"

"Thomas, Steve and Joe."

"What did they do?"

"Thomas pinned me up against the wall and stuck a screwdriver into my stomach. I honestly thought they were going to kill me there and then."

"Did you get injured?"

"A little."

He stood up, pulled up his shirt, pulled up a layer of fat, and hoped that the officer could detect a small scab on his belly.

"What caused that small wound?"

"The screwdriver. He didn't stab me. He was just pressing it into me as he threatened me. He was threatening to winkle-pickle my innards out. I'm not joking officer. I nearly shat myself."

"I see and what did he say?"

"He was just reminding me not to say anything to anyone about the knife, but I really got the conviction that when they got their chance, they would kill me too, like I was a loose end and that feeling hasn't gone away. That's why I'm talking to you now. Self preservation."

DI Blanch pulled back from the questioning and allowed DS Starchley to ask some questions.

"Kevin, going back to the first instance of Lenny threatening you. Prior to that had you had any dealings with him in any way at all?"

"Absolutely none."

"So they just picked on you to hide the knife because they perceived you to be weak, pathetic and vulnerable and therefore likely to be compliant, is that right?"

"Definitely."

"And you were genuinely terrified of them?"

"Totally."

"And you're willing to testify in a court of law that it was definitely Thomas that you gave the knife to, just as the riot was commencing."

"Absolutely."

"Kevin, I've been scribbling down all the days and times and places you say you've been met or threatened by Lenny, Thomas and co. We will check the internal CCTV records to see if they tally up with your accounts. Are we going to find any inconsistencies at all?"

"Absolutely not. I am telling you exactly what has happened, where, when and who with. CCTV will corroborate me."

Kevin looked at them both with strength and conviction in his eyes.

"Thank you, Kevin. You have been very helpful indeed."

The officers wrapped up the interview and got Kevin to sign the tape labels etc.

He asked them what was going to happen next and DI Brand answered.

"Kevin, I'd appreciate it very much if you don't reveal any of the details of what we have discussed today to anyone else, ok?'

"No problem."

"Good. That's very important, not least for your own protection. Also for your safety, I'm afraid that you will be locked up in your cell for the afternoon whilst we deal with the others. We'll be arresting Thomas shortly and he'll be removed to the police station for questioning. Whatever the outcome, he won't be coming back here, you'll be pleased to know. In all likelihood, we'll have Steve and Jo moved to other wings immediately and they will also be investigated regarding their roles in all of this in due course. How's that sound to you?"

"Brilliant!"

"Is there anyone else you think you need to be protected from?"

"No, I don't think so."

"Good. You're our star witness. We've got to make sure you stay safe."

Kevin smiled at them. He liked the sound of that, and he was starting to feel in control and a lot safer.

"Oh and before you go back to your cell, we'll have a quick look at your mattress."

That worried him. He didn't want anyone seeing his suicide note.

Chapter 24

The following day, DI Brand convened an urgent meeting with DCS Bertrand in the morning. DS Starchley joined them. DI Brand brought him up to speed with the new intriguing developments. Mr Bertrand considered all the known facts and played them through his mind to see if they were sufficient to form a charge.

"Ok, so let's look at the possible loopholes. Let's presume that the knife was originally intended for Marshall's use because he was the first one to approach Spartan about hiding it. Is there any evidence that he wanted to kill anyone? Had he made any death threats to anyone inside?"

"Not as far as we know, boss. We believe there to have been bad feelings towards Mako, because as we know, Mako gave three of his boys a bit of a pasting, but in relative terms, that was just a storm in a teacup."

"Yes. Steve Devenish, Joe Ashley and Palmer Trinket if my memory serves me."

"Yes sir, very good."

"Would that be sufficient to want someone dead? I'm not sure that seems likely. So that's still a bit of a mystery and we can hardly ask Marshall about it, can we?"

He paused for thought.

"Then if we put Bennett in the frame, does he have the motivation to kill Marshall? I mean, it's not like this was a crime of passion. They didn't have an argument or anything like that, did they? It looks very pre-planned. What would his motivation have been?"

"Just to become the big fish in the little pond?"

Mr Bertrand pondered for a few moments and then continued.

"Hmm, maybe, but we don't have any evidence to support that idea do we?"

More pondering, then, "You say for all the four occasions which Spartan claims to have been threatened by the others, particularly Bennett, the CCTV confirms that exactly as he says?"

"Yes sir! You can see them coming and going in the corridors exactly as he described. Right time, right place, right people, right order, every time."

"So that's good evidence to support Spartan's credibility and version of events?"

"Absolutely and unusually for an inmate, Spartan is the perfect witness. Apart from his unfortunate car crash which put him in prison, he'd never even had a parking ticket before that and that's forty-eight yeast of unblemished history. Married, reliable, hardworking, upstanding member of the community with two kids. No convictions. Not even a tattoo."

"Just a halo."

"Yes, that too."

"And Spartan swears that it was Bennett that he handed the knife to moments before the killing occurred?"

"Absolutely and don't forget, Spartan's claim that Bennett threatened him a week later is borne out by CCTV records too and, we did a search of Bennett's cell yesterday afternoon and we found a screwdriver hidden inside his mattress."

"And Spartan stated that Bennett used a screwdriver to threaten him, right?"

"Exactly. He seems to be a very reliable witness."

"Did you have a look at his mattress?"

"Yes, sir. There was a cut in the side of it just like he described, with sticky blue tape over it."

"Anything still in there?"

"Well, I didn't force my hand into it. You know what tricks these inmates get up to with syringes, razor blades and fishhooks, but I felt the mattress from the outside. There was definitely nothing in there. You'd know. It's only about two inches thick if that."

"Well, looking at the circumstantial evidence, we know for sure that it must have been one of the eighty who were in there with Marshall at the time of the incident and we've more or less eliminated all the other potential suspects, all seventy-nine of them. Bennett has a record as long as his arm and an awful lot of that involves violence. We know he has threatened people with knives, but he tends to prefer a cosh when he's actually assaulting people, yes?"

"True, but using a knife is hardly out of the question for someone like him, surely?"

"We only have one witness, but he's a reliable witness, who puts the knife into Bennett's hand, literally, just moments before the killing and as far as we can tell, Spartan has no reason to lie?"

"Absolutely not. I mean, it was Marshall who picked on him in the first place, just because he's such a wimp."

"Ok. It also seems very likely that Marshall was taken by surprise, which would fit in with a surprise attack from one of his buddies. You're going to interview Bennett this afternoon, yes?"

"As soon as we can, sir."

"You two interviewed him originally, didn't you?"

"Yes, sir."

"So, what do you think he will be like?"

"I'm ninety-nine percent sure that he will either go 'no comment' or just deny everything. He's not going to admit anything."

"Ok. Which means that we're not likely to have any more than we have right now."

Mr Bertrand paused looking very thoughtful indeed. After weighing all these things up in his mind, he delivered his conclusion.

"Well, on balance, I think we still have enough circumstantial evidence to charge him with murder. If anything else positive comes out of the interview, that will be a bonus. After the interview, go ahead and submit the papers to CPS asking them to support a murder charge. With a bit of luck, they'll at least go for manslaughter."

Mr Bertrand looked very pleased. "Well done, you two. You've done a great job. Good luck with the interview this afternoon."

With that, he headed off to the golf course and the other two, to the custody suite.

The previous evening, Kevin had been released from his cell after tea and he did join the scrabble game. There were rumblings around the room. Everyone knew that Kevin had been interviewed and that Bennett had been arrested and that Devenish and Ashley had been moved off into different parts of the prison, but nobody knew exactly what Kevin's role had been. The rumours had already started circulating, but they were vague, various and sometimes, unbelievable. Playing scrabble, sitting next to the big ginger, was the safest place for him to be right then, so he was ok with that.

Saturday afternoon brought him the visit from Susie that right up until the morning before, he never thought he was going to see. As usual, they sat opposite each other, but today, he sat bolt upright and Susie commented.

"What's happened to you? You look different. Last time I saw you, you said you were becoming a different man. Could that be different in a good way?"

She nursed a little twinkle in her eye and smiled mischievously. Kevin was clearly more confident today and certainly a lot less upset. More capable even and they hadn't even started talking yet. He looked at her seriously.

"Susie, do you really think you can cope for the next four years as a single mother?"

"Do me a favour! What kind of stuff do you think I'm made of? It'll be a walk in the park."

She smiled at him confidently. He smiled back, thankful.

"Hun, I'm not coming back to my old job."

"Sweetheart, you'll find another one. You're a great salesman and you know your photocopiers!"

"What I meant was that I don't intend to go back to that sort of shitty job."

She was taken aback and looked a little worried.

"Oh! Ok, darling. What's brought that on?"

"I want to do something more purposeful with the rest of my life."

"Ok," she said slowly and thoughtfully. "Well, you've got plenty of time to think about it, I suppose."

"I want to be an English teacher."

He looked at her face closely, wondering how she would react.

"Well, that's a bit of a surprise! You enjoying the English lessons in here that much?"

"It's more than that honey. It's about helping the less fortunate, not just about doing any old job just to pay the bills."

"Hark at you! Going to prison is turning you into some kind of saint?"

She was kind of mocking, jokingly, but he could tell that she was impressed.

"I can qualify whilst I'm inside, well maybe not all of it, but most of it. I've already got a degree. I just have to do the teacher training bit. I can probably do most of that by distance learning or online. I'll find a way. I'm pretty sure that Mr Blanchflower will help me."

He sounded so enthusiastic and certain.

"Kevin, that sounds fantastic. What's happened to you? Last time I visited you, you were so down in the dumps, I was really afraid for your mental well-being and now you're more like, well, a superhero. Ready to take the world on."

She couldn't help herself. She started to cry. A sense of relief flooded over her so completely, she couldn't cope with it. He instinctively held both her hands. He didn't need to say anything else. She knew him so well and he was so happy that she was feeling encouraged and relieved by his progress. A guard walked quickly over to them and ordered them to stop touching.

"She is my wife you know and she's upset," Kevin said rather sternly, grimacing at the guard and holding on firmly.

"I'm sorry, Kevin. It's the rules. Please."

They released their hold very slowly, defiantly.

"Babe, I'm going to make the best of it in here. I'm beginning to learn how to cope and not all the people in here are bad. Terry's a really nice guy, so long as you don't get on the wrong side of him, in which case he'll probably just kill you with his bare hands and Liam's been replaced in our scrabble-babble rabble with a really interesting young Nigerian lad, who tells great stories."

"Oh! Did Liam get bored of it?" she asked curiously, wiping away her tears.

"No, darling, he got released."

This wasn't the time nor the place to mention Liam's sad demise.

"Oh, lucky him. Let's hope he stays out this time. eh?"

Kevin smiled. "Yes, darling, I think he will."

Susie added, "There's hope for us all, eh?"

"Yes, darling, there's always hope for us all," he replied quietly, smiling sincerely.